TEMBERLAIN'S

ASHES

Cover design by Kathryn Rosa Miller
www.kathrynrosamiller.com

TEMBERLAIN'S ASHES

AGE OF AXION
BOOK TWO

D.M. WOZNIAK

If thou is dying or sickly, give.
If thou is sentenced, give.
If thou cannot provide, give.
If thou feels unwanted, give.
If thou wishes to be part of something greater, give.
And thy sponsor shall be forever honored.

– The Rules of Giving

PART ONE

THE AZUREMAN

VOIDREAMING

Temberlain ignored his thirteen fellow officers in the *Apsides'* executive mess. They were enraptured with an almost-childlike nostalgia—a form of homesickness rooted more in contentment than sadness. Relaxed, leaned back, feasting on organic food and wine from Efful. Retelling tales of old shrouded in lore. Uncharacteristically close to drunkenness.

He ignored the captain, who was laughing at his own joke, despite the fact that to not laugh was to half-insult the Virel Arm chancellor, leader of the section of galaxy through which their axionship now traveled. He ignored the ashen, a trembling boy who attempted to get his attention with a new course of pink tenderloin from the galley. He ignored the passing field of stars, visible through the massive stern-side window running wall to wall and floor to ceiling.

Temberlain ignored all these things, for he was not dwelling on the past. He was focused on the future.

The Age of Axion.

There had never been a time so prosperous. It was evident all around him.

The massive dining table was a hand-carved relic from the treepeople of Sidarche. Temberlain studied the grain of the knotted wood. The impressive craftsmanship of the joinery. Beneath him was an elaborate wrightworm rug from Jupre, a planet ten light years from Sidarche.

Here were two gifts from conquered worlds unknown to each other. Each was impressive on its own, but combined, they illustrated the full breadth of the Halcyon Confederacy.

And our power is growing every day.

"Officer?" asked the ashen boy, drawing Temberlain out of his thoughts. The servant was hoisting a plate of sliced bovine. Being the only one in the room with hair on his head, he was obviously not from Efful. An Agh-Severian from the look of him. Scrawny, red tinted. Like the kind of ugly bird that could stand on one leg. Temberlain had forgotten the species' name. He'd forgotten the ashen's name as well.

"Can't you see, fool?" said Officer Cordialle, head of security. "He doesn't want any." He forcefully nudged the boy back with his forearm. With the wine's help, his motions were exaggerated, his disdain and impatience a little more evident.

The boy stepped on Temberlain's shoe, nearly tripped, and tried his best to balance the heavy platter while bracing himself with one emaciated red arm on the table's edge.

He didn't succeed.

The platter crashed onto the table. Slices of meat flopped over within a pool of their own blood. Another careless swipe of the servant's arm toppled Temberlain's wineglass. Dark purple liquid splattered over Temberlain's impeccable white uniform.

Immediately, talk in the room ceased. The only sound was the muted hum of the ship.

Temberlain didn't say a word. He looked down at his soiled uniform, arms out at his sides.

"I am sorry, Officer," the boy said. He looked at the damage he'd caused then began silently picking up the slices of meat and placing them back on the platter.

"Let me see your number, Ashen," Cordialle barked.

The Agh-Severian hesitated only a moment before rolling up his left shirtsleeve. On his forearm was a small blue number.

"Only a two," Cordialle spat, his voice full of disdain. "Who in your family gave?"

"My parents," he said, without taking his eyes off the bovine he was collecting.

Cordialle let out a sharp laugh. "I'm surprised it's not higher. Drivel from Agh-Severia don't usually make it past thirty years of age. Polluted atmosphere and all. One would think your number should be well past ten by now." He chuckled.

"Cordialle, let him be," said Officer Berbsby, the woman with eidetic memory. She was responsible for FTL navigation. "Life expectancy on Agh-Severia has dramatically improved since colonization."

"How did you land this job with a number that low?" Cordialle said to the ashen, ignoring Berbsby. "Being a two, you should be sanitizing waste vats, not tending to the empowered."

The boy mumbled something under his breath. Temberlain couldn't make out the words.

Cordialle's eyes grew large. "What did you say?" he asked, his voice taut and almost as high-pitched as Berbsby's.

"Nothing, Officer."

Cordialle pushed his chair back from the table. "No, I heard you perfectly clearly. You said 'Same thing.'"

The servant stayed silent.

"Same thing? You think serving the esteemed captain and his officers is equivalent to cleaning shit?"

The boy shook his head.

"Azureman!" Cordialle barked.

The tall figure standing sentry on the far wall awakened. His matte-silver suit was almost the same shade as the slatted metal wall at his back. The blue face mask, almond shaped, began to faintly glow—the shade of the clear-blue sky of a desert world behind a polarized membrane. In the low-lit room, the featureless face looked as if it were floating.

"Officer?" the azureman said with a clear, masculine voice that seemed to come from everywhere in the room.

"Place this idiot in soteria," Cordialle said.

Temberlain flashed a disapproving look at the officer and noticed Berbsby do the same.

The red-skinned boy backed away. Within a few steps, he reached the far edge of the executive mess and stood there, his palms to the metal wall, head shaking.

The azureman nodded and began to slowly walk around the table toward him.

"Please," said the boy. "I . . . I'm not ready to give. And who would be my sponsor?"

The muscular head of security stood, approached the servant, and wrapped his hand around the ashen's throat. With a squeeze, he forced the boy's eyes upward. "I will not tolerate such insolence from an ashen."

"Cordialle," said Berbsby.

The azureman came to a stop next to Cordialle and the boy.

"Move aside, sir, for your own safety," the azureman said.

Cordialle dropped his hand from the boy's throat and backed away. The servant immediately fell to his knees, head down, weeping behind black tendrils of hair.

The azureman opened his chest. A bright light enveloped the room.

"No," the boy moaned. "Please."

The azureman reached out gently, palm up. "Give me your hand."

"Please," the boy repeated. Now bathed in white light that was starting to undulate, as if underwater, his skin looked more pinkish than red. Turning to the captain, he pleaded, "I'm not ready to give."

"I repeat, give me your hand," the azureman said, in his emotionless voice.

"Cordialle, stop this nonsense," the captain said.

Through squinted eyes, Temberlain watched Cordialle. Behind an outstretched hand meant to protect him from the light, Cordialle's eyes darted back and forth. The sickly glow illuminated the axiongraph on his creased forehead.

It was the mark of an empowered—a matte black drawing of axion. His looked like a sideways *S* with a dozen concentric arrows emanating from it. Temberlain thought that the ostentatious placement and design suited Cordialle. Temberlain's was much more subtle. His axiongraph was located on his bicep—a design of a ghantstag's head, antlers curved like a double helix.

"Azureman, stand down," Cordialle said, his voice barely audible.

The azureman took his outstretched hand, once meant for the cowering boy, and used it to touch his own chest, between his breasts. Temberlain was close enough to the azureman to see the circular structure in the breastplate collapse within itself. Arcs of lightning tracing metallic petals. A blooming flower in reverse.

Dimness descended upon the room again. The boy's sobs grew, an outpouring of emotion like a rush of water in a cave. The room itself seemed to Temberlain like a cave, the blue tinge to the darkness from the azureman's face mask returning.

Cordialle took a few steps back to the table and sat down. He looked at the captain and other officers with a smile despite the frowns. "All of you need a sense of humor."

"Putting someone in soteria isn't funny, Cordialle," said Berbsby.

"I wasn't actually going to do it," he said. "You thought I was serious?" He shook his head, almost in disappointment, and then took a quick sip of wine. "Boy needed a lesson, is all."

Temberlain studied the shaking servant from Agh-Severia and frowned.

This is wrong.

Ashen were valued resources. In this world of the living, they had a job to do. This boy was uniquely important, as he assisted the captain. And like all resources, the boy would perform that job to the best of his ability when there was the least amount of friction. In Temberlain's view, fear was never a long-term motivator. Fear created friction.

The enervated—ashen who were placed in soteria—were a different type of resource. A far more permanent resource. Converted. Trapped in axion, they were infinitely valuable.

Being placed in soteria wasn't something to be feared. It wasn't something to be used as a threat. If the people feared axion, then the empowered would be reduced to using force to place the ashen in soteria. War would spread throughout the entire galaxy. War was friction.

The masses need to want it. Games like Cordialle's only thwart the strategy.

Temberlain shook his head subtly as he looked through the immense back window at the passing stars. At this speed, they were straight concentric lines. The ones near the middle were strings of vibrating color against the inky blackness of space.

"Berbsby," the captain said, drawing Temberlain out of his thoughts. "When will our comms be back online?"

The captain's chair was slightly swiveled away from the table. He was looking at the field of stars as well.

"Soon, Captain. The engineers will have their repairs complete by end of rotation."

The captain sighed. "I don't like being in the dark. We travel alone, you realize."

"Yes, Captain," Berbsby said.

"Sir," Temberlain said to the captain, rising from his chair. "Your permission to be excused?"

"Eh?"

Temberlain motioned to his uniform, which was already becoming sticky. Under normal conditions, he could simply use axion to remove the stain. It would take microrotations.

But he'd been drinking. Axion under the influence was highly frowned upon. Even the imperious Cordialle wouldn't do such a thing in front of the captain.

The captain nodded once.

Temberlain extended a farewell palm to the other empowered officers, who'd already moved on to other topics. Berbsby was now discussing the Virel Arm chancellor's plans for HC342, a planet ten times the size of Efful and within the 0.01 AU habitable zone of a nearby white degenerate.

"Imagine the ashen resources on a planet that size," Berbsby said.

"You are assuming there *are* ashen," said another officer.

Berbsby nodded. "All data points suggest it should be teeming with cognates. HC342 has been around for a very long time. When we're close, we'll start picking up the signals."

A third officer grunted. "That's good. I'm sick of planet runs where we come away empty-handed. Fucking tropicats and hydrogenzoens."

The captain laughed, but his chuckles deteriorated into pensiveness. He clinked the rim of his glass with his knife three times.

"To HC342," he said, raising his glass to the dimmed, sodium-lit ceiling. "May there be plentiful ashen."

"May there be plentiful ashen," everyone echoed, raising their glasses. Except the azureman, whose face mask was dark once again.

THE LEMON TREE INN

I close Chimeline's diary.

It's small—slightly larger than my hand and adorned with a white-leather cover and a pink painted rose. Its appearance reminds me of the Book of Unwanting, which she used to read when we were on the road southward. The one that Blythe gave her. It seems a lifetime ago, though it's been only a fortnight. I can picture her standing in the half-shade of Yerla and Yisla's ramshackle house. I'd been upset with her. The moment she was free from the clutches of her former life, she'd latched on to the effulgency.

So much has changed in such a short amount of time.

Looks aside, this book couldn't be more different. It's . . . fascinating, and almost all the pages are still blank. I don't even know what to call it. It's not a diary if the words aren't *her* thoughts and memories. It's not dreaming if they're not *her* dreams.

She's voidreaming, except that she's linked to someone *else's* mind. And not just any someone.

Temberlain.

"Good morning."

I look up from the spartan desk, startled. I had assumed Chimeline was still asleep.

Earlier, I'd parted the curtains a bit so that I could read her writings, but now, the early-morning sun blasts through the gap, a golden beam that picks up the dust in the dim room almost like indivisibles in the void.

Chimeline rubs her eyes and rises slightly from her crumpled pillow. Her dark hair is matted awkwardly, her usually straight bangs pushed aside.

"Morning," I say, returning her smile.

Her eyes flash to the book, but she doesn't say a word.

"I finished it," I add, motioning to it. "At least what you've written so far."

She nods.

I gently tap the bandaged fingers of my right hand on the cover—the three middle knuckles are still swollen and painful from my fight with Mander on the beach. "I must admit, I'm having trouble understanding it," I say. "There are so many . . . strange words."

"I told you," she says with a yawn, lying back down. Her tone has a sharp edge. I sense that she doesn't want to discuss it.

I cross the small room and sit on the edge of my bed, facing hers and the window. The street below is visible through the slightly parted yellow curtains. A woman is watering plants on a balcony. They drip on the walkway below. Even though it's barely sunrise, I hear people about. Some merchant with a deep Xian accent is yelling about rotten fruit.

"Temberlain's Ashes," I say, looking at Chimeline's huddled form. Our beds are identical, but while my feet dangle off the edge when I sleep, her bed somehow manages to look enormous. Her small frame is tucked within its center. "Is *that* the Temberlain you're writing about?"

"I think so," she says, her words muffled beneath the covers.

"I didn't know he was a real person."

"Neither did I."

"I assumed they were children's stories, meant to frighten us into behaving," I add, as I slide my bare feet against the rough floorboards.

Silence stretches out to the point where I wonder if she's fallen back to sleep. Then she says, quietly, "Well, apparently, we were wrong."

"What do you mean?"

"He *was* real."

I'm sure she cannot see my frown. "So some effulgent went on a rampage hundreds of years ago and destroyed an entire city? Burned it down to the ground?"

She slowly shakes her head. "I don't know. I only know what I've seen. Which is what you've read."

I run a hand through my hair. I'd hoped she'd have more clarity on what she'd written. It was her voidream.

"But who is this *azureman*? Why was he about to put a child in soteria?"

"I don't know."

"What is FTL?"

"I don't know."

"And that phrase . . . Halcyon Confederacy." I frown in thought. "Do you think it has anything to do with Mander's book? He titled it *Halcyon Roadmap*. Maybe there's some sort of connection."

"Dem, how many times do I need to tell you? I don't know."

I let out an exasperated sigh. "Well how am *I* supposed to understand it, then, if you don't?"

She's quiet for a long time.

"You're not the only one who's upset," she mumbles.

"What?"

"I don't understand what's happening to me."

I approach her bed and kneel at its side so that we're eye to eye. I find her shoulder beneath the sheets and give it a gentle squeeze. "Give it time," I say, trying to keep my voice as light as the room. "That's why I gave you the book, so you can write down your voidreams. The more we can learn—"

"Dem?"

"Yes?"

"Can we not talk about this now?"

I try to hide my frustration. *If not now, then when?* This is the perfect time to talk about this.

She turns her body away from me, favoring the window.

The curtains blow in a rare breath from the outside, and I wonder what sort of yellow fills the room now. Is it the color of sunlight? The color of friendship and happiness? Or is it gold? The color of valor. The color of duty before love.

"Just one last question," I say to her back, feeling the pace of my voice increase. "You said that you believe the enervated are giving you these visions."

"Yes."

"Then why are they choosing someone who's been dead for hundreds of years? How is that helpful to our cause? Why aren't they showing you what Mander was doing in the Celestium? About his cursed plan to reach out to his people—"

"I don't know, Dem," she says curtly, getting out of bed. The sudden movement causes the specks of dust to twirl about in a storm. She walks through them, oblivious, her nightgown shimmering.

"I'm writing down everything that comes to me because you asked me to," she adds. "But that's all that I know. If you read it, then you know what I know."

"I'm just looking for clues on how to end voidance across the land. How to undo the damage Mander began. How to perform eleutheria for all."

She ignores me, opening the armoire with a squeak. There's only one garment hanging in it, but she stares at it as if there are hundreds to choose from. Then she spins to face me.

"Did you ever think that maybe the visions are just that? Simply visions? Some random effect of the horror that happened to me in the Celestium?"

I shake my head. "No. You're an axionlighter now. What happened to you wasn't chance. There's a purpose—a design behind it. I'm convinced of it."

She laughs once, softly. "You should listen to yourself. You sound like Blythe."

I hesitate before replying. "I know in my heart that it's not chance. I wouldn't have caught up to Mander without you. We wouldn't have found the book, either."

This silences her. She turns back to the open armoire.

In the Celestium, she touched Mander's voidstone, the one that had liquefied into a pool of white. She was in soteria—trapped inside the void— for the briefest amount of time. The room was collapsing. Marine stepped forward and tried to save her, but her attempt went horribly wrong. My estranged wife's body fell inside that hideous pool, and her soul was taken forevermore, her body left behind.

No. Not forevermore.

Instinctively, I look at the desk. Next to the white diary rests an emerald swatch of fabric, which contains the only voidstone I have left. Blythe and I tried to perform eleutheria on it, but we failed.

Marine is inside, refusing to leave.

It's so strange. I buried her body in a hilltop cemetery, here in Winter's Baiou. Blythe officiated the private ceremony. Commander Reddles paid for the headstone. We said goodbye to her.

But she's still *right here*. A fingertip away.

"Can you turn for a moment?"

"Hm?" I glance her way. She's pulled out the sundress that's a shade of yellow deeper than the curtains. She raises her eyebrows in expectation.

"Ah," I say, complying. I study a crack in the plaster while she changes.

Chimeline is the opposite of Marine in every way. The love between my former wife and me was black sand. Tephra. The love of destruction. We were ladders for each other to climb. Marine would have engineered the perfect moment to disrobe in front of me and become offended had I not given that moment its undivided attention. Instead, Chimeline asked me to avert my eyes.

This one of her many attractive qualities, and it draws my mind back to something I've been avoiding.

The journey to find Marine gave me a lifetime's worth of education—about me and everything I used to hold true. And along the way, new truths were discovered. Chimeline and I grew close.

The Celestium changed all that. Whatever feelings blossomed between us on the way to this Southern city . . . they've become infinitely more complicated. Sometimes I feel that Chimeline is lost to me. There's a piece of her that the void owns now. She is an instrument of the enervated.

As for me, I'm no longer the master voider. I have renounced voidance. The only voidstone I carry is nearly weightless and contains a single soul—that of my former wife.

But I am still the master of my intellect. I haven't renounced reason. I carry my faculties, heavy with experience and loss. And it is with these skills that I will see this mission through.

I have nothing else.

My thoughts turn to the massive voidstone that was pulled to shore less than a mile from here. It was Mander's sadistic prize—a relic he'd searched for his entire life. He'd manufactured a war between two kingdoms to attain it.

Blythe and I have performed eleutheria on it every day for the past week, from morning to sunset, and we're nearly done. It is exhausting work. The chains are heavier than the voidstone now. If it weren't for them, the wagon-sized stone might float.

After we finish, we'll turn our attention to the thousands of voidstones scattered across the land. And to their owners, a group that Blythe refers to as the Black Army. All voiders must be unarmed. Peacefully.

Many of them dispersed after Mander fell. Most returned to the citadel to await new orders from the king—or the new master voider he'll put in place. Rumor has it that some abandoned their duties altogether, preferring to sell their services to the highest bidder—Xian intendants, hilma-plantation owners, wealthy cross-border traders.

Some remain here.

One of them was murdered days ago, or so goes the rumor. While he slept, his throat was sliced from ear to ear.

Effulgents and graycloaks continue to trickle into the city from across the land, the result of Blythe's daughter sending out pigeons. Any day, I expect Reddles to return with word from the king. Will His Majesty bear another letter commanding my beheading? Or, after reading the *Halcyon Roadmap*, will the king come to his senses and realize that it was Mander—not I—who was deceiving him all along?

I cannot shake the cryptic last words in that tome: *They're coming*. Who's coming? When? And for what?

I hold my head in my hands as I think of it all. The world was simpler when we were fighting an imaginary war.

"I'm done, Dem. You can turn back now."

Chimeline stands in front of the armoire holding a small mirror in one hand while struggling to put an earring in with the other.

I approach her from behind, take the mirror, and hold it with my uninjured hand so both of hers are free.

"Thank you," she says quietly.

I nod, and for a moment everything is silent. For a moment, I can pretend that things are perfect between us.

"Listen," I eventually say. "I'm sorry that I keep hounding you about the visions."

Before she can respond, a crashing sound erupts, as if a large stack of crates has been thrown to the ground. The Xian merchant outside swears. Then, through the thin walls, come the shrill wails of a newborn.

This place is a far cry from my former home, the Royal House. I used to wake to the soft echoes of the women's choir practice and the ruffling of nesting falcons in the towering heights. Elrich brought me morning coffee about this time, brushed my cloak, reviewed the day's schedule with me.

Despite all those luxuries, I wasn't happy.

We're near the shore of Xi Bay and close to where Mander's estate had stood before it collapsed into ruin. The inn is situated in the same large market square I visited on my way to see him, when I was famished. I traded my black flaxen cloak for a plateful of fish and eggs.

Commander Reddles graciously set us up here before he left to deliver Mander's large tome to the king. It was decent of him. None of us has any gold from our journey, and the times of my signing promissory notes are over. There is no Royal Bank I can pull from. My private gold has surely been confiscated as well. But Reddles had a favor to call in. Years ago, he saved the life of a young calvary soldier, and that soldier's parents happen to be the innkeepers of the Lemon Tree Inn.

Our new home.

Footsteps come up the hallway stairs just outside our door. Heavy treads. At least two men with boots. There are over a dozen rooms on this level, and these visitors could be headed to any of them, but instinctively I know they're for me.

Blythe and Chireseal. Earlier than usual.

The footsteps stop on the other side of the door.

Muffled disagreement.

A fist pounding.

"Alright!" I say, walking over. I twist the skeleton key and open the door.

Blythe stands there with a tired smile on his hairless face. But the other man—the white-hooded effulgent Chireseal— pushes into my room.

"We're late," he says, walking past me.

"Excuse him, Dem," Blythe says, coming in after his companion and clearing his throat with a fist to his mouth. "He's overly concerned that we start eleutheria as soon as possible."

"What's the rush?" I ask.

Blythe softly closes the door behind him. Chireseal heads to the window and peers through the curtains, parting them slightly further with a finger. He looks down at the street.

I glance back at Blythe, who shrugs. For a moment, the only sounds are the happenings outside.

With his other hand, Chireseal pulls off his white hood, revealing his hairless Effulgian face. Unlike Blythe, he has murky hazel eyes and a square jawline. He's also older and shorter than Blythe, but not by much. The jewels in his face are the most striking thing about him. A dozen or so glittering, colorless gems are somehow embedded in his skin. They rise across his left cheek to meet his earlobe. This may be the tenth time I've seen him and they still take me off guard. Effulgents typically avoid ornamentations of any kind, and these seem too garish even for a nobleman's adolescent child. I've asked Blythe privately about the man, but my friend knows as little as I do. Chireseal came with the first of the influx of effulgents. He claims to be from a temple north of Northinglight.

He drops the curtain. "We need to finish. This morning."

"Why?"

He wipes his face with his hands and sits in the desk chair, which groans in complaint. He starts tapping his foot. "Just . . . please, get your sandals on. We should have finished yesterday. We were almost done." He shakes his head.

"Blythe and I were exhausted," I say. "Being inside the void all day—doing eleutheria—it's not easy."

He exhales, his lack of empathy evident. "Right, right. Yes, I know. Let's just get going."

Hesitantly, I head to the foot of the bed to get my sandals. "Chimeline and I are going to have breakfast in the common room downstairs. I'll meet you after that."

"There's no time for that!"

"Why not?"

"Let's just eat on the way," he insists.

I look from Chireseal to Blythe. "Is something wrong?"

"Yes," says Chireseal immediately, turning to meet me with his swamp-colored eyes. "The Axiondrive is still here."

"We're going as fast as possible."

He places his fingers to his temples.

"Is it the voiders?" I ask him.

"What?"

"Do they pose a threat, since we're performing eleutheria?"

Chireseal laughs sharply. "No."

"Then what is it?"

He rises and walks back to the window, ignoring the question.

I turn to Blythe, who bites his lower lip anxiously.

"Do you know what's going on?" I ask him.

He shakes his head. "I do not, my friend, but I will be happy when we are done. Multiple weights will be lifted today."

"Both of you, listen," Chireseal says. "I know it's impossible for you to understand this, but something . . . is going to happen. Soon." He points out the window. "And if that Axiondrive is on that wharf when it does, it's going to be really bad. Which is why we need it emptied."

"The Axiondrive is surrounded by Reddles' men," I say. "It's safe from voiders."

He laughs again in disagreement.

I pull on my white shirt. "What bad thing is going to happen?"

He doesn't answer.

"Did you pray upon this?" Blythe asks curiously.

Chireseal looks at him. "Yes. The Unnamed himself bestowed his immense wisdom on my insignificant soul."

Blythe places his palms upon the desk. "And? What did the Unnamed say?"

I dig my feet into my sandals.

Chireseal looks at Chimeline, then at me, but his attention seems mostly focused on Blythe. His expression softens, becomes less urgent, almost to the point of sadness.

The filtered morning sun glitters off the gems on his face, causing pinpoints of light to speckle the plaster walls.

"After we're done today, just promise me something."

"Yes," Blythe says. "Anything."

"Get as far away from this place as you can."

THE PORT OF YAMERIND

"Something's not right with Chireseal," I tell Blythe under my breath.

"How so?" he asks.

"Every day, he's hounded us with questions. About Mander, the Axiondrive, voiders, Xiland. He never shuts up. Now he's suddenly silent. He won't even walk with us."

Blythe looks up from the gray cobblestones and stares at the strange effulgent, who storms a few paces in front of us. Well past him is the glittering Port of Yamerind—the maritime commercial hub of Winter's Baiou. Here, there is no beach. The cobblestones extend to the deep, dark, and accommodating shoreline of Xi Bay. A dozen wharves jut out, some short and some long, some light and some dark, almost resembling the keys of a giant's piano. Several two-, three-, and four-masted ships are docked against them. They are here to be loaded and to discharge passengers and cargo—but today, like the days before, the port is silent. No workers or sailors toil. Only local fishermen sit with their feet over the lengthy stone edge, their lines cast out. And to the east, within the shadow of a ship, a trio of voiders stand waiting, their black capes fluttering in the salty breeze like war-torn flags.

Blythe nods then gazes back down at the street. "I imagine it's due to the recent revelation."

"Recent revelation?"

"Whatever it was that the Unnamed told him. He must be under much pressure."

I bite my lip, but I can't keep silent for long. "You actually believe that?"

He exhales. "We've been over this before."

"I know. I know. But he doesn't *seem* like an effulgent."

"And you don't *seem* like a voider."

"That's because I'm not one. Anymore."

At first, he doesn't reply. But then he says, quietly, "You never seemed like a voider to me, Dem. Despite the lies of your upbringing, you saw the truth."

I stop Blythe with a grip on his shoulder before we take a set of shallow stone stairs down to the main section of the port.

"There's something about him that reminds me of Mander," I say.

Blythe purses his lips and furrows his hairless brow. "He's nothing like that evil man."

I glance at Chireseal, who's still walking. He hasn't noticed that we've stopped.

"If he were like Mander," Blythe continues, motioning toward him, "he would never condone eleutheria, on an Axiondrive no less. He would give his life to stop it from happening. Chireseal has done the opposite."

I hesitantly nod. "You have a point, but that's no reason to blindly trust him. We don't know the slightest thing about him. Just that he comes from a village far north of Northinglight. A village I've never heard of, I might add. And he has a strange accent that I cannot place, and gems jammed into his face like some hilma addict who ran headfirst into a tavern window."

The strange effulgent talks to someone near one of the jutting wharves about fifty feet away. A well-built Xian man. Probably a fisherman asking for a prayer. The view of his face is blocked.

I look around.

Everything is ordinary. It's a day like any other. Warm sun on my face, furled sails rippling gently, ropes clattering against wooden masts.

I fear that they're all diversions from a chaos yet to come.

"Do you think he's right?" I ask, paranoia seeping in.

"About what?"

"That something bad is going to happen."

Blythe groans then nods once. "If the Unnamed revealed it, then it will be so. There is no alternative."

I shake my head at the man's impenetrable faith—it's something I have come to both covet and reject in equal measure.

A few metallic *clinks* echo out in the morning air. I turn toward the sound.

Several gold coins glimmer in the morning sun.

"So prayers cost gold now?" I instinctively say.

But then I realize it's Chireseal who is paying. The effulgent drops his gold into the Xian's palm, one coin at a time. In return, the man gives Chireseal a rolled-up piece of parchment. Chireseal opens it, scrutinizes its contents, and then coils it back up with a nod.

The Xian turns and walks down the length of the shoreline, and for the first time I'm able to see his face.

His black eye patch nearly blends in with his dark skin.

"That's Colu," Blythe says.

"I wonder what that was all about," I say, frowning.

Blythe shrugs.

"I haven't seen Colu in days. I figured he'd left the city by now. Gone south."

For a moment, I watch Colu walk westward down the port's edge toward the surrounding storefronts and palm trees in the distance. He's oblivious to us, counting the coins in his hand instead.

"Hello?" comes a loud voice.

We both turn toward the water.

Chireseal stuffs his parchment into a leather sack and extends his arms out at his sides. "Today?"

After fifty feet we reach him where he stands. Here, the cobblestones meet the deep water. We head eastward. Chireseal dons his white hood and looks down at his feet, most likely to avoid the harsh morning sun. I block it with an outstretched hand.

"What was that about?" I say, picking up my pace to walk by his side.

He doesn't answer me.

"Why did you give Colu gold?"

"For information," he mumbles.

I glance back at Blythe. His lips are pursed.

We pass another empty wharf that juts out to sea. The next one, up ahead, is longer and bears a massive four-masted ship. In its shadow wait the three voiders.

"What information?"

As we continue walking down the length of the port's edge, the area directly east of the galleon slowly becomes unobstructed. Behind it, a stone landing juts out into Xi Bay another hundred feet or so. Two smaller three-masted frigates are lined up on the opposite side of this landing. The vessels create a cavernous effect as we progress between them, down the middle of the stone promontory that is roughly one hundred feet square. The water on three sides is so dark it appears black.

The Axiondrive rests in the center surrounded by fifty armored Northern soldiers.

Even though I've come here every day for the past five days, the sight of it still awes me into silence.

I stop in place.

A voidstone this large. It's impossible to fathom.

The power it wields.

The souls it contains.

It's about the size of a horse-drawn wagon—one capable of carrying four to six people. It's shaped like an oval, mostly symmetrical but not precise. I've been close to it many times, so I know that its edges are not continuously curved but made of thousands of minuscule flat planes and dimples instead, as if the entire piece were crudely hewn with a chisel and hammer. But it's impossible to notice this from afar, as there is no glimmer to the voidstone, no shades of gray or arcs of reflection despite the intense morning sun. It seems to soak up the very light, letting nothing out except darkness and hatred.

Thirteen massive chains are woven into its sides.

I'm still not sure how Mander did it. It must have been the same technique he used in the Celestium, when he fused the throats of Colu, Chimeline, and Blythe to the vertical membrane. Two types of indivisibles intrinsically linked to create something new. A bond stronger than hardened steel.

From these thirteen spigots morph the blunted remains of iron chains, like severed umbilical cords. For the longest time, these chains undoubtedly extended hundreds of links long, repurposed anchors leading all the way to the galleons.

It was how Mander raised the voidstone out of Blackscar.

But now, all thirteen links have been cut as close to the surface of the Axiondrive as possible. Some of them are intact—a single link as large as a small child and weighing at least a hundred pounds. Others have been snapped cleanly apart, surely with voidance.

Fifty of Reddles' men surround the Axiondrive in a precise square formation. They stand motionless, their torso armor glittering in the sun. Their bright-red knee-length tunics underneath sway in the breeze. They have been ordered to not let anyone except Blythe and me through.

The three voiders step out of the galleon's shadow. One leads the others, and they walk intently toward us. A remnant of the voider congregation that refused to leave.

"Oh, no, not you people," mumbles Chireseal. He puts his hand on his temple and rubs it. "We don't have time for this." He raises his voice and starts to repeat himself. "We don't have time—"

The voider in the lead cuts him off with an outstretched hand.

"I'm here to talk to the former master voider, not you," she snaps. "As you like to say, *be nothing*."

Chireseal lets out a short, disbelieving laugh, and his mouth stays open.

With her caramel-colored skin, silky accent, and lean and short stature, she's clearly from Chimeline's homeland—Scorpiontail. This woman must be a submaster of the university there. Her hair is chin-length and graying. She appears to be close to my age. The two men behind her are much younger and overweight, also from the archipelago. They hang back, refusing to look me in the eye.

Although she's nearly a foot shorter than I am, she boldly steps up and looks me up and down. "Democryos, is it not?"

"It is. And who are you?"

"You are speaking to the new master voider of Scorpiontail," blurts one of the roundish men behind her.

The woman rolls her eyes, clearly annoyed that the man spoke for her.

"Is this true?" I ask her.

"It is," the woman says matter-of-factly. "I am Gaigane."

"But . . . Aphelime . . ." Although I exchanged letters with the elderly master voider from Scorpiontail as recently as the past winter, the last time I saw her with my own eyes was over five years ago. The night before my wedding. She'd given me the gift of sands. And her warning eventually came true.

"She passed on," Gaigane says. "A fortnight ago. Just before I was sent here. Glory and honor to her lasting memory."

"Glory and honor to her lasting memory," the two men repeat in unison.

I nod solemnly, and for a moment I am at a loss. "Aphelime was a friend of mine," I eventually say, quietly. "Someone I respected greatly. You have my condolences."

For a moment, everything is peaceful, and a sad smile crosses Gaigane's face. But then she looks at Chireseal and Blythe and her wrinkled brow furrows. She looks back at me. "Rumor has it that you've renounced voidance."

I nod once, slowly. "That is true."

"And that you want to rid the land of voidance."

"That is true as well."

She glances at the massive voidstone in the center of the stone wharf. "What do you call it? What you're doing?"

"Eleutheria," I say.

"And what do you believe it is that you are doing?"

"We're freeing the enslaved. The poor, wretched, trapped souls—twisted and perverted by a dark and arcane art. These beings are tortured every time we use voidance. I seek to end it once and for all."

She shakes her head. I hope that it's in sadness, but I know better than to expect understanding out of her. "Emptying souls from a voidstone," she mutters. "Like wine out of a skin."

"Precisely."

"Sounds like nonsense," she says. "It is delving—and delving is for fools."

I nod carefully. "Yes, it is delving. Using voidance to enter a voidstone is the only way to free them. But eleutheria is far from nonsense."

She shakes her head again.

"You are welcome to experience it with us," I say. "It will open your eyes to the wrongness of our supposed gift."

She cranes her head back like a snake ready to strike. "You think *I* am a fool, Democryos? I will not join in your folly."

I point to the Axiondrive. "But we've been doing this every day. Surely you've heard the stories, or else you wouldn't be here. We haven't been lost in the void. We're alive and well."

She sniffs loudly.

"When we've completed eleutheria, we'll be able to move that stone," I add.

"Even though it took thirteen galleons to raise it."

"Yes."

The subtlest shadow of doubt crosses her face. Perhaps it's due to my confidence—or because, according to her, we should be dead as a result of what we're doing.

"I've heard these same stories from the effulgency my entire life, Democryos. Ever since I was a young girl. Souls in a voidstone. It was nonsense back then, and it is nonsense now." She looks me up and down again. "It is sad that a man of your station has succumbed to the drivel of the weak. I had heard great things about you."

I extend my hand. "Join me, and I'll prove to you that I'm right. I'll prove that our very institution is wrong." I feel the two men's gazes on me, but when I glance at them they look away.

"Our institution creates wonder and prosperity in this land. It creates progress that would not be possible without—"

"It doesn't matter if you have good intentions. It doesn't matter if you're from the Northern Kingdom, from Xiland, from Scorpiontail, or wherever. Voidance is an abuse, plain and simple. There are living beings in those stones around your neck, and every time you enter the void you put them under the whip."

She crosses her arms. "Prove it."

"Join us in eleutheria and I will."

"I told you—I will not delve," she says.

I drop my hand. "Then wait here," I say. "By sundown, we'll be finished. The voidstone will be light enough to move."

Gaigane purses her lips and turns around. "Give me your training ring," she says under her breath to one of her men. He hesitates then removes a gold ring from his middle finger and hands it to her.

"What about this?" she asks, turning back and holding up the ring by its underside, letting it glitter in the sun. The voidstone is about the size of a pea. "Can you do eleutheria on this?"

Blythe and I exchange a serious glance while Chireseal groans.

The two of us nod in unison.

"How long?" she asks.

"A halfbell," I guess.

"Far less, Dem," Blythe utters. "Far less."

"Then show me," Gaigane says.

Chireseal clears his throat. "We really don't have time for this. It's the drive that's—"

"We *do* have time for this," I say, cutting off Chireseal with an icy gaze then letting that same gaze fall upon Gaigane. "If this is what it takes for the master voider of Scorpiontail to believe the truth, then so be it."

"Wonderful," she says, smiling wide as she hands me the ring with mock enthusiasm. "I cannot wait to be educated."

I grasp its gold setting with my bandaged hand. Blythe has already stretched out his hand in anticipation, and I accept it with my other.

"Ready?" I ask him.

He nods.

With a forefinger I touch the pea-sized voidstone tucked safely within the ring's setting.

The world disappears.

Blythe's instincts were correct—it takes us no time at all.

When we return to our sunlit existence, Chireseal lies on the ground with his hands behind his head but Gaigane and her two voiders still stand in front of us, nearly in the same place they were before. They're watching us intently.

"It is done," I say, letting go of Blythe and handing the ring back to Gaigane.

"Ah!" Chireseal says, getting up and rubbing his palms together. "That wasn't too painful. Now, we progress! From training rings to Axiondrives."

I ignore him.

"I thought it was supposed to float away," Gaigane says. She bounces the ring in her palm a few times, as if expecting it to rise.

"The gold has weight," I say. "If you remove the voidstone from the setting, it will."

"Oh," she says, her smile returning. Then she laughs. "Of course. The ring has weight."

The two men behind her laugh as well.

"But its power is gone, Gaigane."

She stops laughing. "What do you mean?"

"There are no more souls," Blythe says.

I nod. "The souls are the power source. Without souls, there is no voidance. Like a ship's sails without the wind."

She looks at me darkly.

"Try it," I say.

She hesitantly places the ring on her finger. It's far too large, so she braces it with her thumb. Then she touches the black stone with the index finger of her other hand.

Like most voiders, she closes her eyes. It's not necessary, but had they been open, she would have seen nothing different. Complete blackness. No indivisibles. And she would have heard the silence of a grave.

Simultaneously she withdraws her finger, exhales sharply, and opens her eyes. Then she closes her mouth, her jaw muscles rippling beneath her skin. Without a word, she hands the ring back to her voider.

"Is something wrong with it?" the voider asks as he grasps it, but she doesn't answer him.

"You destroyed a voidstone," she says to me, teeth clenched.

I nod. "And hopefully your stubbornness as well."

The voider behind her gasps then hands the ring to his peer. Behind Gaigane they huddle, analyzing the ring as if it were the first voidstone they'd ever encountered.

"Do you believe me now?" I ask her.

Gaigane places a fist to her mouth and looks at the massive Axiondrive. Her black cloak's sleeve slips down to her elbow, making her look as vulnerable as a child dressed up in her mother's clothes. For a moment, the only sounds are the waves hitting the stone wharf and the ropes clattering against the masts of nearby ships.

"Do you believe me?" I softly repeat.

Gaigane turns to face me, her short, graying hair fanning out momentarily. "Two of my voiders were found dead in their sleep last night."

Her words are unexpected. "I'm . . . sorry," I say.

She narrows her eyes. "Their throats were cut and their voidstones taken."

I open my mouth in shock.

She takes a deep breath and looks around at the wharf and the tiered buildings rising in the distance. "At first, I thought it was a simple murder, robbery. We expect such crime in these barbaric lands, especially after a war. Then a Northerner was also killed—and his voidstone taken, using the same technique. Three is a pattern. Someone is murdering voiders and taking their voidstones."

My mouth stays open as I ponder the implications.

"I don't know what to say."

"It wasn't you?"

I exhale in surprise. "Of course not."

"You're the only one I know who has a motive." She glances back her men. "Maybe you're trying to destroy all the voidstones you can get your hands on."

I shake my head. "No. Not like that. Not through murder."

She grunts then looks at Blythe. "What about you, Effulgent?"

He shakes his head, looking down at his sandals. "I am only a graycloak now."

She scowls. "I don't care what you call yourself. Did you murder my voiders?"

His head snaps up, eyes wide. "Do not be ridiculous!" he shouts, as if he were trying to gain the earshot of the fisherman in the distance. "That is owning the dark."

"I don't know what that means."

Chireseal groans. "It means that it's bad, alright? Murder is bad. We all mourn your fallen comrades. Quite tragic. Are we done here?"

Gaigane turns to him. "You think this is funny?"

He clears his throat. "No. Listen, we're simply in a hurry," he says, pointing to the Axiondrive. "We've got a job to finish, and we have nothing to do with whatever's going on. I'm sorry it happened, but it doesn't concern us."

She glances to where he points and opens her mouth but then closes it again without a word. Her brow furrows.

"Fine," she eventually says. "You keep delving then. Keep doing eleutheria. Keep destroying what makes you special. Throw away the greatest voidstone ever to be discovered in the land." Her lips form a snarl. "But you better stay away from Scorpiontail. Stay away from *me* and *my* voiders. Stay away from *our* voidstones. Are we clear?"

I nod distantly, but she pushes her finger into my chest.

"If I find out that you're behind these murders, that you're destroying our voidstones, then may Temberlain help you. You'll be a dead man. Your effulgents and graycloaks won't protect you. Your trapped souls won't protect you. The Unnamed himself won't protect you. I'll rip you apart, Democryos. Indivisible by indivisible."

There's nothing I can say. My mind still reels.

She knows the truth, and still she doesn't care.

EXODUS AND ARRIVAL

Once more I stand in front of the white room, my body its fourth wall. A doorway to freedom.

But this is not the land of the living. This isn't a room. I don't have a body. There is no door.

Blythe and I are inside the Axiondrive. Using voidance, we're traveled beyond the curtain of everything we know. We're part of it now. The fabric of power.

The exodus continues—and it ends today.

Spheres float toward me. Thousands of enervated. No reflections bend upon their curved surfaces. Yet there is light. There is nothing but light here.

If I turned around, I would meet the most terrifying black. The way through the stone to the outside world. I would surely be lost if it weren't for Blythe by my side. Using their common tongue, he speaks to the enervated. Is it *he* who is guiding *them* to freedom, or the other way around? After all this time, I get the sense that it's both. Regardless, his voice is reassuring, the only lighthouse in this storm.

At this moment, though, both of us are silent. The spheres approach.

My mind, my soul—my *existence* here—almost retreats in expectation, as if someone has handed me a hot kettle. I know what to expect. Blythe and I first experienced this when we performed eleutheria on a small voidstone in the destroyed remains of the temple. We had the same experience in Gaigane's ring moments ago. I've come to understand that it is a burden I must shoulder. The cost of their freedom is my sharing in their memories.

The wave hits.

The spheres pass through me, leaving visions of color and emotion. Painted pictures thrown into my eyes. If I had eyes. Flashes of pain, happiness, anger, fear, confusion.

Life.

An older man embraces someone much younger in a multicolored robe and sash. A wife? Daughter? He parts from her and walks up sandstone stairs, barefoot, never looking back. A pyramidal structure looms above, and a tall man in silverplate is there to meet him.

The man in armor . . . his face smooth and blue . . .

Another sphere.

Darkness and blood. But it's warm here. A murky pool. The feeling of belonging, as if being wrapped in the arms of a lover. I feel two heartbeats. One is small, the other shaking, pushing the pool of liquid around like a tide pool on the edge of a sea.

Then coldness . . .

Another sphere passes through me.

A young boy, tanned and windburned. He looks to be from Scorpiontail, except his surroundings suggest he's anywhere but. He's in an ice cave lined with white furs. Dogs lie about, whimpering. Or wolves. His hands are missing, and his wrists are wrapped in tourniquets made from torn clothes and oiled twine. He cannot pet the animals, but they get up and circle his feet, brushing up so devoutly he almost loses his footing. Then they growl toward the mouth of the cave. A man stands there waiting. A silhouette in the white-cold sun.

Thousands of these.

Sphere after sphere.

The wave eventually ends.

As the visions fade like sunspots behind closed eyes, I realize that the room is empty. After days of seeing the spheres packed together, rushing, wave upon wave . . . it's finally empty.

Blythe speaks to me, but not with his lips and tongue. Outside of this place, we have bodies, somewhere. Arms clasped, hands touching the Axiondrive, my voidance at work, allowing all of this. Through evil we destroy evil.

We can back up now, he says. *But be careful, Dem.*

Alright.

I follow his instructions. The white door shrinks in front of me, the corners becoming rounded. In time it becomes a circle, then a dot. But I hesitate before turning around. Besides Blythe's voice, this dot is my only point of reference in the unending night.

Dem, we need to hurry. This is the last of the enervated. They will wait for us, but only for so long. They want to go home.

So do I.

I face the darkness, and together we fly.

In some respects, everything is the same. Just as I've done every other day this week—every other time we've finished eleutheria—I take a moment to reacclimate to the light. To reacclimate to the *living*. In the span of many breaths, I relish the sun on my face, the feeling of rough stone and sand against my palms as I lie on the ground. The decaying smell of the sea, the beating of my heart, the breeze through my hair. The cries of the gulls. Even the painful tenderness in my fingers. All the little things that are only *here* and never *there*.

But this time, something is different. Despite our massive accomplishment, an elusive and haunting image remains, much like the dancing spots behind my closed eyelids.

Those men in silverplate. I've seen them before.

Chireseal gently laughs, pulling me out of my thoughts. I blink rapidly, forcing my eyes open and slowly sitting.

"You did it," Chireseal exclaims, hovering over me, clearly ecstatic. Then, turning around, he places both hands on the Axiondrive and gives it a good push. The massive thing wobbles and moves a few inches, the iron chain fragments dragging against the stone with a harsh scrape. Some of the soldiers turn in place.

"You actually did it," he repeats.

I look up at the blue sky. The sun is still strong and shadows are small—it must be around midday.

Blythe, lying next to me, sits and grabs my shoulder. "It is finished," he adds, a proud smile on his face, and I return it with a nod while wiping my brow with my shirt.

"I had my doubts about you two," Chireseal says, still rocking the empty voidstone. Beads of sweat fill his diamond-studded face.

He stoops next to us, focusing on Blythe. "That was really something. I've never seen anyone do that before on their own."

"Dem and I worked together," Blythe says.

He shakes his head excitedly. "Sure. Of course. But what I mean is without an eleutherian dri—" He suddenly becomes quiet, patting his face dry with his white cloak. I hear a muffled word.

"Eleutharian *what*?" I ask.

He clears his throat. "Nothing. I mean—you did this entirely by yourselves. You know. Just two people holding hands." He laughs. "It's not as if you had instructions written down . . ."

Blythe and I look at each other in confusion.

"Anyway," he says. "Great work."

I give him a distant nod then open my eyes wide.

It's not as if you had instructions written down . . .

I didn't see them. I read about them.

"Blythe," I softly say.

"Hmm?" He looks up from the ground, where he's tracing sandy grout lines between stones with a short twig.

"I know who they are."

Blythe frowns.

"The silverplated ones," I add.

"In the memories of the spheres?"

I nod. "I think they're called azuremen."

Chireseal sharply looks my way, eyes as piercing as his gems. "What did you say?"

"Azuremen."

Blythe looks up to the sky, squinting. "Azuremen," he repeats slowly, his lips pursed. "I've never heard that word before." He then meets my eyes with a patient expression. "But I gather you have?"

I nod. "In Chimeline's diary."

"She keeps a diary?"

"She just started it last night—"

"Where?" Chireseal asks. "Where is this diary?"

I'm surprised by how animated he has become. "Somewhere safe. Why? Have you heard of them?"

He looks toward the blue horizon and shakes his head quickly. "No. No, of course not. It's just a curious thing, is all."

"Dem," Blythe says, interrupting the awkward silence. "I'm confused. Why would Chimeline write about the silverplated ones? Did she meet one of them?"

I shake my head. "She saw them in her voidreams."

"Ah. Like when she knew about Mander's book hidden in the rubble."

"Exactly. The enervated revealed that to us, through her. And I think they have more to reveal."

"About what?"

"I don't know yet," I say. "But I aim to find out."

"Chimeline," Chireseal says slowly, almost chewing the word in his mouth. "Is that the woman you're sleeping with?"

I snort, insulted by his assumptive and demeaning tone. I cannot believe that this man is an effulgent.

"She is a friend," I mumble.

He seems unruffled. "Seriously? I would've sworn she was your woman."

"May I reminder you, Brother, that one never owns others," Blythe says to Chireseal. "Chimeline is nobody's woman and Dem is nobody's man."

The effulgent exhales through closed lips. "Yes. Yes, of course, graycloak. I am humbled by your reminder to never own the dark. Your words keep me on the path of unwanting." His voice is so flat and devoid of emotion that I cannot tell if he's being contrite or cynical.

Blythe smiles and nods, looking between the two of us. "We are all on the path together, are we not?"

"Of course." Chireseal clears his throat. "But back to this . . . friend of yours. Tell me more about her."

"Indeed," Blythe says. "The Unnamed has bestowed something special on her."

"Blythe," I say, a warning in my tone.

I glance at Chireseal. While he is an effulgent and has supported our endeavors in eleutheria, I cannot shake the feeling that something is off about the man.

I don't trust him.

"Let's not trouble our friend here with all the horrible events leading up to Mander's death."

Blythe blinks rapidly. "Alright, Dem. If you say so."

"She's been praying recently," I explain, looking back to Chireseal and feeding him a lie he should be able to swallow. "Reading the Book of Unwanting. Perhaps she's been having revelations."

Chireseal puts his palms together, and at first I believe that he's about to pray, but he just puts his fingers to his lips, thinking.

"What about you, Brother?" Blythe asks him. "You said that you had a revelation about finishing today. Have you had any more?"

His eyes move back and forth rapidly, as if he's consumed by a multitude of thoughts. The rest of his body is a statue. His pale face, white hood, and glittering diamonds are a stark contrast to the matte black Axiondrive behind him.

"I'm afraid not, Brother," he says with an exhale. "But I will, in time. Revelations always come with sufficient prayer, like the sun after the long night."

"Well said."

Chireseal raises a hand to his brow, shielding his eyes from the sun. "Speaking of revelations, looks as though we finished not a moment too soon."

Blythe and I follow his gaze northward to the stepped wharf that leads up to the city.

A single soldier on horseback approaches the square formation surrounding us. The saddle is ornate—and features King Andrej X's colors.

One of the soldiers guarding the Axiondrive breaks formation and walks out about a hundred feet to meet him on the wharf, leaving a precise gap in the line.

I cannot hear their conversation, and for a moment we watch in silence. Then the man on horseback lowers his visor and pulls off his helmet, nodding to the other soldier. His angular face is covered in sweat, and his short grayish-blond hair is matted down.

I inhale sharply.

"It's Reddles," Blythe says.

I nod, looking on raptly.

With his free hand, Reddles removes a rag from his saddlebag and wipes his face clean as he continues to converse with the soldier. Then the men clasp each other's forearms. The one on foot takes the reins and Reddles dismounts.

"That was a very quick trip," Blythe notes.

"Yes, it was."

"He must have had the blessings of the Unnamed during his travels."

I don't say anything.

Commander Reddles approaches us carrying only his helmet.

I stand, and Chireseal and Blythe follow.

Reddles passes through the gap vacated by the missing soldier, entering the square formation. He glances at the massive black stone that reflects none of the midday sun then looks to Chireseal, his wary expression dissolving only when he sets his gaze on Blythe and me.

He gives us a curt nod. "Dem, good to see you again," he says stoically. "Blythe."

"I am pleased to see your safe return, Commander," I say.

"The Unnamed has willed it," Blythe adds.

Reddles nods politely, but his weak smile fades as he looks toward the tiered heights of the city to the north. It almost seems as if he's avoiding something, and my chest tightens in response.

"Did you deliver the message to the king?" I ask, excitement and trepidation vying for control.

"I did."

"And? What did His Majesty say?"

Reddles looks back at me, and instantly I can tell that my fear was founded. His countenance suggests he's shouldering a heavy burden.

He takes a deep breath. "I gave it to him. The book. Told him everything that happened."

"Did he believe you?"

He shrugs and looks down briefly at his helmet. "I suppose so. But . . ."

"But what?"

"It was too late," Reddles says, looking back up at me. The sweat has returned to his face, but he doesn't have the rag to wipe it anymore.

"What do you mean 'too late'—too late for what?"

He looks down again, cradling his gold helmet as if it were a newborn.

"Well, did he at least read it?" I ask. "Does he understand that Mander betrayed him—betrayed me? Betrayed the entire kingdom?"

"None of that matters anymore." He points to the Axiondrive. "Only *this* matters now."

I glance at it. "What do you mean?"

He takes a deep breath. "The king is here, Dem. In Winter's Baiou. Right now."

I'm taken off guard. "What?"

"He ordered me to guard the stone, personally, until they retrieve it."

"Who's *they*?" Chireseal asks darkly. "Who's going to retrieve it?"

Reddles ignores his question.

"Why did the king come all the way here?" I ask in disbelief.

"There's to be a gathering. His Majesty wishes to address the people directly. He'll explain everything."

"When?"

"Tonight. At sundown. The Union. My men are making their rounds across the city as we speak."

Chireseal mutters under his breath as Blythe asks, "Is he to speak of eleutheria? Of the work we are doing here?"

"No."

"What, then?" I ask.

"Do you remember the last line in Mander's book?" Reddles asks me.

"*They're coming*," Blythe answers without hesitation. "Mander's final writings concluded with *They're coming*."

Reddles nods then swallows. "Well, they're here."

VOIDREAMING

The noise and light increased the further Temberlain went.

Back in the executive mess, the hum of the ship was muted, the light taking on the warmth of fellowship. Here, in the claustrophobic alleys of this city of a ship, noise-canceling technology wasn't considered a worthwhile investment. It was loud enough to require the raising of voices just to be heard. The light was harsh enough to pick up the most insignificant specks of dirt.

Or people.

Temberlain shook his head as he passed dozens of crew—most from Efful, but some Agh-Severian and Dodogh rabble as well. They were all ashen, yet they walked purposely in the opposite direction, toward the executive mess, as if they were empowered. Temberlain caught the various insignia on the shoulder patches of their uniforms. A few from the vats. Five from the common galley. Two from vacuum hardline. They even wore emergency FTL-differentiation vests.

Temberlain wondered why such an odd group was together and stationed near the captain, but the question was quickly replaced by embarrassment. As the group passed, they looked at the stain covering Temberlain's shirt, the whites of their curious and strained eyes showing.

He turned a corner.

The hallway opened into a massive multistory space, easily the largest room on the axionship, if one didn't count the drive chamber. Since the ship was at FTL, the immense window was heavily tinted, but Temberlain could still see starlines, a disorienting array of gray curving ever so gradually as the ship navigated other dimensions. Temberlain walked around its upper gallery edge at least fifty feet above the crowd, glancing down at the common mess, where most of the crew, empowered and ashen alike, ate and gathered. Normally the crowd would be sparse at this hour of rotation, but this was a celebration meant for all. Two hundred years had passed since the first axionship left the gravity womb of Efful, destined for the stars.

Junior officers and their assistants sat in tight formations, raising glasses of wine and singing songs from home, their voices echoing against the transparent starboard wall. Even the ashen—most from worlds beyond Efful—wholeheartedly joined in the singing, causing Temberlain to smile. Here they were, the conquered, joyously belting out tunes that glorified their own conquest.

This is the way we conquer. Not with friction. Not with fear, but with . . . patience.

A few of the more sober crew members looked up to see Temberlain walking along the glass-walled edge of the gallery. One empowered even stood and saluted. With a sigh, Temberlain returned the gesture. He was eager to change into a fresh uniform and rejoin his comrades, preferably before dessert.

On the opposite side of the second-level gallery, the open space narrowed into another tight hallway and the boisterous sounds of the common mess were replaced by the nondescript hum of the ship. The field of dim starlines was gone as well. Temberlain was now surrounded by an elongated cocoon of white. Doors to the left and right were laid out before him. He was in the officers' wing. His cabin was fifth in the distance.

Then the white became red.

The ceiling, the floor, the walls—all of it was suddenly cast in a deep crimson. It permeated everything like the immense propulsion flames of planetfall transports. The light undulated from nearly black to bright red to black again.

The emergency lighting meant one thing only: the ship was nearing FTL differentiation.

Which was impossible.

Temberlain hastily took the fabricreader out of his pants pocket and pressed the corner as it snapped into a firm screen. The screen's glow enveloped him like a salve, causing him to squint. It depicted a health dashboard of the Axiondrive and downstream power flows. Axionship biofunctions. Anti-gravity. Propulsion. Weapons systems. FTL navigation.

WARNING. DIFFERENTIATION APPROACHING. ONE HUNDRED MICROROTATIONS.

Temberlain ignored the earsplitting announcement and focused on the screen.

Every metric was nominal. There were no issues or errors of any kind.

He tapped on the screen to select *FTL Navigation.*

It didn't refresh.

He tapped it a second and a third time.

Nothing.

Scrolling, he found the officer comm team and clicked on Berbsby, activating her commplant. FTL navigation was her area.

Nothing.

Fuck.

There was no plan to break FTL this soon. This ship was set to travel for at least another hundred rotations before differentiating. Which meant one of three things.

One: it was a glitch.

Unlikely. The emergency lights wouldn't be triggered by accident—the ship has too many fail-safes.

Temberlain exhaled as he snapped off the fabricreader and stuffed the cloth back into his pocket. He took a few steps toward his cabin. His thoughts moved faster.

Two: it was a drill meant to catch everyone off guard, including the officers.

Also unlikely—especially now, in the midst of a celebration.

Which left only one other possibility. This was actually happening.

We're falling out of light speed.

Temberlain swallowed hard.

He had to get to his cabin, quickly, and brace himself for the quantum turbulence. If he didn't strap in, the dimension lessening would toss him around as though he were a rag doll.

WARNING. DIFFERENTIATION APPROACHING. SEVENTY-FIVE MICROROTATIONS.

Temberlain extended his palm on the lock as the announcement filled the hallway, drowning out the sound of the door hissing open. Inside, his Effulgian daylight lamp flickered on, but it was faint against the emergency light, which also pulsed inside his room. His cramped quarters were thrown into angular patches of white against pulsing red. It was nauseating.

He stumbled in, letting the door shut behind him. The hum of the ship was muted.

Temberlain pulled his soiled shirt out of his pants and had barely unclasped two buttons when he felt the hard barrel of a serrater against the side of his head.

"Move and you die," said a man's guttural voice, his throat doing more work than his tongue or lips. Dodoghian accent. "Use axion and you die. If you so much as *think*— you die."

Ashen.

"Nod if you understand."

Temberlain cautiously bobbed his head.

"Put this on," said another. Female. Still guttural but higher pitched.

Temberlain tried moving his head left toward the woman, but the man on his right pushed the serrater barrel forcibly into his temple, causing him to wince.

Something was placed into his hands.

He looked down.

His differentiation vest. In the red light inundating the small room, it didn't look red but gray.

WARNING. DIFFERENTIATION APPROACHING. FIFTY MICROROTATIONS.

"Put it on," the man ordered, pressing the weapon into him harder. Temberlain's head leaned to the left.

Sudden understanding hit him.

The ragtag ashen crew he'd passed earlier. They'd been headed to the executive mess.

They'd been wearing differentiation vests.

They knew this was going to happen. They were prepared for it.

The man rapped the side of his head with the serrater. Stars blended with the strobing lights for a moment.

"Alright," Temberlain groaned, raising the vest and slipping his arms through. He pressed the activation button and the vest closed against his chest.

"Now stay," the man said, as he gave him a rough push.

Temberlain felt his suit forcefully connect with the wall behind him. His core became immobile, firmly attached.

His left arm was lifted out at his side. A snapping sound and the coolness of metal against his wrist.

A dark blur passed in front of his face as the woman tossed the other restraint to the man, who caught it deftly.

A pull on his right arm.

There were locking his arms into place.

As he was about to brave another glance left, the two ashen crossed the small room and leaned back against the opposite wall, facing him. They activated their vests with punches to their chests. Their stocky bodies snapped into place, but not before the man dropped something on the floor between them.

Instantly, the air between Temberlain and the two Dodoghian turned hazy. Ripples against a vertical plane, as if they floated underwater.

A membrane grenade.

All detail was lost. Temberlain could make out only their general shapes—uniforms, dark and unruly hair tied into knots. No facial details or insignia. Still, the woman seemed familiar. Her voice . . .

WARNING. DIFFERENTIATION APPROACHING. TWENTY-FIVE MICROROTATIONS.

The man holstered his serrater and gave Temberlain a look of hatred so smoldering it was recognizable from behind the haze. The bastard knew that he was safe from the use of axion with the membrane between them.

Temberlain leaned his head back against the wall.

The ashen crew had found a way to trigger an emergency FTL differentiation and were performing a mutiny.

But why?

He looked at the two Dodoghian.

They could have killed him. They had a serrater and had caught him off guard, rendering the use of axion impossible. Instead, they'd forced him to put on the vest.

They needed him for something.

He shook his head at the absurdity. The thought of an axionship being taken over by ashen was . . . it was simply unheard of.

The woman said something in Dodoghian and the man replied. It sounded as if someone were choking to death.

"You won't get away with this," Temberlain snarled.

This silenced the man briefly. He cocked his head sideways.

"You can't possibly commandeer this axionship," Temberlain continued. "Once the captain finds out—"

"The captain is dead," the man interrupted. "As are your fellow officers. Your security. Your comms team. Everyone. Lucky for you, we need you. So shut your mouth and do as you're told and you might come out of this alive."

Sweat broke out over Temberlain's body and his mouth turned dry. He felt something he hadn't felt in years.

Fear.

The wine spill.

He'd been separated from the others deliberately. The mutineers had wanted him and him alone to come back here. They wanted him alive.

But why?

Temberlain peered through the ripples at the woman and then remembered. Despite the haze, her face was clear in his mind.

She worked in the drive chamber as a vacuum hardline engineer. The conduits connecting the inner chamber resources to the torus. She was part of his team. He didn't know her name, but he remembered her number. Sixteen. Her family were incredibly gracious givers.

The Axiondrive. This has something to do with the Axiondrive.

Temberlain clenched his teeth in frustration.

WARNING. DIFFERENTIATION APPROACHING. TEN MICROROTATIONS.

He could still use axion. The membrane only prevented the use of his power past the vertical barrier, which cut his room in half. It was meant to protect the two Dodoghian from Temberlain. Not Temberlain from himself.

If what they said was true—that the captain and the others were all dead—then he had to escape. Whatever they were planning, they would kill him when they were done with him.

He tried turning his head to view his bound wrist, but the protective vest prevented his head from swiveling. If he could see the brace on his wrist, he could subtly loosen it with axion.

I need a mirror.

The only reflective surface in his room was the cabin's monitor, which was turned off and behind the membrane.

An idea hitting him, Temberlain entered the world of axion.

Instantly, everything changed, softened, grayed. Gone was the loudspeaker, the reddish hue, the guttural language. He felt as though he'd dived into a dark embrace, a solace from the turmoil of the moment.

It was wonderful.

Colorless axion particles leisurely floated around Temberlain. The enervated protested, as usual, but he commanded them to be silent, and the dissonant chorus faded for a moment.

Do your job, and I'll do mine.

He saw the Dodoghians' membrane before him. It was all he could see in that direction, an opaque landscape. But despite its power, it was still a surface, a painter's canvas. He could turn his side into anything of his choosing.

Temberlain floated closer.

Starting near the floor, he began manipulating the axion particles on the surface of the membrane, drawing upon his axiongraph. In another place, he could feel the phantom pain of his living body. An icy burn upon his bicep—the design of a ghantstag's head. It started radiating up his arm. An echo of pain.

Creating a reflective surface wasn't difficult. It simply required the movement—the precise alignment—of the particles into arrays. Like soldiers upon a battlefield. By controlling the spacing between them, he could reflect almost all the light shone on them.

The enervated complained, but Temberlain ignored them.

On the membrane's vertical plane, he began to see a reflection of himself. Or the axion version of himself. He saw his body writhing with life—the glorious shimmer. There was nothing in the realm of axion as beautiful as living matter.

He saw his FTL vest. He saw the wall at his back. The wrist restraints.

Beginning at the floor, he began cutting through the wall, following his form as if he were a child tracing a drawing. He sliced through the particles with ease, ignoring the dust and residue that erupted. He worked via the reflection he'd created.

He assumed the world outside was complaining. The loudspeaker would be reading down the time in microrotations. The Dodoghians would be cursing in their guttural slime.

None of it mattered.

The wall broke free of itself before he finished, his weight causing it to snap into pieces. As his body fell backward, out of his cabin and into the hallway, he let go of axion. The physical world returned.

Callous light. Red and black and white.

A microrotation later, his body hit the floor, knocking the air out of him amid a cloud of dust. It was then that he realized he'd spent more time than he should have in the world of axion—his entire arm was numb and ice cold.

Coughing, he raised his head off the floor.

Through the opening that roughly resembled his form, he saw his reflection. Around its edges, the arms of the two ashen moved behind the haze. But they couldn't do anything. They were still forced up against the wall and trapped behind the membrane, prisoners of their own prison.

Temberlain flexed his biceps, breaking the particles of wall at his shoulders apart.

WARNING. DIFFERENTIATION INITIATED.

A violent gust of wind blew through the officers' wing.

Temberlain was thrown down the hall in the direction of the common mess. His body, still attached to remnants of the wall, fluttered like a moth with putty-colored wings in the firelight. He flew sideways, but the sensation was that of falling.

Down became up. His cabin door was now above him, receding from view.

He shot out of the narrow wing and hit the curved wall of the common mess, falling, sliding upward into the cavernous ceiling as if caught inside some gigantic white sphere. Spotlights slid underneath him. Pieces of the wall he was attached to fell away, along with his wrist restraints. Then he saw the destruction—hundreds of others caught in the chaos. Darting fish in a red aquarium. There were multiples of everyone. Of himself. A mosaic of Temberlains. A reflection in a bee's eye.

Shooting pain behind his forehead.

Then, all multiples converged as gravity returned. Red became black and black became white.

Down became down.

Temberlain fell. Past the glass railing of the balcony and toward the common mess a hundred feet below.

04

"The more I read, the more confused I become," I say, as I close the white-leather-covered diary. "I'd been hoping for the opposite."

But these words are for me only. Chimeline, Colu, and Blythe and his daughter, le-Daerke, are too consumed in their own conversation to acknowledge them.

The five of us huddle around one of the Lemon Tree Inn's common room plank tables. Even though the place is nearly empty, we sit in the back, out of earshot of the bar. Diamond-paned windows surround the room on three sides and more than half of them are open, letting in the late-afternoon breeze.

My hunger surfaces. I take a few pieces of softened cheese from the pewter plate, followed by a sip of honeyed lemon water.

Leaning back in my chair, I listen to my friends, biding my time. I want to speak to Chimeline about her recent writings.

"I still cannot believe that you finished!" le-Daerke says, beaming proudly at Blythe. "Despite Reddles' dire news, we shouldn't discount the glory of what the two of you accomplished."

Blythe is the first to notice that I've put down the book and am paying attention. "Ah, Dem." He leans over and clasps me on the back. "I was just going to suggest to my daughter that we do not own the light—we should not be prideful about this. Yet I agree that it is something we should be humbly thankful for. The Unnamed provided us the way of unwanting, and we followed the path, as we should."

I smile, reflecting on the progress we've made on so many levels. Back when I first met this man, he would have never used the term *daughter*, nor would he have encouraged her to come up with her own name—something she'd lacked her entire life.

"Father," says le-Daerke, leaning forward and placing her elbows on the table. "I would like to learn as well."

He turns to her. "Eleutheria?"

She nods in my direction. "I would be honored to partake in it. With Dem. On all future axion fragments that we confiscate."

Blythe frowns. "Confiscate?"

"From the Black Army."

He shakes his head. "Daughter, we do not confiscate. Confiscate implies taking. Taking is owning the dark."

le-Daerke looks away, out the window, and my thoughts react in a similar way.

Some things never change.

Outside, a man shouts something in the far distance. It sounds as if he's repeating something, but I cannot make out the words.

"You're missing the fucking point," Colu says. He downs his shortglass of sugarcanex and slams it on the table. "As usual."

Blythe clears his throat and straightens in his chair. "I am simply trying to instill a lesson."

Colu laughs as he pours another glass of sugarcanex from the nearby bottle. "A lesson," he says, in a deep and mocking voice. "Sounds more like you're trying to instill the same stick that's in your ass into hers."

Chimeline cracks a subtle smile.

"You are a crass man," Blythe answers. "No doubt caused by that hideous drink, which you consume as if it were water."

"Let's not argue," Chimeline says brightly. "I agree with le-Daerke. We should all be celebrating that eleutheria was done on that horrible thing."

"Absolutely," le-Daerke replies, looking back at us but mostly at her father. Her eyes take on the fiery glow of the sunshine from the nearby window, but this flame is tempered by her pristine white robe of the effulgency, which shines with a blue-tinged iridescence. Her normally flowing sleeves are rolled up and her hood is down. While her smooth and hairless body is the result of Blythe's effulgent heritage, her moderately dark skin is the gift of her Xian mother, le-Sante, a woman I have never met.

For a moment, as the playful bickering ensues, I watch on, lost in thought.

This group cannot be the result of randomness.

Long ago, Colu and le-Sante were lovers, but le-Sante left Colu to bear Blythe's child. Colu was a mason before he was a helmsman in the Xian navy. Over the course of years, he'd helped build the temple that Mander destroyed in a heartbeat with voidance. By the time I met Colu, he had deserted the navy, lost an eye, and become a mercenary at a hilma plantation run by one of my former students. Chimeline was sent to kill me with the very same moonspit she used on Mander—without which he would have never been caught. Now, the enervated call her an axionlighter. Marine, her soul still trapped within the voidstone, said that Chimeline is as powerful as any voider in the land. But for some reason Chimeline runs from this strange new gift, refusing to speak to me about it, even in private. Meanwhile, I have lost everything. I've shifted from master voider to master of nothing.

A too-thin Northern boy of about ten approaches our table. His hair is almost as long as Chimeline's and his cheeks are oily. At first glance, his buttoned-down shirt makes him look respectable, but then I notice that his collar is ripped, and set-in stains mar his sleeves.

He heads straight toward Colu.

The one-eyed Xian removes a silver coin from his pocket, flicks it in the air, and catches it with more dexterity than any sober, two-eyed man I know. "Greeveson, right?"

"Yes, m'lord." The boy eyes both the coin and the food.

"Any trouble?"

The boy shakes his head, handing him a small, tightly rolled-up scroll with a black waxen seal.

Colu sets down his silver piece in front of him then takes the scroll, snaps off the seal, and unfurls it. He nods to himself as he reads the parchment. "You did good, boy."

Colu sets down the scroll, which springs back into its former coiled shape. Then he slides the silver piece to the boy.

"Thank you, m'lord," he says, while eying the plate of cheese.

"Oh, dear Unnamed," Chimeline says with an exhale, pushing the pewter plate toward him. "Take a seat and have your fill, young man."

"Thank you, m'lady." He slides in next to her and begins feeding himself with one hand and pocketing additional pieces with the other.

"What was that all about?" I quietly ask Colu, leaning in while motioning to the boy.

The Xian hesitates then raises an eyebrow. "Insurance."

"Insurance?" I repeat.

Colu picks up the scroll, fidgeting with it. "Let's just say hanging around you lot has been extremely profitable for me." He hands it to me. "Shitloads more gold than I made at the plantation, and it's only been a week."

I analyze the seal which still sticks to the edge. It bears the imprint of a rat surrounded by its own tail.

The mark of the famed Baiou Rats.

"But unexpected income creates unexpected problems," he adds.

"You're doing business—" I turn my head in both directions to make sure there's no one in earshot then lower my voice further. "You're doing business with a thieves' guild?"

I hand the wax circle back to Colu.

Chimeline looks to the boy at her side, her mouth open.

Colu shrugs. "They have quite a legitimate bank." He purses his lips. "One that isn't any kingdom's bitch."

Chimeline furrows her brow.

"I don't understand," I say. "What's wrong with the Northern Bank?"

He laughs. "You kidding me? They won't accept a hefty deposit of gold from a Xian. Or they will, and I'll not see one fucking coin again." He taps the table with his scroll as if he were a drummer.

"What about the Bank of the Jewelled?" le-Daerke asks.

Blythe frowns at her.

Colu nods. "Sure. The Xian bank is good. But it has its own risks."

I look at him inquisitively.

He exhales, still tapping the scroll on the table. "I was a deserter, remember?"

I slowly nod. "Right."

"So the Rats' bank is my only safe option," he says, glancing at the young Greeveson. "A company who will look kindly upon my gold without any judgment."

"il-Colu, have you ever thought that giving away your gold would be the safest option of all?" Blythe asks. "For your soul."

Colu shakes his head as he continues to tap the table. "No. Never even crossed my mind."

"Oh, speaking of things crossing minds," I say. "We saw you this morning, on the wharf. Conducting business. Chireseal paid you for something."

Colu nods. "Map of Xiland. Gave me ten gold for it." He looks to Blythe, smiling wide. "You effulgents are the biggest suckers in the land."

le-Daerke clears her throat and Colu adds, "Well, some of you are."

"A map of Xiland?" I ask. "Why would he want that?"

Colu shrugs again. "I don't know, and I don't care."

More shouts from outside. Then something new—the sound of marching. We all look toward the open windows.

About two blocks away, dozens of soldiers walk down the street, sunlight reflecting off their polished armor. They clearly aren't local guards, nor do they seem to be the scrappy remnants of the war. They must be fresh from the citadel, with the king. Some branch off and enter nearby buildings.

The soldier in the lead is the one who's been shouting the entire time—I catch the words *majesty* and *Union*.

"They're gathering the masses," Chimeline says. "For the king's reception."

"I suppose so," I say.

"What do you think he'll say?" le-Daerke asks.

"Based on what Reddles shared," Blythe says, unusually darkly, "the king wants the Axiondrive secured. He's probably intent on continuing the evil that Mander started. To use it for black arcana."

"But it's useless now," Chimeline adds.

"The king doesn't know that," I add with a sly smile.

She returns the expression.

"What about the other thing?" Blythe says, his voice still heavy with worry.

We all look at him, and he taps a finger on the plank table.

"Reddles said that 'they're here.' Do you think the king will mention this supposed arrival?"

A palpable silence blankets the table.

"Nothing in our effulgency writings say anything about this," le-Daerke finally says. "Isn't that right, Father?"

He purses his lips. "Yes."

"I don't see any emissaries yet," Colu adds, peering out the window and tapping the scroll. "Nobody new besides these annoying soldiers who have nothing better to do."

I shake my head. "Perhaps tonight we'll find out."

Narrow shops underneath red awnings line the street across from us. An apothecary, a chandlery, and a barber. Next to these are doors that open to stairwells that lead to the living spaces above. Individual soldiers leave their ranks and enter them. Shutters above open and people lean over decorative iron railings, taking in the commotion below.

The lead soldier stops, causing the entire formation to halt. The din of metal and marching boots evaporates in the late-afternoon sun, causing an eerie silence.

Somewhere, a baby cries.

The leader raises his head, unfurls a scroll, and begins shouting its message.

"Greetings and celebrations! King Andrej X has arrived in Winter's Baiou! By His Majesty's order, all citizens are required to report to the Union at sundown today, to receive the honor of his presence! All must head toward the light! Any disobedience will be subject to punishment! May the Unnamed bless the protector of the Northern Kingdom!"

Once the soldier ends his announcement, the formation picks up again, passing directly in front of the Lemon Tree Inn.

"Head toward the light?" Chimeline asks, nose crinkling.

"Well, I imagine that in order for the people to see the king, more than just street lanterns will be needed. Maybe they'll use voidance to light up the Union."

"What a stupid time to gather an entire fucking city," Colu says.

Blythe nods, ignoring the curse. "I don't know why the king couldn't wait until tomorrow, so he could leverage the gift of daylight. The Unnamed always provides, if only we allow him to."

Chimeline gasps, covering her mouth with her hand. We all turn toward her.

"That strange effulgent knew this would happen," she says. "The one with the gems."

"Chireseal," Blythe and I say in unison.

She nods.

I lean back and run my hand through my hair.

"He said that something was going to happen," Blythe says to me.

I hesitate. "You're right."

Chimeline motions toward the open window. "I think Chireseal meant *this*. The king's arrival."

The large wooden front door of the Lemon Tree Inn busts open and hits the wall, causing the front barroom to go silent and still. The silhouette of a tall soldier stands within the doorframe, the golden sun at his back.

He enters slowly, looks around, then approaches the innkeeper, who wipes his hands with a rag before pushing his brass glasses up the bridge of his nose. The soldier wears the same uniform as the ones guarding the Axiondrive: torso armor, a red short-sleeved shirt, and a knee-length tunic. He's not wearing his helmet. Despite the dimness of the room, his fair skin is evident. He must have come straight from the citadel, otherwise the Southern sun would have made its mark.

"Did everybody hear the proclamation?" he asks, too loudly, as if he has not yet acclimated to being indoors. The owner immediately nods.

The soldier points to him. "It is your duty to check upon your patrons. Check all the rooms upstairs. Make sure everyone has heard."

"Yes, sir."

The soldier turns in place and addresses the common room. "Did everyone hear the proclamation?" he shouts again.

A weak chorus of affirmation sounds from the dozen or so people in the room, whose heads are buried in their glasses. Our group, nestled against the far wall and furthest from him, doesn't say a word, with the exception of Colu.

"Cock-brained idiot," he mumbles under his breath.

"Where is he now?" Chimeline whispers to me.

I face her and the far wall. "Chireseal?" I ask, keeping my voice low.

She nods.

"I have no idea. Reddles commanded us to leave the Axiondrive. Blythe and I came back here. I assume he went back to his temple." I look at Blythe. "Do you know?"

He shakes his head, so I ask Colu. "What about you? Have you seen him?"

"Not since morning."

"You, there! In the back!"

By the time I turn toward him, the soldier is already walking briskly past tables, coming at us.

"Fuck," Colu groans, subtly hiding his scroll somewhere underneath the table.

Greeveson flees. He ducks around a table on the way to the front exit, but the soldier lunges at the last moment and grabs the boy by his shirt collar, easily lifting him in the air so that his feet kick uselessly.

Chimeline grabs my arm.

"Where are you going, you little shit?" the soldier says, pulling him near.

"Let go of me!"

The soldier rips the boy's collar down further, studying the back of his neck.

"Just what I thought I saw," he says. "Mark of the Rats."

The boy keeps flailing and screaming until the soldier strikes him hard across the face with his open hand. Greeveson slackens, his knees buckling, but the solider pulls him upright again. "Stand!" he shouts. Then he roughly pats the boy's cheek a few times. Greeveson goes quiet and still. "That's better."

Behind me, Chimeline utters a rare curse.

"What's a Ratling shit doing in this establishment?"

The soldier glances back at the owner, who shakes his head. "I don't know who that there boy is, sir. Never seen him before."

The soldier grasps the boy's neck and takes a few more steps toward our table.

The man's size and strength are now evident to me. He's at least six and a half feet tall, and his arms and legs are massive. He reeks of body odor and oil from his breastplate.

He eyes all of us, his expression menacing, while walking around the table, pulling the young Greeveson along. "Any more rats sitting at this table?"

The soldier passes behind me, and I feel him roughly tug down my putty-colored tunic at the neck before releasing it. He does the same with Blythe's dark-gray shirt.

"We are not thieves, soldier," Blythe answers. "We follow the way of unwanting."

The soldier grunts while rounding the corner. He looks le-Daerke up and down curiously. "You an actual effulgent?" he asks. "Or an actor?"

"Actor?" Blythe asks incredulously.

He motions to the window. "From that troupe playing in Southpoint Square."

My mind flashes to the recent destruction of the temple. The felling of the bell tower, with all of us in it. My chasing after Mander through the park. The tent full of actors.

"I am not an actor," le-Daerke says.

"Never saw me an effulgent in a common room before," the soldier adds, raising an eyebrow. "May I remind you that lying to His Majesty's men carries a heavy sentence. You'll be taken to the giving house."

Giving house?

"Lying is not on the way of unwanting, and the way of unwanting leads to the most unlikely of places," she says serenely.

He seems to ponder her answer for a moment then motions to her neck while clearing his throat. "Well then, Your Effulgency," he says, in a slightly softened tone. "Please reveal your neck. I still need to confirm."

She complies without another word.

"Please," Greeveson murmurs. "Let me go." He fidgets, twisting in the soldier's hand, which is still around his neck.

The soldier eyes the boy in annoyance then shakes his outstretched arm. "Shut up, Ratling."

The boy winces, a tear running down his cheek.

Something on the soldier's forearm catches my attention. It's a tattoo, but I cannot discern its design in the shadows. It seems to carry a faint blueish glow—undoubtedly caused by the reflection of the sun on a windowpane. I peer closer, but he rounds the end of the table.

His attention falls next upon Colu, and his somewhat-respectful demeanor vanishes.

The soldier practically rips Colu's thin white undershirt downward. After a pause, he releases it with a disappointed groan.

"What about you, Xian?"

"What about me?" Colu asks. He keeps his head straight instead of raising it to meet the soldier's stare, adjusting his shirt and then taking a drink.

"Didn't you hear the news? You lost." The soldier looks up at the others in the common room, realizing that he has a captive audience, and his voice becomes almost as loud as the proclaimer outside. "Your ports are burned down. Your ships are sunk. We own Xi Bay now."

"Good for you" is all Colu says.

The soldier hesitates and frowns. I detect the faint air of disappointment, as if he were hoping he could goad Colu into some type of altercation.

He steps behind Chimeline. The back of her yellow dress is already low enough that any mark upon her skin would be evident. Still, he traces a single finger across her neck and shoulders while rounding the table. Chimeline tightly shuts her eyes.

He finally comes to stand in the same place where the conversation began. Then he bows mockingly, slowly walking backward with the boy. As he crosses an angular patch of sunlight, I'm able to see his outstretched forearm clearly.

"Remember," the soldier calls out. "Sundown. The Union. Head toward the light." The boy squirms again, and the soldier slaps him even harder than the first time. Greeveson cries out but only once.

I barely hear his words. I barely hear the child's scream. My body is paralyzed in both revelation and fear. The two visions—the one in front of me and the one in my mind—overlap.

The soldier. Temberlain. The present. The past.

His tattoo. It's not a picture, nor is it a design. It's a number. The same type of squared-off blue digits from Chimeline's voidream are inked there. Chimeline's voidream are inked there.

The digits *04*.

THE UNION

"I think I may understand what's happening with Temberlain in your voidreams," I say to Chimeline.

We walk close to each other northward and uphill, on one of the wide thoroughfares of Winter's Baiou. A violet dusk is settling upon the bay city. Up ahead, Colu, Blythe, and le-Daerke are focused on their own discussion. And surrounding us is an ever-thickening and diverse crowd: voiders, effulgents, soldiers, the wealthy and the common folk, Xian and Northerner, the young and old—everyone. The windows lining the street are all dark. The ornate iron balconies are empty as well, but lamplighters perch upon rickety ladders swallowed by pools of passersby, breathing golden life into the night. For now, they are the only ones not heeding the king's order.

"Really," she says. It's not quite a question.

"Well, not *all* of it," I admit.

She shakes her head softly as she observes the crowd. "I don't understand any of it, Dem. It's one thing to dream, but it's quite another to know that these dreams *mean* something. That our very lives may depend upon them. It can be very overwhelming. Especially having to write it all down after the fact." She taps her chest right above her heart. "But I *feel* it. In here."

"I know," I say. "It must be hard, but it's important that we continue to study their message."

Chimeline doesn't respond, so I continue. "For example, what does *ashen* mean? Or *FTL* for that matter?"

Even though we're close enough to touch, I must keep my voice elevated. Everyone around us is consumed in frenetic conversation, all speculating on what the king will say.

She doesn't answer.

"Temberlain and the crew . . . they're clearly traveling," I say. "And I have some ideas about what their vessel might be."

A man carrying a child upon his shoulders roughly brushes past, intent on getting to the Union before us. Colu yells out a curse.

"You do?"

I nod. "Do you remember when we first met Blythe? When he brought us into his temple?"

My memory takes me to the small farm village of Fiscarlo. It was after the airship crashed. When we regained consciousness, Chimeline and I found ourselves locked in cages, but by the end of our visit we were his guests of honor. Blythe was convinced that we'd been sent to him by the Unnamed to teach him a "lesson," and I'm not so sure that he was wrong.

"Yes."

"Do you remember the relic that he showed us?"

"I think so," she says, nose wrinkling. "The blue metal, on the altar. The piece that reflected the light in a beautiful way."

"Yes. Blythe said it was from his ancestors' ship. A very large vessel. Bigger than a city." I spread my arms above the crowd, toward the clay rooftops, which are slowly becoming black against the glimmering stars. "Bigger than Winter's Baiou."

After a moment, she looks at me. "You think that's where Temberlain is? In one of those ships?"

"I'm fairly sure." My next thought appears. It's as if one of the lamplighters is at work in my mind. I squeeze her shoulder and pull her closer. "But not just any ship. *Our* ship."

"Ours?"

I point to the ground. "The one that crashed in Xi Bay."

She blinks a few times but says nothing.

"Think about it," I say, extending my fingers individually as I work through my logic. "One, we know that a crash created Blackscar."

"Okay."

"Two, the Axiondrive was all that was left. Well, that and thousands of voidstones scattered across the land, along with other debris, like that blue fragment Blythe showed us."

I extend a third finger. "Three, Temberlain's people had to have been here after the crash. Maybe Temberlain himself."

"Blythe's ancestors," she says, lost in thought. "Their early writings."

"Yes."

"And Temberlain mentioned an Axiondrive," she adds. "You think his Axiondrive is ours as well. The one here."

"Exactly."

She takes a deep breath, and for a moment we walk in silence.

"There's another thing," I say.

"What?"

"Temberlain," I say. "He called it entering the world of axion. What he did with the mirror. Cutting through the wall. He was using voidance."

Chimeline nods. "That's what I thought as well."

I smile in the darkness, full of excitement and contentment, reveling in that familiar feeling of fitting a missing piece in place. I'm reminded of my discoveries back in the university laboratory, of when results of a voidance experiment perfectly matched my documented hopes and predictions.

Looking at Blythe, I'm eager to share this news with him, but the timing isn't right. There are too many people around.

When I look back at Chimeline, her face is full of concern.

"What's wrong?" I ask her.

She bites her lower lip. "Nothing."

"Doesn't this . . ." I extend my arms at my sides. "This discussion make you happy?"

Her expression shifts from worry to annoyance. "Why would I be happy?"

"Because we're figuring things out."

"Figuring things out?"

"Yes! What happened to Temberlain! What happened to his ship. What the enervated—"

She turns away from me in a huff, shaking her head and mumbling something.

"Wait. Chimeline, what's wrong?"

But before I can get an answer, a column of white light rises into the sky less than a mile ahead. It penetrates the wispy clouds, and its brightness rivals that of the waning moon.

The crowd gasps, and most people stop in place, craning their heads in awe.

Colu, Blythe, and le-Daerke all look back at us, shock upon their faces.

"Head toward the light," le-Daerke says slowly, remembering the proclamation.

"Let's keep moving," Blythe says, and I nod.

This avenue doesn't follow a purely straight path to the center of the city. It angles every so often as side streets jut off like broken glass shards. Because of this, we cannot see where the column of light originates. Instead, it appears over rooftops, a maze of a city lying between it and us. But we know where the maze ends.

It's coming from the Union.

"So wasteful," Blythe says above the crowd. "Subjugating all those poor souls for a hideous display of power."

I look at the column again and run my hand through my hair as we navigate the throng.

"It's black arcana, is it not?" Blythe asks.

I nod. "They must be using parallel voidance."

"What's that?" Blythe asks.

"It's when you break one large problem down into manageable sections," I explain. "Each voider can handle their own section without threat of voideath."

"There must be hundreds of black arcanists alive in the city," le-Daerke says.

"I suspect so." Then I pause in thought. "What do you mean by *alive*?"

She doesn't answer.

We round a slight bend in the street and squint.

Up ahead—perhaps five blocks away—lies Union Square, bathed in a cold white light. It bleeds from that open space, filtered between the three- and four-storied buildings on either side of us and causing sharp shadows to extend in our direction.

As we pick up our pace, I think about Mander. His power was unmatched in many ways. The hidden laboratory. The way he brought down the temple. The way he fused the indivisibles of my three friends to a membrane in the Celestium. Voidspeaking. So many techniques that were unfamiliar to me—and to the entire university. Each was a marvel in its own sickening way. The man seemingly had no limits when it came to voidance, and when I look at the column of light in front of me, I am reminded of this.

Union Square is the largest square in the city. It makes the forested park where the ruined effulgency temple once stood look like a playground. This area is four blocks by four blocks—an enormous negative space hewn from the architectural landscape of Winter's Baiou. Three-, four-, and five-storied buildings surround it, and in the center is a massive fountain with a tall stone pillar. At least twenty streets lead here, some wider like ours, some slender. People flow in through all of them—men, women, and children. And almost all are silent, heads up in awe.

Despite the fullbell, we're bathed in cold daylight.

Above the fountain is a floating disk-shaped white membrane, where the column of light begins. Now that my eyes have grown accustomed to it, I am again taken by its power. There is no warmth, yet our shadows follow us on the ground. In the spaces between the disk and the surrounding rooftops is the night sky. It's a muted color I've never seen before. Part gray, part orange, part silver.

The stars are absent.

It takes another tenthbell to pass through Union Square to its far side, where the Union itself lies. The round building, with its gold-plated dome, would be impressive in any other place or on any other day. It houses the city's elect and judges, and functions as both a courthouse and government center. Three massive doors are sheltered behind twelve stone columns lining the elevated front. At least thirty stairs lead to the wide landing, but the King's Guard prevent the throng from climbing them.

We stand about fifty rows of people from the front. We're more toward the right corner of the square than the center.

The doors open and a wave of silence rolls across the sea of people. More of the King's Guard emerge and stand to the side.

King Andrej X steps out, arms wide, a tongue of purple cloak trailing him.

But I'm not looking at him. I stare, speechless, at the three other men who have emerged.

They're adorned in silver armor. And the almond-shaped masks upon their faces are a reflective blue.

Chimeline inhales and squeezes my arm.

Blythe looks back at me, eyes wide.

"Dem," Chimeline says. Her voice trembles. "Those are—"

"Azuremen," I say.

"We need to go," she whispers. "We're not safe here."

I look around. Thousands of people surround us. We couldn't leave if we tried.

"Dem, I'm serious. We need to go."

I continue to look around in concern. The people all crane their necks for a better view, except a nearby wealthy woman adorned with jewelry. She peels back a shawl around her plain maidservant. The younger woman nurses a baby. Everyone seems oblivious to us.

My thoughts, much like the crowd, vie for clarity.

While I don't share Chimeline's petrification, I understand it because of her diary. The empowered threatened to place the red-skinned boy in soteria, somehow, using these men.

Yet, behind this dread is the feeling of excitement.

The enervated must have a purpose behind their messages. It can't be mere coincidence that imagery from Chimeline's voidreams is now appearing right before us.

First was the tattoo on the soldier's arm, matching the description of the ashen's tattoo in her dream. Next was my discovery concerning Temberlain and the Axiondrive.

And now this.

She pulls hard on my arm. "Dem, we need to get out of here."

"I believe you," I say. "But we can't move through this crowd. And even if we could, we would draw attention. It's safer if we just stay."

My words don't seem to help.

"I don't want to be here."

I wrap my arms around her and bring her head into my chest.

GREETINGS, SUBJECTS. GREETINGS TO THE CITIZENS OF OUR VICTORIOUS NORTHERN KINGDOM.

The king's voice booms from everywhere at once. I see his lips move, but the sound doesn't originate there. It comes from above and reverberates off the ground and buildings like the echo of a thunderclap. Any meager noise remaining in the crowd instantly dissolves.

I COMMEND YOU ALL, SOLDIERS AND CITIZENS ALIKE. THE PEOPLE OF WINTER'S BAIOU PLAYED A CRITICAL ROLE IN OUR VICTORY. AND THAT ROLE HAS NOT GONE UNNOTICED.

As his voice rolls across the square, the king takes a few more steps toward the edge of the landing.

FOR FAR TOO LONG MY PEOPLE HAVE SUFFERED. FOR YEARS, XILAND EMBARGOES WEAKENED OUR ECONOMY. RICE ROTTED IN OUR FIELDS. FISH ROTTED IN OUR BARRELS. ALL DUE TO OUR INABILITY TO LOAD OUR SHIPS AND SAIL THEM OUT OF XI BAY.

He places his hands on his chest and takes a deep breath.

NOW THAT WE HAVE CONTROL OF XI BAY, THE RICH HARVESTS OF OUR KINGDOM WILL AGAIN BE THE BRIGHTEST JEWELS IN THE LAND.

The crowd erupts in cheers.

"Fucking liar," Colu mumbles under his breath.

WHILE YOU WERE ALL BRAVELY FIGHTING FOR YOUR KING, I HAVE BEEN WORKING HARD ON FORGING A NEW ALLIANCE. ONE THAT WILL FORTIFY OUR REALM IN HISTORIC WAYS.

GONE ARE THE DAYS OF WAR AND AUSTERITY. WE NOW ENTER AN ERA OF PEACE AND PROGRESS. AND TOGETHER—WITH OUR NEW ALLIES—WE WILL FORGE AHEAD, WELCOMING WEALTH, HEALTH, AND HAPPINESS.

He looks down for a moment before gazing at the crowd again.

BUT PEACE ALWAYS COMES AT A PRICE, MY GOOD PEOPLE. AND WHILE MANY OF YOU HAVE ALREADY DONE MUCH, THERE IS STILL MUCH MORE TO DO. WE ALL MUST GIVE. IT IS IMPERATIVE THAT WE ALL DO OUR FAIR SHARE.

BEGINNING WITH VOIDERS. THERE WILL BE NO MORE MASTER VOIDER. YOUR MAJESTY WILL ASSUME ALL RESPONSIBILITIES ASSOCIATED

WITH THAT OFFICE. TOMORROW AT SEVENBELL, ALL VOIDERS ARE TO REPORT HERE FOR YOUR NEW ASSIGNMENTS.

Colu, Blythe, le-Daerke, and Chimeline glance at me.

Running my hand through my hair, I think upon the king's words. This is the last thing I expected. I was sure that he would have already named someone else to replace me—someone weak who would never question authority. As for the meeting tomorrow, what new assignments would be given? Now that the war is over . . .

AS FOR EVERYONE ELSE, YOUR HOMES ARE IN DISREPAIR. MEN HAVE GIVEN UP ON THEIR TRADES. HILMA ADDICTION IS ON THE RISE. TOO MANY CHILDREN CANNOT READ. GOLD IS SCARCE AND BREAD IS SCARCER. THERE IS A BLIGHT OF CONFIDENCE WITHIN OUR KINGDOM.

A rustle moves in the throng, as if the first winds of winter are shaking dead leaves free.

BUT ON THIS NIGHT, WE GATHER AT THE UNION BECAUSE WE CHOSE HOPE OVER FEAR, UNITY OVER WAR. ON THIS NIGHT, WE PROCLAIM THAT OUR HALCYON DAYS ARE AT HAND. THAT PROSPERITY AND GREATNESS ARE OUR NEW FUTURE. OUR ONLY LIMITS ARE OUR DREAMS. AND OUR DREAMS WILL TAKE US AS FAR AS OUR WILLINGNESS TO GIVE.

King Andrej X turns in place and motions to his guards, who flank the center opening to the Union. They spread out and open the other two doors—one to the left and one to the right. Due to my low vantage point, I can see only the shadowed underside of the gold dome through the doors, a soft maroon.

The king turns back to the crowd, his hand against his forehead as he scans the people. My chest tightens as his gaze falls precisely on me, but it doesn't linger.

I ALSO SEE MUCH OF THE EFFULGENCY IN MY AUDIENCE. YOUR SHINING WHITE ROBES GLITTER

IN THE VOIDLIGHT. WORD HAS REACHED ME THAT YOU HAVE AMASSED HERE IN RECENT DAYS, WHICH IS FORTUNATE INDEED. I COULD NOT HAVE PLANNED IT BETTER MYSELF.

Blythe turns to le-Daerke and places an arm around her shoulder.

The three azuremen, who have been motionless, turn to the king and nod in unison. The king nods back then continues.

TO THE EFFULGENCY, I SPEAK TO YOU NOW. PLEASE, COME FORWARD AND APPROACH THE UNION. WE WISH TO HONOR YOU.

Suddenly, the soldiers of the King's Guard shift in their formation, creating a small gap in its center. They push the crowd in front of us backward, forcing us more toward the corner of the square. A narrow channel emerges to our left. Upon the elevated landing the king steps aside, motioning with his arms, first to the massive square and then to the place where he previously stood.

PLEASE, ALL OF YOU, LET THEM THROUGH. LET ALL THE EFFULGENTS AND GRAYCLOAKS IN MY AUDIENCE STEP FORWARD.

Blythe and le-Daerke briefly look at each other with statuesque expressions and then nod once. le-Daerke pulls up her white hood, and they both step forward.

"No!" Chimeline calls out, leaving my arms and grasping le-Daerke's robe-covered arm before she's able to disappear into the crowd.

le-Daerke looks at her in confusion while Chimeline forcefully pulls her back toward us. Blythe returns as well.

"Don't go up there," Chimeline says to the two of them.

Blythe furrows his brow. "It is the king's command, my child."

Peering over the heads and shoulders of people to my left, I see two effulgents pass through. I cannot see their faces—just the bridges of their noses, as their white hoods are pulled up. Up ahead, another effulgent and graycloak begin slowly climbing the steps toward the king and azuremen, pulling up their robes so as to not step upon them.

le-Daerke motions to the top of the steps. "The others are going."

"No," Chimeline insists. "Stay here."

I briefly look at the landing and then back at her. "Did the enervated tell you something?"

She shakes her head. "They didn't have to. They're filled with fear!"

YES, YES. COME FORWARD. WE WILL WAIT.

The wealthy woman next to us leans in, addressing le-Daerke. "Your Effulgency, please, go up there," she says. "We all wish to honor you."

"We do not seek glory among people," Blythe says to her, and everyone in earshot. "It is owning the light. But I suppose it is the king's command, after all."

Colu's one eye studies le-Daerke and then Chimeline. He seems concerned. His jaw is clenched, and he grasps the hilt of the sword strapped to his hip.

"This is not a command you should obey," Chimeline whispers again, still clutching le-Daerke.

"Listen to her," I say. "I . . . I don't understand what is happening. But I know by now to trust her. With our lives."

"Please let go of me, Chimeline" le-Daerke says. "We need to go."

"Child," Blythe says, looking at Chimeline. "You must learn to place your trust in the Unnamed." He points to the king. "Baseless fear is owning the dark."

WE HONOR YOU BECAUSE OF YOUR SPIRIT OF NOTHINGNESS. YOU HAVE ALWAYS FOUND MEANING IN SOMETHING GREATER THAN YOURSELVES. YOU HAVE TAUGHT US ALL ABOUT THE WAY OF UNWANTING. THAT THE ROAD TO GREATNESS IS PAVED WITH SACRIFICE.

"Here, let me assist," the woman says next to us, raising her arms, which are covered in colored and jangling bracelets. "Everyone, we have an effulgent here! Please, let her through."

"No!" Colu booms loudly. He turns in place to look at the wealthy woman and then the others who have begun to give us space. "She's no effulgent."

Chimeline lets go of le-Daerke's arm in shock.

"She's from the troupe," Colu says. "We're all from the troupe."

The woman with the bracelets opens her mouth wide then exhales. "Oh, the comedy?"

She places a hand on my shoulder, as I'm the closest one to her. "I absolutely adore that production."

Blythe turns on Colu, outrage and confusion on his face. "You mustn't li—"

"Shut it," Colu interrupts.

I look around. There are over a dozen effulgents and graycloaks on the landing now, and still more progress through the crowd. Everyone has begun to speak again in this period of waiting. Colu's outburst, our hesitation, the woman's advances—it's all swallowed up by the surrounding chaos.

Colu roughly pulls down le-Daerke's hood. "Are you wearing clothes underneath this?"

Her expression is one of both confusion and offense.

"Are you wearing clothes?" Colu repeats, his voice urgent.

le-Daerke blinks a few times then nods once.

Before I know what's happening, Colu produces a small dagger from his belt, grabs le-Daerke's cloak near her throat, and cuts it straight down the middle in one smooth motion. She inhales sharply as he rips it off her shoulders, and it falls to the ground in a shimmering puddle. Underneath, she wears a gauze-thin long-sleeved white shirt and loose gray pants tied at the waist.

"il-Colu!" Blythe barks. "You are owning the dark!"

"I love it," the woman says, clapping once, then laughing while covering her mouth with her hand, which has more rings than I can count. "You don't even break character! Very impressive!"

Blythe bends to pick up the robe, but I stop him.

"Let it be," I say.

"Dem, that drunken fool has just—"

"Let it be," I repeat, looking at all my friends before letting my gaze settle on Chimeline. "We must trust her instincts."

"We must trust the Unnamed!" Blythe quickly follows.

"What if it's the same thing?" I ask. "What if the Unnamed is using Chimeline?"

This briefly silences him.

Blythe eventually exhales and looks toward his fellow effulgents and graycloaks up on the elevated landing near the king. There are over two dozen now.

"I don't understand," he says, though he shakes his head in surrender. "As far as I'm concerned, you are all owning the dark."

EXCELLENT! DO WE HAVE THEM ALL?

The king's words silence the crowd once again.

YES, YES, I DO BELIEVE WE HAVE ALL OF THEM.

He motions to the three open doors of the Union.

PLEASE, ALL OF YOU, STEP INSIDE. STEP INSIDE OF THE UNION. WE WISH TO HONOR YOU.

The soldiers of the King's Guard stand at attention on each side of the three open doors. At first, the few dozen effulgents and graycloaks look to each other in confusion, but they eventually acquiesce and slowly enter the inner darkness. I strain to see if one of them is Chireseal but can't tell from this distance.

THAT'S RIGHT. GO INSIDE.

A single azureman follows them. He's the last to enter before the guards close the doors with three echoing *thuds*.

EXCELLENT.

The king wipes his palms together, smiling.

THE EFFULGENCY HAS SERVED US WELL, BUT IT IS TIME FOR THIS INSTITUTION TO CHANGE.

THE WAY OF UNWANTING SHALL NOW BE CALLED THE WAY OF GIVING, AND OUR EFFULGENCY TEMPLES SHALL BECOME GIVING HOUSES ACROSS THE LAND.

Blythe's expression changes from one of annoyance to one of confusion. "He can't do that," he says, first to himself and then to his daughter. "He can't do that," he repeats.

le-Daerke doesn't answer. She only looks back with a worried expression, first at her father, then at Chimeline, and finally at me.

NOW IS THE TIME TO PROCLAIM NEW RULES. THE OLD ONES OF THE EFFULGENCY—*ONE SHALL NOT OWN THE LIGHT*, *ONE SHALL NOT OWN THE DARK*—THOSE HAVE SERVED US WELL, BUT THEY SERVE US NO MORE. INSTEAD, WE WILL NOW HAVE NEW RULES OF GIVING. IT WILL BE EVERY CITIZEN'S RESPONSIBILITY TO BE ABLE TO RECITE THESE BY HEART. FOR THE ONES WHO CAN READ, THESE WILL BE POSTED IN THE SQUARES. FOR THE ONES WHO CANNOT, IT IS YOUR DUTY TO LEARN FROM THOSE WHO CAN. OUR GIVING HOUSE ATTENDANTS WILL BE HAPPY TO TEACH ALL WHO ENTER.

The king clears his throat. It sounds like rolling thunder.

IF THOU IS DYING OR SICKLY, GIVE.

IF THOU IS SENTENCED, GIVE.

IF THOU CANNOT PROVIDE, GIVE.

IF THOU FEELS UNWANTED, GIVE.

IF THOU WISHES TO BE PART OF SOMETHING GREATER, GIVE.

AND THY SPONSORS SHALL BE FOREVER HONORED.

As the echoes of his words fade to nothing, the crowd remains silent, each person turning to their neighbors in confusion.

YOU WILL ALL COME TO UNDERSTAND IN DUE TIME. YOU WILL ALL COME TO UNDERSTAND

THAT GREATNESS IS NEVER FREE. IT IS EARNED. FOR THOSE WHO GIVE THEIR LIVES FOR THE GREATER GOOD, THERE IS NO GREATER HONOR. FOR THE REST OF US—THE SPONSORS—WE SHALL BEAR NUMBERS THAT QUANTIFY OUR INTENT.

The king holds up his arm, pulling back his cloak. I see a blue glow.

THIS NUMBER MEANS EVERYTHING. NOT JUST FOR YOU, BUT FOR YOUR FAMILIES AS WELL. IF YOU ARE GOOD SPONSORS, IT WILL GROW. THIS IS THE KEY TO UNLOCKING YOUR DREAMS. WHETHER IT IS GOLD THAT YOU WANT, OR THE HEALTH OF A LOVED ONE, ANYTHING IS ATTAINABLE. YOUTH FOR THE RICH OR WISDOM FOR THE YOUTH. HARVESTS FOR OUR FARMERS. WIND AT OUR SAILORS' BACKS. ANYTHING IN THIS NEW KINGDOM IS ATTAINABLE. ANYTHING AND EVERYTHING.

Suddenly, white light flashes from behind the closed doors of the Union, through the slender crevasses between them and over their thresholds. It lasts only a moment, as if bolts of lightning struck within.

The king ignores this light, but the two azuremen briefly turn toward it. I see the curved white lines reflected in their blue visors.

"Good Unnamed," Blythe utters.

Chimeline falls to her knees.

GO NOW. ALL OF YOU. BACK TO YOUR HOMES, AND DREAM. DREAM OF THOSE WHO ARE OLD, DYING, OR SICKLY. DREAM OF THOSE WHO CAN BE OUR GIVERS. MAYBE IT IS YOU. SOME ARE DESTINED TO GIVE. IF THIS IS YOU, DO NOT FIGHT IT. THAT IS NOT ON THE WAY OF GIVING.

I stoop to Chimeline, putting my arm around her. She's crying uncontrollably.

Above us, the crowd stirs, their confused whispers cresting like a swarm of locusts.

AND THEN DREAM OF WHAT YOU WANT IN THIS LIFE. DREAM OF OUR SPONSORS. MAYBE IT IS YOU. THERE IS A PLACE FOR ALL OF US IN THIS NEW KINGDOM.

Blythe squats, his face twisted in disbelief. le-Daerke hovers near.

Chimeline struggles to get the words out. "They're . . ."

She makes a fist and her jaw clenches, either out of rage or uncontrollable sadness. But then she reaches out and gently touches Blythe's face with shaking fingers. "I'm sorry, Blythe. I'm so sorry."

"What's going on?" Colu asks from above.

"They're dying," I utter. "All of them."

Colu doesn't say a word. None of us do. Blythe only shuts his eyes.

They're being placed in soteria.

GREATNESS FOR THE NORTHERN KINGDOM! GREATNESS IS THE WAY OF GIVING!

A scattered few in the crowd erupt in applause, repeating the king's words, but most do not. They don't understand what's happening.

Blythe suddenly stands and wraps his arms around his daughter, clutching the back of her bald head with his hand. I hear muffled weeping, but I don't know who it's coming from.

The crowd slowly disperses, as if sleepwalking. They've been told to dream and are already acting as if they are. No one talks. No one looks at the brightness above.

Still huddled near the ground, I embrace Chimeline and look past her, staring at le-Daerke's shining puddle of a robe.

It's being trampled upon by strangers.

THE END OF THE RIVER

The five of us shuffle out of Union Square without a word, heads down like the rest of the sleepwalking crowd. We exit through a diagonal corner, into a street much narrower than the thoroughfare we entered through. Everyone seems to have a destination. One by one and family by family, people take even narrower alleyways with muted deliberation, not needing to look up and read the clay street-name placards on the buildings' brick and stucco sides. Younger children are carried, asleep upon their fathers' shoulders. Mothers cradle babies hidden in drab-colored rags.

The massive column of white, now at our backs, continues covering everything in an eerie glow that is not quite daylight and not quite moonlight. Even though I cannot feel the light at my back, I know it's there, some ghost's hand upon me, pushing me down.

I get the strangest sense that it's not for us to see them. It's for *them* to see *us*.

My body yearns for sleep. The familiarity of home. The soft darkness of bed. For the briefest moment, I pursue a childlike fantasy—that this is all some dream. That when we wake up, Winter's Baiou will be as it once was. The old rules. The old powers.

No. The world will never be the same. And sleep is a distant shore.

We can't go back to the inn. Not now. There are two people I desperately need to speak to: Reddles and Chireseal. And while I don't know where the latter is—or if he's even alive—the former's whereabouts are certain.

The commander guards the Axiondrive at the Port of Yamerind.

Reddles traveled here with the king and azuremen. He may know what the azuremen plan to do. How many there are. What the voiders have to do with all of this.

After a quarterbell, the column of light disappears, returning Winter's Baiou to the mercy of warm lamplight, glittering stars, and bruised, purple streets. Ours is nearly empty. A few people walk with us, all headed toward the southernmost section of the city. The waterfront.

"About time they extinguished that fucking thing," Colu mumbles, breaking the silence.

Blythe and le-Daerke's faces are drained of emotion. With their hairless skin, they tend to look like stone on a normal day. But tonight, they have become it. No muscles move. Their eyes are pebbles. If they stood in one place, if only for a moment, I would believe that they were statues erected to the memory of their kind.

Chimeline isn't faring much better, although her emotions are plain to see. She's tangled in thought, rubbing her temples with her fingers. Twice I catch her looking up at the waning moon and stars, and while I wonder what's on her mind, I never ask.

A few blocks later we stop, and for the first time since leaving Union Square, Blythe and le-Daerke awaken from their pensive state, looking around in all directions.

A forest lurks up ahead, green swallowed up in the darkness. A park within the city. Then I see the white-and-red-striped tent. The black stage.

Blythe extends his hand to his daughter. She accepts it, and they slowly walk forward. The only sound is the grating dust and sand on the cobblestones beneath their sandals.

The three of us follow closely.

Once we round the pillared corner of a Xian bathhouse, the remains of the temple and bell tower are visible in the distance, barely illuminated by the meager orange glow of nearby lampposts.

I'm surprised that the ring of debris, at least fifty feet in diameter, is still there. I had imagined that all of this would have been cleaned up by now, a scar trying to heal. Almost a fortnight ago, I climbed out from within its center, miraculously untouched. I then pursued Mander through the park, ultimately losing him.

Within the ring, the massive brass bell reflects the meager light. Movement comes from inside. A black cat slinks away.

Much closer is the temple itself. Wooden pews, row after row, most of them naked under the night sky. The vaulted ceiling above is torn away, revealing ribs of wood.

"The effulgency is in ruins," I mumble. The words aren't meant for anyone but me, yet Blythe hears them.

Still clutching his daughter's hand, he turns to face me.

"It may seem that way," he says. "Yes, our temple is destroyed. Our people have been placed in soteria." He turns back to his daughter. "And we may very well be the last of our kind." Blythe's face contorts in the orange shadows as he fights off tears. "But I will not own the light and I will not own the dark. None of us should. The Unnamed continues to guide us."

I admire my friend in profound silence. His unwavering conviction in the face of such evil is the very definition of faith. A kind of faith that's as unattainable to me as voidance is to him.

"The effulgency will live on," he continues. "No matter how many temples fall to dust, no matter how many are placed in soteria, the effulgency will prevail. For it is not made of bricks and stone and flesh and bone."

He's crying now, pointing to the ground with his free hand, his jaw clenched. "It is made of a love that can never be taken, because it is freely given."

Blythe lets go of his daughter and wipes his moist face with his shirtsleeve.

"I'm sorry," Chimeline says, her voice almost breaking. "I'm sorry that I couldn't stop it from happening. Or warn you. Your people." She shakes her head rapidly. "Nothing in my visions led me to believe they would do such a thing. I felt the enervated's fear, but I . . . I didn't know."

Blythe approaches her and places his hands on her shoulders. "It is alright, Child. It is clear to me now that the Unnamed is working through you, guiding us. My faith was lacking."

Chimeline briefly shuts her eyes and gives a hesitant nod while Colu emerges from the shadows of the trees.

I look upon him in shock and confusion as he storms into the warm light of the nearby lamppost. I'd had no idea that he even left.

He carries two wigs, one blond and one black.

"Can you hold this?" he asks me, but it's not a question. Before I'm able to answer, he dumps them into my hands.

What remains in his hand is a glass vial.

"il-Colu, what are you doing?" Blythe asks.

Colu ignores him. Delicately, he approaches le-Daerke and lets a few drops fall upon her bald head. We all watch in silence. Her mouth is slightly open, breathless. It's as if he's anointing her, reenacting some sacred tradition of the effulgency.

He pockets the vial and extends a hand to me. "The dark one."

I pass him the wig.

"il-Colu?" Blythe growls.

Colu places his hands within the wig's center, fanning the tendrils out, ensuring the front is facing accordingly. Then he raises it over le-Daerke's head and sets it down, smoothing it out.

He backs up, studying her for a moment. His mouth twists into a wry expression.

"What?" le-Daerke asks.

"You look like your mother," he whispers.

le-Daerke looks down, not quite hiding a somewhat-haunted expression.

"il-Colu!" Blythe snaps. "This is unnecessary and ridiculous. We don't have time to play childish dress-up games and rekindle memories lost."

Blythe's words seem to break the spell. Colu takes a step toward him, removing the glass vial from his pocket.

"You think I'm doing this for me?" Colu asks.

Blythe takes a step backward, palms raised. "I do not pretend to understand the reasons for your actions when you are clearly not on the way of unwanting."

"They're hunting the effulgency. Which means you need to blend in."

Blythe blinks a few times then tries backing further away, but Colu crosses the distance and grasps him by the shoulder. With his other hand, he lets a few drops of glue fall upon Blythe's head.

"il-Colu! Refrain, at once."

Colu pockets the vial and extends his hand in my direction without a glance. I place the short blond wig in it.

"Stop!" Blythe says, struggling in Colu's grip. "I am not about to hide myself like some back-alley thief!"

"Yes, you are."

"And what if I refuse?" Blythe screams while squirming, but Colu tightens his grip further. "Are you going to strike me again? Hit me in the face like you did on the way into this city?"

Colu doesn't answer. Instead, he wraps his other hand around Blythe, bringing him into a full embrace while still grasping the wig behind the man's back.

"Because that's what you do, isn't it?" Blythe continues, his voice quieting and breaking while he continues trying to push himself away. "Violence and drinking that poison is always your answer, you fool."

Colu says nothing. He just stands there, hugging Blythe tightly in the darkness.

Blythe's resistance slowly washes away with his tears. He stops fighting Colu's embrace and eventually returns it, wrapping his arms around the larger Xian man, grabbing his shirt with clenched fists.

As he sobs uncontrollably into Colu's shoulder, I turn away, raising my head to the stars. They're out of focus, due to my own eyes' welling up. But I continue to listen, remembering.

Before, when he held his daughter's hand so formally, Blythe's cries were constricted. He was still holding on to his dreams. He was determined to fight. These cries are the opposite. They are the sound of a man giving up. He's being washed away—freed from his own unrealistic expectations of himself. Just as I was on the balcony of the plantation house, after Cleanthes overdosed on hilma. I was ready for anything—for nothing. But then Chimeline was there. I grabbed hold of her with everything I had because she was all I had left.

This is eleutheria, in its own way.

"I'm sorry," I hear Blythe say amid weeping, his voice muffled. "I'm so sorry, il-Colu. You are not a fool. It is I who is the fool."

When I turn back, I see Colu placing the wig upon Blythe's bald head.

"I must look ridiculous," Blythe eventually says, sniffling and wiping his face again with his sleeve while looking at all of us.

"You always did," Colu answers.

le-Daerke nervously breaks the silence on our brisk walk to the Port of Yamerind.

"I don't know how you people deal with such idiocies," she says, flicking back the dark hair covering the side of her face. "It's driving me mad. I can hardly see where I'm walking."

"You need to brush it," Chimeline says, by her side. "And use a tie. I will show you in the morning."

"If there is a morning," le-Daerke mumbles. "Only the Unnamed knows what will happen between now and then."

This silences Chimeline for a moment. She bites her lip before adding, "Morning will come, as sure as your beauty. The long black hair suits your skin color."

Blythe loudly clears his throat. "Do you think the commander will talk to us?" he asks, changing the subject. Instinctively, I assume it's his own way of rebuking Chimeline's reference to le-Daerke's appearance.

I nod. "He's a reasonable man. And we have a history."

"But he takes his orders from the king."

"So?"

"What if his orders are to keep silent? What if he knew what was going to happen to us?"

I shrug. "Well, we're here. We're going to find out one way or another."

We descend past rows of palm trees. The buildings and streetlamps are behind us now. Docked ships and jutting wharves lie a few hundred feet away. I smell the salt of the sea but cannot make out the Axiondrive or Reddles and his men in the waning moonlight. Everything is quiet. Even the wind is still.

"Dem," Chimeline says, grabbing my forearm and forcing me to a stop.

"What?"

She motions to the shoreline.

A hundred feet away is the square area where we performed eleutheria. The stone wharf sits between massive docked galleons, their ropes and sails snapping in the night.

Between them, random reflections glitter in the darkness. I strain my eyes, trying to make out the details.

"I can't see anything, Chimeline."

"Something's wrong," she whispers.

"What is it?" Blythe asks, squinting.

She doesn't answer.

"Can you tell us what you see, Child?" Blythe gently asks her.

She rubs her temples with her fingers while shaking her head, eyes closed. "I don't see anything. I *feel* something."

I glance at Blythe. He studies her with fatherly concern. It's eerily quiet.

"Where are the guards?" le-Daerke asks with a frown.

I begin descending dozens of stone stairs windswept with sand. I take them two at a time, until I leave all palms and foliage behind and step onto the grand wharf itself.

Momentarily, I stop. I am not prepared for what I see.

"Good Unnamed," says Blythe, out of breath. The group comes up behind me.

Over fifty mangled bodies lie strewn about on the stone ground. The reflections I saw from above were their chest armor. I see the moon disfigured in pools of blood, black as oil.

Frantically, I walk about looking for the man I came to see.

I find him.

His uniform is ripped away. His hair and skin are gone. Under twisted pieces of chest armor are muscles and bone and blood. All pink and white and red in the moonlight. Like the bodies on the green when Mander used waves of voidance.

Reddles' star medallion is the only thing that identifies him. Still dangling around his neck and over muscle and sinew, it shines like the true-north star, the brightest of them all. O'Eridani, the End of the River.

"Dem?" Blythe says.

I look up. He stands in the exact center of the wharf, his palm to his cheek.

"The Axiondrive is gone."

WHITE HEART, BLACK HEART

I look up from the commander's barely recognizable body. Blythe stands fifty feet away, in the center of the pier, where the Axiondrive used to be. His moonlit light-gray clothes create a sharp relief against the galleon's black-painted hull at his back. To his left, Colu, Chimeline, and le-Daerke hover near the dark water's edge, silhouettes against the sea.

I cautiously navigate the twisted remains of soldiers and moon-filled puddles of blood.

By the time I reach Blythe, he's pacing in a small untouched area, putting his hands to his new hair before quickly pulling them away.

"It was the Black Army, wasn't it?" he asks.

I give him a somber nod. "It's too perfect and devastating to be anything but voidance. They obviously wanted the Axiondrive."

Blythe looks at me doubtfully. "Badly enough to kill His Majesty's men over it?"

I turn to the sea and exhale. "I don't know, Blythe."

"I thought that your black arcanists followed the rule of law," he says. "That they would never condone murder."

"That is true," I say. "I would have never allowed this. But when Mander died, my voiders scattered. Rumor has it some sell their services to the highest bidder."

"You mean someone paid gold to a black arcanist to do this?"

I look back at him. "Maybe."

Blythe exhales in disgust. "Gold. A material almost as vile as axion."

Nearby, Colu brandishes a dagger and stoops. He looks up at us with his one eye.

"This soldier is still alive," he says.

I approach and crouch by Colu's side.

The soldier's eyelids and lips are burned away. His eyes wobble like a fortune teller's baubles, randomly predicting a future. He mouths something but his teeth click. A gurgling noise becomes a fountain.

"He's trying to tell us something," I say.

"He's dying and nothing more," utters Colu. He cocks his head in my direction. "Unless you can heal him?"

Even if I were to resort to voidance, the only stone I have on me is the one containing Marine. It's not powerful enough to boil a cup of water.

But what if I *did* have a full voidstone? Is it justifiable to save this man's life in exchange for the torment of countless souls?

"My healing days are over" is all that I say.

Colu grunts as the two women come forward from the pier's edge. Chimeline's eyes are wide with fear. She looks down at us, shaking her head distractedly. "We need to go, Dem."

The moon sits directly behind her head creating an aura of white light around her black hair.

"Effffffffgrh—"

I glance back down at the dying man. His spherelike eyes have found me. Blood pours down his cheek.

"One of them is coming," Chimeline says.

"Who?"

She looks to the rising buildings in the distance. "An azureman."

I turn in that direction but see no one.

Chimeline grasps my shoulder. "We need to go. Blythe and le-Daerke are in danger. And so are we."

My initial thought is that Chimeline is simply paranoid due to all this carnage. Despite the azuremen's hideous powers, I don't feel directly threatened by them. None of us have committed any crime. However, we are at the scene of one, and I remind myself that I'd be a fool to ignore Chimeline's instincts.

Standing, I study in more detail the rising shoreline, the buildings that seem stacked upon themselves as they fade into the night. Weak golden light seeps from a few windows. The distant streetlamps give off more illumination, but it's scattered and diffused behind palms and foliage.

"How far away is he?" I ask her.

She points to the same wide stairs we descended moments ago. "He's coming from that direction. He'll be here within a tenthbell."

I glance down the lengths of the pier. It goes on for at least a mile in both directions.

"Alright, this way," I say, grabbing her hand.

"So we're just leaving him?" Colu asks.

I nod, continuing to walk. "We have to. There's no time."

"What are you doing?" Blythe asks.

I pause, looking back. Colu has his blade against the soldier's throat.

"Ending his suffering," Colu whispers.

"His suffering is not yours to end!" Blythe says. "It is for the Unnamed! Put that blade down!"

Colu groans then puts away the dagger in a flash of moonlight.

"Everyone, let's go," I say, continuing.

Once we're past the field of bodies, our pace quickens. We head west, keeping the sea to our left. The bottoms of our sandals slap the stone, creating an echo.

"Don't run," Colu barks. "Step lightly."

As we round the stern of the massive galleon, more piers become visible. They're all adorned with ships but none as grand as the one we left behind. To our right, the wide stone walkway ends abruptly with sand, palm trees, and grasses that rise into tiered bluffs. A winding road runs parallel to us about fifty feet above, but the bluff is too steep to climb. Over this, stucco buildings loom.

Up ahead, another path juts north in the moonlit distance, perhaps rising to the road above, but it's at least a few hundred feet away, past three piers full of smaller ships, one-masted sloops and two-masted schooners. Only a chaotic bundle of nets, bamboo cages, and rope lying in the middle of the wide walkway—most likely left by fisherman in haste—offers any type of concealment.

"There," I say, pointing to the mess.

As we near, a stench wafts over us.

The cages and nets are full of dead crabs. A rusty bell-shaped anchor lies nearby, still tethered.

Rounding this disarray, the five of us duck down in a tight huddle. The bundle of rope and wooden cages is about four feet tall and six feet wide and dense enough to give us cover. We're at least a hundred feet away from the dead.

"Child, is he still coming?" Blythe whispers.

Chimeline nods, sitting on the stone ground with her back to one of the cages. She doesn't even attempt to keep watch.

We wait. The only sound is the soft clanging of ropes and ruffling of dropped sails caught in the easy wind.

"He's here," Chimeline whispers.

We all hunch closer to the ground and each other, peering over the chaos of nets, except Chimeline, who covers her head with her hands.

A single azureman emerges.

He walks out from the cover of the palm-covered stairway we took moments ago into the wide expanse of the port.

He walks leisurely, yet upright—as a commander would.

The moon reflects off his body, which is covered entirely in silver armor. His smooth almond-shaped face mask emanates ambient blue light.

We watch as he steps over the bodies without even looking down. It's as if they're litter. He heads straight to the center clearing, where the Axiondrive used to be.

For a moment, none of us breathe.

The azureman stands in place, not turning. Not moving. He's a living statue staring at the sea.

"What is he doing?" Blythe whispers.

I shake my head.

Then, sudden movement.

The azureman turns his head sharply, looking around then down. He takes a few steps, still looking at the ground, until he stands directly over one of the bodies.

"Fuck," Colu says.

"What?"

"That's the same one. The one who was still alive."

The azureman brings a hand to his chest and a piercing yet eerily silent light radiates forth. I briefly see a circle of petals on his chest before all shape is swallowed in white.

Chimeline inhales sharply.

Despite our distance, it's clear in the contrast of white against black that the soldier's body lifts a few inches into the air.

As the light goes out, his dead body drops back to the ground.

le-Daerke gasps. "He just put him in soteria."

"That man was one of the King's Guard," Blythe says. "He didn't even attempt to save his life."

"Or question him," I add.

Chimeline continues to keep her head down but says in a shaking voice, "He's questioning him now."

For a moment I stare at her in confusion. Then I drop down, grasping her shoulders so that we're face to face.

"They're speaking in soteria?" I whisper.

She nods then closes her eyes tightly.

Everyone else joins me, huddling close around her behind our cover.

"It was an effulgent," she whispers.

"What do you mean?" Blythe asks.

"The soldier. He's . . . he's answering the azureman's questions." She swallows hard. "It was an effulgent who killed them all."

"You said this was voidance," le-Daerke says to me.

"It was."

"An effulgent cannot use voidance."

I turn to her. "Mander did."

"Yes, but he was a monster. An abomination."

"Daughter—" Blythe begins.

"He was dressed in white—and hairless," Chimeline says, her eyes tightly closed.

"No," Blythe says. "This makes no sense."

"Sure it does," Colu says. "Some fucking effulgent wanted revenge for what just happened to your people."

"That's not our way!" Blythe says with a gasp. "And we don't even know—"

"The timing isn't right," I say, motioning to the array of bodies in the distance. "Based on the condition of the bodies, those men were probably killed around the time that we were at the Union. Not after it."

"He had a wagon," adds Chimeline. "And horses."

Colu leans back, his one eye unblinking.

"What is it?" I ask.

"It was that strange fucker from Northinglight," he says, bringing his hand to his cheek. "Diamond face."

"Chireseal?" I answer.

"Listen to you two," Blythe says. "You didn't trust that man from the very first time we met, and now you're grasping—"

"I sold him a large wagon and four draft horses yesterday," Colu says.

I stare at Colu and then at Blythe, whose face is now twisted in anger and confusion.

Chimeline opens her eyes. "He's telling the azuremen about us now."

Her words douse all conversation. My chest tightens.

"Everyone stay down," I say, as I rise slightly and peer beyond the maze of nets.

The azureman has moved away from the soldier. He now stands on the edge of the field of bodies, facing us.

I quickly duck back down, swallowing hard.

"What?" le-Daerke asks.

"He knows we're here."

For a moment, none of us says anything.

"We should run," le-Daerke says.

"No," says Chimeline. "It's too late for that."

"Well, hiding like this is owning the dark," Blythe says. "Let us turn ourselves in and tell him what we know. We haven't done anything wrong. In the end, he still answers to the king."

"Idiot," Colu says. "He just killed the king's soldier. He'll kill us just the same."

I look at Chimeline. "What do you think we should do?"

She meets my eyes and swallows once. "I think Colu's right."

"So we fight?" Colu asks, grabbing the hilt of his sword even though I doubt he could draw the long weapon, stooped as he is.

"Yes," she says, standing. I follow her lead.

"He's going to see us!" le-Daerke says.

"He already does," I mumble.

The other three hesitantly stand as I turn toward the azureman.

He slowly approaches, posture as straight as before, hands at his side. He's already covered more than half the distance and is about fifty feet away.

We shuffle out from behind the tangled web of nets and cages.

Colu brandishes his sword.

The azureman keeps walking.

Blythe and le-Daerke clasp hands and lower their heads in prayer.

"I've killed men with thicker armor than that," Colu spits, drawing out his sword.

Forty feet away.

I push down my fear, intent on using logic and reason—the only weapons I have left.

"We had nothing to do with the bloodshed," I call out to him. My voice carries through the night air.

He continues walking, unfazed.

"And we had nothing to do with the theft of your Axiondrive." I cringe at my choice of words. It was never this man's Axiondrive to begin with.

He still approaches. Thirty feet away.

"How many of you are there?" I ask.

Silence.

One more try. A lie this time.

"I know who you are and where you're from. I knew Mander. I knew about his Celestium and I knew about him using voidspeak to reach you. The three lighthouses. The *Halcyon Roadmap.*"

He stops in place, twenty feet away. His head smoothly turns to me and tilts ever so slightly.

"Where is the Axiondrive?" he asks. His voice is clear and loud despite the mask.

I briefly turn to my friends. Do I tell the truth or lie? Everyone besides Colu stares at the ground.

"I don't know," I eventually say.

A weak breeze sails through.

"Lying to us will be harder in soteria."

Us?

The azureman raises his hand, palm forward with fingers half curled, not quite forming a fist. In the center of it glows a small circle that turns from black to blue to red.

Colu advances, bringing his sword up past his shoulder.

A red star fires out of the azureman's palm, moving faster than anything I've ever seen. The air distorts. It heads straight toward the approaching Colu, but just as it reaches him, an intense white glow explodes out of Chimeline. The azureman's star erupts into a storm of sparks as it collides against an invisible curved sphere inches from Colu's face. A clap of thunder echoes out into the night.

A membrane.

Colu retreats in shock while the azureman turns to face Chimeline. In his blue visor I see our distorted reflections. Chimeline's shining form is like a flickering candle flame.

He tilts his head again. Then he raises both of his hands. His palms go from black to blue to red.

Dozens of stars come at us, but every single one of them hits a large curved membrane surrounding our entire group. They deflect off and explode into red rain and a sequence of thunderclaps that shakes my bones to sand.

Chimeline's legs begin giving out. I hold on to her from behind. My hands find hers. They're already freezing cold.

The azureman stops firing and takes several wide steps, until he's within arm's length of our membrane, which still ripples violently.

He taps his chest with one hand.

The armor there opens like a blooming flower of death. Bright light blinds me. I partially cover my eyes with my outstretched hand.

The light curls and pulls. It moves like smoke upon glass. Like fog upon the warm surface of a lake. I've seen this light before. The puddle in the Celestium. Behind the closed doors of the Union. A moment ago, with the soldier's body. But this time, it's right here in front of me. *My* soul is its intended target. And while reason tells me that Chimeline's membrane keeps us safe, every indivisible of me pleads for death before I can be taken in this way.

Colu shouts a battle cry and charges forward through Chimeline's membrane, sword held out in front of him.

He thrusts it right into the white heart of the azureman.

The light immediately changes.

The air beyond the membrane darkens. Shadows overtake everything. I can hardly even see the glint of Colu's sword, the glittering night sea, the azureman's blue visor, the moon. It all goes near black. As if I am already in the void.

The azureman doesn't make a sound, but beyond the swirling shadows he looks down at his chest then at the still-screaming Colu. The petals in his armor are slender, slightly-curved lines. The sword is stuck there, preventing the iris from closing.

The azureman bends his knees, shifts his weight, and then suddenly whirls around, swinging his arm like a club and striking Colu's right side.

With a bone-crunching sound, Colu flies through the air and lands on the stone ground many feet away, unmoving.

Chimeline goes limp in my arms, her head falling against her chest.

The membrane oscillates violently. Patches of darkness spread across the curved surface like ink stains upon parchment.

Together, we sink to the ground.

The light coming out of her begins flickering off. Then on again. Then it stops completely.

"Chimeline!" I cradle her head.

She's unconscious.

I look up. The azureman stands before us. He's only six feet, but he seems like a giant. Meager light swirls in tidepools around his armor's slender opening. Dark clouds pull the air but also push, as if we're in a storm with no direction. Chimeline's hair rises off her face.

Our membrane has all but vanished. Ripped gauze.

The azureman grabs the blade sticking out of him with both hands—the hilt is too far away. He pulls and the shaft moves slightly.

"Dem!" comes a shrill voice.

I stare into his chest opening. Before, the light was so strong that I couldn't even see, but the iris is almost closed now. It's like staring at the sun during an eclipse.

Black. I see a black object within the white.

A voidstone.

"Dem!"

I turn toward the voice.

It's le-Daerke, pulling free from Blythe's arms. She throws me something in the darkness.

A flash of gold.

Letting go of Chimeline, I instinctively reach out and catch it.

As the chain wraps around my closed fist, I feel the object's heaviness and know immediately what it is.

I don't have time to ask le-Daerke—even with a look—why she had a voidstone on her. And not just any voidstone. A full one, not yet brought to weightlessness by eleutheria. One as large and intact as any voider would possess.

I don't hesitate. I enter the void.

Chimeline's membrane sits ragged in front of me, its indivisibles broken and decomposed. I move through them, through the air between, toward the azureman. His indivisibles do not glisten with life as my friends' do. It must be his armor. Everywhere it resembles a membrane. I can't see the structure of anything behind it. Except for the iris in his chest, which is a maze of complexity.

I move straight into it.

There. A voidstone. As large as a fist.

Or a heart.

It's suspended in some type of setting within his body. Like a gold necklace but three-dimensional. A dozen or so pulsing strings lead into and out of it.

Veins.

I cut through them all in one fell swoop.

The voidstone falls inside his chest cavity then tumbles out through the meager opening between two petals, hitting the hilt of Colu's sword on the way down.

I let go of the voidstone, one kind of darkness replacing the other.

But this darkness is euphoric. The soterian light has vanished. The night is as the Unnamed meant it to be.

The azureman falls forward.

I spin and take Chimeline's unconscious and frigid body with me, rolling to the side. The azureman collapses to the ground where we just were. With a loud, reverberating *ring*, Colu's sword breaks in two, the hilt-end flying.

The largest voidstone I've ever seen—aside from the Axiondrive—slowly rolls away. It's roughly spherical, about the size of an orange. It comes to rest against Colu's motionless body. Blythe, kneeling there, eyes it fearfully before looking up at me.

"Did he perish?"

With a grunt of exertion, I turn the azureman's body over. His armor is incredibly heavy. His chest is still split apart, metal petals dilated. I briefly inspect them with my fingers—they don't give at all, and the edges are razor sharp. The tip of Colu's sword is still inside.

"I think so," I say.

"Colu is hurt badly," Blythe adds, after a pause.

Briefly, I shut my eyes in frustration and worry, but I cannot help Colu or Chimeline now. Not yet.

I run my hands over the helmet. It has lost its blueish hue and is now a muted gray. There are no seams.

"I can't get this off," I mumble to myself.

"Watch out," le-Daerke says, approaching.

I lean back in surprise as she brings down the rusty anchor upon the azureman's visor.

A hairline crack forms as the anchor tumbles aside.

le-Daerke cries out in exertion as she picks it up again, but I intervene.

"Let me."

It must weigh fifty pounds.

I raise the anchor over my head and drop it down with all my might.

The crack lengthens.

I do it again.

And again.

It takes about a dozen hits, but eventually the visor breaks into large shards of metal. One of them drops to the stone ground with the crystalline sound of glass.

There's only darkness behind the visor.

le-Daerke and I exchange a confused glance.

Working my fingers inside the man's face, I remove more shards of metal. They come away easily, eventually revealing an opening.

My jaw drops. I blink once in disbelief.

What remains is . . . impossible.

"Father," le-Daerke says. The word is filled with horror. The same horror that I feel.

Blythe looks up sharply from Colu's body then scrambles over and falls to his knees by her side.

"Good Unnamed," he says, looking down. He peers more closely, studying the remains of the head. "What is that? Colored string?"

The three of us all stare at it, speechless.

It's impossible for me to vocalize the complex sensation of my reality crumbling.

I'd always suspected that the azuremen were harbingers of change. From the very first moment, when they were nothing more than wispy concepts in my head. Now, they have climbed out of Chimeline's voidreams and are here, right in front of me, a fearful promise fulfilled. What lies before me is an abomination. What I see now—with my own eyes—creates more questions than it does answers.

The azureman doesn't have a face.

PART TWO

NORTHERN MARKED / SOUTHERN MARKED

VOIDANCE, VIOLENCE, OR VIRTUE

I scramble over to Colu's unconscious body and inspect his wounds in the darkness.

The entire side of his chest is caved in. He has multiple cracked ribs—at least four, maybe five. His breathing is shallow. His face is swollen and bloodied. The eye patch is pulled down, revealing his empty eye socket.

As I put the patch back into place, his eye opens a sliver.

"Stay with me," I tell him.

Herrophilus, my great submaster of healing, where are you now?

Yet in one significant way, he is here. His teachings are enough.

While the war may have been a ruse, it caused us voiders at the university to fine-tune our healing practices—specifically to create triage voidance that took only heartbeats to perform instead of the fullbells required for complete healing. Because in the field of battle, heartbeats are all you have.

I remember Herrophilus' lecture on flail chest—when ribs are broken due to blunt trauma. The area can't hold its shape when the subject takes a breath.

I eye the voidstone on the ground that I used to defeat the azureman. The one le-Daerke threw to me. Its gold setting and chain glint in the night.

"Blythe," I say.

He looks up, and I motion toward it.

"Throw me the voidstone."

For a moment he looks down, forehead creasing. Then he picks it up by the gold chain using his index finger and thumb. After swinging it once, he lets it fly through the night air. It hits the ground a few feet from me and slides into my leg.

"What are you doing?" Blythe asks me.

"I need to stabilize him."

le-Daerke and Blythe lean in, conversing. Then le-Daerke looks at me, straightening her shoulders and narrowing her eyes. "You're not going to use black arcana, are you?"

I pick up the voidstone by its gold setting and feel torn. She's not wrong to judge me. This is the new hideous question: when is voidance justified?

I know the answer.

Never.

le-Daerke continues, unfazed. "Dem, do not confuse my intent. The only reason I gave that hideous thing to you before was to kill the azureman." She points at Colu. "But this? This is not the way of unwant—"

"If we don't do something, Colu will die."

le-Daerke blinks once then looks to her father. "We cannot allow this."

Before Blythe can answer, a raspy sound comes from Colu. He's trying to say something.

"She's right," he wheezes, through pained breaths. "You need to get out of here."

"Colu, we're not going to—"

"Just go."

le-Daerke brings a hand to her mouth.

I turn to Blythe and shake my head. We can't just do nothing.

Instead of answering me, Blythe eyes the voidstone in my hand, his expression haunted and resolute.

Suddenly, he scrambles over and grasps my hand. Balling it into a fist, he forces us both into void.

There's deafening noise in the colorless darkness. The voices of the enervated.

But then a single strand rises above them all, next to me. Blythe.

The wind dies like a wave crashing upon the shore. Only a few strands are left behind. They weave in and out like braids in a rope.

Then, silence.

Dem? Can you hear me.

Yes.

I spoke with them. They say it's alright. But you don't have much time. Whatever you do, you must be quick.

I . . . understand.

My simple reply betrays the multiple thoughts swirling around me in the darkness. The enervated have given their permission for me to use voidance on Colu. Quite literally, it is a transfer of pain from one being to another.

I fly forward into the glittering light of Colu as my thoughts shift from humility to fear.

They said I must be quick. Why? Because the pain it too much for them to bear? Somehow I think not. Somehow they know that time is not on our side. It's not just the sunrise arriving soon.

I don't fuse the fractured bones. I simply create a membrane inside his chest that acts as shield. It covers his lung, protecting it from being punctured, as well as raises his ribcage, allowing him to breathe.

When I leave the void, Colu's breathing is much better, but he's still in obvious pain—perhaps even more than before.

Blythe stares at him, his mouth open. "The light . . ." he says. "It was so . . . beautiful."

I hastily remove the weathered leather pack from around Colu's waist.

"Everything living looks like that in the void," I say distractedly, but then I glance at Blythe briefly. The look of admiration upon his face reminds me of my former students, and I regret that I don't have the time to devote to this teachable moment.

I open the pack, which I'll use to pick up the azureman's massive voidstone, resting against Colu's leg. In the darkness of the nighttime port the voidstone almost disappears, making it seem as if a piece of his body is missing.

"Blythe, can you help Colu to his feet?"

He nods as distantly as a ship out in the bay.

"Blythe," I snap, louder. "We need to get out of here."

He blinks. "Alright."

"I'll carry Chimeline," I say.

Not wanting to enter the void, I'm careful not to touch the large black sphere with my bare hands. It falls into the pack and clatters among Colu's belongings: a few gold coins, the vial of clippings glue, the Baiou Rats' scroll, a whetstone. After adding the much smaller voidstone that le-Daerke threw to me, I close the pack tightly, hoist it around my waist, and cinch the leather ties. It hangs awkwardly. The azureman's voidstone must weigh five pounds.

"Where are we going?" Blythe asks.

"I'm not sure," I say, looking around.

The small northerly path I noticed earlier sits less than a hundred feet in the distance. It seems to head up to the road above, back into the heights of the city.

I pick up Chimeline's cold body and rest it over my shoulder. "This way."

Blythe helps Colu to his feet.

Without another word, the five of us leave the azureman and head toward the path. Upon reaching it I feel my spirits rise—steps lead upward and curve out of sight behind tall grasses and palms. It's a more private route than the one we took to get here.

The climb is difficult, but soon we reach a slender gravel road that runs parallel to the port. The stairway continues on the opposite side, but it's nestled between stone foundations instead of sand hills and shrubs. Lit by small hanging oil lamps, it leads into a dense neighborhood of rising stucco buildings.

We take it.

"What's the fullbell, you think?" I ask Blythe amid deep breaths.

"Hmm," he groans. "Threebell? Four?"

"Fishermen are usually out before dawn," Colu grunts. "Port's still empty."

I nod in agreement and lean against a stone wall for a brief respite. The others do the same. The windows up ahead are all dark.

"The bells," le-Daerke says, after a moment of silence. "Nobody is ringing the bells."

I glance at her in confusion. But once I see the sadness in her eyes, I understand what she means.

The effulgency temples.

The sound of the effulgency bells has been with me my entire life. For the most part, I simply took them for granted. They were just *there*, like chirping birds in the morning or the orange glow on my walls at night. In the worst of times, while I searched for Marine after she left me, their sound was menacing—a stubborn voice carrying a message I had no wish to hear.

But it was I who was stubborn. And their voice is something I now profoundly miss.

"They'll ring again," I tell her, continuing to climb. "As the Unnamed is my witness, they'll ring again."

We reach an intersection. The road here is wide enough for only two people to walk side by side. The buildings are three or four stories and stacked next to each other, preventing side passages. Oil lanterns hang over the alleyway on iron links, their light meager. Deep shades of purple and orange blanket the unforgiving stone and stucco, creating the illusion that they're softer than they really are. Far above, the stone is bathed in the moon's rays.

These are the homes of the rich, with priceless views. At this fullbell, all the windows are shuttered and padlocked. Darkness lies behind them.

Except for one.

Up ahead, an orange light glows behind closed shutters.

"There," I say, taking a right down the alleyway.

Soon we reach the home. I look up and see smoke rising within the narrow channel of moonlit sky between rooftops.

"They've got a fire going," I say.

Placing my hand on the iron doorknob, I pull up on the heavy latch.

It's locked.

I sigh deeply, exhausted and frustrated.

"Dem, these are private residences," Blythe says. "We cannot just enter."

Ignoring him, I think of my options.

There are three ways to do this: voidance, violence, or virtue.

Virtue.

Forming a fist, I knock on the door, just loudly enough to hopefully draw the attention of someone inside while not waking the neighbors.

We wait.

I shift Chimeline to my other shoulder.

From far away comes the weak, echoing sound of shouting.

Not just the shouting of one or a few but of many.

"That's coming from the port," Blythe whispers.

"No shit," Colu groans.

Movement from inside.

The warm glow behind the shutters moves. Behind us, black shadows on the purple wall follow, like thieves ready to strike.

For a moment, the distant shouting is the only sound.

Then, much louder, the rattle of a key being inserted.

The door opens a few inches.

Behind a thick black safety chain, a stocky older man in gray-striped bedclothes and an ivory necklace stands with a brass oil lamp. He's obviously been up for a while. His eyes aren't tired or creased but clear as he studies the five of us.

"May I help you?" he says. His voice is deep and formal and his back is straight, as if he takes his position quite seriously. For the briefest of moments I'm reminded of Elrich, my young footman at the Royal House, and wonder what has become of him.

"We need assistance," I say quietly. The closest shuttered window is only feet away.

He narrows his eyes.

"What is wrong with these two?" He indicates with a subtle leaning of the lamp.

"There was an altercation. They need healing."

For a moment, he studies them.

"You should take them to a voider for healing," he says. "Or an effulgency temple for praying over. I do not understand what sort of assistance this home can—"

"We need privacy," I say urgently.

The shouting has gotten louder.

The servant tilts his head. He heard it too. Clearing his throat, he says, "If you will please stay here, I will wake my master."

He begins closing the door, but Blythe, still supporting Colu, steps forward.

"Those are effulgency beads, are they not?" Blythe asks.

The servant blinks then looks down and pulls up his necklace, revealing a length of pea-sized ivory beads from underneath his gray bedclothes.

"Why, yes, they are," he says, running his fingers across them devoutly.

"You were saying your morning prayers to the Unnamed before we interrupted you," Blythe adds.

The servant blinks again then nods.

Blythe tugs his blond wig and winces as it separates from the skin of his scalp. Once le-Daerke sees what her father is doing, she assists, pulling it off completely. Glue flakes float in the lamplit air like dust, and behind them I see candlelight flicker awake in a window down the alleyway. Someone on the third floor opens their shutters. They clang against the stucco walls, echoing out into the night.

The servant raises his light, inhaling sharply. "Your . . .Your Effulgency." He gives a bow.

"There are no closed doors on the way of unwanting," Blythe answers.

The servant blinks a few more times and then suddenly slams the door.

Shouts come from the intersection.

I hear a rattling chain falling against wood.

With a meager squeak the door opens wide, revealing darkness behind a perfect globe of flickering light surrounding the servant.

"Inside," I whisper. "Quick."

Blythe enters first, supporting Colu. I push le-Daerke ahead of me with a hand on her back, looking down the length of the alley.

I enter last carrying Chimeline and stop the servant just as he's about to slam the door. I guide it gently closed and he nods in understanding before quietly reattaching the safety chain and locking the door with a key from his pocket.

"Douse it," I command him.

He twists the small key on the side of the oil lamp and the flame disappears, leaving us in near darkness.

For a moment, the four of us stand there, saying nothing, only listening. A *drip, drip, drip* comes from a water clock somewhere in the room.

Outside, the clamor grows.

Suddenly, a rush of men pass by—the hard, echoing clatter of armor and marching feet. There are no windows in the foyer, but in the dimness I can make out an adjoining sitting room past a wide opening and supported by flanking columns. Its window must be the one from which I saw the servant's lamplight. Beyond its shutters, silhouettes flicker, one by one.

Eventually, the group fades into the distance, leaving behind only incessant faint shouting and barking dogs. I hope that they're not palehounds tracking our scent. If that's true, we're done for.

My vision has adjusted. I see details. A black-and-white diamond-tiled floor. Forest-green walls. An elegantly carved staircase leading to the second floor.

"You have a fire going," I say, looking at the servant who stands in the center of us all.

"I do, sir," he says.

"Where?"

He hesitates, looking toward the stairs and then back to me. "It's in my master's suite."

"Let's wake your master, then."

THE TAX COLLECTOR

A fullbell later, both Chimeline and Colu have regained consciousness.

Chimeline rests by the fireplace—the bedroom's only source of illumination—wrapped in white snow-leopard furs from Northinglight. They're a luxury borrowed from Levi's pregnant wife, Ghanesa. Chimeline is on the floor, weak but attentive, her head propped up by a goose-feather pillow.

Colu lies nearby, on Levi's millionescent-wood desk. It's so large that we were able to push all of Levi's massive leather-bound journals and a brass scale full of ingots of gold aside and still accommodate Colu's body.

The hard surface is vital for him, as he had trouble breathing on the soft four-poster bed. A rag that Ghanesa soaked in aloe covers his face. His eye patch lies by his side.

The bedroom has two bleached white-leather chairs near the full bank of southern-facing windows, but Blythe and le-Daerke do not sit on them. Instead they stand against the clear glass looking out at the predawn sky from our elevated height. An anxious sun hides to the east. Xi Bay and the Port of Yamerind are in the distance, still bathed in the velvety shadow of night. The moon is gone, sunk below the horizon. It wants no part of this.

Dozens of soldiers swarm the bay, their torches like fireflies.

le-Daerke sucks in air between her teeth. "I see two other azuremen now," she says, her palms to the window. "They're carrying the dead one away."

"It's not dead, Daughter, if it was never alive to begin with," says Blythe.

Geodrey, the servant who let us in earlier, returns with a large silver tray of coffee.

"Thank you, my dear man," Levi says.

"The smallbreads and dates should be done in a halfbell, my lord," Geodrey adds. "And I will get more water for the lady and the Xian."

Levi approaches the dresser. He waves off Geodrey's attempt at assistance and fixes himself a cup of coffee.

Levi is perhaps ten years my senior and still bears a full head of hair and a tailored goatee, which is all brilliantly silver. He wears gold bracelets and necklaces. A ruby ring. Silk bedclothes.

Ghanesa is in bed, sitting upright against the headboard. She's wrapped in a storm of lightweight silk shawls, her hands resting protectively on her round belly. She must be half Levi's age and has hair as black as Chimeline's. Had she not been sharing the man's bed when we barged in, I would have taken her to be his oldest daughter.

Levi is a tax collector and has done exceedingly well for himself.

In almost every respect, he reminds me of the man I used to be. This could be the Royal House. Instead of managing gold, he could be managing souls. One marked difference, though, is his blessing of a child. I remind myself that it was Marine who never wanted children, not I.

"Dem," Levi says, motioning to the silver pot of coffee with his own full, steaming cup. "Partake in the breaking of my fast. All of you, please."

"Thank you," I say. We have come far with Levi in such a short amount of time.

There was chaos at first. Levi thought he was being robbed and grabbed a dagger from beneath his mattress. Ghanesa screamed. But once Geodrey rekindled his lamp and the couple understood that they were in the presence of an effulgent and a graycloak, they quickly settled down.

I explained to the couple and servant what had happened, more or less: The genocide of the effulgency behind the closed doors of the Union. Blythe and le-Daerke's need for disguises. The King's Guard, decimated. The azureman's attack. What we saw behind the mask. There were some truths I omitted—such as Chimeline's being an axionlighter. And I left out any mention of Chireseal. Even though I desperately want to discuss the strange effulgent with Colu, I don't want to reveal any more to our hosts than necessary.

"Show them the note," Ghanesa tells her husband, as I fix myself a cup of coffee.

He looks at her and tilts his head as if to say "Are you sure?"

She nods. Her face is full of concern.

"Yes, yes, I suppose that I should."

He walks over to his millionescent table, sets down his cup next to Colu, and opens a drawer underneath. He rifles through its contents.

Colu grimaces. "Got any sugarcanex?"

Levi lets out a short laugh. "Little early for that, don't you think?"

"Pain knows no fullbell," Colu answers.

Levi mutters a sound of agreement then finds what he's looking for. He peers at the note in the darkness.

"Geodrey, light a lamp, will you, my good man?" he asks, without taking his eyes off the parchment. "And fetch our valiant soldier here some fifteen-year vintage."

Geodrey awakens a nearby square lantern—a much larger one with a ring at the top for carrying—and sets it on the desk next to Colu then leaves the room.

"Dem," Levi says, motioning me over. "Come see this."

I cross the room.

"This arrived yesterday, just before the assembly."

"A messenger brought this to you?" I ask, taking the parchment from him.

He nods. "I was not home at the time, but it bore the king's seal."

I unfurl it and hold it up in front of the lantern. The light pours through the semiopaque golden paper, the black ink easily legible.

To my most loyal head publican of Winter's Baiou:

A new era of great prosperity is upon us, which will impact every facet of our kingdom, including your bestowed responsibility.

Effective immediately, you are no longer to arrest any citizen for evading taxation—the squander of what is rightfully due to Your Majesty for securing their safety and prosperity.

Instead, you and your men are to escort these criminals to the nearest giving house—a former effulgency temple—where they will be handed over to the ones stationed there. As their sponsor, you will gain a number that, I assure you, will be worth far more than the gold ingots you currently attain.

Instruct the men who work for you of this command.

Your Majesty of the Northern Kingdom,
King Andrej X

I hand the parchment back to Levi.
"Do you know what it means?" he asks me.
I glance toward the windows, unsure if I should rip open such fresh wounds—Blythe and le-Daerke are listening intently. But I need to be truthful, even if it hurts.
"Now that the effulgency is . . . gone," I say, "it seems that the azuremen are converting their temples into something else."
"Giving Houses," Blythe says, coming near. le-Daerke stays by the window, forehead to the glass.

I nod. "The king said as much last night."

"But what *are* they?" Levi asks.

"I assume they're going to be used for placing people in soteria," I say.

"In soteria?" Levi asks.

I run my hand through my hair, struggling to come up with an explanation this man will understand.

"Everything the effulgency has proclaimed is true," I say. "Voidance is powered by souls—immortal souls trapped within voidstones. The azuremen are somehow able to add to this supply. They imprison people in soteria after the death of their flesh. They extract the soul and place it into a voidstone."

Levi stares at his lantern, and for a moment everything is still.

"That's worse than death," Colu says, his voice deep and raspy.

I nod.

"And the number?" Levi asks.

I roll up my sleeve and point to my forearm. "Sponsors—those who bring in people destined for being placed in soteria—will have numbers upon their skin."

"You mean tattoos?"

"Something like that. The number somehow represents status. The higher the number, the greater the status."

"But what does it give you?"

"I don't know."

Gentle sobs from the other side of the room draw our attention.

It's Ghanesa.

She leans forward, arms wrapped around her pregnant belly.

Levi runs over to her. "What's wrong, love?" he says, delicately laying a hand on her. "Shall I fetch Octelia?"

Ghanesa shakes her head then gathers her hair aggressively into a ponytail.

"Are you in pain?" he continues.

"No!" she says with annoyance, before sniffling and taking a large breath. "It's what that messenger said yesterday."

He looks at her in confusion.

"She mentioned my baby," she cries.

Ghanesa wipes her face with the back of her hand while Levi turns to me.

"My wife was home when the messenger delivered the scroll. Apparently, she noticed that Ghanesa was pregnant and casually said something to her. I didn't know what it meant. Neither of us did." He turns back to her. "Can you repeat what she said to you, love?"

She swallows and nods. "She said that I'd get a number if I took the baby to a giving house."

"Once it's born," Levi says.

"No!" she yells. "She said tomorrow. Today."

Levi looks at me then Blythe.

"She said to think about it," Ghanesa continues, gritting her teeth and speaking slowly, as if remembering the words one by one. "She said it was a great opportunity. That it would be painless," she adds, her sobs returning. "She never said that the baby would be put in . . ."

"In soteria," I say.

"Yes!"

"But the child isn't even born yet," Levi says.

"It is born to the Unnamed," Chimeline says suddenly, drawing our attention to her. Even le-Daerke turns from the window.

Wrapped in the white furs, Chimeline slowly rises and takes small steps toward the bed. "The Unnamed knew your daughter before she was formed in your womb. She already has a name."

"A name?" Ghanesa asks. "But . . ." She looks at husband. "We haven't come up with a name."

"This name is not made of letters. It cannot be said with words."

We all stare at Chimeline.

"Wait," Levi says. "So, it's a girl?"

Chimeline nods.

Levi takes a gulp of air and bends to hug his wife. "We're going to have a daughter, love. A beautiful baby girl."

Ghanesa smiles, but it quickly fades to resoluteness. "Levi, I'm not going to let some blue-dressed bitch kill my baby."

"No one's going to kill anyone, love." He sits down next to her on the edge of the bed. "It was only a suggestion. Not a command."

"What do you mean 'blue-dressed bitch'?" I ask.

Ghanesa gives me an icy stare. "She was very well dressed. Adorned with jewels and smelled like perfume. Blue silks. Unlike any other messenger I've seen, king's seal or not."

I frown in thought as Levi kisses her forehead. A moment passes, and they begin speaking to each other softly. I retreat, giving them space.

Chimeline approaches me.

"Are you feeling better?" I ask her, putting my arm around her shoulders.

She nods but seems distracted.

"What is it?"

"Marine wants to speak with you."

I stare at her, taken aback.

The white furs slip away from her shoulder, so I place them back around her gently while thinking of the implications.

It's unnerving to think that a part of Chimeline is always in the void—that she's able to talk to Marine's soul as if the woman were standing in this very room. It makes me wonder how often they speak to each other, and about what. Or whom.

"Dem?"

"Alright," I say, shaking my head to clear my thoughts. "You mean, right now?"

She nods.

I walk over to the window and dig out Marine's voidstone from my pants pocket. The stone is still wrapped in Mander's emerald silken fabric.

le-Daerke takes a step away, giving me privacy, just as I did with Levi and Ghanesa.

I feel as if I'm standing upon a grave holding a bouquet of flowers.

Carefully, I unravel the blue-green swatch.

Something is wrong.

Black dust covers the voidstone. Ash.

Grasping the stone tightly between two fingers with the fabric, I bring it up to my face and blow the black dust outward. It drifts to the floor like soot from a charred log.

How strange.

Dirt must have gotten into the fabric wrapping somehow.

I grab the voidstone with my bare fingers.

The world becomes nonexistent. I barely see the indivisibles in front of me. I turn in place. Blythe and le-Daerke should be glistening with the radiance of life. Instead, it's as if I'm searching for the moon through a midnight fog.

It's because this stone is weak.

It's good to . . . to feel your presence again, Dem.

For a moment, I do nothing but listen to her voice. Its sound—the tone, pitch, and overall quality—perfectly matches the voice she had when she was alive. It brings back the bittersweet past.

Hello, Marine. You can . . . feel me?

Yes. In the darkness beyond the white. Sometimes I think this room has gotten larger. Or maybe it's just becoming home to me.

There's absolute silence here. Of course there would be. She's the only soul remaining.

I wish you would visit me more often, Dem.

If I had eyes to shut, I would shut them. Out of guilt. Frustration. An uncertainty bordering on vertigo.

I'm sorry. I know you must be lonely, trapped in here by yourself. But we've been on the run. There hasn't been time.

The guilt spills over, since this is a lie. I could have made time for her. The problem is, I don't know what to say when I come to visit like this. It's twisted. She's dead. I buried her.

I'm not alone. I speak with the enervated in the other white rooms. I speak with Chimeline. When I say that I wish you would visit me more often, it is not for my benefit. It's for yours.

Her words are not filled with hurt or blame. They float over me, emotionless.

What do you mean?

There's a span of silence. Then she speaks again.

You need to teach her.

Chimeline?

Yes. Like you taught me. She has so much strength but no control. I've been explaining things to her. Membranes. Dynamic voidance. How to speak in the enervated's tongue. But there's only so much I can do. I'm just a voice.

My first instinct is to object. The idea of teaching Chimeline seems repulsive to me. I've renounced my past. I seek eleutheria, not more voidance.

But within a single beat of my heart, I know that Marine is right. The enervated have called Chimeline an axionlighter for a reason. She is the greatest of weapons— perhaps the *only* weapon—in our fight against the azuremen and the new kingdom that Mander has brought down upon us. The remains in the Port of Yamerind are a testament to this. We'd all be dead without her.

Dem, she has the blessing of the enervated.

I know.

So teach her. Think of the possibilities. The greatest of teachers and the greatest of voiders. With the two of you working together, we stand a chance.

But how, Marine? We're not at the university.

Have her heal the Xian man.

I would shake my head in this darkness if I could.

Tampering with the indivisibles of the body . . . it's too risky as a first lesson, Marine. One wrong move could kill him.

Trust her.

I turn toward Chimeline. She's right next to me, facing away. The subtlest form of radiance. In here, *she* is the fire, not the massive hearth beyond.

Life. Glorious life.

I wonder if Marine is jealous—if she can see what I can see. Feel what I can feel.

If there's anything that can be gleaned in this perverted darkness, it's not jealousy from Marine. Coldness toward me, perhaps. But not Chimeline.

Alright. I'll show her.

Thank you, Dem.

I pause for a moment. *What about you?*

What about me?

Are you ready to leave? To move on?

She doesn't respond.

Blythe and I need to perform eleutheria on you. If we don't, you run the risk of them taking you. If the azuremen find this voidstone on me, you'll be suffering in torment— possibly for eternity.

I know.

Do you want us to do it now?

Her reply is instantaneous.

No. Chimeline's not ready. So I'm not ready.

I pause. *But if I'm teaching her—*

You can't teach her how to speak their language. I'm the only one who can do that.

Her curt answer makes sense, but I suspect that she's hiding something. Perhaps she's afraid to let go.

Marine, I just want you to be safe. Safety is the only thing left that I can give you.

Dem, now is not the time for wants. Not for you. Not for Chimeline. And not for me.

Her words shock me into silence. Although the message itself is harsh and cryptic, the delivery is soft and unemotional. This could be Blythe talking, not the wife I once knew.

My frustration builds. Her body is dead—she's trapped inside of this place and outside of time. The risk of the azuremen seems irrelevant to her. She doesn't see what I see.

Marine, what happens in the outside world impacts what happens here. Chimeline and I will figure things out. The longer you remain, the greater the risk that you'll be taken. It's time for you to move on. Let me do this for you.

Dem, you're not doing it for me. You're doing it for you.

Her reply stings me, as if I've extended too much voidance and let the wind cut into me. And her next words sting as well.

Right now, our duty is our prison. Not this white room.

I don't reply.

Go, Dem. Teach Chimeline. Help her save Colu. Then help her save us all.

VOIDREAMING

Temberlain frantically drew upon his axiongraph as he tumbled toward the floor of the common mess a hundred feet below.

As he attempted to create a cushion of air beneath him, it became immediately obvious that such a maneuver was impossible, like trying to control a jettisoned waste pod with thrusters.

At the last microrotation, he resorted to a spherical membrane, wastefully growing it out in all directions.

He hit the floor hard, the impact knocking the breath out of him.

The membrane saved him from serious injury, but pain still tore through him, both ice and fire.

His head snapped back. The FTL restraints on his wrist cut against his skin.

He let go of axion, returned to the world of white light. The world of the living.

Well, not quite.

Over a hundred people lay strewn about, empowered and ashen alike. Most ashen writhed in pain, some of their limbs bent in hideous directions. Salvation through axion wasn't an option for them. Even some empowered who hadn't thought fast enough lay still, either unconscious or dead.

Temberlain felt something wet on the side of his head. He brought his hand there, and it came away red.

Bleeding through the ears. Differentiation.

The screams escalated, echoing throughout the common mess.

But Temberlain paid no attention to them. As he raised himself up on his palms, he turned to the massive translucent wall. Gone was the heavy tinting. Gone were the starlines that had streaked past like cloudrops on the window of an innership passing through atmospheres.

Replacing this view was a planet more beautiful than words could describe. The whites, blues, and greens were so vivid they seemed to create the words, the very idea of color.

Temberlain had had this feeling before. Every few hundred rotations they'd break out of FTL. Perhaps nine out of every ten differentiations ended within murky nebulae, deep-space assembly stations, or lunar training grounds. Lifeless places that stirred no dreams in men. But occasionally, like an oasis hidden within the deep recesses of a Dodoghian desert, a habitable planet would await them. A world as beautiful as this.

Where are we?

Serrater fire. Staccato buzzing.

Temberlain pulled his gaze from the window just in time to see a fellow empowered—someone from Cordialle's security team, based on his insignia—rise to his knees and aim his weapon. But he was too late. A red pulse came from the gallery above and cut him in half.

Temberlain turned away as the blood splattered, followed by the smell of burnt flesh. A black arc smoldered on the white floor, stopping a foot away from him.

Temberlain's hand slipped on blood. His face hit the floor, and he bit the inside of his mouth. That's when he saw it.

A serrater.

The silver weapon, smaller than a palm, lay right in front of him. Maybe it had been there before. Maybe it had slid across the floor as the one who'd held it slid apart.

He reached out and grasped it.

But instead of aiming it toward the gallery, he backed away kicking. Taking shelter behind a large, upturned circular table, he knew that it wouldn't save him from serrater fire, but it gave him a moment to think.

The ashen need me alive.

Another dead empowered awaited him behind the table—the one who had saluted him earlier. The hideous angle of his lopsided head told him he hadn't perished from a serrater but a broken neck.

The buzzing in the room escalated into an echoing cacophony, a swarm of bees in his ear.

This is impossible. Ashen overcoming empowered.

But it was happening. And it wasn't even much of a fight. The mutineers had the clear advantage from the elevated gallery. They were also not disoriented—they had used their FTL restraints.

All around him were the sounds of his fellow empowered dying.

This is not a battle I can win.

But perhaps it was one he could survive. They seemed intent on taking him to the drive chamber. Whatever they were doing, it was related to the Axiondrive.

Behind the cover of the overturned table, Temberlain stuffed the serrater into the back of his pants, feeling the autosizing give a little. His shirt was already untucked, and it covered any hint of the weapon. There was so much blood on it that the original wine stain was indiscernible.

Flipping over the dead body, he searched it for a serrater.

He found one safely harnessed in a holster.

He freed it.

I have to make a run for it. Get out of the common mess. Get word to Efful.

The nearest exit lay about fifty feet in front of him. The massive room narrowed into a funnel-shaped hallway underneath the gallery level, a white circular door at its end. It was closed, but a serrater would burn through it—faster than axion.

He scanned the room.

Between the door and him were two empowered—a man and a woman, each caught within a similar predicament. Instead of tables, they took shelter behind spherical membranes of their own making.

Temberlain watched in horror as multiple red serrater bolts hit the two membranes from all directions. Both surfaces rippled violently, throwing off rainbows of color like oil in water. They changed in size before his eyes, shrinking then growing. A battle between the empowered's natural talents and the cheap display of stolen power in the ashen's primeval hands.

The woman fell to her knees behind her translucent membrane. Her face was twisted in torment, eyes closed, shuddering. Her hands clutched nothing.

A sudden wind blew through the room, moving directly toward her.

Then, without warning, her membrane collapsed.

A pinprick of silence.

The massive and earsplitting shockwave of pressure she'd created detonated in a cone-shaped area in front of her.

The wave destroyed everything in its path. Tables, chairs, ashen, even the glass railing in the gallery a hundred feet above. Everything blew apart—almost melted, like flakes of snow caught within the heat exhaust of an innership.

The far wall of the room instantly became red and caved in, as if some phantom giant had punched his fist straight through it.

A few ashen tumbled from the gallery to their deaths, their bodies breaking and splattering against the white. Massive shards fell.

It was hard for Temberlain to gauge numbers, but the woman's attack must have eliminated at least half of the mutineers in the common mess.

After a moment of stunned silence, the empowered went limp and fell forward.

The remaining mutineers wasted no time. A fresh torrent of serrater fire rained down upon her, tearing her body apart.

But it was futile. She'd already succumbed to axionilation. Death by axion overexertion.

What a glorious way to die under the circumstances.

Their attention then turned to the other empowered, who was pinned within his own sphere. He was further away from both Temberlain and the circular exit—more toward the left, past the destruction the woman had caused. A legless ashen crawled on the floor behind him, leaving a trail of blood.

Temberlain ran for it.

Jumping over glass shards, tables, chairs, bodies, and limbs of empowered and ashen alike, he sprinted toward the funnel fifty feet in the distance.

Risking a glance above, he saw the ashen in the gallery directly overhead. A few had noticed his movements. They shouted madly, aiming their weapons, but not firing. One gripped the edge of a remnant of the railing uselessly, as if preparing to jump.

Temberlain lost sight of the group as he passed underneath the gallery ceiling. He fired his serrater twenty feet ahead—not on pulse but on beam. His aim was sloppy due to his speed, but he was able to cut through, creating a circle in the middle of the door. The edges faded from red to black. Bright light burst through from the other side.

The circle began to fall outward.

As he sprinted toward his makeshift exit, the gallery ceiling suddenly began to collapse.

Large pieces of malineum and glass rained down. They filled the space between Temberlain and the door, a mound of silver with glowing red edges from the heat blocking his way. Something hard hit his left shoulder and then his head, knocking him to the ground.

Pain spread across his back; black spots spread across his vision.

Up billowed a cloud of white dust, enveloping him.

Temberlain coughed, trying to breathe. The only things he could see from his prone position were bright-red pulses on the far side of the room—the serrater fire of at least a dozen ashen concentrated on a single point in the haze. The last empowered, besides himself.

Temberlain tried to move, but something heavy covered his back, pinning him down. Malineum from the ceiling. As he struggled, his back touched an edge and he screamed in pain from the burn.

The firing stopped. Only the echoing of marching feet and shuffling suits remained, whispered secrets in the crowd.

The shuffling became louder. It sounded like running. Guttural Dodoghian voices, but a few Effulgian as well.

"He alive?" said a man, his voice urgent.

"Better be."

Dark shapes, inches away. Boots crawling in the wreckage, stirring up the white cloud just as it was settling. Someone pulled the weight off him with a groan. He turned his head to see a huge slab of malineum being pushed in the other direction by a large ashen. It hit the mound of debris with a bang, sending up another cloud.

"Which arm?" someone asked. "Left or right?"

"Right."

The ashen forcefully turned him onto his back, causing fresh tendrils of pain to shoot across his head and back. The black spots returned, his world spinning.

Someone grabbed his wrist and tugged on his arm, roughly pulling it up and sideways.

"Rip his shirt off."

"What?"

More Dodoghian, all shouting over each other.

Temberlain didn't know what was happening. He only knew that escape was impossible. So he did the only thing that he could.

He entered the world of axion.

It was there, awaiting him. Even though his body was immobile, his mind was free.

He would follow the woman's courageous example. He would die right here and right now, taking as many of these animals with him as he could.

He counted fourteen. Five were clustered over him, clawing at his shirt and tearing it off while pulling his arms to his sides. He felt their actions, but the sensations were gone, as if he were watching this happen to someone else. Nine stood behind them. Through the particles he saw their glistening forms.

He began constructing a pressure differential.

The particles in the air began coming toward him from all directions as he wove a small parabolic membrane across his chest. Within the world of axion, the cloud of dust was disappearing into it, but he imagined that in the outside world nothing appeared different.

He drew upon his axiongraph as he'd never done before.

The numbness began.

Within a microrotation, the pressure within the membrane became noticeable. A microrotation later—a single heartbeat—it risked collapse, but Temberlain worked the axion in parallel by applying continual layers, strengthening the membrane while continuing to pack more of the room's air inside, again and again, a recursive path with destruction at its end.

Axionilation, come.

Suddenly, the colorless world was severed from him. He was torn from its soft and dark embrace and into chaos and light.

And white-hot pain.

Temberlain watched his membrane prematurely collapse.

The pressure wave was enough to knock half the ashen off their feet, but not enough to break skin and bone.

The agony in his right arm increased.

Temberlain's head lolled to the side, but he fought to remain conscious. He lay on debris, his back slanted up against a pile of malineum. His shirt was off, his chest entirely covered in blood. The black spots returned. The world spun.

As the ashen slowly got to their feet, Temberlain desperately tried entering the world of axion again, but nothing happened. As if he were ashen. It was a feeling that he'd never experienced.

"How . . ."

He instinctively turned to look at his axiongraph—reassurance in this moment of need. The familiar ghantstag's head, the antlers in a double helix.

It wasn't there.

Neither was his arm.

Just above his bicep, his limb ended in a charred husk.

Temberlain tried to scream, but instead, the black spots took over, and this time he knew that they would not be denied.

HOW WE RECEIVE THE TRUTH

"You did well," I tell Chimeline, as we return from the void to the bedroom, which is full of sunrise. "You rushed the hard-callus formations, though. Next time, arrange the indivisibles and then pull back, letting them go about on their own. The body knows what the body needs."

She doesn't reply.

"How do you feel?" I ask, peering around her black hair to see her face. She looks tired.

"I'm fine."

"Any numbness?"

She shakes her head.

"Good."

"I'd give my left nut for a little numbness," Colu mutters, before pushing himself up to a sitting position with a wince. "Does that mean we're done here?"

I hold up two cautionary palms. "Take it slow," I say. "Yes, your ribs are fused, but your body just went through about three weeks of healing in less than a fullbell. It might be in shock."

He swings his legs over the side of the millionescent table while doing his best to suppress his grimace.

"Thank you, il-Colu," Chimeline says.

"For what?" he says with a grunt.

"For allowing me to learn from your injuries. Dem could've healed you in half the time, with very little risk."

"Bah! You did fine."

She smiles at the compliment, and I realize that I don't remember the last time she smiled at me that way.

Gingerly, he lowers himself and tests his footing before standing on his own.

"Fucking Unnamed," he utters, touching his chest with both palms and taking a deep breath. "It's like it never happened."

le-Daerke makes a *tsk* sound and crosses her arms. "You shouldn't say such things about the Unnamed."

Colu glances at her before searching the table for his eye patch. As he pulls it on over his forehead, he says, "You're right. I've got so much to be thankful for."

le-Daerke doesn't respond. Instead, she shakes her head and joins Blythe, who's in the midst of preaching the way of unwanting to Geodrey.

Levi departed a fullbell ago to check in on his publicans. Ghanesa is downstairs with her maidservant, Octelia. Only Geodrey remains. The stoic middle-aged servant changed out of his nightclothes and into his formal uniform fullbells ago. He looks awkward sitting on the floor next to the other two, his posture straight, as if he's trying too hard to prevent himself from relaxing.

I walk past them, toward the bedroom windows.

The sun rises. Ships sail out to sea. Fishermen toil on the wharves, emptying nets and barrels. Men with carts load their catches, taking them up to the city. Soldiers patrol. Life continues.

Except in one place.

The area where the bloodshed occurred remains empty, a negative space surrounded by normalcy while desperately trying to blend in. All the bodies have been carried away. Only dried stains that look black in the morning light remain.

As for the Axiondrive, its absence is palpable, as if the weight we recently released with eleutheria still hangs in the air.

"We should leave," I say, to nobody in particular.

"We can't," Chimeline says.

I turn to face her. She's taken off Ghanesa's furs. They're carefully folded and sit on the foot of the bed. Ghanesa must have lent her clothes as well—Chimeline now wears a colorful one-shoulder transitional dress with a Northern cut and a Xian pattern.

"Why not?"

She looks at Colu leaning against the table then at the three sitting on the ground. "They know who we are," she answers, not quite meeting my eyes.

"The azuremen?"

She nods.

"But we killed the one that was after us," Colu says. "Before anyone showed up."

"It doesn't matter," she says. "What that one azureman saw, they all saw." She wrinkles her nose in contemplation. "They share a common . . . mind."

For a moment, no one says anything. From downstairs, Ghanesa calls out for Octelia.

"They are always in the void," I surmise. "So they communicate like the enervated, across voidstones."

"Yes," she says, finally looking at me.

"Fantastic," Colu says sarcastically. "Then we must assume the King's Guard knows, too. Not to mention the city watch."

le-Daerke adds, "The Black Army will be hunting us as well."

"Why do you say that?" I ask.

She looks at me as if I'm daft. "We all heard what the king said. There is no more master voider. That hideous man is in charge now. The Black Army will be his arms and legs."

Colu takes another deep breath, as if testing out his lungs. "We might as well hunker down here for a bit," he says. "Let all this shit blow over."

Blythe shakes his head then meets my eyes. "We need to find the Axiondrive."

I nod in agreement while looking at Geodrey. His mouth is open in confusion. I briefly contemplate asking him to leave, but he's part of this now whether he knows it or not.

"What else do you know about Chireseal?" I ask Colu. "Anything that might help determine which way he went."

Colu shrugs. "Already told you. Yesterday was the first time I met him. He wanted a large wagon and four draft horses."

"Did he mention why?"

He shakes his head.

"And you didn't ask?"

"Why the fuck should I have cared what he wanted it for? Man offered two thousand."

"You said he also wanted a map of Xiland."

"Yeah."

"And that was it?"

He nods and places his palms on the table, leaning back against it.

"He didn't mention a city? An area?"

"No."

"Why would an effulgent from Northinglight take the Axiondrive south?" Blythe asks.

"Perhaps he is simply running away," Chimeline says. "Hiding it."

Colu grunts in agreement.

I run my hand through my hair. "Alright. Well, whatever the reason Chireseal left, it still doesn't explain the bloodshed," I say, turning back to look out the window, as if I could still see the dozens of bodies there. "The use of voidance."

"The bloodshed would be justified," le-Daerke says softly. "The voidance not."

Blythe gasps. "Daughter! The spilling of blood is owning the dark!"

"The death of a few soldiers who are clearly not on the way of unwanting in order to protect millions of souls from an eternity of torment? I see the justification, Father."

"We freed those souls, Daughter. Their torment was at an end."

"Empty though it might be, perhaps the effulgent sought to keep it from the hands of the azuremen, lest those souls be replaced."

A heavy silence blankets the room.

"Regardless of his reasons," I finally say, "we have to find him."

"I agree," Blythe says.

"Why is it so important to find him?" Colu asks.

"There's more to him than what he seems. He knew about the azuremen coming. He warned us to leave. I wager he knows how many there are. What their plans are. Maybe even how to stop them."

"If he knew how to stop them," Colu says, "then he would have."

I nod. The man's right.

"None of you have to come," I say, "but Blythe and I are going after him. Chireseal has answers that we desperately need. Besides, we have a responsibility to hide the Axiondrive, so that it's never used again."

Chimeline doesn't hesitate. "I'm coming with you."

Colu sighs. "You'll need someone who knows Xiland. Might as well be me."

le-Daerke glances at her father before turning to me. There is a passion in her eyes—an intensity that's almost scary. "I will journey with you on this road until its end."

Colu mutters something unintelligible and looks at the floor, shaking his head.

"I would go, too, were I not needed here," Geodrey says. "Your cause is the Unnamed's. But my duty is first to Levi."

I nod. "I wouldn't think of asking you to leave, Geodrey." I meet each gaze. "Tonight, then. Under the cover of dark."

"We'll never get through the city gates, even at night," Colu says. "And they have our horses at Grenaden's

Stables." He scratches the back of his head. "Horses are as good as gone. But I think I know a way out."

He looks across the room, to the window, with a narrow eye.

"Years ago, they rebuilt the sewers," he continues. "Only the Xian half of Winter's Baiou. City was growing like mad and the rich didn't want the shit flowing into their beaches. So the emperor had the entire system redesigned."

"I remember," Blythe says. "The roads near the temple were all torn up. It made it difficult to receive the stone shipments for construction."

Colu laughs darkly. "Yeah."

"You worked on these sewers?" I ask.

"Briefly."

"Where do they lead?"

"Xi Bay. Southwest of the city." He taps the brass scale full of gold ingots resting on the table next to him, forcing the lighter side down. "The outlets will all be barred. We'll have to find a way through."

"How?" Chimeline asks.

He lets go of the scale. The weighted end slams down.

"Voidance, I guess."

le-Daerke shakes her head. "Absolutely not. We're not touching one of those cursed stones again unless our lives depend upon it. And even then, it must be discussed."

Colu shrugs.

"It's settled then," I say. "We'll wait until dark and use the sewers to leave the city. We'll figure it out as we go."

"What then?" Blythe asks.

"Chireseal shouldn't be that difficult to track," I say. "I'm sure that the locals won't have missed a white-skinned effulgent with gems on his face."

Blythe nods. "Very well, then."

"Agreed," Colu says.

With the matter settled, I purse my lips and turn to le-Daerke. A question has surfaced. "Where did you get that voidstone?"

"What voidstone?"

"The one that you threw to me."

The resoluteness drains from her face and she looks at her lap.

"I have been wondering the same thing," Blythe says softly. After a moment of silence, he adds, "Daughter, can you please answer the question?"

She doesn't. All she does is shake her head meagerly while continuing to look down.

"Daughter?"

When she looks up, her face is twisted and her eyes are wet, reflecting the morning sun. "Father, do not ask this of me."

He blinks rapidly. "Why not?"

"Because how we receive the truth is just as important as how we deliver it."

Geodrey clears his throat while standing. "Um, if you will excuse me, Your Effulgencies," he says. "I need to check upon a few things downstairs."

He leaves in a hurry, his footsteps heavy on the stairs.

Once the sounds diminish, Blythe turns back to le-Daerke. "What is that supposed to mean?"

She doesn't answer, but she doesn't have to. I frown as her meaning becomes clear to me. Or, at the very least, I understand her point. Too often we demand the truth but fail to accept it. She probably fears that the answer will incriminate her somehow. Or perhaps that she will be unfairly judged.

My mind flashes back to Fiscarlo. She admitted to her father that she burned down my student's house. She bared her soul. In response, Blythe rode out of town without looking back.

And here it is again.

There was a time when I would have reveled in any division between these two. A time when I would have piled on to her words to create as much suffering as possible. But that time is long gone. I feel only sadness now—that these two people, who clearly love each other, seem to be standing on opposite ends of the world.

In some ways, they remind me of Chimeline and me.

"You don't need to answer now," I say. "I'm sorry I brought it up."

But Blythe leans in. "Where did you get the voidstone?"

"It belonged to one of the . . . one of the Black Army. The dead ones."

"You mean the murdered voiders?" I ask.

She hesitates, unable to meet my gaze.

"I gave it to her," Colu says suddenly.

le-Daerke's head snaps in his direction.

"What?" I ask, turning to him as well.

He shrugs. "I thought one of the effulgents would be the safest place. For your etherian shit."

"Eleutheria," Blythe corrects.

"So how did *you* come upon it?" I ask.

Colu fixes his gaze on the scale again, forcing the lighter side down with his index finger.

"I killed the voider it belonged to."

For a moment, none of us say a word. Ghanesa shouts downstairs.

Blythe stands, his hands fists. "You murdered him?"

Colu nods but keeps looking at the scale, placing gold ingots from the heavy side to the lighter side, seeking equality.

"It was you?" Chimeline asks, but her voice is not full of condemnation, only curiosity. "The one hunting the voiders?"

Colu doesn't respond.

"How many?" I ask. "How many have you killed?"

"Does it matter?"

Blythe and I alternate our gazes between Colu and le-Daerke, but Blythe speaks up first, to his daughter.

"And you knew about this?"

"I never told her I was responsible for the killings," Colu interjects. "I only said I came upon them."

Blythe swivels and takes a step toward him, raising his voice. "We vouched for you!" he says, shaking his fists. "We proclaimed your goodness to the enervated! They saved your life and they *suffered* for it!"

"I didn't ask you to."

Blythe raises his hand to his bald head and turns abruptly, walking to the windows. "Good Unnamed. To think that we did all of that for a murderer. A man so clearly off the way of unwanting that there is no chance at redemption."

"You knew what kind of man I am," Colu says, his voice composed, as if he doesn't even care to argue. "You knew I've killed more men than I can count. And I would do it again."

Colu places one last ingot on the lighter side. The scale balances perfectly. He nods to himself. Then he puts his palms on the table, leans back against it, and looks at me. I wonder if he's trying to gauge my reaction to his admission, but it's impossible to tell. His countenance is as level as the brass scale by his side.

I don't know what to think.

Voidance must come to an end. With that, I cannot disagree. The question is how.

While I had thought that it could be done peacefully, I'm no longer sure. The encounter with Gaigane stung like the namesake of her homeland. She witnessed eleutheria. The master voider knew the truth, yet she still would not accept it.

How we receive the truth is just as important as how we deliver it.

The voiders Colu murdered could have been my former students. Have I saved their greatest lesson for last? A lesson about loss that involves giving up the very thing they've dedicated their lives to? What if they can't pass this final test? What is the price of failure?

While I don't agree with what Colu did, I can't fault him for it either. He's not the enemy.

I'm ripped from my thoughts by the sound of someone hastily climbing the stairs.

Geodrey bursts into the room, panting. He eyes all of us with a haunted expression before speaking.

"There is no good way to say this, friends. You must leave at once."

"Overstayed our welcome?" Colu asks.

Geodrey shakes his head. A tear falls down his cheek, and he quickly rubs it away, as if it were a spot on a silver spoon. Under all his forced formality, he seems to be barely holding it together.

"My master, Levi, has turned all of you in."

THE WATER CLOCK

"He's a stupid man!" Ghanesa cries, meeting us at the foot of the stairs as she wipes tears away with one hand and cradles her belly with the other. "A stupid, shortsighted, spineless man!"

"What damage is done?" I ask her.

She turns to Octelia. "Show them."

The older maidservant hands me a piece of parchment. Her hand shakes.

Ghanesa:

You must leave the house by tenbell. Only you and the servants. Under no circumstances are you to inform our guests. Tell them you are headed to the square for victuals for their stay.

I'm sorry, but I had no choice.

Levi

I hand the parchment back then look at the massive water clock standing opposite the foyer's front door, underneath the staircase. It's taller than I am—a vertical slab of white marble three feet wide and six feet tall. At its top is a bejewelled bowl from which water slowly drips. Encircling the bottom is a waist-high walled pool lined with turquoise and beige tiles. Inside, the water is about knee height, nearing the mark of ten stones.

"Is this accurate?" I ask, pointing to the pool of water.

"Absolutely, my lord," Geodrey says.

I sigh. It's nearly tenbell.

But then a wave of gratitude and empathy comes over me. Ghanesa didn't need to do this. She could have lied, as her husband instructed.

"Do as he says," I tell her, giving her a serious yet patient glance. I give Octelia and Geodrey the same look. "Leave. All three of you. You don't have much time." I motion to the parchment. "Pretend you never showed this to us."

"What will you do?" Ghanesa asks.

"We'll think of something."

She lets out a sound of utter agitation, putting the back of her hand against her forehead. "I cannot believe Levi would do this to the effulgency." She glances at me. "And their companions, of course."

"He's not stupid," I say, trying to soothe her feelings. "He was thinking of you."

"He was thinking of himself!"

There's nothing I can say to that. She's right, of course. A man doesn't become the head tax collector in Winter's Baiou any other way. Turning us in was an instinctive act of self-preservation.

A pause is filled by the dripping of the water clock.

"A voider is coming," Chimeline says.

We all turn toward her. Her eyes are closed.

"Where?" I ask. The foyer doesn't have any windows, but I peer into the next room, at the window there. I see little past the shutters, but even if they were open, the other side of the narrow alleyway would be the only view.

She squeezes her shut eyes, as if she's in pain. "He's near the wharf."

"Just one?" I ask.

"Yes."

"Bah," Colu exclaims. "We should be able to handle just one." He storms into the other room and cautiously peers through the shutters.

Chimeline shakes her head, bent in concentration.

"What is it?" I ask.

"This one is different," she says.

I flash Blythe and le-Daerke a worried glance. Blythe puts his palms together, his fingers near his lips.

"Different how?" I ask.

"Never have I felt so much . . . hate."

"An azureman, then," Blythe says.

She shakes her head forcefully. "No. Those . . . things don't have souls. They are like stone beings. This man has a soul. But it's being overtaken. Like some trained palehound."

"All voider are little more than beasts," le-Daerke says.

Blythe gives his daughter a look of disappointment.

"Whoever he is," I say, "I have no intention of confronting him head-on. Not while we have the time." I turn to Ghanesa. "Does your house have a back door?"

"Forget it," Colu says, walking briskly back into the room but from a different direction. "Guards surround us. Keeping their distance, but I counted at least a dozen." He's adjusting the ties of a new scabbard, in which sits a beautifully-adorned sword.

"That's Levi's," Ghanesa says in shock. "It was a gift from King Andrej IX!"

"No sword this fine deserves to be hanging on a wall," Colu says.

She glowers but says nothing.

My gaze alternates between him and the clock, which marks tenbell.

It's too late. Our only advantage was Ghanesa's warning, but that has dripped away.

I study Chimeline. Her head is bowed, and she's rocking back and forth in distress.

"We could use voidance," I add.

"No black arcana," le-Daerke says.

I hold out my hand in explanation. "Only if the enervated give us—"

"The Unnamed will provide," says Blythe soothingly. "One way or another."

Colu laughs darkly.

Blythe eyes him, his serene expression morphing into one of scorn. "Your lack of faith is appalling."

"We don't have time for bickering," I say. "We need to figure a way out of here."

I turn to Ghanesa. "You need to go, now," I say, more forcefully than before. "You don't want to be here when the voider comes."

Ghanesa needs no more prompting. She moves toward the door.

"My lady," Geodrey says, clearing his throat. "I will be two steps behind you. Let me gather a few essentials, and I'll meet you at the market."

"Yes, yes," she says distractedly. "Do hurry."

Ghanesa opens the door and steps through into muted daylight. The sun must not be high enough to extend its reach beyond the tall buildings. I can see only one other building, on the opposite side of the narrow alley, painted a robin's-egg blue. She looks in both directions.

"There is nobody here," she says.

"They're there," Colu says. "You just can't see them."

A warm breeze drifts through the foyer carrying the smell of charcoal and cooked meat.

"Ghanesa," I say, getting her attention.

She looks back at me, her face constricted in fear.

"Thank you," I say.

She looks down briefly, gathering her silk robes around her despite the warmth. Looking up, she nods. "Simple truths are the bricks by which the way of unwanting is built."

Blythe smiles wide then bows. le-Daerke approaches the open doorway, but I stop her with an outstretched arm and a shake of my head.

She nods in understanding then addresses Ghanesa.

"May the Unnamed bless you and your child," le-Daerke says.

Ghanesa shuts her eyes briefly. Then, taking a deep breath, she looks past le-Daerke—past all of us—into the foyer, as if this might be the last time she sees it. "Octelia," she says sharply. "It's time."

Before the maidservant steps through the open doorway, Geodrey meets her. He puts a hand on her forearm then leans in and kisses her on the cheek.

"I love you," he says quietly.

She narrows her eyes. "You're coming right after," she says. "As is our lady's command."

"Yes. Of course."

She doesn't look convinced. The last thing I see before Geodrey shuts the door is her furrowed brow underneath wisps of gray hair and her parchment-toned hood.

Dim, cold light returns. For a moment, Geodrey simply stands there, one hand on the iron handle, the other pressed gently upon the wood door.

"We're fucked," Colu mutters, his hand on the hilt of his new sword.

Geodrey glances at him then looks at me. "There is a way. My lady doesn't know of its existence. Only my master and me."

Colu and I exchange a glance.

"I'm not following," I say.

"When Levi commissioned this home, he had a secret route built."

"A secret route?" Blythe asks with a frown. "There is no such thing on the way of unwanting."

Geodrey crosses the small foyer, headed toward the water clock. "That may be true, Your Effulgency, but a tax collector has more enemies than friends."

"All the more proof that gold tarnishes the spirit."

Raising his foot over the water clock's ledge, Geodrey begins to step into the pool. Then he hesitates, pulling back.

"One of you will need to do it," he says, turning to us. "My pants will get wet. It will look suspicious."

"You want me to step inside the water?" I ask.

"Yes, my lord," Geodrey says.

I waste no time despite my lack of understanding. Stepping over the ledge, I enter—pants, sandals, and all—letting the cold water rise to my knees.

"Push against the stone slab, my lord. Hard."

I do as he says. Once, then twice.

With a loud cracking sound, the marble slab pulls away from the wall a bit, as if on a spring, revealing a dark sliver. The water in the pool around my feet instantly drains through the opening, disappearing somewhere behind the wall.

"You'll need to pull, now, my lord."

I stick all my fingers into the dark crevasse and pull toward me until it's barely wide enough for a person to pass through. It takes all my might—the stone slab must weigh hundreds of pounds.

Inside, it's pitch black.

"Where does this lead?" I ask Geodrey.

"South, my lord," he says. "To the sewers."

Blythe smiles widely and looks up to the ceiling. "I learn from this lesson. The Unnamed always provides, even in mysterious ways."

This time, Colu remains silent.

"The steps are steep, and a little uneven," Geodrey says, fetching a lantern from the foyer table and lighting it with the flint that had been sitting next to it. "And now they are wet as well. So you will have to be careful. In a tenthbell, you'll reach a gate to your right. It should be unlocked. It leads directly into the sewers beneath the city. From there, head south. You can tell the direction by the way the sun hits the walls from above. It's morning so keep the sunlight to your left."

Colu takes the lantern from Geodrey and steps into the empty pool, which is large enough to accommodate both of us. Geodrey then rushes toward the rear of the house.

Colu raises the lantern through the dark opening.

With the space illuminated, I can see rough-hewn stone. Large sandstone blocks and mortar cover the walls and low ceiling of the narrowly descending stairway.

"Dem," Chimeline says from behind me. "He's close."

Colu turns to me. "I'll go first and wait at the bottom."

I nod and turn to Chimeline. "You next."

Colu steps through without hesitation. The glow from the lamplight fades, the darkness in the gap returning.

Chimeline gathers up her dress and steps over the ledge.

Geodrey returns carrying a large decorative jug full of slopping water. With a groan, he sets it down on the floor.

"Geodrey," I say, without taking my eyes off Chimeline, who steps through the opening. "Get out of here."

"I will soon, my lord. Once I close this door, I must refill the pool."

le-Daerke steps into the empty pool as Chimeline disappears into the darkness. Blythe turns to Geodrey before following.

He wraps the man in a tight embrace then pulls back and gently fingers the ivory beads around the man's neck. "Be nothing," Blythe says.

Geodrey's smile shows no teeth. "Be nothing."

Something in the corner of my eye catches my attention. It comes from the shuttered window in the adjoining room.

The silhouette of a large man looms past the numerous wooden slats.

He stands perfectly still in the alleyway.

"The voider's here," I say under my breath. "Go!"

Blythe steps in and enters darkness, and I follow. Geodrey was right—the stairs are indeed slippery from the water. The three at the bottom look up, helplessly waiting within the halo of Colu's lantern.

"May the Unnamed protect his child Geodrey, body and soul, from all evil," Blythe mumbles in prayer. He slips on a stair and I reach out, grabbing his forearm. "Dem, you should offer a prayer for the man as well."

"Geodrey is going to be fine," I tell him, bracing myself with an outstretched hand against the rough ceiling inches above my head. "He's Levi's man. The voider will do him no harm."

"Are you sure?" he whispers. His voice echoes in the darkness like the wind in the void.

"Yes," I answer.

It's a lie.

After I descend another step, I turn to say goodbye.

"Geodrey, thank you—"

I'm interrupted by the unforgiving sound of stone upon stone. He's already shutting the door.

MOONLAKE

The five of us stand at the bottom of the stairs wrapped in stone, silence, and flickering gold light. Fog drifts around our feet, snakes of dampness trying to lure us into the darkness. Yet we seem incapable of moving, as if we were built with this place and then forgotten.

A symbol is crudely inscribed into the stone wall at the foot of the steps, about eye level. I brush my fingers over the circular pattern, leaning in to inspect it.

"Baiou Rats," Colu says.

I mutter a groan of inquisitiveness.

"Levi was into some shady business, it seems," he adds.

The faraway sound of flowing water echoes throughout the tight cavern.

"Won't the black arcanist see us here?" le-Daerke asks, her voice the barest of whispers.

"No," I answer.

"Even with the use of black arcana?"

I shake my head. "The stone is thick. Too many indivisibles. Unless he knows exactly what he's looking for and purposely navigates through them."

While I'm confident in these words, I don't reveal a darker truth: It doesn't matter what we do. If we cannot use voidance defensively we don't stand a chance against the forces against us. Running will serve only as an illusion. It's like telling a dying soldier on a foreign field that everything will be alright.

Our fate lies in Geodrey's hands now. A man whose only weapons are faith and charity.

And after that?

I fear the answer to that question.

"Let's move," I utter, and we plod south, through the rough-hewn darkness.

Geodrey told us the truth. Through an unlocked gate, another world awaits.

Colu douses the lantern but still carries it by his side. The light in the space turns from gold tinged to a melancholy blue. Weak natural light seeps in from somewhere.

The sewers are built from gray stone blocks. The stones are laid precisely, the obvious work of skilled masons. About ten feet wide and ten feet high, the space is all straight lines except for a barrel-vaulted ceiling

In the center of the floor runs a swiftly moving current of dark storm water about three feet wide. Black as oil, it reflects the filtered sunlight from a street grate above. I don't know its depth. As I stare at the currents, my imagination runs wild. I see other things moving. Dark, slippery forms headed to the bay, miles from here.

On either side of this narrow canal is an elevated stone pathway. The five of us slowly walk on the right side, more spread out than before. The way is mostly clear, but now and then we step over shadowed piles of litter, and the soft scurrying of rats causes us to stay near the water's edge. The rubbish makes me wonder if vagabonds have also made this place their home.

The smell isn't as acrid as I had assumed, perhaps because the air down here moves, preventing stagnation. A musty salty-sweet odor wafts past us.

Colu and le-Daerke take the lead. They walk next to each other and converse quietly. A few paces behind them is Blythe, head bent downward except for when we pass a street grate in the center of the barrel-vaulted ceiling. Only then does he look up, as if trying to listen to the echoing voices in the sunlit world above. Chimeline and I take the rear.

Based on what I remember of the city's layout, we'll travel like this for several fullbells before reaching the southern edge of the city.

"Did you want to continue our lessons?" I ask Chimeline. "While we walk?"

She doesn't answer.

"We don't need to be in the void. There are many fundamentals we can discuss. Lessons that I used to teach at the university."

"I'm not in the mood."

I shake my head in frustration. "We don't have the luxury of doing this when the mood suits you."

She stops in her tracks. "Excuse me?"

I stop as well, touching her arm apologetically. "I'm sorry. I just meant that perhaps it would be wise to use our time efficiently."

She recoils, folding her arms. Her expression is as hard as the stone blocks behind her. But I remember Marine's words.

"We need to do this, Chimeline. It's important."

Her folded arms tighten further. "Why?"

I resist the urge to roll my eyes in exasperation. Shouldn't this be obvious to her?

"If Blythe and his daughter are found, they'll be killed. Simply because they're effulgents." I raise my arms and let them fall back to my sides. "In fact, we'll all probably be killed. Because, apparently, everyone knows what we did to that azureman."

"I know that, Dem."

"Then what's the problem?"

She's the one who rolls her eyes, and then she continues walking.

"Chimeline," I call out, striding to catch up. "Wait. What's wrong?"

She doesn't respond.

"Look, I'm only trying to help. You're an axionlighter. I won't pretend to know exactly what that means, but I do know that you need to understand voidance to unlock your full potential."

She shakes her head, not looking at me. "You're unbelievable."

My forehead creases as I try to make sense of her foul mood.

Suddenly, she spins toward me and pounds my chest, nearly pushing me into the center canal. "Is that all I am to you? An axionlighter?"

A startled bird flutters in the small street grate. The sky beyond is perfectly blue.

"Of course not," I say defensively. But I'm lost in confusion.

For a moment, she looks at me as if studying a cryptic tome at the university library—deeply furrowed brow almost hidden underneath unkempt bangs, head cocked, lips tight. Then she brings her hands to her temples, her black hair a storm.

"Ugh!" she screams, then heads toward the others.

I catch up to her, reaching out for her hand, but she swats it away.

"Please talk to me," I say.

She just shakes her head in the blue-gray dimness. A rat scurries past, but she doesn't even flinch.

"Chimeline," I say, stubbornly getting in her way and stopping her from walking one step further. She tries to step around me, but I match her movements.

"Something's wrong," I say. "Ever since the Lemon Tree Inn." I point to the black water at our side. "It's as if I'm on the other side of this canal and there's a darkness dividing us. I don't under—"

"That's just it," she snaps, her dark eyes finding mine and becoming fiercer than I've ever seen. "You don't understand! You want to teach me voidance? Now?"

"I thought it would be a good—"

"Oh, because it's a quiet moment, right? What better time to hone your weapon!"

I hesitate, unsure how to respond.

"Just like you study my diary," she continues. "You study the voidreams so intently, as if they're your books back at the university. Perhaps because they're the key to winning some sort of war—I don't know. But did you ever think to ask me how I *feel* about all of this? No. You care more about Temberlain's Ashes than you do about me!"

"Chimeline—"

"And when we have a rare moment of privacy, just now, what do you do? You decide that it's a good time to train me. To make me a sharper weapon in your war. You don't care about how I feel. You don't ask how my visions affect me, or how the voices of the enervated have haunted me. How I cannot even sleep anymore."

She hooks her hair behind her ear before continuing.

"You can't sleep?" I ask her.

She ignores the question. "Do you remember the beach? When I was near voideath?"

My mind flashes to the moment after I pushed Mander beneath the waves. I nod.

"You told me that I was special. That it was nothing to do with me being an axionlighter. And that you were a fool not to have seen it earlier. Do you remember?"

I nod again.

"Those words brought me back to life, Dem! Not that stupid fire you built." She wipes tears from her face with the back of her hand. "Now I shudder to think that those words were only lies. It's all different now. I am nothing more than a weapon to you. You're just like my father."

I am struck nearly speechless.

Just like her father?

"Marine told me to teach you" are the only words that come out of my mouth, and I instantly hate them. I sound like one of my former students, blaming others for my shortcomings.

"Stop," she snaps. "You were this way before you ever spoke with her."

For a moment, all I can do is stare at the black water. It's the sound of her rushing away from me.

"Let's walk," she says. "We're falling behind."

I nod, and for a minute, we walk side by side in silence. It seems like a profound improvement.

"I want to tell you a story, Dem," she says, her voice subdued. "About my father. But it will be the only story about him that I'll ever share with you."

I don't respond.

We take another few steps and she breathes deeply, as if in preparation.

"It was a warm winter night—almost like a summer night—in Jwoei, on our island in Scorpiontail. We lived on the shore, but there was a freshwater lake a mile inland. My father woke me long after I had gone to bed. He had a bottle of sugarcanex with him. I could smell it. He told me to get dressed. Said that we were going for a walk."

"Wait. How old were you?"

"Twelve." She looks up to the ceiling. "It was a place called Moonlake. The moon was full that night, and the moonfrogs were all glowing green. I remember I saw the light through the palm trees even before we descended to the beach."

"Moonfrogs," I say softly. "That's where moonspit comes from. The vial of poison that you used on Mander."

"Yes. Once a month, during the full moon, the females glow to attract mates. The green is a slime that covers their skin. They . . . copulate, and after the males impregnate the females, they die. Even they cannot withstand the toxin. Of course, I didn't know any of this back then. I was only a child."

I have no idea where this is headed. I continue listening.

"As we sat together on the beach, my father took swigs of sugarcanex from the bottle and told me who I was destined to become. That I was to be a weapon against powerful men, and that he would teach me. This teaching was his way of loving me, no matter how sick it would make me feel."

From the small grate in the ceiling comes the rush of foot traffic. A staccato series of light and dark as dozens of soldiers march down the street. A man shouts orders. I hear the word *perimeter*.

"He captured one of them, near the bank," she says quietly.

"What? You mean a moonfrog?"

She nods again. "He held the glowing thing in his hands. He'd built up an immunity to the poison and would only sweat. I remember his face becoming a dark red."

She cups her hands and holds them out, as if acting out a scene on stage. "'Take it,' he told me. 'Hold it in your hands.'"

"What did you do?"

"I did as he said. But then he blurted, 'Let it go!' I didn't want to. I thought it was so beautiful and perfect underneath the full moon. It almost looked white. It glowed in my hands. But he swatted it away. The slippery little thing jumped back into the water. And almost immediately I started to feel sick."

"How?"

"My heart beat too fast. I broke out in sweat and the world started to spin. Then my father took the bottle of sugarcanex and poured it all over my hands. When the bottle was empty, he tossed it aside and held me close. He told me that everything was going to be alright. Every month, every full moon, we would come back here, and he would make me stronger. Into a woman capable of destroying kingdoms."

She begins to cry. I'm not sure if her story is over or if she's simply overcome by the memory. Regardless, I stop walking and pull her into my arms.

This time, she accepts the invitation, clutching me tightly. I wrap my arms around her as she sobs in the dimness, the intimate sound overtaking the rushing black currents. And as I hold her close, she reveals why she told me the story.

"I was his weapon. And now I'm yours."

I close my eyes in understanding. Chimeline has been used her entire life—a life that's never belonged to her. And now I'm as guilty as the men from her past.

Mander's psychotic attempt to put Chimeline in soteria brought me face to face with my feelings for her, but I have abandoned those feelings in recent days. The thought of losing her was unbearable—*is* unbearable. But rather than deal with them, I've pushed them to the periphery. I neglect the people who matter to me most. I always turn my attention toward something else. Before, it was the university. The institution of voidance. Now, I'm obsessed with its very destruction.

In the darkness behind my eyes rise the memories of those I've abandoned, looking much like the dark, slippery forms I imagined in the currents.

Anaxarchis curled up in the bottom of the well, a cut-up moon.

Cleanthes stretched out upon his piano through a haze of hilma smoke.

Marine floating in turquoise, seaweed partially covering her pale face.

Chimeline flashing white.

They rush away.

"I'm sorry," I say, opening my eyes to a dim world. "I'm so sorry."

She continues sobbing into my shoulder.

"I've been so focused on Chimeline the axionlighter that I've forgotten Chimeline the woman," I admit. "I can't imagine what you're going through, but I can promise you that from now on, we'll go through it together."

I don't know how long the silence lasts. Long enough that when I brush aside her hair, I catch sight of Colu, Blythe, and le-Daerke at the far end of the sewer. The three of them watch and wait patiently.

"So no more constant voidance lessons?" she asks me.

I run my hand gently though her hair. "When you're ready, I'll teach you, but not a moment before."

She wipes her cheek before she looks up at me, almost in disbelief. As if I'm not the man she once knew.

"I used to teach that voidance was of the mind," I say. "That only by honing the mind could one make herself stronger." I feel my jaw clench in conviction. "But I was wrong. I've lost so many people because I cared only about the mind and neglected the heart. Well, I'll be Temberlain's Ashes if that's going to happen again. I will not lose you, Chimeline. I love you."

The last three words slip out unconsciously. Even though I've never said them to her before, they seem natural.

A small smile breaks across her face before she puts her cheek against my shoulder.

"I love you, too," she says, her voice almost lost in my arms.

THE TEMPLE AND THE BAZAAR

All the sewer outlets into Xi Bay are barred so we backtrack, following a trail of litter instead. There are a few vagabonds now, silent watchers huddled within their birds' nests of homes against the sweating stone, away from the rushing currents, their white eyes orbs floating in the dark.

If they can get in, we can get out.

After fullbells of searching, Colu approaches one of them and shows him his scroll with the waxen seal of the rats. The vagabond says nothing in reply but he reveals his neck underneath soiled rags. Then he leads us toward our escape.

It's a narrow vertical passageway that resembles a chimney with rusty iron rungs. A service entrance. Two damaged metal panels open onto the brush-hidden side of a paved street a half-mile outside the southernmost gate of Winter's Baiou.

We rise under the light of a half-moon.

For a moment, I stare back at the city that spat us out. It has the audacity to gleam against the matte purple of the coming night, trying its best to lure us back. But we know better. Beneath all that beauty is a building darkness. Somewhere within those walls, evil spreads.

When I turn away from Winter's Baiou and toward our destination—the sparse, moonlit Xian countryside to the south—I don't feel as if I'm entering a wilderness. I feel as if I'm leaving one.

Before we take another step, we collapse in exhaustion. It's been almost two nights since our last sleep.

After what seems like a few fullbells, Colu wakes us up. Then we walk straight through the remainder of the night.

Before dawn, we approach the first sign of civilization, a small town that might not even have a name. Much like Winter's Baiou, it's on the shoreline of Xi Bay, but that's where the similarity ends.

We stop a mile outside, in an area sheltered by boulders, sagebrush, palms, and frankincense trees. Perhaps we're being overly cautious. In some regards, we're infinitely safer than we were a day ago. We are no longer in the city. But the azuremen are still out there. So is the voider whose silhouette I saw through Levi's window. I fear that all of them are the kind that have no regard for the boundaries of the kingdoms of men.

We send in le-Daerke.

With her dark wig and even darker skin, she'll blend in with the townsfolk. Chimeline ties up le-Daerke's hair in a messy bun to get it out of her face. Colu wants to go with her, but everyone agrees that both his eye patch and temperament are too memorable. So he gives le-Daerke his gold to procure food, water, horses, and, most importantly, information on Chireseal. After she leaves, we fill the time by performing eleutheria—not just on the azureman's massive heartstone, as we've started calling it, but also on two of the three stones that Colu gave to le-Daerke. The fruits of his murders.

The third we keep full of souls in case of emergency. A dark insurance for a dark age.

In the fourth is Marine. Refusing to leave.

Afterward, I lie on the sandy ground, shirtless, guiltily basking in the warmth of this world to recover from my time in the void.

Until I feel soft fingers on my beard.

Squinting my eyes open, I see Chimeline next to me on the sand. The noonday sun filters through her black hair. Her bangs have grown out in the weeks since we met. Now she keeps the shorter center section swept to the side, trying her best to blend it in with the longer hair. She looks so beautiful yet out of place in Ghanesa's colorful silk dress. A red desert flower. She's not dressed for this kind of journey.

"You're exhausted," she says, moving her hand from my face to my bare chest.

"I'm fine," I say, which is somewhat of a lie.

"They know what you're doing," she says, smiling with pride. "Every single time you do this, they know. I hear them. Countless souls, scattered throughout creation, crying out in gratitude."

I match her smile. Her simple words bring me more strength than resting for fullbells in the sun. She leans down and kisses my lips. I tenderly touch the side of her face before she pulls back.

Blythe stands and walks away, fidgeting with his beads. Colu is asleep on a flat section of rock.

Chimeline hands me a water jug. "Your lips are dry. You need to drink."

"Thanks," I say, downing a sip, and then another. She's right—I'm parched.

"What are you going to do with them?" she asks, motioning to the odd collection of voidstones in the sand. Three of them sit underneath my thin white shirt. I covered them up after eleutheria so they wouldn't float away. The still-full one sits naked in the sun, contained in its gold setting and chain, while Marine's is wrapped in the emerald fabric.

"The empty ones?"

She nods.

"I don't know," I say, shrugging. "Blythe thinks we should let them rise, as we did before."

"I don't think that's a good idea."

"Why not?"

She points upwards. "To the very same place the azuremen came from?"

I slowly sit and put my shirt back on. The motion causes the three stones to float just above the sand. They gently ricochet against each other.

She's right. Days ago, the world was simpler. After eleutheria, a voidstone was useless. But now, with the arrival of the azuremen and the giving houses, any empty voidstone is a cage ready to be filled.

"Well, it's either that or bury them," I say. "They can't be destroyed."

"Isn't that how you found the voidstones to begin with?" she asks.

I raise my eyebrows. "What, in the ground?"

She nods.

"Yes."

"Then I think we have only one option for the moment."

"Keep them on us," I say.

She nods again.

"Just put 'em in my pack," Colu says, from his nearby rock. I'd thought he was asleep. His eye is still closed, but he points to the sand below him, where his pack rests. "I'll guard 'em with my life."

"Alright," I tell him, and he mutters a groan of acknowledgment.

Chimeline scrambles over and returns with the leather pack. Carefully, without touching the azureman's large stone with my bare skin, I stuff the two empty stones inside. Despite the heartstone's size, it's now weightless.

"I greatly admire you," Chimeline says. "You were the master voider. Not many men could turn away from such power."

"You give me too much credit," I say, as I forcefully tie up the pack. "A fool who becomes wise too late is still a fool."

She furrows her brow. "Too late?"

The full voidstone sits in the sand, creating an ample depression. Holding its gold chain, I hesitantly place it around my neck. The weight sickens me.

"I could have stopped all of this, Chimeline. If I were smart enough."

She wrinkles her nose.

"The azuremen. The war. You becoming an axionlighter. All of it."

She shakes her head. "You can't blame yourself. Mander fooled an entire kingdom."

"I know," I say with a sigh. "But I was the master voider, and it happened on my watch. And there were so many warning signs. Signs that I should have—"

She places a finger on my lips. "We're stopping it now. Together."

I move away her finger and pull her in for a kiss.

When we pull apart, my gaze rests on the emerald fabric between us, a brilliant contrast to the golden sand.

I look into the distance, past Chimeline, past the low sagebrush and the boulders. On the hazy horizon, the lo-Kimer foothills rise hundreds of feet into the air.

"You still speak to Marine," I say, turning to her. It's not a question. Marine admitted as much.

She hesitates then nods.

"Do you know why she refuses eleutheria?"

She bites her lip.

"I've tried multiple times to convince her," I add. "Even just now, after freeing thousands of souls in the other stones, we tried again. She only says that she's not ready. She says that she's still translating for you. So that you and the enervated can understand each other."

"That is true." She tilts her head. "Mostly."

"Mostly?"

She brushes back her sideswept bangs. "Marine has been incredibly helpful. I can understand much of what they say now and can speak a little back to them. There are some words I struggle with, but . . . I could get by without her. If I had to."

I exhale in vexation. "You see? This is what troubles me. I fear that you're some sort of excuse and that she's hiding something. That there's some other reason." I point to the emerald swatch. "If something happens to this voidstone— if it's confiscated, lost, stolen—her soul will be forever trapped in torment. Used for voidance. And we have the power to free her *now*. I just don't understand her reluctance."

"I think you have to trust her. Give her time."

"Give her time for what?"

She shakes her head. "I don't know. But I have the feeling that she's working something out."

A hot gust of wind ruffles her red floral-patterned dress and blows sand around us. We shut our eyes momentarily.

"There's something else," I say, unwrapping the emerald swatch of fabric.

Black ash dissipates in the air.

"Did you see that?" I ask.

"See what?"

"The ash." I shake my head in bewilderment. "This happens every time I unwrap the stone. The black ash is always there." Using the fabric, I pick up Marine's stone and raise it toward the sky, letting it eclipse the sun. "I know it sounds crazy, but I think her stone has gotten smaller."

"What?"

"It's almost as if it's shedding. As if . . . it's continuously losing its shell."

"I thought that voidstones couldn't be destroyed," she says. "Or divided."

"They can't." I wrap the stone back up carefully and place it in my pocket. "Can you do me a favor?"

She nods.

"The next time you speak to her, can you ask her about this?"

"The black ash?"

"Yes. I just want her soul safe."

She looks at me with her dark eyes and smiles sadly. "Of course."

Fifty feet away, Blythe stands underneath the shade of a frankincense tree, his back to us. He looks southward, his effulgency beads grasped by his side. In the distance is the road down which we sent his daughter.

"I think it's sweet how you care for the well-being of her soul," she says. "Especially considering the pain she caused you in life."

I turn back to her. "I've forgiven her. But mine is the easy job. As for Marine . . . well, let's just say that I'm not sure the feeling is mutual."

Chimeline nods in understanding. "You're out here, alive and free, while she's still trapped inside."

I grimace. "Much of what happened was my fault. In fact, I feel somewhat indebted to her."

"Why is that?"

I shrug. "If it weren't for what happened, I don't know if I'd ever have realized the error of my ways."

"I'm indebted to her as well," Chimeline says. "She saved me in the Celestium. That white pool was for me, not her."

Another gust of hot wind blows, and Chimeline responds by tying up her hair in a hasty bun using a string from around her wrist. She then sweeps aside her lengthy bangs, which aren't quite long enough for the bun.

"Marine knows about us," she says evenly.

I raise an eyebrow.

She shakes her head while looking into the hazy, mountainous distance. "I didn't even have to say anything. She knew. Within the void, such things don't require words. She feels what I feel."

I follow her gaze and contemplate her words, which remind me of our vast differences when it comes to the void. My experience is technical. It has always been about the indivisibles and nothing else. Hers is emotional. About relationships with those enslaved.

She puts her arm around my waist and leans her head upon my shoulder.

"Inside, there is no such thing as a lie," she adds. "Sometimes I think that the heart and the soul are the same thing."

"And what did her heart and soul tell you?"

Chimeline continues to stare at the mountains. Finally, she replies. "I think that's what she's still working on, Dem. It's why she can't yet say goodbye."

The apparition of le-Daerke shimmers a long way off on the dusty road.

"She doesn't have the horses," Blythe notes, a hand against his forehead to shield his eyes from the afternoon sun.

"Told you," Colu says with a groan. "Not enough gold."

Blythe shakes his head. "The Unnamed creates beasts of the soil and gives them to us. Humankind creates gold to take them away."

Colu laughs once, kicking sand. "Right."

"What about your promissory note?" I ask Colu. "From the Baiou Rats?"

"No rats would be in that shit-fuck town."

"How far away is the next one?"

"Twenty, maybe thirty miles," Colu says, pointing south along Xi Bay, which glistens through the foliage, a few hundred feet away and east of the road. "They're all small though. Fishing ports that live off Winter's Baiou. None of them have much."

"It will take a day to walk there on foot," I say.

Colu spits on the ground. "Let's just steal them."

"The horses?" I ask.

"We are not stealing anything," Blythe says.

I agree with Blythe, which Colu must sense, because he keeps looking at me. "We're never going to catch Diamond Face on foot," he says pointedly.

"Why must you always resort to owning the dark?" Blythe snaps.

"But you just said that horses are free!" Colu briefly raises his arms.

"Stealing is wrong."

"So is traveling on foot."

le-Daerke's arrival interrupts us. We leave our hidden camp and approach the road a hundred or so feet away, meeting her there. On her head she balances a large wicker basket, heavy with something. My mouth begins to water as I realize my head aches from dehydration. Underneath her wig, her brow is deeply furrowed. Her expression seems to have nothing to do with the weight upon her head.

Colu quickly steps forward and takes the basket.

"I'm sorry," she says. "I couldn't get horses."

"It's alright, Daughter," Blythe says. "The Unnamed will provide."

She nods once and then alternates her gaze between her father and me. "We need to talk."

"Let's get off this road," I urge. "We can talk as we go."

The five of us head back toward our hidden camp. Our prior footsteps in the sandy ground are a subtle path weaving in and out of the sagebrush.

"Did you hear any news of Chireseal?" I ask her.

She looks sideways at me and nods. Sweat drips off the bridge of her nose. She must be exhausted.

"He came through here?" Blythe asks.

"Yes." She wipes her glistening face with her sleeve. "But he was quick and silent about it."

"How so?" I ask.

"I asked almost everyone in town. Nobody saw him, except for the farrier."

"Farrier?"

"One of Chireseal's horses had a bad shoe that dug into its hoof. It needed to be adjusted. The effulgent woke the man at night and paid him handsomely for his trouble."

Blythe scoffs. "This strange brother of ours sure relishes dealing with gold."

"When was this?" I ask.

"Two nights ago," le-Daerke says.

We reach our camp. Blythe upturns the wicker bag on a clean, concave section of rock, and its contents pour out: a leather water sack, head-sized bloodfruits, and tongue-shaped strips of dried meat. le-Daerke leans against a tall boulder within a tree's shade.

We immediately pass the food and water around. Everyone begins feasting except for le-Daerke. She looks straight ahead at nothing.

"What else?" I ask, as I bite into the bitter but nutrient-rich bloodfruit, keeping my knees parted as drips of bright red fall to the ground.

le-Daerke looks at me for a moment, blinking rapidly. Then she turns to her father. "I visited the temple."

Blythe straightens.

"There was no effulgent there," she continues. "Or graycloak. The temple has been . . . changed. It is now a giving house."

"Just as the king proclaimed," Blythe says with a deep sigh.

"Wait," Colu says, straightening from his leaning stance on the rock. "All that giving house shit was in the Northern Kingdom. We're in Xiland now."

The only sound is my bloodfruit dripping onto the sand.

"Those azuremen aren't over here, too, are they?" he continues.

His one-eyed gaze passes over each of us but settles on le-Daerke. "Did you see any of them?"

"Azuremen?" She shakes her head. "No."

"What about Xian voiders?" I ask.

She shakes her head again.

I run my hand through my hair. "I don't know, Colu. Maybe since we're so close to the border, they converted this temple too."

"No," Chimeline says quietly.

We all turn to her.

"It's not just happening in the North," she says. "These intruders are desecrating temples across the land. Xiland. Scorpiontail. It's happening everywhere."

For a moment, only the dry wind through the sagebrush answers.

"Fucking Unnamed," Colu says.

Blythe flashes him a disapproving look.

"It's a place of horror," le-Daerke says, shivering despite the warmth of midday.

Blythe swallows hard. "What did you see there?"

"The stained-glass windows have all been broken and cleared out. The wooden sign carved with the way of unwanting lay charred in a firepit outside. Inside, the pews have been removed. There were some townsfolk. But they were not there for the way of unwanting."

Blythe closes his eyes. We all wait for le-Daerke to continue.

"A man appeared to be in charge. He wore rich, shimmering blue garments, like the feathers of a peacock." le-Daerke points to her forearm. "A bell rang. People came, and he began handing out gold coins to everyone with a number. The higher the number, the more gold they received."

"They have reduced a sacred space to . . . a bazaar," Blythe says.

"He saw that I was numberless, so he asked if I was there to give. Or if I knew someone I could sponsor."

"What did you say?" Blythe asks.

She shakes her head. "Nothing."

"Souls for gold," I say, after a moment of silence.

"What do you mean?" Blythe asks.

I tap my wrist. "If you take someone in to be put in soteria, you get a number. The more people you take in, the higher your number. And the higher your number, the more gold you receive."

"Souls for gold," Colu repeats. He spits.

"No wonder they're executing all the effulgents," Chimeline says. "This is the antithesis of the way of unwanting."

Blythe fishes out his effulgency beads from underneath his gray tunic. le-Daerke looks down at the sandy ground while rubbing her temples with her fingers.

Chimeline, who has the water sack, crosses the clearing between the rocks and hands it to her. "You're parched," she says. "You must drink."

le-Daerke gives her a thankful nod and takes the sack, letting a trickle of water fall into her mouth.

"Did you see the act of giving itself?" I ask her. "How they place people in soteria?"

She flashes me a worried look as she hands the water sack back to Chimeline. "There is a ritual—up where the altar used to be."

I frown. "Ritual?"

"After the man in blue finished passing out gold, a mother and daughter approached him and said that they were ready to give. The man greeted them in a friendly manner and walked them up to the altar."

"What did he do? Use voidance?"

"He wasn't a voider."

"Are you sure? He may not have been dressed in black, but he could have had a voidstone beneath his blue robes."

She shakes her head.

"Then I don't understand how he placed someone in so—"

"There was a black box, in place of the altar," le-Daerke says, her voice growing louder and more resolute. "It was large. As tall as a man. Cube shaped, metallic. And perfectly smooth. The mother and daughter both walked up there . . ." le-Daerke pauses before continuing. "I tried to see what was happening, but I was in the back. There was a flash of light. It was so bright it blinded me for a moment. It blinded all of us. When I regained my vision, the daughter had received a mark on her arm. The number *01*. And the mother was gone."

I shake my head in confusion. "Where did her body go?"

"I don't know!" le-Daerke shouts. Almost as quickly she looks down and rubs her temples again.

When she looks up at me, her eyes are more red than white.

"What has become of us?" she asks, her face wrought with pain. "How did we let this happen?"

Despite the harsh sun, a memory of blackness fills my vision. So long ago, yet recent. It was the night Chimeline and I stumbled upon Mander's rogue laboratory in the wilderness of the Second Ring, near the bank of the River Xi. A collection of macabre applications of voidance.

A large black cube stood within that barn. Slightly larger than a man. Seamless. Impervious to voidance. Heavy enough to require a stone foundation instead of wood. At the time I had no idea what it was, and I never got the chance to question Mander about it.

A fool who becomes wise too late is still a fool.

Leaning back against the rock, I shake my head in disbelief, caught again within a trap of guilt. Mander had been planning for this day for years, right under my nose. There was a time when I could have stopped it, had I the wisdom to look for it.

But that time has long passed.

VOIDREAMING

Within the tight confines of the lift on its way down to Torso level, Temberlain stared past his armed captors at his refection in the door.

The crude blackened stump just past his shoulder symbolized everything that was happening—to him and the empowered at large. The usurping of the natural order by those who had no understanding of what it was like to wield true power.

His physical pain was muted. The ashen had given him an injection to bring him back to consciousness and keep the agony at the periphery. Which meant that they needed more than just his DNA codec. They needed his cognition, however dulled.

But for what?

He wasn't even distraught about losing the limb. It was mere flesh and sinew and bone. If he survived this mutiny, the axionship's neoteny team could grow out a new one.

It was severance from axion that hurt the most.

Temberlain reminded himself that it was temporary. His axiongraph was gone, but his capability to harness axion remained. That was a gift that could never be taken away by these animals. They nervously spoke among themselves in their dribbling Dodoghian dialect, breaking intermittently into graceful Effulgian. He caught their words. "Now he is ashen, like us."

No, you fools. I'll never be like you.

A wave of nausea came over him as the lift shuddered and accelerated.

Something was wrong. It usually followed the outer curve of the ship like a graceful silver drop of mercury, all direction and velocity imperceptible. Perhaps emergency FTL differentiation had damaged it. The entire ship seemed to mimic Temberlain. Both bodies were in shock.

All seven ashen in the lift braced themselves against the reflective walls or each other. One of the ashen roughly grabbed Temberlain's remaining arm. A soft feminine voice announced that fifty microrotations remained until Torso level.

One of the ashen called out "Drive chamber."

Why there? They've already got control of the ship.

A green-blue glow drew his attention downward.

In the corner, one of the ashen had a fabricreader in her hands. The vacuum hardline engineer. Temberlain couldn't remember her name, so she was Sixteen—the number on her forearm. Almost as wide as she was tall, her body was muscular despite years of working in zero G.

She was checking the evacuation pods. Dozens of perfect circles lined the fabricreader in a matrix. Half were green, meaning that she'd already brought them online. They were ready for occupants.

Sixteen tapped on the yellow ones, activating them on the resulting screen and going back and forth between screens to check on their startup progress. Grunting at a few reds.

Temberlain closed his eyes.

The view from the common mess. Of course.

The presence of a habitable planet was no coincidence. Given that the axionship had no velocity of its own, the planet must be dangerously close. Undoubtedly, the ship was already caught within its gravity well, being slowly pulled in.

It was also near enough for the evacuation pods to reach.

The ashen must have come out of FTL in this system purposely. They had no intention of commandeering the ship long term.

They were leaving it.

He did the mental math. FTL comms had been down for at least half a rotation before they broke free. Based on the rate of FTL travel, the permutations were almost infinite. Triangulation was impossible.

Without a new ping, the chances of Efful finding them—of locating this exact planet in this exact system—were as low as the chances of discovering a diacrystal seashell in the Garthenic Ocean.

Why do they need me? The ashen are in control. Pods are coming online.

The feminine voice announced that the drive chamber was approaching.

Temberlain opened his eyes. "Why are we going to the Axiondrive?" he asked no one in particular.

Sixteen glared at him with bloodshot eyes. "No questions," she barked.

"Whatever it is that you want me to do, you're going to have to tell me eventually," he said. "Why not just tell me now?"

"Shut your mouth."

"But—"

She shouted a Dodoghian word. "We'll tell you when we tell you. Until then, keep quiet, or I'll remove your tongue as easily as your arm."

Not wanting to test her threat, Temberlain went silent. He needed to devise a way out of this.

In the common mess, he'd attempted axionilation, which in hindsight was foolish. He'd thought that death was imminent, but in the bloody chaos he'd forgotten how he'd arrived there. The ashen at dinner. The wine spill. The two waiting for him in his cabin.

As long as they needed him alive, he had the opportunity to escape.

I've got to get word back to Efful.

As subtly as he could, he moved his remaining hand behind his back and searched for the serrater hidden within the autosizing of his pants.

It wasn't there.

His heart dropped in disappointment. The lift shuddered and moved again, and the sensation made him retch. As the bovine and wine from dinner came up, he turned his head into the corner.

The ashen complained in guttural unison.

They must have searched him while he was unconscious. He was naked from the waist up, covered in drying blood. The tip of the serrater would have risen above the hem of his pants, easily seen.

There was only one way he could regain the advantage. He needed to find axion. Fragments were buried inside each serrater. Inside every lift. In every maintenance extraship on Torso. All he needed was one.

Even the smallest piece would give him enough power to kill these seven. Then he'd work his way to the CC and turn back on FTL comms. A single microrotation, a simple distress call, and these ashens' dreams of mutiny would be cut short, their impending awakening immortalized in the annals of history.

The lift doors opened.

AL-KIMER-VIS

"You can wipe that smirk off your face," Blythe calmly says to Colu. "Let it go and be nothing. Your provocations will not work on me, for I do not own the dark."

Colu points at him. "You may not own the dark, but you *do* own a beautiful Xian horse."

Blythe sighs and looks toward the late-morning sun perched above the lo-Kimer foothills.

He and his daughter ride together on an elegant gray horse. The drab color suits them. Colu's is dark brown with white spots, and apparently the oldest, though I cannot tell the difference. Chimeline and I share a chestnut-colored mare. We're taking up the rear.

Our road sharply turns left as it circumvents a looming outcropping of rocks, and I take the opportunity to gaze back down the path we just traveled.

Our elevation is noticeably higher—we've been steadily climbing.

I cannot even see the small town we left behind in a rush during the night, and Winter's Baiou is barely discernible in the haze. The massive Port of Yamerind, with all its impressive wharves and masted galleons, is a mere collection of tinder sticks and white confetti jutting out into the sparking blue.

The region between the border city and us exhibits a gradual shift in color. While the North's foliage is verdant, our area has a more muted tone.

"Shitload better than walking, isn't it?" Colu asks me, then spits.

I ignore the question as I continue to scan the landscape. "The important thing is that we're gaining ground on Chireseal. He's got four draft horses, and the Axiondrive weighs nothing."

"Those drafts are Northern inbreds." I hear Colu pat his horse's neck tenderly. "And these beauties are Xian."

I turn to him. "I take it that means they're faster?"

"Faster. Steadier. Handsomer. Better in every way."

"How so?" le-Daerke asks curiously. "I've heard that Xians are the standard to which all other breeds strive but never understood why." Blythe, sitting directly in front of her, shakes his head slightly in disappointment.

"They *are* the standard," Colu agrees, admiring all three of our horses. "While these are no warhorses, they'd fetch over a thousand gold each. The hostler was an idiot not to guard them, especially these days. Lots of men running around with the war still inside them."

"But why are they worth so much?" le-Daerke asks.

Colu extends his hand to the dry wilderness. "Because of this. For centuries, Xian horses lived out here. The rough terrain breeds strength. Something your Northern green fields could never create." Then he points toward the mountains. "And even further, past the lo-Kimer Pass, in the deepsands." He takes a swig from his water sack and spits the liquid back out, hitting the vertical tan rock wall that our road embraces. "Out there, most are kept in the family tents, with the children. And any hot bloods are butchered for meat."

"Hot bloods?" I ask.

He shrugs. "Bad temperament. Any sign of untrustworthiness."

"That is horrible," Blythe says. "They should be set free to roam."

Colu shakes his head. "Roaming means fucking. And then the hot blood gets passed to the foals."

Blythe sputters to himself in outrage. The only coherent word is *unwanting*.

Colu ignores him. Leaning forward, he hugs his horse's graceful neck and extends his hand toward its head. "See this bulge?" he asks le-Daerke.

He points to a small bump upon its forehead, almost between its eyes.

"Yes," le-Daerke says.

"Only Xians have it. Called the jibstay."

"Jibstay?"

Colu nods. "Our voiders studied them. Found that the bone structure helps the animals breathe in the desert. Filter out sand."

Chimeline whispers something in my ear while sharply squeezing her arms around my waist.

I turn slightly around. "What's that?"

She hesitates. "Oh, nothing. I was just . . . thinking to myself."

There's something unsettling in her tone, so I try turning in the saddle more, but it's impossible.

"Is everything alright?" I ask her.

Another hesitation. "I think so."

"Are you going to have another voidream? I don't want you falling off our horse."

"No, it's not that."

"Chimeline, if you need to talk through anything—"

"I don't."

After a moment, I close my mouth, deciding to let it go in light of our recent conversation in the sewers. Her blunt reply is uncharacteristic but almost assuredly related to being an axionlighter. I remind myself that I have no idea what she's going through.

I turn forward again. The other three watch us in silence, their conversation about Xian hot bloods halted.

We silently climb to a steeper section of the road, which is rounding the gigantic outcropping and looping back west. A gust of dry wind whips through, peeling away the dust that the horses kick up and sending it into the sagebrush wilderness.

We enter shade cast by the looming rock.

Soon, the road turns southward again and Colu stops his horse, prompting the same from us. He points into the distance. Another valley lies down below. "There. al-Kimer-vis."

Xi Bay is miles to our left, almost out of sight. From it, a narrowing inlet cuts in, ending in a small river.

I remember this area from university maps. Kimer Dagger. The town of al-Kimer-vis sits at its very tip.

To the right and west are the lo-Kimer foothills, rising from the ground like a stretched-out, slumbering giant. Rolling hills covered in sagebrush transition into even-higher smooth plateaus of gold. It all gradually fades into the distance as far and as high as the eye can see.

Unlike our last stop, al-Kimer-vis seems large enough to be considered a proper town. There isn't a wall surrounding it, but impressive domed and flowing structures make it resemble a city made of sand. Banners and tents of all colors dot it like jewels in the midafternoon sun.

"Should we bypass it, as we did the other town?" Blythe asks. He places a hand against his forehead as he warily gazes at the city.

"No," Colu says without hesitation.

I turn to him sharply, but Blythe speaks up first. "May I ask why?"

Colu turns to me. "You want to get to Gemface, right?"

I nod.

He points to al-Kimer-vis. "We need to go in if we want to keep going south. There isn't a road that goes around."

I put my hand to my forehead as well. "What about that one?" I ask, pointing to a dusty road leading west and up toward the mountains. It's sparsely dotted with travelers.

Colu exhales through his nose deeply. "That goes through the pass. "

"The pass?"

"Deepsands," he adds.

"Maybe he went that way to hide the Axiondrive," le-Daerke says.

Colu groans. "I seriously doubt Gemface would go there. Unless he doesn't know what the fuck he's doing."

"I don't understand why he wouldn't," Blythe says, ignoring the crassness. "It's a road like any other."

Colu shakes his head. "It's a wasteland, alright? Gemface wouldn't last a fullbell there."

"So you think he's headed south," I say. "Through the city and continuing on."

Colu shrugs. "Where else? Maybe all the way to the Jewelled. Maybe not. But certainly the country south of here. It's the only safe route between the sea and the mountains."

For a moment, we sit on our horses in silence. Then Colu's mount neighs in impatience.

"Besides, we need to stop for supplies," Colu eventually adds in a softer tone. "Need to buy shit. Food. A tent or two. Canex."

"You and your poison," Blythe mumbles.

Colu gives him an icy stare.

"I agree," I eventually say. "It's a good opportunity to ask around. Maybe find a clue or two about Chireseal. Who knows, he might even still be here, in the city."

Everyone nods except for Chimeline.

"I don't think we should be stopping," she says, rubbing her temples. "For anything."

"We're almost out of food and water," I reply gently. "And I'm assuming our horses need a rest, Xian or not."

Colu shakes his head. "Horses are fine."

"We'll stop in town anyway," I announce. "But we'll make it quick. In and out with no trouble."

Colu laughs. "Trouble part is entirely up to you."

"What's that supposed to mean?" I ask.

He looks at Blythe and then at me. "You two are as white as mother's milk. And the war is still a fresh wound in these parts. Try not to be your usual asshole selves."

I glance at Blythe. He has no expression whatsoever.

"Fine," I tell Colu. "You do the talking."

He nods then gives his spotted horse a kick, and we all begin our descent.

al-Kimer-vis is so strange that it could be a mirage.

We enter a cloud of dust and merge with dozens of others on camelback or horseback from the west, carting loads of hides. There are herds of bleating goats. Crimsonhawks on leashes. Wicker baskets full of seeds and snakes. Xian nomads coming and going, bringing their huntings and gatherings and leaving with all the things that the wilderness could never provide—spices, frankincense, hilma, fabric, rugs, weapons, palehounds.

It's where the wandering and the everlasting collide.

Swallowed up within the coiling streets, the buildings of the city breathe with life of their own. While Northern architecture strives for straight lines—as if humankind could stubbornly make order out of chaos—Xian design seems to understand what it cannot control. The curved stone structures connote the feeling of movement, as if they're sand dunes sculpted by the wind. Fabric tents flutter like palms. There are no linear streets. No grids. al-Kimer-vis seems to know it wasn't here first, and it won't be here last.

I'm glad to see a few Northerners about, but they blend in as I could never do. They're already tanned and wear Xian clothing. They're oblivious to where they are. They're part of it.

The stares are everywhere, and they are not kind. Despite the overwhelming diversity blowing in and out of this place, Blythe, Chimeline, and I are not threads in this patterned rug. We are not tiles in this mostly dark-skinned mosaic.

Most of the women cover themselves in patterned silk scarves and cool-toned dresses—blues, whites, grays. The men wear white. The workers have less clothing—some are even naked except for loincloths—while the wealthy stroll about with headscarves and grasp gold-painted canes carved into the shapes of snakes or effulgency beads. Some of these sticks are adorned with gems, which Colu says indicate the person's social status in the Jewelled, the sprawling capital well south of here.

We ride tightly together through a curving street, surrounded by a whirlwind of chorus, color, and shape. Colu straightens in the saddle and tilts his head to both sides, stretching his neck.

"There," he says, kicking his horse ahead, parting the crowd.

Our destination is not a building but a large, open-walled, white-tented area at least a hundred feet square nestled between buildings that twist like the cutoff trunks of gargantuan trees. There are tethering posts in front.

Colu gets off his horse first and ties it off. Then he walks up to le-Daerke and helps her off. "Gimme the gold," he says to her.

"What gold?"

"The rest of what I gave you," he says.

"Oh." She digs in her small bag and procures three large coins and a few ingots.

"That's it?" he says loudly.

"I had to purchase food and drink."

"Fuck, Woman!" he exclaims. "Didn't the effulgency teach you how to barter?"

Chimeline gracefully gets off our horse and ties it off while I struggle.

Colu grunts. "Some of us will be sleeping under the stars."

Blythe clears his throat. "The sky is the richest canopy of all—"

"Given freely by the Unnamed," Colu finishes mockingly. "Listen," he says, his gaze falling upon each of us. "Stay here. All of you. I mean it."

I nod.

"I'll ask about Gemface," he adds. He gives an ingot to le-Daerke. "For the water boy."

Colu walks off to the white tent full of customers.

A small Xian boy no older than seven approaches. He carries a dark wooden bucket full of water that splashes about—it's obviously much too heavy for the child. Using both hands, he pours its contents into the trough.

le-Daerke drops the ingot in the empty bucket. The boy smiles, revealing missing teeth. He sticks his hand in and retrieves the ingot.

The inside of the bucket briefly glows blue.

As he withdraws his hand, I catch the digits *01* glowing faintly on his forearm.

For a moment I stare at him, speechless, and get the sense that the other three are doing the same. Of all the oddities in al-Kimer-vis, this is the one I hadn't been expecting.

"Where did you get that?" I ask him.

His smile vanishes.

"It's alright," Chimeline says soothingly, putting her hands on her thighs as she leans to match his height. "We just want one of those numbers too. Can you tell us where you got it?"

He looks into his empty bucket.

"Did you get that here?" Chimeline asks, motioning toward his arm. "In al-Kimer-vis?"

He nods once then scurries away.

I run my hand through my hair and look at Chimeline as she straightens. "It's like you said. It's happening everywhere—even down here."

She nods sadly and looks lost in thought as she gently touches the face of our chestnut horse.

I curse. "How did they make it this far south so quickly?"

"I don't know," she says distantly. "But this disease is rampant."

A thought comes to me like blown-in sand through an open door. "Where are all the voiders?" I ask.

Only le-Daerke seems intrigued by the question. She purses her lips. "You mean the Xian ones?"

I nod as she surveys the crowd in the street. "Have you see any?" I ask.

"No. But they could be mixed in."

I shake my head. "They'd stick out," I say, thinking of their flaxen cloaks—a custom that knows no borders. "Nobody is wearing black in this sun."

"Maybe they all went back home," Blythe says. "The hideous war is over."

In some respects, Blythe is correct. The Southern voiders had reassignments, just as our Northern ones did. And now that the bloodshed is over, they should have dissolved back into normalcy. Returned to the Xian university in the Jewelled, or to their former stations.

But I shake my head. "Home?" I say, pointing at the ground. "Home is places like this. The town of al-Kimer-vis is large enough to warrant the permanent assignment of dozens of voiders, given its population."

"Dem."

It's Chimeline. She stands a few feet away staring down the length of the bustling street, which curves out of sight.

I squint, trying to make out details in the hazy air. "What? Do you see one?"

She looks back at me at the same time as I see it. It's almost out of sight—the gold dome, shining like a second sun. A man stands on the elevated stone steps in front of the open doorway.

He's not wearing black but brilliant blue.

"That is an effulgency temple," Blythe says pensively.

"No," Chimeline answers. "It's a giving house."

THE SPONSOR

"What is that sound?" Blythe asks.

I hear nothing except the chaos of the street. Two screeching peacocks. Vulgarities from a Xian man on horseback carting a small wagon as he's forced to navigate around us.

After he passes, I notice it: a high, repetitive ringing floating above the noise, bright as the day.

"It's not deep enough to be the effulgency bell," Blythe adds.

"But it's coming from the temple," I say.

A few angry shouts accompany it. There's commotion in the street far ahead, but the man in blue on the giving house stairs remains motionless.

Braying, then a scream.

I turn to the group. "Chimeline, you and le-Daerke stay here with the horses. Blythe and I will see what's going on."

le-Daerke nods coolly but Chimeline looks deeply worried. "Colu said to stay here."

"I know what he said."

She rubs her forehead. "Dem . . . we need to keep moving. I have a bad feeling about this place."

"Look," I say, motioning to the distance while trying to summon my patience. "It's just up the road. We're going to be quick. I promise."

She doesn't look convinced, but I don't have time to change her mind. She reaches out, and her fingers move through mine before I step away.

"Blythe, let's go," I say, over my shoulder.

As the street curves to the right, it becomes clear that the giving house sits at the center of a T intersection—it's on the left side of our street and at the end of a perpendicular one that comes from the right.

The crowd thickens as the ringing becomes louder.

Some people in front of us are now backtracking, trying desperately to leave. A man on horseback—the same one who swore moments ago—curses again as he turns his horse and cart around in a tight circle. Two women in his way skillfully avoid being trampled, the wicker baskets balanced upon their heads not even tipping.

Blythe and I reach the edge of the throng. It wrestles with itself—the people in the front want to turn back while those in the back want to see what's in front.

The entire intersection is clear except for four people.

In the lead is a young Xian man, perhaps in his twenties. Clearly wealthy, he has a pure-white headscarf, cloak, and walking stick, which is adorned with turquoise jewels.

In his other hand is a brown leather leash.

On the opposite end of it, about ten feet behind, is another man. He rings a small brass bell and is covered entirely in thin gray gauze except for two slits in his face—one for his eyes, and one for his mouth. I can see dark skin and pus-yellow eyes. The gauze bandages are spotted in blood. He's hunched. Around his waist is another rope that leads to two bandaged men behind him, much closer together.

The people next to me begin covering their faces with their shirts and cloaks.

"Lepers," Blythe mumbles, exhaling while shaking his head.

Carried over the dry wind is the scent of rotting flesh.

The man in blue, standing on the steps of the giving house, raises his arms at his sides. The sleeves of his robe look like dripping wax. As he raises his hands higher, the sleeves slip down a bit, revealing a blue metallic-looking ring that covers one of his wrists. It could either be a shackle or bracelet.

"Welcome!" he says, loudly enough to subdue the crowd. "I see a sponsor and three courageous givers in my midst!" His tone is welcoming, congratulatory. Ecstatic.

The wealthy man in the lead—the sponsor, I assume—hesitates, tapping the bottom of his cane against the street bricks a few times, faster than the tempo of the bell. Then he quickly ascends the stairs and clasps forearms with the man in blue, a formal Xian business gesture.

They both look down at the three, who seem to be having a hard time making the climb. There are only seven stairs.

"Come now," the man in blue says to them, as if speaking to children. "The pain and weariness of this world will soon be over."

The sponsor leans in, speaking privately with the man in blue. The latter nods, taking the leash. Both step out of the way and hold open the doors to the giving house as the three lepers slowly enter, one by one.

Into darkness.

The ringing stops.

The man in blue smiles wide while the sponsor looks anxious. He grasps his white robe at his chest, directly over his heart. Then he looks down and lets go.

I inhale sharply.

Blythe turns to me. "What is it?"

I lean close to his ear without taking my eyes off the proceedings. "That man is a voider."

"Who is?" Blythe asks.

"The sponsor."

Blythe looks confused.

"He just reached for his voidstone," I say.

The man in blue puts his arm around the sponsor and they enter the giving house, shutting the doors behind them.

Suddenly, people flow past us, back into the intersection like the rising tide.

"What does it matter?" Blythe asks.

I glance at him. "What does *what* matter?"

"If that man is a black arcanist."

I'm about to answer but feel myself getting pushed from behind. "Come on. This way."

We walk to the edge of the street to get out of the way of traffic and give ourselves some privacy. A scriber's shop is steps away. Sweet, earthen-smelling smoke from a hanging silver frankincense censer curls through the green tent's opening, making me light-headed.

Sitting down on a cracked stone step in a meager patch of shade near the corner, we look directly across the intersection at the giving house.

"It matters because I need to understand what has happened to them," I say.

"What makes you think something happened?"

I put my elbows on my knees, forming a fist with both hands. "They've all disappeared, Blythe. The last time we saw any voiders was at the Union. And I've seen none in Xiland except for him." I point with my index fingers at the closed doors. "And he's not wearing a black flaxen robe. He's hiding from someone."

"You forget about the one who came for us."

"At Levi's house?" I shake my head. "Chimeline said that one was different."

"A trained palehound."

I raise my eyebrows. "Whatever that means." A moment of silent passes. "But you have to admit, it's odd that the azuremen didn't send more voiders after us. Right?"

He nods in thought.

"There were dozens in the city," I add. "And there should be dozens here."

"Dem, if I may be frank, the disappearance of black arcanists is not what troubles me. What troubles me is that the rich are rounding up the poor and the sick, placing them in soteria, and becoming richer as a result. It is a grave injustice."

I bring prayerlike fingers to my lips and nod. "I don't disagree." I look sideways at Blythe, but he still stares intently at the giving house.

"We need to talk to that man," I say.

Blythe breathes through closed teeth. "You promised that we would not intervene."

"I know, but we need to understand what we're up against."

He groans. "Well, now is your chance, my friend."

I turn back to the giving house in surprise. The doors have opened. The sponsor steps through into the harsh sunlight, pulls back his white sleeve, and looks at his arm.

"That was fast," I say, as we both stand.

"Most evil deeds are."

Cane in hand, the sponsor quickly descends the stairs and heads across the intersection in our direction, toward the place he originally came from—the perpendicular street to our right. The man in blue stands within the doorframe of the giving house, arms out against the wood, looking smug in the shadows.

"Turn around," I tell Blythe, as I face the green scriber's tent.

I hear the *click, click, click* of the sponsor's walking stick as he passes behind us.

Braving a glance, I catch him disappearing around the rounded, twisted corner of a sand-colored building that looks as if it were carved from the side of the rock. His face is even smoother and younger close up, which makes his walking stick all the more ridiculous.

"Let's go," I tell Blythe.

He groans again but stays by my side. "The way of unwanting, Dem. The way of unwanting."

We allow a handful of strangers to merge between. A woman with a basket on her head. Two older women holding a clothesline from which silks hang.

For another tenthbell, we weave in and out of the crowded, labyrinthine passageways, following the sponsor. Many other Xian men wear the same style of white robe and headscarf, but only the sponsor's cane is adorned with turquoise gems.

He turns into a dim alleyway—a narrow channel covered by taut tarps in various colors tied to iron hooks set into the sand-colored buildings.

The rest of the crowd continues straight ahead.

We follow, into the alley. And within an instant, the three of us are alone.

With the sunlight filtering through the tarps, even the shadows in the cool dimness seem to be painted with color.

An emaciated palehound is curled up against the side of a building. It looks dead, although I don't smell any rot.

The sponsor keeps walking a few steps in front of us, oblivious to our presence. The taps of his cane echo against the buildings. The deeper we go, the darker it becomes.

As my eyesight adjusts, I realize that the alleyway is becoming narrower. Twenty feet from the sponsor lies a dead end. The sensation is one of being stuck inside a natural crevasse. The sides of the buildings to our left and right are stucco. No brick or mortar. Just seamless, vertical, slightly curved walls.

This place is abandoned. There is no destination. No doors or windows of any kind.

Yet the man continues to walk as if an entire village is laid out before him.

I stop, signaling Blythe to do the same.

A gust of wind causes the tarps above to flap violently. The colored shadows ripple.

The sponsor stops ten feet from the dead end.

He turns around—first his head then his entire body.

I see his furrowed brow. I see him reach again for the voidstone near his heart—a voidstone that is obviously not there.

Rushing as fast as I can, I close the distance between us.

He has no place to go. He raises his cane, but the alley is too narrow for him to use it as a weapon. It clatters against the stucco wall uselessly.

I grab onto his cloak. Using my momentum, I push him into the curved side wall then cover his mouth with my hand just as he begins to shout for help. His cane falls to the ground, the sharp, hollow sound echoing. Behind us, the palehound awakens with a growl.

"I'm a voider!" I hiss. "I'm not here to hurt you!"

The palehound begins to bark incessantly.

The Xian man is shorter and weighs less than I do. He's wiry, all thinness behind the cloak. As I push his shoulder against the wall he winces but looks at me with wide eyes. They go to my chest then back to my face.

He tries to say something.

I hesitantly remove my hand from his mouth.

"Why are you following me?" he asks in a rush, nearly out of breath.

"You are the first voider I've seen in Xiland. Where are the rest?"

He narrows his eyes. "How did you know? I'm not carrying."

I grasp my shirt above my heart in illustration and he exhales. He looks momentarily at the blank wall before giving me an accusatory look. "You of all people should know what's going on." The next word is almost spat out. "Northerner."

A *shh* sound briefly commands my attention. Glancing behind me, I see Blythe kneeling on the ground, his arms raised in front of the palehound, whose red teeth and gums are bared.

Turning back to the voider, I ask, "What do you mean?"

"They came from the North!" he shouts.

They?

"You mean the azuremen?" I ask.

He blinks in the dimness. It's evident that he's not heard the term before.

"Covered in armor," I add. "Blue visor."

His amber eyes meet mine. "Yes."

"Are they here? In al-Kimer-vis?"

He tilts his head in contemplation. "One came through here two days ago. Word has it there are more in the Jewelled."

I open my mouth but no words come out. My thoughts swirl too quickly to catch any one of them individually. The azuremen have been here, too. How is that even possible?

"We assumed they came from the North," he says.

"No," I answer. "It's the *same* in the North. I don't know how, but they've come to all kingdoms at once. The destruction of the effulgency. The turning of temples into giving houses. It's everywhere."

"The confiscation of voidstones," he adds, his voice almost a whisper.

"What?"

He narrows his eyes as he studies me. "You honestly don't know, do you?"

"Know what?" I ask, raising my voice in impatience.

"Do you still have yours?"

Taking my hand off the man's shoulder, which is pressed up against the wall, I fish out my necklace from beneath my shirt. The stone is still wrapped in gauze to prevent it from touching my skin, so I hastily undo the twine using my teeth then let the strip of fabric fall to the ground.

For a moment, he looks at my voidstone in both disbelief and adoration. Then he smiles, laughs genuinely, and wraps me a tight embrace.

"It is wise that you wrapped it up," he says, his voice muffled against my shoulder. "If they saw it, they'd send the marked after you."

Behind me, the palehound goes quiet.

The marked?

The sponsor pulls back, keeping both hands on my shoulders despite being a few inches shorter than I am.

"My brother from the North," he continues, before I have a chance to say anything, "if what you say is true, then the old war was nothing compared to the one ahead of us. And in this war, you and I, we are not enemies."

"We were never enemies," I tell him.

The Xian nods, understanding evident in his eyes. There is a bond between voiders that no race or country can sever. And despite the knowledge that I have of the evilness of our gift, it does nothing to destroy this feeling of kinship. Whether I use it or not, voidance will always be a part of me, as it will him. One could not erase it more easily than draining my body of all its blood.

"So the how did they confiscate your voidstone?" I ask him.

The man swallows, his smile vanishing. "He gathered us up. At the temple."

"The azureman?"

He blinks then nods. "There were a few who refused and he—"

Screams from the mouth of the alley draw our attention.

Two children enter, one chasing the other. Their laughter and taunts echo off the walls as if they were ten times their number. The one in the lead kicks a brown leather ball. It ricochets off the wall and rolls down the narrow passageway.

A woman stands behind them in the entrance, her motionless body almost a silhouette against the sunlit street.

Seeing the palehound and the rest of us, the two boys stop in their tracks. The ball rolls beyond their reach.

The palehound's attention remains on Blythe, but its aggression has become outright passivity. Blythe still kneels, and the palehound licks his face, its tail wagging so forcefully I can hear it tap against the stucco wall. One of Blythe's hands is on his blond wig, ensuring that it doesn't fall off.

The ball rolls past the two of them and comes to rest against my feet. I give it a good kick back to its young owners.

"It isn't safe to talk here," the voider says. "And you need to put that stone of yours away."

I turn back to him.

His headscarf is lopsided from our scuffle, so he takes it off briefly, revealing corkscrew locks. Clean shaven. He must be twenty years old. Practically a student.

He nods toward Blythe. "The palehound likes him. Never seen that before."

"You have never seen kindness?" Blythe asks, without taking his eyes off the creature.

The Xian voider rolls his eyes. As he puts the headscarf back on, the sleeves of his white robe fall to his elbows, revealing a number on his forearm.

"Seven," Blythe says sharply, as he stands. His eyes are fixed on the glowing blue numbers like a hunter's aim on a doe's heart. An awkward silence hangs in the alleyway.

"Seven souls!"

The voider alternates his gaze between the two of us. "A halfbell ago it was four. Now it's seven. What's the problem? You're not sponsors yet?"

I shake my head. Blythe exhales in disgust.

The man shrugs. "Listen, I don't like it either. Gathering up lepers in the deepsands is a pain."

"They are not outcasts in the eyes of the Unnamed," Blythe says. "Only you are." His voice is calm yet booming, reminding me of the first time we met.

The voider raises his eyebrows. "You still follow the effulgency?"

Blythe straightens. "The way of unwanting has no beginning and no end."

The Xian clears his throat. "Listen, I only do it because we need the gold," he says. "It's too risky to sell our services, like other voiders are doing. Word would get around. Then the marked would come."

"Who are the marked?" I ask him.

He looks at me with a horrified expression then shakes his head. "Not here."

He picks up his cane.

I turn to Blythe. "Go back to the others. Tell them I'll return in a fullbell."

For a moment, Blythe's eyes dart between the Xian voider and me. Eventually his eyes lock onto mine, and he takes a deep breath. "Do you know what you're doing?"

I nod. He continues to stare at me.

"Very well, then."

Without another glance at the voider, he turns and walks down the alleyway. The palehound follows, overgrown claws clicking upon the bricks.

Both disappear into the sun-bleached street.

The voider exhales once in disbelief. "I paid ten gold for that palehound." He shakes his head quickly, as if to clear his thoughts. "It's time for you to meet the others," he says, the surprise on his face replaced with excitement, and maybe a little dread. "An escaped voider from the North. This is news indeed."

He taps his cane. "Come with me."

The sponsor walks, without hesitation, straight into the end of the alleyway.

Through the stucco wall.

A HEARTH IN RUIN

We pass through the membrane into smoke-filled darkness.

A large abandoned forge about fifty feet square lies before me, although the walls are gently curved. The ceiling is at least two stories above, and chains hang most of the way down from a massive beam that spans the entire section. It must be from a millionescent.

Dozens of small paned windows are embedded in all four walls, near the ceiling. Some of them are missing. Small birds flutter in the open squares and perch upon iron lattices.

Rays of sunlight cut through the room, illuminating luxurious curls of incense smoke coming from silver censers below. The scent in the air is a mix of cinnamon sweetness and old wood.

A tattered circular red rug with Xian geometric designs sits in the center of the rough-hewn plank floor surrounded by mattresses made of straw and stacks of wicker baskets. Thick candles are lit, yellow eyes watching me in the dimness.

Despite the afternoon fullbell, a Xian couple rests together on one of these beds while a third Xian sits on the rug with her legs crossed reading a book in her lap.

They all look up as we enter.

"Welcome back," says the man on the bed.

"I've returned with a voider," the sponsor says proudly, as we approach. "And he still bears his stone."

The woman shuts her book. The sharp sound echoes in the large room. Birds flutter in the heights.

"You brought a Northerner here?" she asks shrilly. "What were you thinking?"

"Relax," he says. "It's happening in the North, too."

The couple slowly get up—a slightly overweight man and woman who look to be in their fifties. Neither of them wears a headscarf, only traditional flowing garments, his white, hers blue. The woman opens a wicker basket and pulls out a silk scarf patterned with crescent moons and wraps it around her bare shoulders. Both have their hair cut very short, and the man's face is speckled with age spots.

"Really," the woman on the rug says, her voice sharp with skepticism. She slaps the book down next to her and stands. She's tall, and probably as young as the sponsor. Wearing a saffron-colored shirt and tan pants, she looks more ready for riding than reading. Her hair is an impressive storm of black.

"Yes," the sponsor says. "A blue-faced man also went to the North."

"They're called azuremen," I say, as we approach the center of the room. "And there were three of them."

"*Three*?" She raises one eyebrow. "Only one came here," she adds contemplatively. "Although there's word that more are in the Jewelled." She takes a breath. "I don't know what to believe."

"At least three came to Winter's Baiou," I say. "For all I know, they're still there."

Our footsteps go silent as we step from the ancient planks onto the red rug.

The woman shakes her head disappointedly as her gaze finds the voidstone hanging around my neck. She gestures to it with an upturned palm. "Seriously? You're displaying it for all to see?" She puts the palm to her forehead.

"Don't worry, I had this hidden," I say, grasping the gold chain. "I only revealed it to your friend, to prove my identity."

She flutters her hand near her face. "Voider or not, you aren't welcome here," she says. "Leave us. Go back to the

North." Not waiting for a reaction, she turns to the sponsor. "Shon, show him out."

"Wait," I say. "I need to ask you some questions."

She takes a sudden step toward me, her eyes fierce. "I don't care. Your very presence puts us in danger, *Northerner*." A snarl accompanies the last word.

"Calm down, Wri," the sponsor says, putting a hand on her arm. "It's okay. We weren't followed."

She looks at him skeptically before mumbling something. Then she takes a voidstone out of her pants pocket and enters the void.

My body tenses. I'm unsure of her intent. But she only stares past me with empty eyes.

Voidsight. Through the wall. Looking for guards. Or worse.

After letting go, she stuffs the stone back into her pocket and sighs.

"I won't stay long," I assure her. "I just have a couple of questions and I'll be on my way." Without waiting for a response, I continue. "Let me start over. My name is Democryos. What's yours?"

She doesn't answer.

The sponsor steps forward and extends a hand. "My name is il-Tortershon, but you can call me Shon." He blinks a few times then his eyes go wide. "Wait. *The* Democryos? You're the—"

"Master voider," the young woman finishes slowly, her piercing eyes set on Shon. "This gets worse with each passing breath. You brought the master voider of our *enemy* into our *home*?"

"I am not your enemy," I say, loudly enough to cause an echo.

She takes a step back and I immediately close the gap.

"You're smarter than this," I tell her. "You know that the world is different now. You have to feel it in your bones. Everything that you once held true is a lie, and these lies have come crashing down."

"You mean the war?" Shon asks.

I glance at him then back to the woman. And I am full of pity.

They don't know. And I don't have the time to teach them.

I want to say *voidance*. I want to say *the way of unwanting*. I want to say *eleutheria*.

"Yes" is all that I say.

The woman's jaw is as tight as her mind. "The war was about breaking trade pacts. About getting your rotting goods out of Xi Bay—"

"No!" I shout, punching my fist into my other palm. "It was about a Northern traitor duping my king—tricking him into starting a war. All for the purpose of raising a massive voidstone at the bottom of Xi Bay. And he found it. And he used it to call his kind home. And now they're here, reclaiming what they believe is rightfully theirs. And no kingdom is safe. The North. Xiland. Scorpiontail. None of it."

They look at me as if I'm mad.

I point at the rug. "Trust me when I say to you that everything you think you know must be brought to ruin and built back up," I say, my voice softer. "All of your former hatreds and gifts must be cast aside. When you look at the world, you need to look at it as a child would, learning for the first time."

The woman looks at me defiantly. "And forget our heritage? Our history? This is our home."

I raise my eyes to the shattered glass and then to the crumbled hearth. "This is not a home. This is a grave."

For a moment, nobody says anything. Only birds flutter.

Shon breaks the silence by extending a hand to me. "Master Voider, your words are wise, and I hear them. We are not at war with each other. We are at war with the ones who want to take away our power."

Again, I am filled with pity and frustration at his ignorance, which only time and humility can erase. Humility he may have, but time I do not.

"Call me Dem," I say, noticing once again the blue number on his forearm glowing in the dimness. My gaze passes over the others before settling back on Shon. "What about your master voider? il-Bartholu. Have you heard from him?"

They look at each other in worry. "Word coming out of the Jewelled is rare these days," Shon says. "Nobody has heard from him or the university. Only that the blue-faced were there. And the scribe said that il-Bartholu had been dismissed."

"Scribe?"

"A royal scribe came here with the blue-faced man," the young woman adds. "The decree bore the emperor's bloodprint."

I put a hand to my chin. "The emperor didn't deliver the news himself?"

She laughs darkly. "No, he would never come this far. We're nearly in the deepsands."

"King Andrej X came to Winter's Baiou. He did the talking, even though he appeared to be a puppet dancing on the strings of the azuremen."

"What did your king say?" the woman asks.

"The rules of giving. The dissolving of the effulgency. The new kingdom at hand."

She scowls. "It was no different here."

"The next morning, they took our voidstones," Shon adds solemnly.

The woman looks at me shrewdly. "How is it that they didn't get yours?"

I take a deep breath. "I left after the king's speech. I thought to escape to the South, where it would be safe."

The older couple walk over. "I only wish that it were so," the man says. "And that our master voider il-Bartholu had been as lucky as you." His voice is as deep as Colu's but calmer, softened by the years.

I nod. "Despite the recent years of silence between Bartholu and me, I hold no ill will toward the man. Only respect." A brief smile crosses my face. "He was at my wedding, but that was a long time ago."

My smile fades as I wonder how Bartholu would receive the truth about voidance.

He doesn't know. None of them do.

"il-Daunt," the older man says, pointing to himself, then introduces the woman, who wraps the silk of crescent moons tighter around her face. "This is my wife, le-Caracant."

I shake their hands.

"You are both voiders?" I ask.

Daunt nods, tapping his pocket. "Only I bear a stone." He glances lovingly yet sadly at his wife. "She was in the Topaz Room and gave hers up. But we can share mine. Isn't that right, my dear?" He pulls her closer, but this does nothing to change her haunted expression. Were her eyes not white, I would mistake her for a hilma addict running short on supply.

Daunt turns to the younger woman with the storm of hair. "This is le-Wri. She is much nicer than she lets on."

Wri groans. She doesn't extend her hand to me but turns, motioning to the red rug. "Make yourself comfortable, I guess, before the marked comes and kills us all."

I sit down on the rug and fold my legs. Daunt and Caracant sit on the edge of their mattress. Wri takes up her former position and hands me the small wicker bowl that was next to her book. "Dates and pistachios are all we have, I'm afraid." She looks up with annoyance at Shon, who paces. "Someone was supposed to return from the deepsands with more food."

"I'll go to the nightmarket," he says. "When the crowds die down."

Wri scowls. "And the freshest fish is gone."

I take a few dates and get right to the point. "In addition to fleeing south, I'm also looking for someone. Someone who came through here."

"A voider?" Wri asks.

I shake my head and run my hand through my hair. "The complete opposite. An effulgent."

"They were all killed."

"This one probably came through after that happened."

She laughs under her breath. "You want to finish the azureman's job?"

"No," I answer. "I believe that he has information. Valuable information."

"Like what?" Shon asks.

"About the azuremen," I say. "Maybe even how to defeat them." I don't dare mention that he stole the Axiondrive.

"How would he know that?"

"Maybe it's written in their books."

She scoffs. "Their books? Their books are a joke." She makes a mockingly petrified face. "Black arcana! Souls being tortured! It's all nonsense meant to fill their temple coffers. They say *be nothing*, but have you ever seen an effulgent look like a beggar?"

I look away, toward the hearth and piles of red ash.

"Anyway, it doesn't matter anymore," she adds. "They're all dead. Which is fine by me. Only good thing to come out of all this."

I stay silent.

"Dem, I've not seen any effulgents or graycloaks since they . . . rounded them up," Shon says.

"This one is different," I say, turning back to them and motioning to my face. "He has diamonds embedded in his skin. Or some type of clear gem."

Her head recoils slightly. "What?"

"I know. It's sounds ridiculous. But he does. And a wagon and four horses. He came through here. A day ago. Maybe two."

Shon has stopped pacing. "I saw him," he says. He kneels next to me, reaching for the pistachios. He cracks one of them open and tosses it into his mouth.

"Where?" I ask.

"In the deepsands." He cracks open another.

"The deepsands?"

Shon chews contemplatively. "I would remember that face anywhere. I passed him on the road back. He was headed west."

"What's west?"

Wri laughs. "Northerner," she mumbles.

"The deepsands," Shon says.

"I've never been there."

"Not many Xians have either," Wri adds. "Nothing is west of here until you reach other side of the lo-Kimer range. Except sand and lepers."

"Did you exchange words?" I ask Shon.

He purses his lips. "Not much. He complained about the smell."

"What smell?"

"I had the lepers with me."

I nod as he continues.

"He told me to stay away from his camp. I didn't realize he was an effulgent. He certainly didn't act like one."

Wri laughs again.

"How long ago was this?" I ask, leaning in.

He cracks open another pistachio and looks unimpressed with what's inside. He lets the contents fall back into the bowl and picks up another. "This morning, around tenbell."

"So it was close to the city."

"Yeah. I got the sense he'd just left."

"Was he in a hurry?"

"Not particularly so," Shon says, pursing his lips. "He was stopped on the side of the road. Grilling something."

"Was he alone?"

Shon shrugs. "From what I could tell."

"Is this effulgent really that important?" Wri asks.

I turn to her. She's staring at me.

"It's the only thing I have to go on," I say. "If we're ever to defeat them, we need to understand them."

She nods and looks down to her lap momentarily. "Well, that's a goal I can get behind. As you can see, we're just trying to stay alive at this point."

I place my hands on my thighs, about to rise.

"One more question," I say.

She nods.

"How exactly did they take away your voidstones?"

Wri and Shon look at each other before he extends a deferential hand to her.

She looks at me. "It happened two days ago. The morning after we were told the rules of giving. In the Topaz Room."

"The Topaz Room?"

"Our Jewel." She points, as if I could see through the wall. "al-Kimer-vis is too small to have much of one. It houses only fifty people, if that. Anyway, we were all summoned. The azureman, as you call him, he was waiting for us inside."

I nod, remembering Xian heritage. Every city in the Southern Kingdom has one habitable sculpture devoted to the emperor, each decorated with a specific type of gemstone. In the Jewelled—the seat of the emperor—all of them are clustered together within a maze of formal gardens.

"What happened?"

She shakes her head and motions to the older woman. "Among us, only Caracant entered. Daunt, Shon, and I hadn't arrived yet. We got into town later that day. Fullbells after it all happened."

"I see."

"They have a list, Dem," Shon says.

I turn to him. "What kind of list?"

He exhales. "All our names. Every voider from the university, by station, by last known location, known relatives and friends, physical description—all of it."

"When we turned in our voidstones to the azureman," adds Caracant in a monotone, "the royal scribe crossed off our names. As if we didn't exist anymore."

Daunt looks down.

"Tell him what happened," Shon says to Caracant. "With Gorloth."

Caracant swallows. "There were about twenty of us in the Topaz Room," she says. "A few in the back tried to leave, but the door was locked. There might have been a membrane. I don't know."

"Regardless, you were trapped," Daunt adds.

She nods. "Three, maybe four of us, started to use voidance."

"Including you?" I ask.

Her eyes go wide for a moment. "No. I would not be standing here otherwise."

"So these others . . . they used voidance in an attempt to escape?" I ask.

She looks up to the broken windows. "Yes. But I think Gorloth tried to attack the azureman."

"Who is Gorloth?" I ask.

"Was," says Wri.

I turn to her. She pops a date into her mouth and speaks while chewing. "il-Gorloth was a huge beast of a man. We studied at university together. Always an impulsive fool."

"The azureman killed him?"

She tilts her head before looking at Caracant. "Not exactly."

Caracant looks at me with her fish-eye gaze. "I was in line to hand in my stone when the azureman snapped up his head. He walked over to the others using voidance. Then he . . . opened his chest. There was a bright light. So bright that I had to close my eyes. When I opened them again, they were all on the floor."

"Dead," her husband adds uselessly.

"Worse than that," I mumble.

"What's that?" Wri asks.

I look at her and then the other three. To say more would reveal that the effulgency had been right all along. They wouldn't believe me.

"Nothing," I say. "He did this to everyone who used voidance?"

"Everyone except Gorloth."

I furrow my brow.

"Gorloth was different. The azureman ripped his stone away from him," she says, nodding slowly while she speaks, as if confirming her own memory. "Then he lifted him by the neck, up against the wall, and . . . I don't even know how to describe it."

"Yes you do," Wri says, without a trace of empathy. "You said 'burning coals.'"

"I did say that, didn't I."

Wri grunts while crawling to one of the nearby silver censers. "We need to refill this anyway." She lifts the ornate silver door of the censer, revealing pitch-black insides. A small silver box rests on the floor at the foot of the censer. From it, she removes a black rock that looks shockingly similar to a voidstone. She holds it up to me. "Charcoal."

She places it inside of the censer. "Watch."

In the darkness, a wave of red sparks momentarily crosses the surface of the coal.

"That's how it looked," Caracant says.

From the same silver box, Wri spoons out cloudy white crystals of frankincense, which she sprinkles onto the burning coal. Then she shuts the door and crawls back over.

"It was as if the azureman painted with Gorloth's voidstone," Caracant says. "He cut him right across the head. *Into* his face." She motions with her hand, starting above her forehead and moving backwards, over the crown of her head. "Gouged away. Black from the stone, red from the blood and sparks. His screams . . ."

"We call him the marked now," Shon says. "Because part of his face looks as if it's tattooed, and he doesn't respond to his name."

"When the red sparks died away, all that was left was a black design," Caracant says. "And the stone was gone."

"It's as if he's no longer human," Wri adds. "Like some animal, doing whatever—"

Suddenly, I cannot hear what she's saying. I'm in a crowd of pain. They scream within me. With me.

Needles pushed deep into my temples.

Shon says something, oblivious. His mouth moves but nothing comes out.

I put my hands to my ears, trying to silence them. The screaming is constant. I feel my face for needles, but there is nothing. Nothing but the wailing wind.

Smoke from the refilled censer curls thick and fresh, covering me. I fall back, my head hitting the rug. I stare at the rafters. Shadows flicker. Black feathers.

DEM?

Her voice is a bird fluttering above the wailing, barely discernible, coming into this dark place from a shattered windowpane.

Chimeline?

Wri hovers over me instead.

YOU CANNOT VOIDSPEAK BACK. BUT I PRAY THAT YOU CAN HEAR ME.

"I hear you!" I scream, but I don't hear my own voice.

Shon joins Wry above.

HE'S HERE. IN THE CITY. HE FOLLOWED US.

Shon puts his hands on my shoulders, shaking me.

WE'RE IN THE NIGHTMARKET. BENEATH THE GOLD—

Silence returns like a soft hammer.

"Chimeline!"

I push Shon off me and sit up, inhaling deeply. The needles release me and sweet air rushes in.

I cough uncontrollably.

"What's wrong with you?" Wri says, leaning back.

"Where's the nightmarket?" I manage to say, while trying to stand. I spit on the red rug, my saliva tasting like metal. I feel dizzy.

"What?" asks Shon.

"The nightmarket!" I say, regaining my balance.

"It's in the center of town," Shon says. "But it's not open until dusk."

"You were just speaking to someone," Wri says after a pause, standing up much quicker than I did.

I nod, distantly. Past the smoke I urgently look for a door but then remember there isn't one. Only the membrane.

"They're in danger," I say.

There. A distorted reflection of a candle. Haziness. The alleyway.

"Who's in danger?" Wri asks. "Who were you speaking to?"

"You're bleeding," Caracant says. She motions to her ear.

I touch the side of my face and my hand comes away dripping red. For a breath, I stare at my blood. Then I remember Chimeline's bleeding. When Mander did this to her.

Good Unnamed.

"I need to go."

"You shouldn't leave," Shon protests. "This is the only safe place in the city."

I look up at him and then let my gaze pass over the four. "There are no safe places anymore."

THE NIGHTMARKET

I hastily turn a corner, following the last of Shon's instructions. For a breath I stand still, staring at what looks to be an island bathed in dusk and floating upon a sea of sand.

The nightmarket.

If al-Kimer-vis is a dream rising out of the barren ground, the nightmarket is a nightmare within the dream. It's lines and colors are a concentrated form, a crux of chaos. The center of a wheel that has broken free from its axle, spinning out of control. Perhaps on some other budding night, it might look different. But all I feel now is tightness and guilt.

A wide thoroughfare stands before me. It encircles the nightmarket—a cluster of buildings connected by a cavernous maze of shadowed alleyways—all covered by countless writhing silk tarps. An entrance lies straight ahead. There's another one far to the left, almost out of sight past the curvature of the street, and a third to my right.

The buildings here are taller than the rest in this city— three and four stories—although the tarps that cover the alleyways hang at their midsections. Peaks and domes loom above them, and their tips are painted with dying sunlight, as if dipped in liquid gold. I give them a passing glance.

It's the lowly spaces between that command my attention. That and Chimeline's final words voidspoken to me.

Beneath the gold.

I run across the sparsely filled, wide street.

The sun is hidden behind the buildings to the west. Shadows are deepening. The air is cooling.

A shiver comes over me as I enter the shade.

Approaching the closest entrance, I see a waist-high wooden gate barring the few dozen villagers waiting, all Xian. I roughly push past them, eliciting shouts and curses, and climb over the barrier.

Ahead of me stretches a gently curved alleyway flanked by dozens of merchants. It's dimmer in here, the waning sunlight distilled. Each stall is about ten feet wide and separated from the others by accordion-shaped floor-standing panels of dark-stained wood.

Behind their tables, vendors are busy setting up within the bright glow of their lanterns. Some give me an odd glance, but most are too distracted to care about a Northerner slipping into the nightmarket before opening time.

I look up.

The silk tarps strung between the buildings bear various patterns: small stars against a blank field, stripes narrow and wide, Xian geometric designs. But they all share a common theme.

They're all different shades of gold.

She's here. Somewhere.

Alternating my gaze left and right, I check every stall as I progress. Because the nightmarket is still closed to the public, the way forward is mostly clear. Some vendors come and go, carting their wares in small wheelbarrows or wicker boxes strapped upon their backs, but I easily weave around them. I look for my friends. Or anything out of the ordinary. Signs of distress. Suspicious vendors. Anything that could obscure people within the small spaces. Voiders. The marked.

I see nothing.

The merchants I've passed are selling jewels, gold bracelets, rings, adorned walking sticks, and vials of perfume. The scent of oranges and sugar wafts over me, and for the briefest of moments I think that Chimeline is near. I spin wildly, trying to catch sight of her, but all I see are strangers.

I near the end of the alley.

Up ahead is a brighter circular space. It must be the center of this wheel. A white stone fountain is awash in weak pastel twilight. As I approach, I see that it's full of water. Above is the clear sky in shades of pink and orange.

Rounding the fountain at a quickening pace, I peer down the eight emanating alleyways. A handful of vendors are setting up and conversing with each other. Above them, silk tarps extend into the dimness bearing various colors. Placards hang over the mouths of the eight alleyways, attached by chains.

Jewelers and Perfumes — al-Cade
Leathers — lo-Per Cade
Clothes — al-Bit Cade
Tea and Spices — il-Huj Paza
Lightmaking — le-Mon Paza
Fruit of the Sea and Land — il-Ref Paza
Furniture and Cookware — il-Div Paza
Carpets — le-Sah Cade

I took al-Cade here. It's the only path covered in gold tarps. Others are shades of red, green, blue, black. le-Mon Paza's silks are white and cream colored. Peering down its curvaceous length, I consider that it's possible that a few of them are dark enough to be considered gold.

I shout out a curse.

"Excuse me, sir."

I step out of the way of an old man carrying a thin brass rod with a lit wick. He uses it to light a lantern perched ten feet above, near the signpost that reads *le-Mon Paza*.

I look in every direction. A few other workers are doing the same.

Small flames soon light up all eight pathways of color, trails of jewels caught within a sunset.

Discordant bells begin to ring, high-pitched and far away.

"Did you see a one-eyed man pass through here?" I ask the lamplighter. "Black eye patch."

"Can't say I have," he says, his head still craned upward.

"He was with a young woman from Scorpiontail," I add. "And a Northerner as well." I wish I had more to go on. Back in Winter's Baiou, I didn't see the man the azureman sent after us. Only his silhouette.

The lamplighter doesn't respond. It's apparent that he's concerned about illumination of only one sort, and it's not of the mind.

I head back down al-Cade.

The first stall contains a middle-aged woman selling perfume. She fidgets with two rings in her nose but snaps to attention as I approach.

"Have you seen a young woman from Scorpiontail?" I ask her, leaning across her table. "She might be with a Northerner," I add, realizing that this could mean either Blythe or her pursuer. "Or a Xian with an eye patch."

She just smiles as she opens a vial. "You buy for your woman?" she asks, her voice torturously slow. "From Scorpiontail? Take back home to her? Try. Try."

I curse and keep walking.

The vendors in the next stall are yelling at each other. Shards of broken glass litter the floor behind their table.

Ten feet past them, an older woman sits alone on a stool, a handful of pearls spread out on a small black velvet cloth in front of her. She almost looks asleep. Her hands are like claws, her fingernails yellow.

I repeat the same questions.

She opens her eyes fully. A large milky-white cataract floats in her left one, looking like one of her pearls.

She places a shaking hand over her left eye and leans in, looking me up and down.

"I'll tell ye what aye's seen," she says. "Two of ye in a day, which is two too many for a woman of my years." She spits on the ground.

Exhaling, I turn to leave but then pause.

I retrace my few steps. "Two of whom?" I ask.

"Ye Northern bastards," she says, waving me away with a claw. "Won the war, ye did. Got yer gold. Good for ye. If ye buying pearls, Mother Charlee is here for ye. Otherwise, shake ye arse out of al-Cade. That's what Mother Charlee told the ugly un."

"The ugly one?"

She points to the center fountain, her finger curled. "Big Northerner." She moves her hand over her face, as if wiping it dry. "Had a mark."

I grasp the edge of the table.

"What kind of mark?"

"Ugly feller."

"You sure he was a Northerner?"

"Aye."

"Where did he go?"

She points in annoyance to the fountain again. "Down one of the other seven. I don know. Too ugly for pearls." Then she directs the scowl at me. "What about ye? Non too ugly but too poor, aye's wager."

I push away from the table and collide with a group of women who yell out in complaint. The nightmarket has opened. People are streaming in. Chimeline's words are streaming in.

He's here. In the city. He followed us.

"Ye Northerners are good fer nothing!"

Chimeline's trained palehound is a monster like Gorloth. He was altered by the azuremen and sent after us because we're a threat to them now. We were able to kill one of the azuremen. Whatever they are. So they're not coming after us themselves. They're sending their . . . creation.

I run back to the fountain and systematically enter each of the other paths—lo-Per Cade, al-Bit Cade, il-Huj Paza—

ten feet deep. Then back out. I study the warm glow and developing crowds. Instead of looking for Chimeline, Blythe, and the others, I search for the Northern marked.

Pushing through the thickening crowd, I ignore the outbursts. The rippling blue silks above me, from midnight to teal, look like sunlight through water. The scent of fish gets stronger the further I go, blown in with the fresh air from the nearby exit.

The crowd thins a few stalls from the end of il-Ref Paza.

Suddenly, the silhouette of a large man fills the dusk-lit archway ahead.

His back is to me, awash in lanternlight. Straggly black hair. Soiled and tattered white shirt. His black leather vest has a rip between the shoulder blades. His pants are torn diagonally below the knee, and a remnant drags on the ground like seaweed.

He raises his head as if staring into the blue silks overhead. His movements are cumbersome but confident.

A momentary chill comes over me. If this is indeed whom I think it is, then I fear what I have just walked into.

He turns around at the exact moment I reach for my voidstone. And when I see his face, I know it is him. The look in his eyes is unmistakable.

It's the Northern marked.

Momentarily, I'm swallowed in both darkness and waves of hope, as if the enervated cover me like the rippling blue. I'm reminded of Mander. The bell tower. The fountain. I dare to believe that this man can do me no harm.

But that feeling is crushed as I'm violently lifted into the air.

Something grabs my arms. My legs. My neck.

My fingers slip away from the voidstone in my pocket.

Within a heartbeat, I hang many feet above the ground, strung up in midair by strands of blue. The silks have morphed into ropes that stretch me between two buildings. They coil around me tighter, cutting off my circulation, cutting into my skin, pulling at my appendages. My neck, armpits, and groin burn with tension.

Below me, the Northern marked looks up in curiosity. There's a deep gouge across his face. His entire skull is indented.

His eyes slowly move to my pocket, where my voidstone lies.

He extends his hand, and a hole instantly burns through my pants. My stone flies into his grasp. Flames erupt on my leg and crawl up my chest before extinguishing themselves. I scream in pain.

"Where is the axionlighter?" he asks me. His voice is deep but quiet.

I cannot bear to look at him.

Instead, I gaze up and out, down the alleyway. I'm strung up at the same height as the silks, and all of them near me have been ripped away, allowing me to see, for the first time, into the heights of the nightmarket.

The buildings are windowless shapes against the twilight sky—daggers pointed toward the coming night. Between them, the stars are ambivalent. A gust of wind peels through, rippling the silks and buffeting my body.

Where are the enervated?

The crowd below has cleared out, but only so far. They seem torn between fear and morbid curiosity. Hands to mouths, some hide behind the wood panels separating the merchant stalls.

"The axionlighter," he repeats. "Where is she?"

Everything holding me holds me tighter, and I scream again.

I finally look down at him. His face collapses further into creases of impatience. The black line of axion is burrowed deep into the crown of his head, where no hair grows. A black river between two hillsides of his skull.

"I don't know" is all I can say, finding it hard to swallow. Hard to breathe. He's using a term he shouldn't know. He's exhibiting power he shouldn't have.

I feel so utterly alone.

"They're trying to protect you," the marked says. "But I will drive this vessel into the ground before I allow them to have their say."

He flicks his fingers at his side.

The blue silks unravel—all of them except the one around my neck.

My body falls then bounces up slightly.

Agony overtakes me. My air is fully taken.

Everything becomes periphery. Spinning away slowly. I no longer control what I see. The daggers of buildings. The stars. All the things that will continue to exist after I'm gone.

The Northern marked. He walks away, toward the fountain, my voidstone in his hand like some black fruit he's about to eat.

His head rises as he sniffs out his next victim.

BENEATH THE GOLD

"Cut it!"

"What if it comes back—"

"Passed the fountain—"

Pain erupts from everywhere at once. Colors blossom in the darkness. I remember them from somewhere far away. Another life. Rippling silks.

"Poor man—"

It was better before. Just let me sleep.

I'm forced open by unseen strings. The Unnamed breathes into me. Burning life, pushing all the way from my mouth into my lungs. My head cranes back.

The silks flutter. Colors become vivid then fade away. Blue. Red.

Gold.

"He's alive."

A man stares at me. He's upside down. One of the voiders from the hearth in ruins. Dark spots cover his face.

Daunt.

His face is expressionless. Oblivious to this world. I've seen the look countless times.

He's in the void.

His face snaps to attention the moment my body relaxes. He blinks as I turn to the side, coughing, taking deeper breaths than I ever have before. A woman kneels on the ground watching me with a mix of horror and concern.

Caracant. She grasps her husband's hand.

"Thank you," I say into the dirt. I don't know if the words are meant for the two voiders or for the thousands of enervated they recently abused on my behalf.

Blood and spit drip from my lips and form a small puddle.

I can't stop shaking.

"There's another marked," Daunt says. "A Northerner. You didn't mention him."

"I—" A fit of coughing overtakes me, and I barely get the words out. "I didn't know."

"He followed you all the way from Winter's Baiou?" Caracant asks.

I ignore the question. I don't have the strength—mental or physical—to converse about the matter. I look at the ground and try to regulate my breathing.

"I have to go," I eventually say. I struggle to push myself up. The colored spots return to my field of vision.

"You're in no condition," Caracant says.

"Let's take him back to the hearth," Daunt adds.

"No." I sit up and gingerly place a hand on my throat. Something is wrapped around it. I pull it loose and hold it up. A remnant of blue silk.

I try piecing together what happened.

The enervated didn't protect me.

I remember Chimeline's petrified expression as the Northern marked came near while we stood in the foyer of Levi's house. Her rocking bath and forth. Her warning.

These marked apparently have some sort of hold over the enervated—a power that blocks their awareness of the outside world. Their ability to rebel. I remember the marked's last words to me.

They're trying to protect you, but I will drive this vessel into the ground before I allow them to have their say.

What does that mean?

I stare down the length of il-Ref Paza. The area around the three of us is noticeably clear. The crowd avoids us as if we're lepers. But closer to the fountain it thickens, the business of the nightmarket stubbornly refusing to be squashed.

I slowly stand.

Daunt and Caracant help me. "Put that away," she chastises her husband.

I look down. He still has his voidstone in his hand.

"Right," he says, pocketing it.

I take a careful step on my own. The world spins as I shut my eyes.

"Go home," I utter, in my momentary darkness. "You've helped enough."

Opening my eyes, I steady myself and begin walking toward the fountain. Directly above me is a blue silk with a turquoise-star pattern ripped in half and hanging down, partially obscuring the way. I pass through it as if it were a curtain.

Within a few steps, the dizziness somewhat subsides and I'm able to pick up my pace to a slow walk. Twice, I lean against the wall of the alleyway between the stalls, catching my breath and balance, before moving on.

Up ahead, the fountain is awash in harsh lamplight. Everything looks different now. Night has fully come. Only starlight glitters beyond the silks. The shadows cast from flickering flames are long and menacing. Strangers sit upon the fountain's circular edge. Some talk, some rest with straw bags between their legs, others cradle babies. The water looks black.

I round it once again, navigating the crowd, peering down the eight emanating alleys. But the nightmarket is even busier now, clogged with bustling shoppers, making it impossible to see down the alleys.

Except for one: le-Sah Cade.

More people leave than enter.

One of them is a woman clutching two coughing children. Her wicker bag has fallen off her shoulder. She doesn't even pause to adjust it.

Trailing her is the acrid smell of smoke.

Pushing forward, I head down le-Sah Cade.

The silks overhead are shades of dark gray. Almost immediately, it's apparent that this alley is devoted to carpetmakers. A man carrying a rolled-up carpet on his shoulder nearly runs into me. To the left and right are smaller rugs hanging on long, thin iron poles mounted to the walls of the merchants' stalls. Others sell oversized ones in stacks on the floor.

It seems that I'm the only one pushing further down the alleyway. Most are headed back toward the center.

About halfway, the smoke in the air is noticeable. It hovers over the thinning crowd in a light haze. It's hard to breathe. My throat burns anew. Gold rings surround the hanging lanterns above, as if I'm walking through a Northern street on a foggy late-autumn's eve.

There's a fire up ahead.

With a sound halfway between a cry and a groan, a distressed stall owner to my left picks up a large bucket of water and pours its contents onto a rug half-consumed in flames, dousing them with a *hiss*. It looks as if he's already done this a few times. Another stack of carpets already sits blackened and saturated with water. Just inside the entrance, a lantern lies sideways on the ground, its glass panes shattered.

Flames still flicker across half of his stall.

The owner leaves with the now-empty bucket, presumably heading to the fountain. Meanwhile, a boy, perhaps his son, arrives with a similar-sized bucket obviously not filled to capacity. He pours, but only a trickle comes out, making no impact on the growing flames.

Part of me wants to help—especially the voider part of me, which will never truly be erased. But I don't carry a voidstone. The only thing I carry is my burning need to find my friends.

From this mess trails a stream of water leading to a depression in the ground. I step to the edge of the puddle.

In its reflection is the Northern marked.

I raise my eyes—the only parts of my body not instantly paralyzed with fear.

About thirty feet away, he stands facing me in the center of the alley. His head is bent slightly upwards and his eyes are closed.

Slowly, he turns to the left and then to the right, as if sniffing out some prey upwind. Directly behind him is the arched and star-filled exit from le-Sah Cade. Smoke trails curl in the breeze.

My friends must be close. Otherwise, the Northern marked wouldn't be here.

Taking a deep breath, I slowly step backward, blending in with the sparse crowd.

Six stalls line le-Sah Cade between the exit and me— three to my left and three to my right.

The stall directly to my left is the one on fire. The one past that is empty. I don't see anything in the ten-by-ten-foot space except some rubbish in the corner. The last one sells fabric tassels arrayed on a wooden table. No customers are present, but the two women working there carry a filled bucket by each handle, coming to assist. Each stall much have a bucket at the ready.

To my right, across the alleyway, a single upscale shop takes up all three stalls. It's thirty feet wide. The floor is made of an elevated deck of wood. Stacks of rugs and hanging runners on iron poles fill the space. A few shoppers in white robes and decorated walking sticks leave in a hurry, fleeing the nearby fire. An older man—presumably the owner—sits at a desk shouting out orders to his half dozen scrambling employees.

Someone roughly grabs my bicep from behind.

"Glad you could join us."

I immediately place the deep voice, as relief washes through me.

Colu.

"Walk with me."

I do as he says, putting more of the crowd between us and the Northern marked. We cut across the alleyway to the right, further from the fire. Colu has changed his attire. Wearing a long, flowing white robe and a black-and-white headscarf and carrying a walking stick, he blends in exceedingly well with the crowd. If it weren't for his eye patch, he'd be unrecognizable.

When we're about fifty feet away from the Northern marked, Colu lets go and turns toward me.

"Where are the others?" I ask him.

He motions to the large shop to our right.

"Where?" I ask.

"See that table? The man with the beard?"

I squint and then nod. "Who is he?"

"Doesn't matter. See the carpet underneath?"

My mouth hangs open. "The gold . . ."

He nods. "Yeah. Underneath is a door."

I run my hand through my hair as I look at the rug. The elevated wooden floor. The table sitting on top. It's a perfect hiding place.

Except that the Northern marked is less than ten feet away.

Now it has become the perfect death trap.

"Does it lead anywhere?" I ask.

"Huh?

"Is there another way out?" I raise my voice. "A tunnel or something."

He shakes his head. "No."

Shouts erupt behind us.

A few other merchants and workers have arrived. They're carrying buckets of water, which they pour directly onto the growing flames in the stall. One carpet, strung up vertically on an iron pole, is entirely consumed in fire, shedding bright-yellow light onto the nearby crowd. People step back, arms outstretched and faces averted.

A high-pitched bell begins to ring.

Colu motions with his cane to the Northern marked in the distance, who now walks in circles with his head craned upwards. "Everything was going according to plan. But then this fucker shows up. I swear to the Unnamed we weren't followed, so I'm not sure how this happened." He spits. "It's almost as if he can smell her."

"I agree," I say. "It's some sort of voidance, I think."

The blackest of smoke streams from the stall. It's getting darker in the alley, and harder to breathe.

Colu leans in, his voice a whisper. "I knocked over that lantern, right before you came. Thought the smoke might distract him. Muddle his senses or something."

I furrow my brow. "*You* caused the fire?"

He knocks his walking stick into my chest. "Look."

I follow his gaze toward the exit.

The Northern marked is on the move.

He walks slowly toward the burning stall and away from the larger one on the opposite side of the alley. Away from the gold rug and table. Away from Chimeline, Blythe, and le-Daerke.

Thirty feet away, over a dozen men frantically attempt to douse the growing flames. The hung-up carpet collapses, sending out a flurry of sparks. More shouts come from behind as people return from the fountain with refilled buckets of water.

"Sonofabitch," Colu says. "It's working. Now's our chance. Come on."

He pushes past me and moves through the thin crowd, hugging the right side of the alley, his white robe fanning out. At first I keep up with him, but then a fresh bout of dizziness comes over me. The smoke has gotten far worse, and I have to lean against the wall to catch my breath, my hands on my knees. I cough. My throat is on fire. The colored silks blossom in my vision for a moment. I try to blink them away.

"You okay?"

Colu leans over, putting a hand on my shoulder.

I try to take deep breaths. My body shakes.

"What the fuck happened to your neck?"

"I'm fine," I utter, standing straight as the colors disappear.

Across the alleyway, the stall is now consumed in fire—a box of condensed yellow, orange, and red tightly contained within the plaster walls. Everyone has backed away.

Except the Northern marked. We both watch as his silhouetted form disappears into the flames.

For once, Colu is at a loss for words. He only puts a hand underneath my armpit and helps me up.

We break from the crowd.

TWIN PILES OF ASH

As Colu and I step onto the wooden platform, I look through the narrow spaces between the floorboards. There is only darkness.

We cross over onto the massive gold carpet, woven in a pattern of dying leaves and diamonds.

I place my palms on the large rectangular table to steady myself. Colu lets go of my arm.

The man with the beard is no longer here. The store is now devoid of workers and shoppers alike. Only a leather-bound book rests upon the table.

Colu rounds the table and begins riffling through its pages. He says something under his breath, but I don't hear him above the incessant ringing of the fire bell.

"What are you looking for?" I ask loudly.

He ignores me for a moment then nods in satisfaction. "This," he says, ripping away a stitched-in bookmark. With a smile, he lifts a small iron key attached to a loop of golden silk.

But then his smile fades as he looks past me. I see the flames' reflection in his eye.

I turn around.

Far across the alley, the Northern marked walks further inside the engulfed store, a translucent sphere surrounding him where the fire doesn't reach.

"We don't have much time," Colu says.

He puts the silk ribbon between his teeth, casts his adorned walking stick aside, and flips the heavy piece of furniture on its side, careful to guide it down to the carpet without making a sound.

I kneel behind the upturned table, catching my breath. About four feet high and eight feet wide, it acts as a visual barrier.

Colu is quicker than I am. He takes off his belt and sword, hidden underneath his white robe. Dropping to his hands and knees, he rolls up the rug, starting with the end furthest into the room and ending closer to the table and alley. Halfway through, he uncovers a small door, three-by-three feet, precisely cut into the wooden boards. A thick iron padlock rests inside a carved circular depression.

The ringing of the fire bell stops.

The silence is unexpected. Even the crowd makes no noise.

While Colu begins to work with the lock, I look to see what's happening.

The overturned table obscures most of the alley from view, but I peer through the space between its left end and a nearby thick stucco pillar at the edge of the store.

The once-burning stall is now extinguished. The room is charred black, full of opaque smoke. The Northern marked stands inside, directly in the center.

In his hands he holds a sun.

A perfect sphere of roiling red, orange, and yellow that's about the size of his head and teeming with heat. Even from fifty feet away, I can hear it crackle like the sound of fresh snow underneath one's boots on an especially freezing day.

The Northern marked walks through the room, sun in hand. He seems to be using pure voidance, but the power required to contain that many indivisibles would bring about voideath in even the most powerful of voiders. The sphere is inches away from him, wildly distorting the air, but it's not causing him any harm. There must be a membrane as well. Parallel voidance.

The dozens of people in the alley seem paralyzed with shock or fear. They hold their hands up against the heat and light, but their feet are stone.

"Fucking thing is jammed," says Colu, but I barely hear him.

The Northern marked exits the smoke-filled stall and enters the alley that separates our line of shops from his. The sunfire creates harsh shadows in all directions.

The puddle of water at his feet hisses and steams as he steps through it.

Finally, the crowd breaks.

People flee in panic, shielding their faces, screaming, heading in all directions—some toward the arched exit and purple night beyond, some toward the fountain and seven other alleyways. Strangers trip over each other, barrels of water, rolls and stacks of blackened carpets.

Colu curses loudly.

I glance back at him. He's frantically digging between the floorboards. Suddenly he leans back and exhales while looking upwards and shutting his eye.

I scramble over to him. "What's going on?"

He carelessly tosses me the golden ribbon of silk, its knot undone. It flutters downward like a torn flower petal.

"Where's the key?" I ask him.

"I dropped it," he mutters.

"What?"

"I fucking dropped it. It fell through."

A single breath escapes my open mouth. The sound is lost among the distant screams. "You're joking."

"Do I look like I'm joking?"

I drop prone to the floor and peer into the darkness between the boards, breathing in the dust and dirt. But I see nothing. No key. No movement. No light.

Sounds of panic continue from the alley.

"Can you use voidance?" he asks me as I search. "Melt the lock or something? Break the wood?"

"I can't."

"I know it's wrong or whatever, but—"

"No, I mean I *can't*!" I yell, as I continue to look between the cracks. "I lost my voidstone."

I feel Colu's eye on the back of my head as if it were the sunfire itself. "What do you mean you lost it?" he snaps.

"That . . . thing took it from me," I explain, without looking at him. "I was coming back to find you and he caught me off guard. Nearly killed me in the—"

I breathe in dust. My throat aches as a fit of coughing comes over me, and I turn onto my side. The spots in my vision return.

"Well that's just perfect," he says. "Makes you about as useful as a one-legged palehound in a pissing contest."

I look at him through narrowed eyes. "I'm not the one who dropped the key."

He laughs once, sardonically. "Oh, right. You're blaming me now. Even though we wouldn't even be in this shit situation if you hadn't run off on some fucking research project."

"We wouldn't be here if you hadn't trapped them underneath a carpet store!"

He points downward. "This was her idea. Not mine."

I pause. "What do you mean?"

He leans in close, his voice becoming a low rumble. "I wanted to take the horses and get out of this city. Everyone did. Fuck you and your voiders."

My ragged breaths are now the loudest sound. The panic in the alley has all but died away.

Colu quietly motions toward the upturned table, the alley, and the Northern marked beyond. "She knew that thing was here, hunting for her," he whispers. "Scared her shitless. But she wouldn't leave. Not without you."

His words cut deep into my heart, and for a moment I'm overcome with guilt that's wrapped in the sudden eerie silence of the nightmarket. It's as if the entire city knows as well.

Colu picks up the ribbon of silk that rests on the floor between us. He shakes his head, running the gold between his fingers.

"Colu," I say, my voice gentler now, almost an escaping breath. "Listen, I—"

There's a sudden cry for help in the alley. A man's voice.

"Wait!" the voice says. "You don't understand! I was going to give it back. I was going to give it back!"

His voice is choked into silence.

I sit up.

Colu and I share a confused glance, then we scramble to opposite edges of the table and peer out.

Only three men remain in the middle of the alley, about thirty feet away from us.

The smallest is a Xian being lifted into the air by his neck. He's a voider—his voidstone necklace hangs over his torn white cloak. Another Xian man, at least a head taller, grasps his neck with a massive arm, like some gnarled tree branch. The voider claws at the arm uselessly. His legs dangle like a child's. Even his kicks cannot reach his attacker.

The third man, calmly coming to stand nearby, is the Northern marked, equally as massive as the Xian strangler. With one hand, he lifts the sunfire above his head and then leaves it floating there, a foot or two in the air. Far above, black silks erupt in flames.

In the harsh light, he watches the other two with a detached curiosity. The voider still hangs uselessly in the air, but his motions change. He stops fighting the hand at his throat and instead writhes wildly, undoubtedly recoiling from the heat of the sunfire. He blindly tries to grasp the voidstone around his neck.

The Xian strangling him remains calm. The sunfire doesn't seem to affect him.

The Southern marked.

Almost as if he could read my thoughts, the large man turns slightly, and I can finally see his face.

A blacker vein cuts through his black skin. His forehead bears a cleft.

The twins look at each other. Different versions of the same horror.

As I look on helplessly, they seem to communicate in silence. Their dead eyes don't move, but they nod in unison before looking at their prey.

The Southern marked lets go.

The voider falls to the ground between the twins and immediately turns onto his side.

I see his face.

It's Shon.

"Where is the axionlighter?" the Northern marked asks.

Shon grasps his neck and tries to take a rasping breath. I find myself gingerly touching my own, remember the blue silks.

With his other hand, Shon finds his stone. He slowly twists his body to face the twins.

The area shimmers around the trio, like sunlight hitting a damp cobweb. I don't know what sort of voidance Shon is attempting, but I fear that he's outmatched.

Within the distortion, the twins look at each other again before gazing back at Shon.

The Southern marked extends an open palm.

Shon's voidstone is ripped out of his grasp and flies directly into the Southern marked's hand.

"WHERE IS THE AXIONLIGHTER!" the Northern and Southern marked say in perfect unison.

Shon looks up helplessly, clawlike hands over his face, alternating his gaze between the malformed twins. He doesn't know.

He shakes his head.

His body rises toward the sunfire, and he screams something unintelligible.

Gritting my teeth, I scramble back to the locked door and call out Chimeline's name into the narrow crevasses between the boards. My hoarse voice is not quite a shout—

I'm as loud as I dare, the sound covered by Shon's inhuman wailing.

"Chimeline!" I repeat.

Nothing.

"Chimeline!"

I keep calling her name until Shon's screams go silent. Until the only sound remaining is the crackling sunfire.

Slowly, I lift my head.

Colu is still by the table. He leans his head back in and puts his back against the large surface. He takes off his black-and-white headscarf, letting it fall to the floor. Then he faces the rear of the store, a reserved look in his eye.

I can't see the alley, but the shadow cast by the table shifts, its angles changing.

The Northern and Southern marked are moving.

Without a sound, Colu looks at me while reaching into the folds of his white cloak. He produces two small daggers.

"Tell me when they're standing directly over me," he says, not even bothering to whisper. "I'll only get one chance at this."

I nod, realizing that I have the better vantage point.

The table's shadow keeps moving, its lines shifting diagonally until they cross over my body.

I feel the painful heat of the sunfire as it appears over the top of the table.

But then this sun is eclipsed by the moon.

Parallel lines of cool-white luminescence move around me. Around Colu. They are everywhere. The ceiling. The walls. Stripes moving as one, as if someone is galloping on horseback through a forest while holding a lantern, causing the narrow trunks of trees to cast moving shadows.

They're coming from below. Underneath the floorboards.

Axionlight.

Colu silently gets up from his sitting position. He's stooping but on his feet. A dagger is in each hand. He's ready to stand. To strike the marked when they appear over him.

In the air, the sunfire nears, its crackling deafening. But it's the glow of the axionlight that has my attention. We're right on top of it.

"We need to move!" I yell, my voice barely audible.

Colu looks at me as if I'm not making sense. Beyond him, the sunfire is only feet away.

The heads of the marked slowly appear over the top of the table. Their faces are distorted in heat waves.

I feel the skin on my face begin to burn.

"Colu! We need to move!"

He ignores me, his face resolute.

Without another thought, I scramble over to him, pulling him away from the table and toward the rear of the store.

He curses as we stumble to the ground.

Frantically we flee, arm in arm, squinting against the brightness of the axionlight. The heat blisters our backs.

An abrupt earsplitting sound echoes in the small space. The wooden floor around us cracks and reverberates, and our bodies collapse.

I inhale dust and for a moment cannot breathe.

Holding my hands in front of me, I try to shield myself from the light. From the heat.

No. The pain from the sunfire, I don't feel it anymore. Something blocks it.

Chimeline slowly rises from an open hole in the floor, arms outstretched, bathed in axionlight. I cannot look directly at her. Between my fingers, the lights converge, intermingle—swirls of her blue-tinged radiance fighting against the red and yellow beyond.

She is beautiful, glorious.

Terrifying.

The upturned table splinters to pieces.

Unable to look away, I see the Northern and Southern marked step through the destruction and approach her, their expressions blank.

The light intensifies.

I cower in the corner, my hands over my head as the crackling and the vibrations grow, threatening to overwhelm me. Colu mumbles a prayer next to me. And despite my shut eyes, my sheltering arms, I continue to see her—a black phantom against orange and blue, arms out at her sides, as if she were a messenger of the Unnamed.

A deafening thunderclap breaks the world.

I feel it throughout my body, as if the very indivisibles that compose me are shaken and redistributed. Then it echoes out a second time. A third.

The thunderclaps roll into the distance. I imagine them crossing the moonlit Xi Bay. The barren deepsands to our west. The frozen plateaus of Northinglight. The labyrinthine gardens of the Jewelled.

Eventually, I open my eyes. Blinking repeatedly, I see that night has returned to the nightmarket.

It's completely dark now. All the lanterns are shattered and snuffed out. I can still hear them sway upon rusty links, as if caught within a breeze. Pieces of loose stucco fall to the ground. Other random echoes of destruction are the only sounds. Outside the carpet store, the overhead silks are gone. The only light is starlight.

Carefully, we crawl toward the epicenter of the destruction.

The wooden floor around the once-locked door is blown apart, boards snapped upwards in a circle with a black hole in the center—the mouth of some hideous creature.

Nearby, Chimeline lies still upon the ground.

I scramble over to her, rounding the hole, while Colu carefully descends the partially intact stairs. He calls out for le-Daerke. A palehound whimpers below.

Chimeline's skin is cold, but she's nowhere near voideath.

She's breathing.

I take her in my arms and hug her tightly, cradling her head into my shoulder.

My body shakes. I fight back tears.

Pushing her dark hair aside, I gaze into the dimness, looking for the remains of the marked. I don't see their bodies. For the briefest of moments, I fear that they've run away, wounded yet alive to fight us another day. But then I hear rustling amid a gust of cool night air.

Ten feet away from me, twin piles of ash stir in the wind.

VOIDREAMING

Temberlain could have been blindfolded and he still would have known where he was. He felt almost weightless. Which meant that he was at the center of it all. In more ways than one.

All axionships followed the same torus-based design, with a center hub connected by a series of spokes, or hardlines. The only difference was the scale. The *Apsides* was smaller than average—it adhered to an exploratory charter in the far reaches of the Virel Arm that favored speed and agility over cargo capacity. A reduced population. Five thousand people on board, 90 percent of whom were ashen. The outer ring was only one mile in diameter, and the cross section a mere three hundred feet. It was a modest version of everything Efful represented.

The one exception to the smaller scale was the Axiondrive. It was as large as one that any core-located trademass ship would contain. Which had always been a source of pride for Temberlain.

Until now.

What are they after?

The lift doors opened, and a hardline lay before him. Its walls were a laid-out cylinder ten feet in diameter. They were translucent but significantly tinted. At the other end of it, a half-mile ahead, lay the hub.

The hub contained three major components. First was the drive chamber, which was connected directly to the other end of the hardline. Above it and clearly visible through the hardline's walls was the ship's mirror, already positioned to the nearby yellow dwarf—a sun as large as one of Efful's three. The mirror reflected its light toward the inside curvature of the torus, the axionship's black morning sky. Opposite this and just underneath the drive chamber was the FTL array. It was out of sight below the hardline's floor grates, but the undulating blue glow from the array was evident, reflecting off the black skin of the hub and other sunlit hardlines in the distance.

Two ashen exited the lift and began moving—half walking, half floating—through the hardline. They used their outstretched arms to keep straight.

"Let's go," Sixteen said, giving him a push.

Here, the gravity was 0.3 g. The Axiondrive's power wasn't limitless, and artificial gravity took as much power as the FTL array. Sixteen's shove gave Temberlain enough momentum to fly down the middle of the cylinder. But he was disoriented. His arm was gone. Whatever drugs they'd given him to mute the pain also muted his sense of balance. His body didn't seem his anymore. It began turning. His shoulder brushed against the translucent wall, beyond which was a field of stars. In the corner of his vision, the gorgeous planet gleamed green and blue.

A fresh wave of nausea came over him.

Sixteen grabbed him by the wrist, pulling him back. Stabilizing him. She nervously muttered something in Dodoghian.

Temberlain glanced over his shoulder. The other four ashen took up the rear, serraters at their side.

Sixteen didn't let go. They floated side by side, like two lovers strolling through a park.

"What are we doing here?" he asked.

She didn't respond.

"If you're bringing pods online and colonizing the planet, you don't need me."

Sixteen ignored him.

"What do you need the drive for?"

Again, nothing.

Darkness bloomed on the other end of the hardline. The translucent walls became matte gray and widened into an alcove that surrounded a circular door. Gravity this close to the hub was nonexistent. The charred bodies of two enervated floated in midair, obviously killed by serrater fire. A few droplets of blood also floated nearby, a child's shiny red marbles. Temberlain saw the enervated's insignia. They were from the drive chamber's security profile. Two of Cordialle's men.

One of the bodies had a visible axiongraph—it crossed the side of the neck and moved onto the bald scalp. A two-headed bleedersnake.

Axion!

An opportunity existed right here. Right now. Any fragment would do. Even an axiongraph on a corpse.

But Sixteen held him tightly. He couldn't reach it.

Temberlain quickly looked away to hide his sudden interest and focused on the closed circular door a few feet in front of him.

The two ashen who'd first exited the lift stood in front of the door, but they slowly pushed themselves aside once Temberlain and Sixteen drew near. One of them peered into the dimness of the alcove. Deep in the shadows was another person waiting. A woman.

She floated forward into the half-light.

An Agh-Severian.

Clothed in a black autosized suit, she looked like a child trying to appear older. Narrow hips, small breasts. A heart-shaped face and long black hair. Skin as red as raw meat.

She carried a silver case.

"What is that?" Temberlain asked.

"You'll find out soon enough," Sixteen answered, pulling him forward.

She pressed his palm up against the door.

A box of white light appeared then turned green.

The door opened like a cat's eye, revealing the drive chamber.

It was a perfectly spherical room, fifty feet in diameter. White walls, saffron-yellow light. White metal walkways hugged the perimeter in all directions—left, right, up, down. Six other circular doors leading to the hardlines formed the only spatial foundation. They indicated the plane of the outer torus.

In the center, black and matte as ash and taking up most of the room, sat the Axiondrive.

SECOND STONE

The abandoned forge seems larger at this late fullbell, its gently curving walls disappearing in the darkness. The millionescent beam that crosses the space is but a shadow. The chains that drop from it barely glimmer. Far above, weak moonlight seeps through broken windows.

Everything hides tonight.

"I told you to never come back here," Wri says to me the moment I enter, looking up from the book in her hands. She stands from her curled-up position in the center of the red Xian rug surrounded by a dozen thick candles.

Her very presence infuriates me, and for a moment I say nothing. I turn my back on her as I watch the rest of the group step through the membrane.

"Did you hear me?" she asks.

I don't look at her. "I heard you. We're staying the night."

Colu carries the unconscious Chimeline. It damages my pride that I'm still too weak to do it myself. She's covered in a light-blue woolen blanket that we stole from one of the nightmarket's abandoned stalls. Its color reminds me of axionlight.

Blythe and le-Daerke follow, looking around in confusion as they stumble through the shimmering wall. The palehound hugs Blythe's side. Taking up the rear is the older couple. Daunt and Caracant talk incessantly to each other in hushed whispers.

"Where's Shon?" asks Wri, addressing the couple.

They look down.

"Dead," I answer for them.

Wri's mouth hangs open for a moment. She tosses the book on her mattress and puts her hands on her hips. Colu storms toward the center of the room and places Chimeline upon one of the straw mattresses.

"What happened?" Wri asks, her voice breaking.

"It was the marked," Daunt says.

"There was a Northern one too," Caracant quickly adds. "His face was the same. Had a burned-in voidstone."

"A Northern marked?" Wri asks, swallowing.

I feel her eyes on me as I slowly step into the circle of light, approaching Colu. "Thank you for carrying her," I tell him quietly, as he stands back up.

He offers a grunt in reply.

"I knew this would happen," Wri says. "I knew it!" She storms off clutching her voidstone by the necklace's setting. I hear the words *followed* and *fools* echo off the walls, but she's speaking to herself.

I don't bother telling that she has nothing to fear, that the twins are dead. To my surprise, Daunt and Caracant stay silent as well.

I sit down on the edge of Chimeline's mattress. She's still unconscious.

Colu unclasps his sword belt and lets it fall to the red carpet with a muted *thump*. He lies next to it and places his hands behind his head, staring up into the hazy heights.

For a moment, I study him in silence, worried that I've made a big mistake in coming back here. But it's the middle of the night and we're short of gold and in no condition to travel.

"Colu," I say quietly. The others are outside the ring of light, out of earshot.

"What."

I hesitate as I think about his admission in Levi's house.

"We're going to sleep here tonight," I say.

"No shit."

I glance once more at the others.

"Can I trust you to keep your knives to yourself?"

"What are you talking about?" he mumbles. He already sounds half-asleep.

"I don't want any voiders mysteriously assassinated during the night. Do you get my meaning?"

His chest rises as he takes a deep breath. "You don't have to worry about me."

I stare at him. His tone is unsettling.

Wri storms back.

"Lucky idiots," she mutters. "I'm shocked that one of those marked didn't follow you back here."

"They're dead too, Wri," Caracant says levelly.

Wri stops in place. "Did Shon kill them?"

Caracant shakes her head. She looks exhausted and seemingly doesn't have the strength to explain.

Daunt points to Chimeline but says nothing.

"*Democryos* killed them?" Wri asks.

I straighten in surprise then turn to Chimeline and realize why Wri said that. I'm sitting directly next to Chimeline.

"No," Daunt says quietly. He motions again, with his head this time. "The woman."

Wri walks in my direction, stoops, and studies Chimeline with a head tilted in thought. She reaches out and roughly parts Chimeline's hair before touching her forehead with the back of her hand. "Strong," she says distantly, before meeting my eyes. "One of your students?"

I nod. It's true enough.

"She was the one in danger," Wri says, her eyes flashing between the unconscious Chimeline and me. "The one you were voidspeaking with."

I exhale.

"You know how to voidspeak, don't you?" she adds, more slowly. I don't answer her, and after a pregnant pause, she adds quietly, "You Northerners are full of secrets, aren't you?"

I say nothing.

She stands and turns in place to address all of us. "How did Shon come to die and the rest of you survive?"

Caracant looks down, her guilt transparent. Daunt shrugs then puts his hand on his chin. "We all hid when the fire started. I don't know how, but Gorloth must have seen him. Cara and I were further back, near the fountain, watching from a safe distance."

"What fire?"

"You should have seen it," Daunt says, perhaps trying to douse the woman's irritation with his almost-childlike excitement. "There was a fire in the nightmarket, and the marked . . . the Northern one . . . he swallowed all the flames into a ball. An incredible feat of voidance."

"Black arcana is not *incredible*," le-Daerke says from the shadows. "It is not a *feat*. It is torture." Everyone glances at her briefly.

Blythe extends a hand in her direction, palm down.

"The nightmarket was in complete chaos," Caracant adds.

Daunt nods. "And during it, the marked—Gorloth—he found Shon. Both the Northern and Southern marked were standing there together in the alley. Shon did what he could. He tried to stop them with voidance. But they were too powerful. They . . . they . . . burned Shon alive."

Wri shakes her head and points a finger at me. "His blood is on your hands."

I raise my eyebrows. "I'm not the one who's been reading all night."

Colu laughs once, still staring up into the dark heights.

"This Northern marked was hunting *her*!" Wri screams, pointing at Chimeline. "Not us! And you come bounding in here like some hot-blooded mare, putting us all in danger!" She exhales in disgust. "I should have put you down when I had the chance."

I ignore her while gingerly touching my throat. It hurts to speak and swallow. Layers of skin are ripped away, but I fear that most of the damage lies underneath. It still feels as if I'm continually catching my breath. I'm just thankful that the incense isn't burning.

"You are owning the dark, Woman," Blythe says, stepping forward onto the rug. "You are the one whose blood is hot. Dem is a man of both faith and reason, and you would do well to listen to him."

She looks at him as if he's a beetle crawling upon sand. "Who are you?"

He adjusts the blond wig. The hairpiece moves about, and dried flakes of glue flutter downward, catching the candlelight. "Friends call me Blythe. And I would like to think that you are a friend."

"We are not friends." Her gaze shifts to the palehound, who walks in a tight circle and then lies by his side. "Shon said earlier that you stole my palehound."

"This creature belongs to nobody," Blythe says levelly. "He is a gift of the Unnamed."

le-Daerke approaches and takes off Blythe's wig then inspects its underside.

Wri snarls in outrage. "You're effulgents."

Blythe taps his fist to his chest. "I am only a graycloak." He looks to le-Daerke. "But my daughter honors me by leading us on the way of unwanting."

"You think that disguise will help you?" Wri asks, smirking hideously. "All of your people are dead. And soon you will be too."

"If that is the will of the Unnamed, then so be it." Blythe shrugs. "But make no mistake—my people are not the only ones being hunted." His eyes flick to her voidstone. "They hunt you as well. And the deaths of these marked will not stop them. Odd as it may seem, we share a common enemy."

Wri's snarl fades and she looks down at the rug, seemingly at a loss for words.

I turn to Blythe and le-Daerke. "Get some sleep, if you can. Both of you. We leave at first light."

Blythe nods. "Where are we going?"

"West," I say. "Toward the deepsands."

Colu turns toward me, fingers still interlaced behind his head. "The deepsands. Are you sure?"

I nod.

"You know there's nothing out there. Gemface is headed to the Jewelled."

I shake my head. "Shon saw him this morning, on his way back with the lepers."

"What lep—" Colu stops and purses his lips then blows air between them. "Whatever."

Wri shakes her head and turns to Daunt. She leads him away past the rug, to a spot that would normally be out of earshot. But there is no other sound, so I pick up a few of their whispered words: *ashes* and *voidstone*.

Daunt's expression becomes haunted, and he swallows. He looks at his wife as if steeling himself to answer Wri.

"What do you mean you couldn't find it?" Wri yells.

Daunt looks at the floor.

"Please tell me that you didn't leave the nightmarket without Shon's stone," Wri continues. "Please tell me that you're not that stupid."

le-Daerke speaks up. "It is best you get used to that feeling of loss. Be nothing! Your voidstones are prisons of the soul. You will all be rid of them in time."

Wri turns toward le-Daerke, looking appalled. "Shut your mouth. I will not have my house overrun by vagabond effulgents! Nor will I listen to their senseless dribble."

Daunt gently touches Wri's shoulder and whispers to her while gesturing toward Chimeline.

"What?" Wri says.

Daunt nods.

Caracant joins them, arms folded, nodding in agreement.

Wri looks at Chimeline. "White as the moon?" I catch her saying.

Daunt says something in reply, then Caracant adds to it.

Wri mutters something then looks at me with an expression that I cannot place. Perhaps hatred. Maybe fear. Meanwhile, Daunt and Caracant continue their hushed discussion in the shadows. Their whispers echo and sound like the fluttering of birds.

My body and mind are overcome with exhaustion, so I lie down next to Chimeline. A gray woolen blanket is balled up at the foot of the bed, and I pull it over us. I smell a man's odor on it. This was probably Shon's bed.

As I wrap my arm around the sleeping Chimeline, I feel a weight—Wri's piercing stare on my back, burning a hole there. It also comes from the scent of the bed. I try to bury my head in Chimeline's black forest of hair, but the lingering smell of the blanket remains, reminding me of Shon.

But mostly this weight comes from the two voidstones inside my pants pocket—both of which are still heavy with souls.

One is mine, recovered from the Northern marked's pile of ash.

The other is Shon's.

THE TRUTH REVEALED

The palehound's barking startles me awake.

"Who's there?" screams a voice in the darkness. It's Wri.

I hear others too. The singing of steel. Colu's blade being unsheathed.

Moonlight falls upon us from the paned windows far above, but it's too weak to reveal any details. I raise my head from the straw mattress, feeling Chimeline's motionless body next to mine. I have no sense of the fullbell.

It must be the middle of the night.

Across the rug, at Wri's bed, shapes move in the darkness. Two. Maybe three.

Sudden cold, bright light.

I hold out my hand, squinting. Within a moment, I see that the light is Wri's doing. An orb flutters above the room like a firefly, casting harsh, shifting shadows in all directions. She's sitting upright in bed and has her hand on her voidstone necklace, which sits between her breasts, inside the deep V cut of her indigo nightshirt.

Within arm's reach of her, a bald le-Daerke looms clutching a golden voidstone necklace. Her black wig is on the floor near her feet.

Colu stands just behind le-Daerke, sword out, looking around the room frantically.

Wri scrambles out of her sheets, using her feet to kick herself backward.

"What's going on?" I say, standing as quickly as I can.

Daunt and Caracant are in bed, getting up slowly. Blythe is stretched out on the rug, rubbing his eyes. His wig is also off, lying next to him. The palehound continues to bark, baring its teeth at Wri, until Blythe leans over and puts his hand on the creature's head, whispering to him. The hound immediately stops, its barks turning into a soft whimper.

"You!" Wri says, letting go of her voidstone. Her eyes focus on this world again—first on le-Daerke then on the voidstone necklace dangling from her hand. "That's Daunt's stone."

Daunt gasps as he runs his palms over his shirt. "How did you . . ." He stands.

"You will torture them no more," le-Daerke says. Her jaw is clenched. Her hands are fists at her sides. Her body is shaking. I'm not sure if it's fear or fury consuming her.

I try to fit the picture in front of me with what I know to be true. le-Daerke holds Daunt's voidstone—she must have taken it from him. And now, she's hovering over Wri. Back in Winter's Baiou, there were multiple dead voiders, their stones taken. Colu admitted to the crime back at Levi's house. I'd warned him not to do the same thing here tonight.

But Colu seems as caught off guard as I am. I don't see hatred in him. I don't see a person who could murder someone in their sleep.

That's what I see when I look at le-Daerke.

Could it be her? All this time, it's been her?

"le-Daerke, what are you doing," I say. It comes out as a statement rather than a question.

She doesn't look at me. "What do you think I'm doing."

"This is not the way to free them," I explain calmly. "Please, give Daunt back his voidstone."

This time she looks at me, her eyes defiant. "I can't do that, Dem."

Her words shock me into silence. She's an effulgent refusing to give something away.

"Daughter," Blythe says, standing. The palehound circles him, panting. "It is owning the dark to work this way. Only through gentle enlightenment should we gather the axion fragments. Perhaps this is a good time to discuss eleutheria."

"Shut up!" Wri screams. Her head makes sharp movements as she studies all of us and nervously fidgets with the gold chain around her neck.

Things are quickly escalating.

If Wri uses voidance on le-Daerke, will the enervated intervene? I think back to the Celestium, when Blythe and I were unharmed by the mirror shards yet Chimeline was cut. Mander was able to pull her across the rift. She hadn't yet been in the void—the white room—the way Blythe and I had been during eleutheria. They didn't know her soul. Her name.

le-Daerke is in danger.

Instinctively, my hand moves toward my pocket. I contemplate voidance but catch myself, forcing the thought away. I will not torment the enervated when there are other options.

"Colu," I say, my arm outstretched. "Put away your blade."

His eye flashes to me, and his expression is one of disagreement. But he acquiesces. The metallic sound breaks the heavy silence.

"Blythe was right," I say, looking at everyone but focusing mostly on Wri and le-Daerke. "We share a common enemy. And when we fight, they win."

Wri gets out of bed and cautiously approaches le-Daerke, coming within a few paces of Colu and her. "Then explain why you're stealing our stones."

le-Daerke shakes her fists. "They were never yours—"

"le-Daerke!" I say harshly, silencing her.

I glance worriedly at Blythe, running my hand through my hair. This is the worst possible moment to be crossing this bridge. Wri's already on edge, and anything I say will be contested. I could say that the rug is red and she'd disagree.

But there's no other choice. I can't think of a lie better than the truth.

"Wri, everything that the effulgents have preached is true."

She looks at me as if I'm speaking utter nonsense.

"That's why the azuremen have killed them all," I add. "Because the truth is their greatest threat."

Wri scowls. "What truth?"

"Voidance is the abuse of trapped souls," I say, pointing to the necklace that she still clutches. "There are thousands of souls in that single voidstone around your neck. And every time you use it, you cause them pain."

Silence fills the ruined hearth. The palehound lies down and stretches, tongue lolling out.

Then Wri shakes her head, grasping her chain tighter. "You actually believe that?"

"Think about everything that has happened since they came, Wri. The azuremen confiscating the voidstones. They want them for themselves. All the countless souls. They view them as *their* property. Not yours."

"Or maybe it's because *voidance* is their greatest threat. That *we're* the only chance at stopping them."

I shake my head, but I have no words to counter her argument. It breaks my heart that she won't see the truth, but part of this heartbreak is that I can understand her perspective. It's not a lack of her intelligence—in truth, it's the opposite. Gaigane had the same reaction.

Reason alone cannot save her.

"Get out," she says. "All of you. I want you to leave. Now."

"But—"

"Go! Return Daunt's stone at once and leave."

"The giving houses," I say, getting her attention back.

She looks at me.

"People disappearing. Lepers. Criminals. The elderly. They're all being placed in soteria."

"In *what*?"

"People are being put *inside* voidstones. And we're helping them. We're helping them grow in power. As the blue numbers on our arms get higher and higher, the souls in the voidstones—"

"Stop!" she cries, the word echoing in the shadow-filled hearth.

Daunt and Caracant look at each other in worry.

le-Daerke continues to stare with hatred at Wri, her shaking arms at her sides.

"I've listened to you, voider," Wri says to me levelly, keeping her focus on le-Daerke. "If I can even call you that anymore. I've listened to you far longer than you deserved. Your words are those of a fanatic. Now go, before things get even more unpleasant."

I nod. The time for words has passed. "le-Daerke," I say, "return the stone. We'll talk about this later."

But she shakes her head.

"Daughter—"

"Just do it, Woman!" Colu says in a hushed tone, interrupting Blythe. "She's a fucking voider. Don't you know what she can do to you?"

"I don't care!" le-Daerke screams, looking at him while pointing to Wri with the same shaking hand that holds the necklace. "That's what they always want! To make us afraid of their power!" She addresses Wri. "You don't have any power over me! And you don't have any power over the enervated either."

"But don't I?" Wri says, an ugly smile on her face. "If what you say is true, then I not only have power over you, but also these *enervated*."

I see le-Daerke's face scrunch up into something hideous—in the harsh, shimmering voidlight, I cannot recognize the serene graycloak I met in Fiscarlo. The one who silently brought bland food to Chimeline and me in our cages, her demeanor made entirely of graceful sunlight. This woman is not the same.

"I should have slit your neck," le-Daerke says from behind clenched teeth, then eyes Daunt and Caracant. "All of you wretches. Like I did the others—"

"le-Daerke," Colu says, his voice full of warning. "You would be wise to hold your t—"

"You are nothing!" she screams at Wri. "Without the enervated's pain, *you are nothing*!"

le-Daerke reveals something in her right hand with a dexterity I didn't know she possessed. It catches the voidlight above. A sickle-shaped shadow passes over the room.

She lunges toward Wri.

I wouldn't have had the chance to react, even if I'd dared.

Wri grabs her voidstone. A popping sound echoes out in the room.

The back of le-Daerke's skull breaks apart. Her brain, grayish-red, sprays through the air behind her and falls onto the rug next to me, even covering the edge of the mattress that Chimeline sleeps on, ten feet away. It sounds like a storm's first rains hitting parched dirt.

For another heartbeat, she stands. Then she slumps to the floor at Colu's feet.

I can only stare at her body, trying to understand what just happened. Trying to admit to myself that Blythe's daughter is dead.

In my peripheral vision, Colu moves.

By the time I look up, the wooden handle of a dagger is sticking out of Wri's chest, directly between her breasts and very near her voidstone. She still clutches the stone with both hands but looks down at the dagger.

The light of voidance dies, throwing us into darkness.

A moment later, Colu shouts out in pain. I hear shuffling in the blackness.

"Dem?" he groans.

I hear him, but it's as if he's far away. As if it's voidspeak. The ghost of the voidlight haunts my vision. It's yellow now, like le-Daerke's eyes in the Lemon Tree Inn, and everywhere I turn, she's watching me.

Flint and steel.

Caracant lights a single candle.

Everything is cast in a warm glow that makes the room look like a completely different place. Colu is on his knees an arm's length before me. His left hand caresses his right shoulder. Blood is flowing, black in the candlelight.

Past him, Wri lies on her bed, arms at her sides, eyes wide open and still, seemingly focused on the hanging chains ten feet above. Beneath her, the mattress is quickly turning dark.

Caracant drops the flint and steel, letting out a moan of disbelief. She looks at her husband, and then they both begin backing up.

"Oh no," Blythe softly cries. He crawls across the rug to his dead daughter and cradles her in his lap. In the weak candlelight, I see that her face is mostly intact. There's only a single hole in the center of her forehead. The palehound comes near and licks le-Daerke's bare feet.

"Oh no," Blythe keeps whispering. He kisses her cheek.

I turn away, out of respect. Out of guilt. Her yellow eyes still follow.

What else could I have done?

Daunt and Caracant flee through the hidden membrane in the brick wall. No one else seems to notice or care. I'm surprised that Daunt didn't try to get his voidstone back—clearly they fear for their lives. Those two saved mine, and I repaid them by bringing horror to their home.

"Can you do anything?" Colu asks me.

I turn to him, blinking, struggling to free myself from my thoughts. He motions to le-Daerke then winces as he takes off his ripped, bloody shirt and ties a tourniquet around his bicep.

I somberly shake my head.

He gingerly touches his bare shoulder. It's hard to see in the candlelight, but a small piece of his shoulder flesh is missing. A grazing parting shot from Wri.

Colu eventually stands and walks over to Wri's body. He roughly pulls the dagger out of her heart and wipes it on her indigo nightshirt before placing it back in the leather sheath tied to his belt. Then he yanks off her voidstone necklace.

He throws it to me. "I hope this was fucking worth it."

PART THREE

A PAIR OF ASHEN

THE PERSISTENCE
OF WATER

Blythe steps out from the cover of verdant grasses and into the rushing turquoise waters of the Kimer River cradling two glass jars topped with wide pieces of cork.

The sun rises to our left over Kimer Dagger, the widening scar that leads to Xi Bay.

The town of al-Kimer-Vis sits behind us, down a dusty road. It's slowly waking, but we're far enough away that it's almost unnoticeable. Only the smell of charcoal pits and the lonely sound of a hammer on anvil are carried over to us on the dry wind. Much nearer are our horses, who bray now and then, perhaps confused about why we've stopped at water before our journey to the deepsands has even begun.

The unending rush of the clear river against stones covers everything.

Colu and Chimeline stand next to me among the grasses, watching Blythe carefully step further into the slender river. The water passes his knees, soaking his clothes. He seems unaware. He doesn't turn back to face us. He doesn't look straight ahead to the South, toward the Jewelled, hundreds of miles away, where everything vital in Xiland seems to come from, including this river. He doesn't look to the right, to the rising foothills, where the greenery is suddenly stripped away into red and umber.

He only stands solidly in the currents, feet wide apart, as he opens the first of the glass jars. He lets the gray ash spill out, and the morning breeze takes it away from him, into the water, into the sky. Two different shades of blue, two different ways to freedom.

I find Chimeline's fingers next to me and attempt to interlace them with mine, but she draws away, folding her arms underneath her breasts.

I glance at her, trying to read her expression, but she's as closed off as ever. It's been a fullbell since she regained consciousness and she's hardly said a single word.

Blythe uncaps the second jar, doing the same with its contents. I'm not sure which one was his daughter and which one was Wri. I'm not sure Blythe knows either.

For a long time, all of us stand in silence, the only sounds the water and the distant clanging.

In my peripheral vision, I see Colu somberly shake his head. "I don't know how he does it," he murmurs.

I glance at him in confusion, and he motions with his head to Blythe. "Forgiving like that."

I look away but eventually find myself nodding in agreement. Blythe's actions are so effortless that they almost come across as wrong.

Blythe adamantly fought to treat his daughter's murderer—a voider, no less—with the same respect, despite all our objections.

He submerges both jars in the river then pours out the water, ensuring that all the remains are scattered. Afterward, he replaces the corks and turns around.

He slips.

Both jars fall out of his hands and land in the swirling current as he tries to catch his balance. He reaches out to a large boulder and grabs hold of it as if hugging the belly of a giant.

The jars float away.

Colu mumbles a curse and steps into the river.

"I'm fine," Blythe says, but his voice betrays these words—it's as tumultuous as the surrounding waters. He wipes his face. I'm not sure if the wetness is from water or tears. "Stay where you are. I can manage just fine, il-Colu."

"I'm already soaked," Colu says, approaching while extending a hand. "Here."

But Blythe doesn't grab it. He's focused on the boulder in front of him, running his palms across its glasslike surface, almost in admiration.

"Blythe," Colu says, trying to get his attention. "It's a rock."

"Do you see this?" Blythe asks, turning to him in excitement before looking at Chimeline and me. "Do you see how it's been split in two?"

Chimeline and I exchange a glance before we take a few steps to the side to improve our vantage point. Once we do, I can see it: a deep, narrow crevasse cuts almost through its middle.

Blythe gently pats the boulder with one palm. "This is the way of unwanting," he says, smiling. He wipes his face again, and then, seemingly for the first time, sees Colu's still-outstretched hand and clasps it by the wrist.

"The water," Blythe continues, as the pair walk to shore. With his free hand, he motions back toward the rock. "It doesn't use brute force for change. It uses persistence. Gentle persistence. Such behavior can change the world." He nods to himself. "May we all remember this place that the Unnamed has provided."

No one says anything. Colu raises an eyebrow while Chimeline turns away. And all the while I contemplate the strength of Blythe's faith. It's always been a mystery to me, but after all that he has lost, the mystery is even greater. Is his resoluteness a facade meant for us or himself? Is his trust in the Unnamed as slippery as the pebbles under his feet?

Or is it as persistent as water?

I honestly cannot tell.

On dusty ground again, Blythe lets go of Colu and steps into his sandals. He pats his palms dry on his chest—the only part of him not drenched—and looks at the three of us as if none of the recent events have occurred.

"Shall we get on our way?" he asks.

"Can you make that out?" Colu asks me.

Looking up, I adjust the white sheet covering my head and body. I peer down the red scar of a road to where he's pointing: at a cluster of dark shapes on the otherwise bleached horizon.

"Is it a well?" he adds.

I reposition myself in my saddle then shake my head. "I see a cluster of low trees. Frankincense, maybe. And a small house. Vulture overhead."

"A house?" he asks.

I shrug, still peering. "Built from stone. Very small. Flat roof."

He grunts. "Yeah. Probably a well. And more lepers."

"How do you know that?"

"If there are vultures, there will be lepers," he says, before dropping his gaze again.

The midday sun beats down.

A handful of travelers dot the path in the miles before and behind us. They ride in covered wagons, their trails of dust extending toward the rising heights of the lo-Kimer foothills. A single white cloud reigns there.

"Dem," Blythe calls out from behind us. "May I have a word with you?"

I glance back and give him a nod, trying not to show my ironic sadness. There was a time when I would have taunted him about his word choice. *"Having" implies ownership, Blythe!* And Colu's mention of the distant well. I think of the shuttered one in the sun-sheltered place in Fiscarlo, where Yerla went for water. Or was it Yisla?

I hated Blythe then. Now I hate what has happened to him.

Gently pulling upon the reins of my gray horse—the one that Blythe and his daughter used to share—I slowly drop back between him and Chimeline, who rides silently on the chestnut-colored mare.

Blythe sits atop a new white Xian horse, a purchase we made just before leaving the city. Colu had found a red velvet bag containing over eight hundred gold hidden in Wri's straw mattress. He used it to buy the fourth horse, which pulls a small covered wain. It's not for carrying people, but the palehound sits in it along with the rest of our belongings, including food, water sacks, and tents.

I push back my white sheet and look at Blythe. He appears contemplative under his blueish hood. Ever since his daughter died, he has refused to wear the wig—he can't be convinced, despite our numerous attempts.

"I imagine that we'll be doing eleutheria again soon," he says.

I nod. "As soon as we have time to rest. Tonight, perhaps."

Blythe stares straight ahead. "How many do you have?"

"Two." Clearing my throat, I add, "Well, actually, there are three. But remember, we decided to—"

"I know, my friend." He gently cuts me off with a wave of his arm underneath the white sheet. "Leave one full, just in case. And Marine's as well."

His mention of Marine reminds me of my broken promise to visit her more often. I haven't checked on her since before the nightmarket. With all that has happened, it's completely slipped my mind.

Is she ready to move on?

"Anyway, that's beside the point," Blythe says. "I have an idea. Chimeline thinks it might be possible. Isn't that right, Child?"

I blink my guilty thoughts away and look at Chimeline, riding on the other side of me.

I cannot see her face behind her white sheet—just the tip of her nose and a few stray strands of black hair. But then she glances at us and I'm taken aback. Usually her eyes are enveloping black pools. But the intense sunlight has transformed them—her pupils are infinitesimal specks floating in seas of cinnamon brown.

"Maybe," she says quietly. "I've asked the enervated. They don't know. This sort of thing has never been done before."

I alternate my confused gaze between the two of them.

Blythe subtly motions to Colu, riding up ahead. "I think il-Colu should partake in eleutheria with us."

I squint at the single cloud in the sky as I struggle to comprehend this. Colu is neither a voider nor an effulgent. Eleutheria requires my voidance to delve and Blythe's ability to speak to the enervated, so they can guide us through the dark. Colu can do neither of these things.

"Why?" I ask Blythe.

"So they know his name."

"His soul," Chimeline corrects.

After a pause, I give a single nod in slow understanding. "So that the enervated can protect him from attacks of voidance."

"Exactly," Blythe says.

"Would it even work?" I ask, again glancing between the two of them. I turn to Chimeline. "Wouldn't it be easier if you just told the enervated about him? Perhaps explain that he's traveling with us and helping our cause?"

"I tried that already." She looks away thoughtfully and then shakes her head. "It doesn't work like that, for them. To have a proper awareness of him, they need to see his soul—to feel it. In soteria."

Blythe sighs deeply. "If le-Daerke had shared in eleutheria, the enervated would have known her soul too. Perhaps they would have protected her."

A wave of guilt comes over me in a different form. "She asked to help us," I say. "Asked *me*. Back at the Lemon Tree Inn. And I was going to show her. I just . . . I never got the chance."

He doesn't reply.

"I'm sorry, Blythe," I eventually say. "I should have listened to her. I keep wondering if I could have done something differently. Done anything to prevent—"

Chimeline scoffs, interrupting me.

I frown, surprised by her reaction.

"If it's anyone's fault, it's mine," she says. "I was passed out, useless, on the bed. Had I been awake, I could have protected her."

Blythe blinks rapidly but doesn't reply.

"You were passed out because you saved our lives," I remind her.

She focuses on me. The white sheet falls down, collecting around her hips and saddle, leaving her black hair shining in the sun.

"Saved you? I nearly *killed* you and Colu in the nightmarket! I nearly killed myself, too. I couldn't . . ." She looks up into the blue sky, struggling to find the right words. "Control them. Control myself."

"It doesn't matter," I say softly. "What you did was enough."

"It *does* matter. Nearly killing you *does* matter, Dem. Being passed out for an entire day *does* matter. What happens the next time we meet a marked? Or one of those azuremen?"

I feel my emotions rising. "We'll manage. We always do. The important thing is that you're alright—"

"You don't care about me," she snaps. "None of you do. And I'm starting to believe that you're right."

"Woman, you are owning the dark," Blythe says.

She wrinkles her nose, but I see anger in her eyes, which suddenly widen. Then she nods slowly. "Yes, I think you're right. That's exactly what I'm doing."

"Those are dangerous words, Child."

She ignores him. "I've been owning the dark my entire life. Why stop now?"

Chimeline snaps open the ring-shaped clip on her ponytail and places it on her wrist. Letting go of the reins, she roughly gathers her hair with both hands, trying to order it back together.

I glance at Blythe. He looks to me in worry, mouthing, *Why stop now?*

Blythe centers his attention back on Chimeline. "I don't see a woman who has been owning the dark," he says. "I see a woman on the way of unwanting."

She laughs again, joylessly. "That's precisely what you're meant to see," she says. She reclasps the ring and runs her ponytail between her hands, looking pleased with the newfound order. "The truth is, I was raised to kill men like the two of you. Powerful men. Some women too."

In a rustle of canvas, the smooth white head of the palehound surfaces from the wagon just behind Blythe, looking like a skull. The creature sniffs the dry air before retreating to the shadows.

Blythe straightens again. "Always remember: the way ahead can be different from the way you took to get here."

"I used to think so, too," she says.

"Used to?" I ask her.

She glances at me. "Do you remember when we left the citadel in your airship?"

I nod.

She smiles for the first time today, and I momentarily envision the moon and stars. "I felt free, then," she says. The smile fades as she squints. "Mander was still out there. He would voidspeak, wondering if I'd killed you yet. But in that one moment, my head was clear. The skies were clear. Everything was clear." She hesitates as the wind passes through. "For the first time in my life, I felt free."

"You *are* free," I remind her.

Chimeline gathers the white sheet around her hips and pulls it back over herself, hiding her face from view. "Am I?"

Colu looks back at us, hunchbacked and forlorn.

Blythe opens his mouth but then closes it again.

"Yes," I say, adamantly. "You answer to no one. Only to yourself."

Blythe clears his throat. "May I remind you both that we all answer to the Unnamed. Whether we admit it or not." He leans forward in his saddle, addressing Chimeline. "As for you, Child, whatever dreams you have in this life, if the Unnamed wills them, they shall come true."

Chimeline shakes her head.

"What is it, Child?"

"The Unnamed wills me to be a weapon, just as I've always been," she says. "My dreams have nothing to do with it."

Blythe's silence tells me all that I need to know, but I bite my tongue. I don't need to argue with a man who has just lost his only daughter.

Chimeline guides her horse very close to mine. She looks sideways at me with a gaze as pure and harsh as the bleached sand and sky. The same expression that she wore the night we met. In the king's dining room, just before the lacquered paneled doors opened, when the muscles on her face were relaxed. No complications with dreams. Only duty. A weapon being prepared.

"I'm ready for you to teach me now," she says.

VOIDREAMING

Temberlain stared at the Axiondrive with admiration and regret, knowing full well that it could be the very last time.

So often he'd taken this room for granted, moving through the circular malineum rungs that made up the spherical cage around this black heart. Checking arterial connections. Enervated capacity levels. Fragmentation on the outer surface.

Now, he floated in place for a precious few microrotations, trying to push the fear away. Trying to forget what was happening. He focused on the beauty. Despite the harsh sodium light, there were zero reflections upon its surface. It appeared as if there were a massive rent in the ship and he were staring into the vacuum of space, the arterial connections posing as glittering stars.

Sixteen nudged him forward into the cylindrical opening of the malineum rungs, and the moment passed.

"Up," she said.

There was no up here. No down. It was a poor choice of words from an animal that didn't know any better. There was only mirror-side and FTL-side.

But, using his only hand, he did as he was told—and without a word of insolence. The tightening fear had returned, along with an instinctive will to live.

At least long enough to warn Efful.

Time was running out. They were climbing toward mirror-side. The Axiondrive was the heart of the ship, and there was a brain behind that heart. The brain was mirror-side.

The control unit.

After progressing a quarter circumference through the circular rungs that made up the large spherical cage, he could see where he'd just traveled, curved out below him.

The Agh-Severian was following.

Sixteen kept close—right on his heels. With her thick torso and wide shoulders, she could barely fit inside the cylindrical ladder. However, the red-skinned Agh-Severian, trailing many feet behind her, looked as if she would float away between the rungs. Her black autosized suit was a harsh contrast to the white walls, but it reflected everything, as if it were wet. Compared to the Axiondrive, her suit didn't even look black.

She still clutched the silver case.

Soon, the seven circular doors leading to the hardlines were all visible below, surrounding the Axiondrive. If he envisioned this room as a planet, the seven doors were at its equator while he sat near the northern pole, mirror-side. One of the seven—the one he'd entered through—was still open. The two empowered corpses prevented it from closing. Outside the chamber, multiple ashen kicked the bodies inward. Once unobstructed, the door sealed shut with a hiss, leaving the living ashen outside.

Temberlain paused in contemplation.

The bodies of Cordialle's men gently continued floating, caught within their predestined trajectories. They collided with the malineum cage in the southern hemisphere, FTL-side, arms twisting between rungs, torsos slowly ricocheting—a macabre dance of the dead. Wherever they went, a trail of red marbles remained, pronounced against the sterile white-yellow walls.

If only I could reach their axiongraphs . . .

Sixteen tapped her serrater loudly against a rung. "Keep moving."

Temberlain slowly climbed on.

Within a hundred microrotations, they arrived at the northern pole.

A large screen was laid out before him. Connecting to its underside was a slack silver ribbon that extended ten feet between the cage and the Axiondrive and ended in an arterial connection weaved into the surface.

"Log in," Sixteen said, beneath him. Even with her guttural accent, he could tell that she was clenching her jaw.

Temberlain looked down past his feet.

Sixteen had already braced herself against the rungs using her back and feet. She held her serrater with both hands above her head, aiming it directly at him. The number *16* glowed blue on her forearm.

Movement, from outside the rungs.

It was obvious to Temberlain that Sixteen could see it as well. Her eyes nervously flashed to the rungs but she didn't move a muscle of her thick body.

One of the corpses was floating near. It must have meandered from FTL-side to mirror-side.

The body was already feet above the Agh-Severian, blocking most of her in Temberlain's line of sight. But he could still see her red face framed within the malineum. Her narrowed pink eyes looked straight at him.

Slowly, the corpse floated further away from her, and then past Sixteen. On the other side of the rungs, it made its way toward Temberlain and the control unit.

Temberlain could see the axiongraph.

It was only feet away from him, but it might as well have been on the opposite side of the Virel Arm. Sixteen would kill him before he had a chance to touch it.

"Log in," Sixteen repeated.

Temberlain felt his options narrowing.

"And then what?" he asked, looking down at the tip of the serrater.

"Just follow my instructions and there won't be any pain. If you don't, I'll put you through as much torture as you put them through."

Them.

Why can't she see that immortality isn't torture? Partaking in greatness isn't sacrifice.

Temberlain looked back at the screen. One thing was almost certain: they still needed him for something beyond his logging in—something that only Temberlain could do.

He glanced once more at the corpse. If he couldn't reach axion soon, he would die.

Temberlain knew that there was nobody awaiting him on the other side. There was no "other side." No god that couldn't be named. Finally caught within the probability of death, Temberlain almost envied the ashen in their simpleness. To be able to cling to a belief like a child clutches a blanket against the coming night . . .

He gritted his teeth. No. He had something better than a god: the assurance that the greatness of his kind lived on forevermore.

And that was something worth dying for.

Temberlain pressed his palm upon the screen.

The control unit awakened, authenticated, then immediately showed enervated levels. The Axiondrive was at 91 percent, which, for a microrotation, made Temberlain second-guess the readout. Ninety-one was high. But then he realized what had happened. Emergency differentiation had brought the ship out of FTL and into a literal state of shock. Power redirection was happening all over the place. He recalled the blue light from the FTL array on his way here, reflected upon the hardlines.

"Good," Sixteen said. "Now, take it offline."

For a moment, Temberlain stared at the screen.

Take it offline.

He'd expected something different. Redirect power to the escape pods, perhaps. More power would allow more of them to come online in parallel. But take the drive down completely? What would that accomplish?

But then Sixteen's previous response came back to him.

Them.

The ashen wanted to let the enervated rest. In their twisted view of reality, that's what was important. Before they abandoned this ship altogether, they wanted—

The Agh-Severian pushed herself through a gap in the rungs and floated gracefully toward the Axiondrive, opening the silver case as she went.

"Off. Line." Sixteen readjusted the serrater in her hands but kept it trained on his face. One of her eyes was closed in concentration. "The next time I ask you, you'll be begging for death."

He swallowed then nodded.

It would take time. Taking a drive offline was rare. Temberlain had never actually done it outside of training. Axiondrives were turned online in the lunar shipyards during preconstruction and remained in that state for their tenure. They were taken offline only during major repairs or rehosting in a new ship.

He placed his palm on the screen a second time.

The sodium lights dimmed as the ship transferred to reserve power.

As if the entire axionship were a living enervated, Temberlain could feel its last breath escape. A palpable silence reverberated throughout the room, and then beyond, like a wave of exhaustion stretching to infinity.

Temberlain felt a tear fall down his face.

Feet away from him and still out of reach, the corpse rotated slowly, caught within the control unit's silver ribbon, spinning in its own chaotic axis.

It symbolized everything. Entropy. The descent into disorder.

He was out of time. He knew it in his bones.

Temberlain readied himself to lunge. If he was going to die, it was going to be on his terms.

But as the moment arrived, the Agh-Severian grabbed something white out of her case and then pushed the case away. A microrotation later, she landed upon the surface of the drive like a cat. Her face was now covered in a silver-tinted mask—an obvious feature of her autosized suit.

"What is she doing?" Temberlain asked himself. His words were almost a whisper. They were built as much out of curiosity as self-preservation.

The Agh-Severian clutched a white disk in her red hand.

"I should let you see this," Sixteen said. "Before you die."

Temberlain inhaled a sharp breath.

Impossible.

The Agh-Severian reverently set the white disk upon the Axiondrive and then pressed a button in its center before pushing herself away.

As she flew backward through the room and grabbed hold of the cage, at least a hundred white wires telescoped out many feet from the disk, spokes in a wheel, humming for a few microrotations before weaving themselves into the black surface. The staccato sound was deafening.

Temberlain had never seen such a thing, but he had heard rumors. Stories passed among the ashen to give them hope. He'd laughed when he first heard about it. And now he was crying.

It was an eleutherian drill.

Everything fell into place. Why he'd been kept alive. Why he'd been brought here.

They were freeing the enervated while freeing themselves.

Out of the corner of his eye, he witnessed Sixteen staring in awe. She still held the serrater, but it was trained off him slightly.

Discreetly, he moved his hand under the screen and tugged upon the silver ribbon.

Meanwhile, the white disk began elongating, becoming brighter. It was still white but was glowing now. The pinprick of light widened into a beacon. The staccato sound sank into a deep humming.

Tangled in silver, the corpse floated nearer.

The Agh-Severian shouted something from across the room, but the humming drowned it out. She pointed to her mask.

White light swallowed the room.

Temberlain embraced his fate. He lunged.

Blindly, he felt for the ribbon then clutched something with his one hand. The man's uniform. He pulled the body in tightly, feeling for the neck. The head.

Sixteen's serrater went off once, a buzzing sound even louder than the humming. The cage broke apart, sending his world spinning. The air was charged with possibilities.

A microrotation later, his prying fingers found the bleedersnake.

Blackness returned.

Axion! At last!

THE WAY OF DISAPPOINTMENT

Squinting, I look at the lone bird, circling above. It's hard to tell its size, but I can easily spot the bright red of its head.

"I think that's a crimsonhawk," I say. "Not a vulture."

Chimeline and Blythe crane their necks but don't reply. Blythe shrugs, so I call out to Colu, riding ahead of us.

"Colu, what do you think?"

He raises his head but only to take a swig of water from his glass bottle.

"Who the fuck cares," he mumbles, after a swallow.

Blythe exhales in disapproval. I study Colu's hunched back. *What's gotten under his skin?*

Three gnarled and barren frankincense trees stand a hundred feet away, giant skeletal hands rising out of the sandy and rocky ground. A short distance away from them is a small cube-shaped windowless structure, its stone walls dry-stacked. Blue sky sneaks through in a few places, where the grout should be. The roof looks to be made of wood and clay, the overhanging beams gray and petrified. The door must be on the opposite side.

A single white horse drinks at a trough.

The palehound jumps out of the wagon and joins in, lapping the water determinedly.

"I've read that deepsanders sometimes train crimsonhawks," I add, looking up again at the circling bird. "They're used to hunt."

As we dismount, a Xian man covered in white robes steps out from around the corner. The palehound stops drinking to circle the man inquisitively.

Pulling back the sheet covering his head, the stranger peers at us, his forehead creased.

He must be at least sixty years old. His dark age spots remind me of Daunt, but this man is even older. He tugs upon his tattered gray beard. His weathered skin looks as petrified as the dark, twisted trunks behind him. Even his cane is this color—unadorned with jewels, it's the first I've seen since arriving in the South that is more about necessity than style.

Blythe's admonishment from several days ago comes back to me. He said that I've only ever traveled to perfect places, and he was right. This Xian man seems to be the opposite. It's as if the Unnamed fashioned him from the very ground and sky. If he happened to stumble upon some human-made luxury, I doubt that he'd understand what it was.

Colu dismounts clumsily and stuffs his sloshing water bottle into his saddlebag. I'm surprised that it's not empty. Mine has been empty for fullbells.

"Greetings," I say to the older Xian man.

He doesn't answer.

"Looks like the well hasn't run dry," I say, motioning to the trough.

"Of course it hasn't," the elder says matter-of-factly. "The Unnamed provides."

Colu chuckles to himself as he leads his horse to the trough.

"Have I said something amusing?" the elder says, his brow furrowed.

"No," Blythe answers, a few feet behind us. "What you said was wise and true." He's busy disconnecting his horse from the wain's yoke.

Chimeline and I tie up our horses and let them settle in with the others. The stranger stares worriedly at us. "You came from al-Kimer-vis," he says, extending the tip of his cane toward the east.

"Yes," I tell him.

Just beyond the trees, the crimsonhawk dives.

Chimeline jumps in place as the bird suddenly levels off then grazes the ground, raising up a small cloud of dust that the wind promptly carries away. The palehound barks and then heads into the well house, its tail between its legs.

After a moment, the bird rises again, flapping its wings, a storm of sand curling below.

It approaches. Something is caught within its talons.

Chimeline takes a step closer to me, looking on in awe.

The bird is massive. Its wingspan must be at least five feet. Its head is bloodred, hence its name, while the feathers of its body are white underneath and tan and spotted above.

The crimsonhawk drops the dead animal at the Xian man's feet—a tanned burrowcat, from the look of it. Then it lands a few feet away, constricts its wings slightly, and takes a few steps while studying us with neck movements that remind me of an azureman.

I turn to Chimeline. She purses her lips, staring at the crimsonhawk, lost in thought.

Past her, Colu lets out a curse of relief. Standing beyond the well house with his back toward us, he's pissing on the ground while singing a deep Xian tune.

With a single swoop of its wings, the crimsonhawk takes flight again, into the bleached sky.

When I turn back to the elderly man, his narrow eyes seem to be measuring us. "Some men have markings," he says. "You one of them, Northerner?" He tips his cane toward me. "You looking for more lepers from le-Mon-Sogara?"

I shake my head and raise my hands, letting the sheet fall to my elbows. "We carry no marks."

He points the cane at Blythe. "You?"

Colu interrupts. "We're looking for a hairless fucker with gems on his face," he says, adjusting his crotch while returning. He laughs.

The older man opens his mouth but says nothing. He puts both his hands on the tip of his cane, shifting his weight upon it as he watches Colu approach the well house.

Colu rubs his palm across his face. "Effulgent with gems." He keeps laughing, shaking his head, and disappears around the corner, presumably entering the well house. "Fucking crazy," I hear, from beyond the stone wall.

"Forgive his crudeness," Blythe says.

"But have you seen this man?" Chimeline asks the elder. "He was driving a wagon through these parts."

"A four-horse wagon," I add.

"No," the elder says immediately, looking southwest, toward the jagged cliffs. "No effulgents out here in the deepsands." He stamps the dry ground a few times with his cane. "No effulgents anywhere, it seems, these days. May the Unnamed help us all."

Chimeline and I both instinctively turn toward Blythe.

Blythe takes a deep breath then removes his head covering. "The effulgency still exists, my son. And the way of unwanting goes everywhere, even to the most barren of places. For that is where one can truly be nothing without the distractions of man."

The Xian man stares at him in disbelief.

"Your . . . Your Effulgency," he eventually says, slowly getting down upon one knee while bracing both hands on his cane. He grimaces in discomfort.

"Please," Blythe says, urgently approaching him and helping him back up. "There is no need for such formalities."

The loud sound of splashing water echoes from inside the well house. "Fuck, that's cold!" Colu screams.

The elder grabs Blythe's forearm for a moment. "You must be seeking safe haven."

Blythe nods hesitantly. "More than this, I seek the one who comes before me."

The splashing is louder—the sound of water hitting dry ground.

"May we talk in privacy, Your Effulgency?" the elder asks.

Blythe looks at Chimeline and me. "These are my friends who are both on the way of unwanting. You can speak freely."

"Balls, that feels good!" Colu yells.

"And him?" the Xian asks, motioning with a tilt of his head.

Blythe sighs. "I am still trying to guide il-Colu. He has a long way to go."

Another splashing sound.

"I will check on him," Chimeline says, walking away.

The elder glances at me, his distrust evident in his creased eyes and the way he tugs on his ratty beard, but then he hesitantly nods.

"There is something happening in le-Mon-Sogara," the man says to Blythe. He glances at me.

"Has your temple been converted to a giving house?" I ask.

He scowls. "Where I am from is too small to even have a proper temple. We have an altar cut out of the rock."

The elder taps his cane on the sandy ground as we wait for him to continue. "Do you know of le-Mon-Sogara?" he asks both of us, alternating his gaze.

Blythe shakes his head.

"I've never heard of that city," I say.

His smile is dry and twisted. "It is not a city. It is a handful of ancient homes built into the cliff. And it should not even have a name, for naming implies ownership."

Blythe nods deeply.

"I only say *le-Mon-Sogara* because that is what the city folk decided to call it a very long time ago. They have the urge to own everything that glitters."

I look at him in confusion.

"It means Light of the Mountainside," he adds.

Chimeline and Colu argue inside the well house. Chimeline's voice is unusually raised.

"Go on," I urge.

He takes a deep breath and grabs his cane with both hands again. "There are sixty-seven of us. Twenty are lepers."

"It's a leper colony?" I ask in disbelief.

Looking down, he draws a line in the sand with his cane. "You could say that."

I take a step back.

"We keep the infected apart," he quickly adds. "They do not share water, food, or pits. I've lived there my entire life, and I am as healthy as the day I was born."

"Lepers are children of the Unnamed, Dem," Blythe says. "Their skin may be in decay, but their souls are pure."

"They are contagious," I answer, thinking back to my days at the university. "Even with voidance, we could only stop the spread if it was caught early. But if not . . ." I shake my head. "It's a horrible disease."

"Black arcana?" the elder asks sharply. "You're a black arcanist?"

I look at Blythe, hesitating. "No," I finally say. "I'm not." I don't feel that it's a lie.

The elder narrows his eyes. "Yet you casually speak of it."

"My friend was a black arcanist but is now on the way of unwanting," Blythe tells him.

"It is of no matter," I say, trying to defuse the situation. "Thank you for warning us, in case we come across your . . . village. We will travel past."

He looks at me with a scowl. "It is not the presence of lepers that worries me, Northerner. It is their *leaving*."

Blythe and I share a confused glance.

"We used to have twenty-three," the Xian man says. "But a black arcanist from al-Kimer-Vis came to visit. He convinced three to go with him in exchange for gold for their families. They were never to be seen again."

Shon.

He draws another line in the sand. "I am deeply worried that word may have gotten out."

"Word of what?" Blythe asks.

The elder purses his mouth, looking southwest.

Chimeline appears from around the corner and leans against the stacked stone. She's touching the side of her head, as if in pain.

"Excuse me," I say, pushing past him.

"Child," Blythe calls out to Chimeline from behind me. "Is something wrong?"

He follows me to the well house.

"Are you alright?" I ask, as I approach.

She nods. "It's fine."

I pull her hand away. There's some blood on it.

Leaning in, I gently part the hair on the side of her head, just over her ear. There's a gash.

"Dem, it's fine," she repeats. "I brushed the stone."

She takes deep breaths, as if trying to calm herself.

Leaving her side, I step over a frankincense tree's gnarled roots and turn the corner.

The open door lies before me. It was previously hidden from view. Inside is a circular well built of the same beige stones as the house and also stacked in the same crude manner.

Seemingly oblivious to my presence, Colu pulls upon the rope, hand over hand, water dripping generously off his brow.

I step out of the harsh daylight and into the shadows of the well house. Rays of sunlight make their way through the walls and dilapidated roof. Thin and curved yellow lines follow the contours of Colu's drenched face and body in the dimness.

"What did you say to her?" I ask him.

Colu ignores me and continues pulling upon the rope. The wooden bucket finally appears. Grabbing it with both hands, he takes a few gulps, letting most of it flow past his cheeks and onto his shoulders. Then he dumps the remainder over his head.

Behind me, Blythe and Chimeline quietly enter. The elder stands in the open doorway.

"Dem, it was nothing," Chimeline softly says.

He drops the bucket at his feet, stumbling a bit, and then leans against the wall to prevent himself from falling.

Finally, I notice his condition.

That bottle he's been nursing all morning wasn't filled with water.

"That's right," he says. "Be nothing."

"You're drunk," I tell him.

He points to Chimeline, slurring his words. "I'm the one trying to save her fucking life. Which is more than what you're doing."

The elder clears his throat. "Your Effulgency, may I have a word with you?"

"Your Effulgency!" Colu yells, bringing his hands to his head. "Fuck, that sounds good. You're an important man, Blythe!"

Blythe looks at the elder. "I apologize for his behavior. il-Colu tends to own the dark. He disappoints us every chance he gets."

The elder glances outside, looking conflicted.

Colu points to Chimeline. "That's what I was saying. You should learn from me instead of Dem. I'll save you a shit pile of heartache. Maybe save your life."

Chimeline turns her back to him.

He pushes himself away from the wall, wobbles a bit, then bows mockingly. "I could show you how to be a disappointment." He belches as he straightens up.

"il-Colu, I cannot believe you have been consuming that hideous drink," Blythe says.

"Shut up," he barks. Then he addresses Chimeline's back and softens his tone. "I'll let you in on a little secret," he says. "Once you disappoint someone so bad . . . you know . . . really fuck them over . . . you can do pretty much anything." He belches again. "I mean, the people around you, they've already given up on you, right? Once that happens, you're free. Can do whatever the fuck you want."

He laughs again, searching the ground. He picks up the bucket and motions to Chimeline. "We should call it the Way of Disappointment," he says, slurring the words.

The older Xian shakes his head. He holds his cane off the ground slightly, as if he's contemplating striking Colu.

"You are a fool and a drunkard, il-Colu," Blythe says. "The words coming out of your mouth make no sense."

"Don't you talk to me about sense, you ass," he shouts. "I heard enough of your shit on the way here." He motions again to Chimeline's back using the bucket. "Woman, I'm talking about you. About you being a weapon. You should tell the Unnamed to fuck off. And anyone else who thinks you should sacrifice yourself just because they think you're special."

Blythe gasps. "You mustn't speak of the Unnamed like—"

Colu interrupts him, his voice a deep shout. "le-Daerke is dead because she thought she was a weapon."

Nobody replies. In the distance, I hear a high-pitched cry of pain cut off by the sound of crunching gravel and sand. The crimsonhawk made another dive.

"Maybe I should leave," the elder says.

"Great idea," Colu answers, without meeting the man's eyes.

After a pause, the elder nods once then walks through the doorway and disappears around the corner. Blythe doesn't seem to notice.

"le-Daerke is dead because she was owning the dark," Blythe says, his voice soft but breaking. "Which undoubtedly she learned from you, il-Colu."

Colu laughs darkly. "Right."

"Everyone," I say, "let's just calm down. le-Daerke's death is nobody's fault."

Blythe's hands are shaking fists at his sides. "I've had enough," he says, turning away and storming out into the harsh sunlight. "I'm dumping that poison onto the barren ground, where it belongs."

"Don't you touch my canex!" Colu shouts out after him.

Through the narrow spaces in the stone wall, I see Blythe head toward the horses. "Sometimes one must resort to destruction to prevent destruction," I hear him say.

"You fucking ass." Colu spits and stumbles around the well with the bucket still in hand.

I attempt to get in his way.

"This poison has become a false god to you!" Blythe cries in the distance. I hear glass shattering against the stones.

"Get out of my way, Dem."

"Colu, you're drunk."

With a forearm, he roughly pushes me up against the doorframe. The back of my head hits the petrified wood hard.

I smell the canex on his breath, the sweet cinnamon and bitter clove. His one eye is dilated, meandering. "Your woman I could never hit. But you? That's another matter."

He exits the well house and immediately stumbles upon a root.

Colu falls to the ground. The wooden bucket shatters under his weight.

He doesn't rise. After a moment, it's apparent that he's knocked himself out.

Chimeline rushes to me and we stand together, my back against the doorframe, her head against my shoulder. I gently part her hair and check the side of her head. The bleeding has stopped.

She tightens her grip around my waist.

I hear Blythe rummaging through the wain, then the crystalline sounds of additional bottles being shattered.

Looking southwest toward the rising cliffs, I see that the elder Xian is already far away, his white robes blending with his horse. Distorted by heat waves, the hovering vision resembles nothing of this world.

Far above, his crimsonhawk floats upon the breeze with an effortlessness I envy.

I DON'T LIKE
THE STARS ANYMORE

"I can see the entire river," I tell Chimeline, pointing at the stars. They hide among red sparks from our dying fire.

"A river in the desert?" Under the thin woolen blanket she stirs sleepily in my arms, running her leg up against mine. "You've been drinking Colu's canex."

"No, look," I say playfully. "Up in the sky. It's so clear."

She rotates her body, taking her head off my chest and facing upward.

I continue to point. "That's O'Eridani, the End of the River. The true north." After a pause, I add, "See that trail of stars? The seven? That's the river. Back in the citadel, I could never see them."

"Because your head was buried in books," she says. She playfully pulls upon my chest hair, perhaps to take the sting of her words away.

I hear Blythe feeding the dog and horses with our supply from the wagon. He speaks to himself in Effulgian, a sound that is layered with the cool desert wind.

"Do you miss it?"

"Miss what?" I ask.

"Your home. The North."

"Not at all," I answer immediately, almost in recoil. "And it is no longer my home."

"Do you think you'll ever go back?"

Her question takes me off guard, and I spend a moment thinking it over.

"I don't know," I eventually say. "It just seems that the Northern Kingdom, its idiot king, the university, all of it . . . it's all so small now."

"Small?"

"The beginnings and endings of countries. Politics, war. None of it seems to matter anymore."

She doesn't respond, but she doesn't need to. Nobody has been more affected by recent events than Chimeline.

"The entire world has changed," I add.

"So have you and I," she whispers distantly.

"You're right," I reflexively respond. "Two months ago, I wouldn't have balked at the elimination of the effulgency. Now, I feel sorrow at what has been done to them. I pity all of those who are using the giving houses without understanding the evil lurking there."

She huffs next to me.

I try turning to her to meet her eyes, but her head is too close. "What is it?" I ask, confused.

She doesn't respond.

"Are you upset?"

"I didn't mean you and I *individually*," she says after a pause. "I meant *you and I*."

I open my mouth. "Oh."

Then her meaning rings clear.

"You know I meant what I said in the sewers," I tell her. "I love you."

"How romantic," she huffs again, the meager exhale audible in the quiet night. But she eventually wraps her hand tighter around my chest.

"The world may change around us, but you and I will be together to face it," she eventually adds. "Until the azuremen and marked are dead and giving houses destroyed and everything else is back to normal, there can be no . . . *normal* between us. It will have to wait. And hopefully there will be a time when everything is done that you and I can be together."

I keep staring at the stars as I speak. "When this is all over, no matter where you are, Chimeline, my place is by your side. I will never leave you."

She pauses and looks at me. "Even if I go to Scorpiontail?"

"No place will be too far. If it's Scorpiontail, then Scorpiontail will be my home."

She slaps my side playfully. "You're in luck. I was only testing you. I don't think I'll ever go back there."

I wonder if she can see me smile. "Well, wherever you decide to go, that will be my home."

She nestles into my shoulder. "Sounds like more dreaming to me."

"It's a promise. As sure as these stars above us."

But with the utterance of these last words, her mood seems to change. I feel her fingernails as she holds me tight.

"I don't like the stars anymore," she says.

"What do you mean?"

"That's where they came from. Even with Temberlain's visions, I still don't understand how it's possible." I feel the warmth of her breath on my skin. "How Mander could reach his countrymen from so far away. How they could sail across an entire ocean of stars."

"I don't know either."

"I can never look at them quite the same," she adds. "If they are home to such hideous things, I want no part of them. They no longer glitter for me."

Her words are wrapped in a stubbornness that is almost childlike, except that I empathize, and even respect her vulnerability. With all this change—horrible change, all going in the wrong direction—perhaps empty declarations are all that we have left.

"Maybe there are good people out there too," I tell her, trying to be optimistic.

"Then why aren't they here?" she replies. "Helping us?"

"I don't know. But across all that vastness out there, it stands to reason that there would be good as well as evil. It's probably no different from our lands here."

"I'll believe it when I see it."

I cannot think of anything else to say to brighten her spirits or lift the mood. Silence seems best, but soon even this is taken away, replaced by a bright and repeating sound in the night, almost like a wind chime.

"Dem and Chimeline," Blythe says from across our campsite, near the well house and wagon. "Please do not walk barefoot. Wear your sandals. There is broken glass in the sand." The tinkling sound continues. "I am picking up the big pieces, but there could still be some hiding."

Lattices.

"Actually, Blythe, could you bring one here?" I ask, leaning up slightly and propping myself up on my elbow.

"A piece of glass?" he says. He's stooped by the well house, bathed in a small sphere of lanternlight.

"Yes."

"What are you planning to teach me now?" Chimeline asks me.

I turn back to her and am silenced by her calmness, intelligence, and beauty. For a heartbeat all I can think about are the stars reflected in her black eyes.

We had a training session before dinner: reconstructing the bucket. The task of weaving indivisibles precisely together is one of the most difficult to master. She healed Colu's ribs days ago, but while the initial manipulations of the body require more finesse, the body is already intent on healing itself. Weaving inert indivisibles—wood and iron— is different. Dead things don't have a mind of their own.

"Lattices," I tell her.

Blythe approaches us by the dying fire and looks worriedly at Colu, who is sleeping faceup near the edge of the reddish glow.

I sit up further. Chimeline holds the blanket to her chest.

Blythe passes me a large shard of glass from one of Colu's broken bottles. "Is this what you wanted?"

"Yes, thank you," I say, reaching up to grab it. "It's perfect."

"Be careful," he says.

Chimeline sits up. "Blythe, why don't you join us by the fire?"

Blythe shuffles back a few steps. "No, thank you. I am going to sleep in the wagon with the palehound."

"You're sure?" she adds.

"I can abide being alone with the Unnamed." He looks up at the stars momentarily. "It seems that this is what is wanted of me." He bows slightly and leaves, but halfway to the wagon he turns around.

"You are sure il-Colu is alright?" he blurts out, then clears his throat. "He did not injure himself in his drunken fall?"

"He's fine," I assure him.

"But he has not stirred since midday."

"I looked him over when I was repairing the bucket," Chimeline answers. "Only his pride is damaged."

Blythe hesitates then nods, pointing to the fire. "I left a skewer of mutton and onion. He may be hungry when he wakes." Then he walks away.

"That's sweet," Chimeline whispers to me. "After all that Colu has done, Blythe still cares for him."

"It is the way of unwanting," I say, shrugging.

"I worry about him," she says distantly, watching his silhouette. Then she leans over to glance at the sleeping Colu. "I worry about both of them. They're both taking her death hard, in different ways."

"And so are you," I add.

She eventually nods once.

Blythe climbs into the wain and we're left fully alone. I give Chimeline ample time to speak more of le-Daerke, but only the cool wind blows. So I hold up the shard of glass in my hands. She and I sit facing each other, the blanket covering us from our waists down.

Carefully, I hand her the piece of glass. "I was thinking it would be good for you to study the indivisibles and lattice structures in this."

"Lattice structures?"

"The pattern in which indivisibles are bonded."

"Why?"

"So that you can understand the pattern and apply it to other materials in an emergency."

"I'm not sure I know what you mean."

I look around. Flat stones border the fire, creating a crude pit. They are seemingly the same stones the well house was built from.

"With stone, for example," I tell her.

I stand, walk over, and grab a stone from the square formation. It's at least ten pounds.

Setting it next to us and getting back under the blanket, I point to the glass in her hand. "A sharp object is just extremely thin. There's nothing much to it. Simply concentrated force on less surface area."

"Sounds easy."

I smile. "Not quite. What's critical is understanding the indivisibles of the material you're working with. Not everything can be sharp. It depends upon the lattice structures."

She looks at me expectantly.

I motion again to the shard. "When you enter the void, I want you to notice the composition of those indivisibles. Compared to, say . . ." I look around then pull upon the blanket. "Wool."

She nods.

"Back at the university, we used to teach that something can be cut when shear *strength* is less than shear *stress*. As opposed to, let's say . . . tensile stress."

"Tensile?"

"Pulling something apart."

I take her hand and gently pull upon the soft skin of her forearm. "Tensile strength represents how hard you can pull on something without it breaking apart." Next, I press the same area with my fingernail. "Shear strength represents how hard you can cut into it without it breaking. Some materials, like wool and skin, have high *tensile* strength and won't fail under that type of load but can be cut very easily, because shear stress is a different type of force entirely."

"I see."

"When it comes to cutting, or really any type of force, it's all about one energy overcoming another. And this energy is largely unseen and unexplained."

She wrinkles her nose.

I look up at the stars, extending my hands. "Look around us. Our entire creation is made up of indivisibles bonded into lattices. Why? What keeps them together? What keeps your indivisibles from simply coming apart? What keeps this entire world from coming apart?"

"Sometimes I feel that it *is* coming apart."

I smile sadly. "Yes, but it is an indisputable fact that something in the void is keeping everything together." I take a deep breath. "We cannot see this energy, but it's always there around us."

"The Unnamed," Chimeline whispers.

Her comment takes me off guard, and I think about it. Never in all my years have I heard such a theory from any student or teacher. It's impossible to prove, but also impossible to disprove.

"Maybe," I eventually say. "But that is beside the point. What I need you to understand, in case you have to do this in an emergency, is that life and death can come down to overcoming this energy that keeps these lattices together. And some lattices are stronger than others. Which is why even the sharpest of blades won't cut through Colu's armor. The lattices in armor are too strong, the bonds too deep."

She taps the broken glass with her fingernail. "Alright, I think I'm ready."

Taking a deep breath, I hesitate as the guilt returns. It is the same feeling I had fullbells ago.

"You're sure that this is alright with them?" I ask her.

She nods.

"It's just . . . I know that we're torturing them every time I teach you. Which is why I use words as much as I can. Theoretical—"

She places her hand on mine and gently squeezes it. "They understand, Dem. Pain is tolerable when there is a purpose."

After a moment, I nod. "Alright, then." I point to the piece of glass. "First, I want you to analyze the lattice structures in that shard, especially at the edges."

"Okay."

"Then, when you're ready, I want you to do two parallel manipulations of dynamic voidance. Like we did earlier. First, you're going to isolate the stone in front of you."

"You mean pack the air underneath."

"Yes," I say. "Just as you did with the bucket. Create a membrane underneath the stone and push the surrounding air indivisibles into that space. The membrane will grow in density and support the stone. But the stone is heavier than the bucket, so you'll need to add more than you did last time."

She swallows. "Then what?"

"With a second manipulation, I want you to hone the stone down. But pay attention to the lattices. How they fail under tensile stress and shear stress. It will be different."

She exhales. "Okay. I'll give it a try."

"Just listen for my voice," I tell her. "I know it's hard to hear—"

She glows white.

Instinctively, I shield my eyes with an outstretched hand, but then realize that the axionlight coming out of her is pale, soft. Nothing like at the nightmarket. More of an ebbing glow, an underwater luminescence, but white. I take this as a hopeful sign of her continued development. The brightness, I theorize, is somehow correlated to the degree to which she uses voidance. Or the degree to which she is overcome by it.

She raises the piece of glass so that it's directly in front of her face. It's hard to make out small details in her expression, but I can tell that her eyes are closed.

"Do you see the lattice structures at the edge?" I ask her.

She must not be able to hear me over the enervated.

Leaning in, I repeat the question, raising my voice slightly and talking directly into her ear. I wait for a response.

Instead of replying with her lips, she voidspeaks to me. YES, I SEE THEM.

Her voice echoes within my mind.

For a moment, I struggle to reply. I cannot voidspeak back to her. Nobody at the university ever taught such a thing. The only one ever to do it was Mander. My mind is suddenly caught up with its limitations.

I wonder who should be teaching whom.

"When you're ready, you can begin," I eventually tell her, the only way I know how—loudly, into her ear.

She doesn't voidspeak back. Instead, I feel air coursing past my fingers, headed into the membrane, becoming trapped. The flattened, rectangular stone I set down rises between us. A few heartbeats later, its surface begins peeling off repeatedly, translucent shavings fluttering to the ground. The sound is soothing—like an oiled whetstone being dragged across a metal blade.

After some time, she stops glowing and opens her eyes.

The heavy stone remains hovering in the night air between us, but more impressive is that the slow shaving continues, flakes still raining down.

I smile at her with pride. "Excellent. Now what do you feel?"

She wrinkles her nose. "Feel?"

I point at her heart. "Even though you've exited the void, there are two dynamic manipulations still tethered to you."

She looks up then nods. "Yes. I can feel it," she says. "Like a sliver underneath my skin. But everywhere."

"Exactly." I grab her hands and hold them tightly. "That sliver is vitally important, Chimeline. It's a reminder that your voidance is still occurring. Voidance that will affect your body if it's left unchecked."

"You mean voideath."

I purse my lips. "In a worst-case scenario."

From the well house, the horses suddenly complain. It's an uneasy sound, almost like discordant trumpets. A few of them raise their heads, pulling upon their leads. The iron rings clang out in the night as they fall back against the stone.

Chimeline turns around and peers into the darkness, the whites of her eyes clearly visible. "I wonder what's gotten into them."

Quickly, I scan the camp for signs of intruders. There's no movement besides that of the horses.

But then a low growl rumbles in the night, captured within a brief silence between the sounds of the stone's peeling and the horses' panic.

I sit up straighter.

"I think that's your answer," I mumble.

"Sounded like thunder."

"Except there's no storm."

Behind us, the horses' trumpeting escalates. They pull wildly at their tethers. From inside the wagon, the palehound begins to bark.

"What do you think is out there?" she whispers.

I squint into the darkness. Nothing is visible except the faraway silhouette of the southern mountains against the star-studded sky. I listen for any sound of movement or another growl, but it's impossible now. There's too much noise from the animals.

"Do you know anything about wild creatures in the deepsands?" Chimeline asks.

"Not especially." I turn in all directions, watching and waiting.

Then I see it.

Movement, directly on the opposite side of the campfire and past the frankincense trees, at the very edge of the ring of flickering light.

Something paces there. Something large.

The animal's back is almost as high as the branches on the gnarled trunks. Three feet off the ground, at least.

Just as quickly as it appeared, it vanishes into the night.

Recoiling in shock, I whisper a curse. I shove the blanket off me and crouch. "Temberlain's Ashes. Did you see that?"

Chimeline nods.

"That must be a . . . Xian mountain lion." I glance at the fire. The skewer of mutton. "It smells our dinner," I surmise. "Or maybe the horses."

"Or maybe us."

Very close to where the beast appeared, Colu lies asleep.

Blythe pushes back the canvas covering the rear of the wain. "What's going on?" he asks loudly.

"We've got company," I say.

I place a hand under Chimeline's armpit, trying to urge her up. "Let's get up slowly. Retreat to the wagon."

"What about Colu?"

"I'll come back for him once we get you to safety."

But before we can take a step, the animal bounds into the weak reddish glow with unfathomable quickness, teeth bared, nostrils flaring.

The creature is massive.

It's only twenty feet away from us—and half that distance to Colu. I get the sense that it could easily reach us in another jump. Instead, it claws the sand a few times.

Chimeline glows white.

She cuts off her dynamic manipulations. The hovering stone falls to the ground. The shaving stops.

Chimeline's axionlight grows even brighter. It eclipses the reddish hue, pushing the visibility outward a vital few feet in harsh waves of white.

More details present themselves. The beast's coat is the color of sand and its fur is short except for around its neck. The cat's underside is white, and its tail is black and impressively long—almost as long as its body.

"Good Unnamed," I hear Blythe say from the wagon.

Chimeline inhales sharply, her entire body tensing.

Simultaneously, the mountain lion lets out a high-pitched whimper. It whips its tail forcefully into the sand a few times—the sound of a bass drum being struck—then collapses. I feel a soft reverberation in the ground.

Kneeling, I glance between the two of them raptly, not wanting to disturb whatever voidance Chimeline's using.

It doesn't seem to be physical. I see no blood coming from the beast.

Her lips move. I lean in, trying to catch her words. But she's not speaking to me.

She's repeating the same cryptic, whispered phrase, over and over again, until it's just breath coming from her. The words disappear.

The cat and Chimeline seem to be entwined in some dance of the mind. A strange intimacy between two consciousnesses. Chimeline's eyes are closed, but I see furious movement behind her shining eyelids. She moans and stumbles, putting a hand on the ground, but still she looks at the creature from behind shut eyes, refusing to lose contact. Refusing to yield.

She's voidspeaking with it?

Chimeline raises her right hand. Her brightness surges.

The mountain lion's legs flail, as if caught in a seizure. A dream perhaps, where it's running away—or toward us.

Within a few heartbeats, it is still.

Chimeline's chest rises and falls.

Slowly, the mountain lion stretches, whips its tail— weakly this time—then rises upon all fours.

It paces in a circle, stumbling, as if learning to walk for the first time. Then it gracefully walks away into the darkness.

Chimeline's axionlight suddenly cuts off, and she collapses into my arms.

THE LAST FACE
TO BE FORGOTTEN

A shuffling of skeletons. Bones rattling against bones.
Where do they all go when their souls are taken?
Inside the black box.
It was right there in front of you, the entire time.
A fool who becomes wise too late is still a fool.
I sit up straight, startled awake.
Colu stands before me, a stack of wood at his feet.
It's dawn.
Chimeline sleeps a few feet away, swallowed in blankets.
Finding her buried face, I put my hand to her forehead, but
her skin feels normal. Her breath is brief fog in the cold
desert morning, disappearing the instant it's born. Her
mysterious injury from yesterday on the side of the head is
wiped clean, yet some fresh scrapes remain.

Colu glances at me but says nothing. He stoops to rebuild
the fire. Clearing the gray ash first, he then methodically
places the sticks from the pile he's just laid down. Dead
parchment-colored brush fills the center. Flint sparks.
Kneeling, he blows with cupped hands. Finally, he leans
over and grabs the leftover skewer of mutton from the low
wall of stone and places it over the wood.

As the first crackles spark, I look at Chimeline again, at
peace and oblivious to what happened fullbells ago.

When she wakes, will she want to talk about it?

Days ago, the answer would have been a definite no. I would have had to pull the details out of her until the point of argument.

But ever since le-Daerke died, she's shown a marked change in behavior. From avoidance to acceptance. Even more than acceptance. She has seemingly embraced her newfound power.

As the fire grows in front of me, so does a fear.

I should be excited about this change. After all, we don't stand a chance against the azuremen without her.

But what is her deeper motivation? What's going on inside of that head, behind her dark eyes, beneath those black currents of hair?

Sometimes I think it resembles a war.

It's as if it's one or the other with her. It's either our love or axionlight, and we can't have both. One has to win. She said last night that there were no point to her dreams.

Our love.

Colu sits in the sand opposite me and drinks from a skin. I know that it contains water because Blythe got rid of all the alcohol.

Behind him, the sky is cloudless and bursting with color, like a pane of glass from one of the effulgency temples. At least before they were all shattered. I'm looking east, directly at the sun, but it's so low on the horizon that I'm able to stare at it without squinting. Reds bleed into yellows, further into purples and blues. Directly overhead, the stars are still out. The moon sits behind me.

"Sorry about yesterday," Colu says weakly.

I draw my attention back to him.

Colu brings a hand to his temple, and it trembles ever so slightly. He seems aware of this, so he suddenly leans forward and reaches for the skewer, turning it once over the fire. As his breath escapes, it's ragged.

Eventually, he looks up at me with one red eye.

"Forget it," I say.

We sit in silence for maybe a tenthbell, just the two of us, as the fire cracks and wakens. Soon, the smells of mutton and onion mingle amid the woodsmoke.

Far across the camp, the palehound jumps out of the wagon, shortly followed by Blythe, who climbs out slowly.

"I thought I smelled something," he says. He stretches and turns toward the sun. "What a blessed morning."

Colu swears under his breath then rises, walking over to him.

Left alone with Chimeline, I check on her again, but she's still fast asleep. When I look up, I see Blythe and Colu conversing. Colu looks at his feet while Blythe rests his hand on the man's shoulder.

I reach into my pocket and take out Marine's stone, wrapped in emerald.

If not now, when?

Slowly, I unwrap the fabric.

When I hesitantly reveal it to the light of day, black ash covers everything. There's even more than last time. It falls away from both the stone and the fabric. But *fall* isn't the right word. It's too light to collect around my feet. Even with no breeze it simply floats away in all directions, becoming one with the air. I try to catch one of the specks but it's impossible.

What remains of the stone is the size of a grape—half of what it was before.

"What is happening?" I mumble.

Bringing a fist to my mouth, I bite my finger in fear and confusion.

I enter the void.

Dem, you've returned.

I hear Marine's ethereal voice, but I'm not listening. It's been so long since I've been in the void, I'm distracted by my very presence. This secret world repulses and captivates me at the same time.

Because she's the only soul in this stone, what I see is almost nothing. Only the murky indivisibles directly in front of me. I search for the glistening forms of Chimeline, Blythe, and Colu, but none of them are discernible. All detail further than an arm's length away is lost to the colorlessness, as if I'm swimming near the bottom of a deep lake.

However, I do see ash.

I float in close, picking out one of the black specks at random, then move in closer. Closer. Following it before it meanders away. If this were any other substance, I'd be seeing the lattice structures by now. But all I see is black. It fills my vision, as if I'm about to delve. To do eleutheria. Yet I cannot enter it as I would a voidstone. It's right here in front of me, but . . . not. A black door, closed forever.

This room has gotten so large. It's like a palace.

This time, Marine's voice has the power to pull me away. The speck of ash shrinks from view and the random indivisibles return.

What room, Marine?

The white one. What other room is there?

I don't have an answer for that, so my thoughts take me to my reason for being here—my reason for facing Marine once again.

I truly think that it is time for you to leave now, Marine. You have stayed long enough in this prison. Chimeline is strong—you have taught her well—and there are new dangers that threaten you. This very voidstone is breaking apart. I do not know how, but it is . . . shrinking.

Shrinking? How curious.

Every time I check it, there's black ash everywhere. Ash that floats away. Your stone is about half the size it was when you were placed in soteria.

Chimeline said something about ash.

If I could nod in this place, I would. *Are you ready, then?*

But instead of answering me, she changes the subject.

Dem . . . I try to remember the Royal House, the sound of birds . . . the sound of the choir singing . . . your curtains that I burned . . . but I can't picture any of them anymore. I've forgotten them all.

I pause, unsure what her point is. Perhaps this is her way of preparing for leaving.

I've forgotten the sky, Dem. Its color. I've forgotten all the colors of your world. They've faded from my memory and have become nothing more than words.

She doesn't sound frustrated—or even sad. Her tone is one of introspection.

Looking down, I stare at my glistening hand with the black voidstone in its center.

Is that what happens in this place? I ask. *Have the other enervated forgotten their worlds as well?*

She laughs, bell-like, at my question, as if it's absurd. *I think that forgiving and forgetting are somewhat the same. If you really forgive, you are able to just let it go. You give it away, as the effulgents teach. What is it? That phrase of theirs.*

Be nothing.

Yes! Be nothing. It floats away. Your fears. Your anger.

I pause as her somewhat disjointed point begins to sink in.

Ah, so you're saying that you've been able to let go of your past. And now that you have, you're ready to move on.

I feel her lightheartedness—if such a thing exists in this place—disappear. It's replaced with a new emotion: red-hot anger. When she speaks again, her voice surrounds me like a cyclone of wind, so close that I jump in place, almost losing contact with the voidstone.

How dare you. You act as if this is easy.

Confused, I hold out a hand apologetically, which she cannot see. *Marine, I'm just trying to under—*

Stop trying to convince me to leave, Dem. You're not performing eleutheria for me, you're doing it for you. Oh, I'm sure it would be so convenient to have me gone, once and for all, wouldn't it? No longer would you have to struggle with the guilt that eats at you every day. You would be free of me. No more weight to carry around.

I frown. *Guilt eating at* me?

I used to be so angry at Mander. At my father. Now I don't even remember Northinglight. I don't even remember Winter's Baiou. And I cannot even see Mander's face. The only face I see is yours, Dem. I cannot let it go. I cannot forgive you.

I am the one who should be forgiving you! I reply. *You made a fool of me! And not just for any man—*

You made a fool of yourself. Do not deny your failures, Dem.

Whatever my failures were, I acknowledge them. But there's something wrong with you if you can forgive a monster like Mander but not me.

Oh, I see. So everything is always my fault. I'm still a child, apparently.

We share a silence, and then I reply.

Look, after you left me, I crossed the entire Northern Kingdom for you.

Right, Dem. And then what? You ran into the arms of the first beautiful woman you found who's half your age. Even though she was sent to kill you.

Marine—

The real tragedy of it all is that she truly loves you—probably even more than I did. And just like me, the only thing you have to offer her is 20 percent of your attention. Just enough for her to keep you warm in the night and for you to teach her the void.

That's just not true. I love Chimeline.

You love the idea of love. Just like you loved the idea of sending your students into the world. But it ends there. You offer her nothing. You give her nothing.

No, Marine. If anything happened to her—

You wouldn't even notice. After a short pause, she continues. *It's time that you take responsibility for your actions, Dem. For all of it.*

All of what? I ask, appalled.

Her reply is immediate, as if she has spent all her time in soteria perfecting it. *The rise of Mander. You pushing me away—pushing me into his arms. What happened to me in the Celestium. What happened to Chimeline. What happened to the effulgents. It's all your fault.*

Her voice is everywhere at once, but she's not shouting. Her words are as smooth and oiled as a blade entering the small of my back. And suddenly, I'm caught within their reverberations.

Somewhere back in the world of the sun, the moon, and the stars, I envision the effulgency bells, hanging still. In that world, time has been stolen. Gone is the fullbell of the common man.

But here, time is beyond reach. It always has been.

I don't know how long I remain swallowed by black, within the void and within my own tormented thoughts. Everything she said is true, but also false. Why can't she see that I'm trying my best to make amends? To do right because of all of these wrongs? Surely that deserves more forgiveness than the pure evil of Mander's vision.

Marine, how many times do I need to tell you that I'm sorry?

You used me, Dem. Just like you used the enervated. We are one and the same. We always were, even when I had a body.

What in Temberlain's Ashes are you talking about?

You abused your position of power.

No. I recoil. *You were the one who sought me out. You were the one who used your beauty and charm to get what you wanted. You knew exactly what you were doing every step of the way.*

And you were the master voider. I was the student. You should have known better. You used me for your pleasure and prestige. You took my body and discarded it when you had more important things to do. Just as you tortured the enervated your entire life by embracing voidance. I was a touch away when you needed it.

You're not being fair and you know it.

Don't talk to me about fairness, Dem. Is this white room fair?

I let go in disgust.

This time, the sunlight doesn't help warm my body. It only reveals what was once hidden.

Three colored, hazy ellipses slowly transform into my friends. They sit around the campfire speaking spiritedly but become quiet as they notice my return.

I take gasping breaths. My hand, which holds the voidstone, shakes uncontrollably.

Good Unnamed. Is Marine right?

"Dem, what's wrong?" Chimeline asks.

She sits on the sand next to me, still wrapped in her blankets while eating scrambled eggs with her fingers. I'm happy to see that she's awake but also desperate to change the subject. All three stare at me in concern.

Focusing on keeping my hands as still as possible, I carefully wrap up Marine's voidstone and put it away.

I still feel everyone's gaze.

"Nothing," I eventually say, staring up at the sky to avoid them. The sun is noticeably higher. I shield my eyes with an outstretched hand. "Just that Marine still won't leave."

I glance back at Chimeline. She doesn't look convinced but thankfully drops the topic. Giving me a forced smile, she briefly raises her plate. "Colu made breakfast. You should have some too before he eats it all."

She's right. I feel dizzy—some food may help.

Nodding, I lean forward, and Blythe hands me a banged-up pewter plate.

As I shovel in a handful of eggs, I realize that my body is indeed famished, yet the eggs have no taste. It's as if I'm in soteria with Marine, forgetting what savoring food is like. Forgetting what colors are like. All is gone in her world except for me.

The last face to be forgotten.

Blythe sighs discontentedly. "We must pray on this more. For Marine's sake."

I don't say anything.

"Is there a reason why she won't get the fuck out of there?" Colu says, pointing to my pocket.

I look down at my plate of eggs, full of confusion and a bit of self-loathing.

Could it be true? Did I use her like I used the enervated? Is my entire life one of perversion? Am I using Chimeline now?

I've always believed that I'm a good man. At least I've tried to be. But if a good man does nothing, is that evil? If a good man uses ignorance as a shield, amorality as armor, does that change the side of the battlefield upon which he stands?

Chimeline fills the silence. "Marine is still working things out, Colu."

He's in the middle of drinking from his waterskin. He spits out whatever's in his mouth. "You women. Even in death you make no sense."

I swallow another bite but taste nothing.

Blythe clears his throat awkwardly. "Dem, I was just telling il-Colu about the mountain lion from last night."

Finally, something else to discuss. I glance at the two of them. "Yes. It was . . . quite the scene." As I swallow another bite, I try to gauge Chimeline's mood. She seems content to speak about it, nodding in interest as well.

"Do you know anything about them?" I ask Colu.

"Xian mountain lions?"

I nod.

"Why you asking me? Because I'm Xian?"

I shrug. "I guess so. They're indigenous—"

"You forget that I've wasted the last few years of my life freezing my ass off in the North. And before that, I was crammed on a galleon like a pickled sardine. Not wandering the deepsands."

After a pause he continues, waving his hand back and forth. "Anyway, I don't know much about them. Just that they're man-eaters. Horse-eaters too."

I nod then finish my eggs and set my plate on the ground.

"Speaking of horses," Colu says, standing. "I need to piss like one. Thanks for saving our asses again," he says to Chimeline, while meandering toward the frankincense trees.

"Ah," Blythe says, pointing up at nothing in particular. "If I may say—"

"I know, I know," I interrupt, before Colu can respond. "We owe our lives to the Unnamed. No one else."

He smiles. "Very well said, my friend."

Chimeline sets her plate on the ground next to mine and shrugs. "It was nothing, really. I was simply trying to voidspeak with it."

"Voidspeak?" I ask. "With an animal?"

"Why not?" she replies. "We talk to dogs and horses all the time. I thought that maybe voidspeaking with it might help."

I hear Colu's piss hitting the sand in the distance.

She holds her hands out in front of her defensively. "I just didn't want to kill it, alright?" she says, raising her voice slightly. "I didn't want any more blood being spilled with voidance."

I nod. "What was it like?"

She takes a deep breath. "When you voidspeak, you enter the person's mind. You have to do this in close proximity first, before voidspeaking over distances. You need to find that special place on the left side, inside their skull." She shakes her head quickly, as if to get rid of a memory. "Mander did it to me when he was experimenting. I felt that exact place inside my own mind, so I knew where to look for it." She gazes at me with an expression that borders on guilt. "That's how I knew how to voidspeak with you."

"It's okay," I tell her. "Go on."

She turns toward Blythe. "So, I did the same thing with the animal, but when I found the place, I sort of . . ." She glances back at me. "Normally, when you do this with a person, there's a tension on both sides." She wrinkles her nose. "A give and take. But with the mountain lion, there was nothing of the sort. I pushed through."

"So once you did this, you were able to talk to it?" I ask slowly.

She shakes her head. "I . . . *became* it. Part of it, anyway."

"What do you mean?"

"I could see what it saw. I felt its hunger. I smelled us. The horses. The animal was very far from home. It was hunting." She takes a deep breath and looks down, bringing in the blankets tighter. "I willed it to leave. But the interesting thing is, when it walked away, I stayed with it for a while and could see through its eyes before finally breaking off."

She continues staring at the sandy ground while Blythe and I share a worried glance.

"Hey!" Colu yells out, by the trees. "Come over here."

"We don't need to see," I say. "I'm sure you pissed more than the horses."

"No," Colu says. "There's writing over here. In the sand."

Blythe, Chimeline, and I look at one another then rise and walk around the dying fire.

As we approach, Colu backs up to let us in.

Blythe inhales sharply.

Chimeline and I exchange a glance before I read the message once again.

THE EFFULGENT YOU SEEK IS WITH US.

LIGHT OF THE MOUNTAINSIDE

By late afternoon we have progressed further southwest, out of the sandy lo-Kimer foothills and up against the heart of the range. Our trail hugs a sheer limestone cliff to our left, lit up in burnt orange under the slowly sinking sun. Every halfbell or so, the trail breaks. We pass entrance after entrance into a gargantuan maze of twisting valleys and deep canyons. Each of these canyons is about a hundred feet wide and many more hundreds of feet high. Sand bottomed, shadow filled, meandering, they are a wasteland leading to more waste. Like one of the garden mazes at the palace except not fashioned by man. To the north—our right—the sand continues into the bleached horizon, which is dotted with low brush and frankincense trees.

"This isn't a heart," I say, as our horses trot past another blue-tinged canyon entrance hidden from the sun. "It's a mind."

"Hmm?" Chimeline says distractedly, from atop her chestnut-colored mare. Her face is surrounded by a white sheet. Only a few unkempt trails of black hair are visible.

Motioning back to the cavern, I explain. "Colu keeps saying that we're in the heart of the lo-Kimer mountains. But this place looks more like a mind to me."

"A mind?" She wrinkles her nose.

I tap my covered head with a finger. "You know the way it looks in the void? Twisting coils, deep folds past the skull?"

She nods slowly. "Ah. Yes, I understand what you mean."

"We're never gonna find this leper colony," Colu yells from the front. A moment later, his voice echoes, as if the maze is mocking him.

Blythe straightens his back while balancing in the saddle of his white Xian horse. The covered wain almost blocks my view of him. "I normally do not prefer names," he says, "but *le-Mon-Sogara* is far more elegant than the filth spewing out of your mouth."

"I just don't know why he couldn't write more in the sand," Colu grumbles. "Like draw a map or something. Or how about just tell us."

"You are the only one to blame, il-Colu. I have given up this anger to the Unnamed, and I suggest you do as well."

Colu laughs as we leave the canyon entrance behind. The somewhat-cooler air from the shadows is replaced by sun-scorched waves, and I pull my white sheet further over my head.

"I'm sorry," Chimeline says, guiding her horse even closer to mine. "I should have warned you."

I flash her a confused glance. "About what?"

"Marine." She raises an eyebrow. "Her . . . condition."

I stare into the bleached horizon as I remember their strange bond. Part of Chimeline is always in the void. "Her condition? You mean the fact that she hates me?"

Chimeline doesn't respond, and I let out a sardonic laugh, still unable to fully process my and Marine's previous conversation. "I mean, she's forgiven *Mander*. But not me."

"Give her time, Dem."

"Time? You honestly think time is going to help? I think time is making things worse."

She opens her mouth but doesn't say anything.

"She accused me of *using* her. Of abusing the power of my station."

"I know."

I shake my head at the absurdity of it all. "She leaves me, for a madman, and *she's* the victim?"

"I know," she repeats. "I heard."

I pause, somewhat surprised. "You heard?"

She nods.

"Of course you did." I look away feeling a mix of annoyance and embarrassment.

"Dem," she says softly. "Despite what you may think, she is working things out. She's learning to let go."

I scoff at that, but Chimeline's cautious tone betrays the sureness of her words.

"Just trust me. She needs time, that's all."

I let out a deep sigh. I do trust Chimeline. In some ways, she knows Marine far better than I ever did. Perhaps she has a more accurate read on the situation.

She stretches in her saddle, arching her back. The sheet briefly falls to her hips before she pulls it back up again.

I have no idea what it's like for Marine to be trapped in that voidstone with nothing more than memories. Stuck with all the various hurt that happened to her in her life. Those memories are floating away, but not the anger. It moved, transformed. It has been refocused. Now it has all converged on one person. Like sunlight directed through a curved glass.

A fresh wave of scorched wind hits me, radiating off the rock to my left. I envision it as Marine's hate—as if I am an insect underneath a voidance-shaped lens, squirming before I smolder to death.

Another break in the cliff lies ahead, but this one is wide enough for the sun to penetrate. The blue shadows fall upon only one side of the cavern, but they are still large enough to contain all of us.

"I'm going to the shade," I say to her.

I give my horse a strong kick, eager to get away from the sun's godlike wrath—out from under this unforgiving glass.

"Good idea," Colu says, as I pass. "Could use a stretch as well."

"The palehound requires water," Blythe adds.

"I thought that hound of yours was on the way of unwanting," Colu says.

"Animals do not know the way, il-Colu. They do not have the power to make that choice." The corner of his mouth twitches slightly. "You, on the other hand, have the ability to choose but lack the wisdom. Better to be this palehound than to be a man wallowing in foolishness."

"Fuck you."

"Colorful language will never fill the void within you, il-Colu. Only through the way of unwanting will you find inner peace."

Colu spits. "I'll show you inner peace."

As the sounds of their arguing are lost in the swirling wind and sand, I cross over into the blue shade. Dismounting in exhaustion, I put my back against the cool rock and slip down into a sitting position.

Something far away to the right, deep within the canyon, catches my eye.

Just before the twisting maze of rock hides it completely, just before the wrath of the sun is replaced by a field of blue and purple, something far up on the mountainside glitters. A gem set atop velvet.

le-Mon-Sogara.

TAKEN AWAY

"You sure this is the place?" Colu asks, as he pulls back on his impatient horse's reins while Blythe disconnects the wain. "Ain't no way Gemface got his wagon up here."

We stand at the trailhead. The rocky path leading up the sheer face of the cliff is clearly too narrow for anything but one horse at a time. I count at least thirty switchbacks.

"He might not have had to," I say, as I lean forward in my saddle, peering around the curved face of the rock that continues past the trailhead. The narrowing sand-bottomed valley disappears into deepening shades of blue. "He could have hidden the Axiondrive anywhere in these canyons."

Colu groans in agreement. The sound is quickly swallowed by a gust of wind—hot and dry, coming in from the sun-bleached stretches to the south.

I look for wagon tracks in the sand. There are none. Even ours are disappearing in the wind.

"Look," Chimeline says, pointing straight up.

I squint as the white covering falls off my face. But I don't need it anymore. We're in the shade.

Far above, a crimsonhawk circles near the glimmering peak.

Heavy chains softly rattle as they fall to the sand.

"Should we just leave the wagon here, then? For someone else to use?" Blythe asks, standing back up and leaning against the covered wain. Despite being sheltered from the sun, his face is covered in sweat.

"Yes," I say.

Colu shakes his head. "That cost me hundreds."

"And it served us well," I say. "Listen, if it's any consolation, it will probably still be here if we return this way."

"Take the dried mutton and fruits," Colu says to Blythe.

"I have gathered up everything that can be given away," Blythe says, pointing to his saddle bags. "To the least fortunate who await us above."

Colu stares at Blythe with a narrowed eye. "Just so you know, I bought all this shit with gold that I found on that cunt who killed your daughter. So you give it to whoever the fuck you want. But it's tainted with blood money."

The palehound jumps out of the wain as Colu's words echo.

"All money is blood money, il-Colu," Blythe says softly. "If you don't know this by now, you are beyond hope."

Colu grabs the hilt of his sword.

"Let's go," I tell them. "I want to get to the top before the sun goes down."

And before you kill each other.

A singular crystalline sound reaches us above gusts of wind that are getting progressively colder.

"That's a leper," Chimeline says. "I heard the same ringing in al-Kimer-vis."

"Then we are near," Blythe adds, fearfully guiding his horse close to the rock face. "Thank the Unnamed."

I nod as I look down and to the right. The trail's edge is perilously close.

We're at least a few hundred feet above ground.

Over my shoulder, the sun is low on the horizon, red and weak. I use my high vantage point to study the labyrinthine valleys below—meandering purple veins surrounded by a field of cracked orange. There isn't a soul around. No tracks, no sign of humanity.

The structure of the rock to my left has been changing during our climb, like the layers in a master baker's cake. Gone is the matte umber that makes up the rest of this mountain range. Instead, creamy white stone surrounds us. Every so often a glasslike ribbon is mixed in, looking like folded candied sugar.

I run my hand across the strange surface. "This must be why this place glitters from afar."

"It's limestone," Colu says. "Soft as butter."

The trail widens as the ground begins to level off. For the first time in fullbells, we all ride side by side.

As we reach the summit, the cliff-top village of le-Mon-Sogara reveals itself and we stop.

Looking on, I'm reminded of the strangeness of al-Kimer-vis—how the buildings in that trading town seemed built out of the sand. There were no straight lines. Everything curved as if formed by the wind. It's now evident that those buildings were all human-made, built out of brick and stone and plaster. al-Kimer-vis was complex but trying to look simple.

le-Mon-Sogara is the opposite.

The buildings here were not built up but taken away. Carved from the very mountain, everything is formed with utilitarian straight lines. The roofs are gently sloped and flat, the windows small, square, and open to the dry air. No glass or wire screens. No silk banners or tented awnings. The only fabric I see are some drying shirts and tunics strung up on ropes between limestone walls.

This is a town that had no other choice but to be simple, caught within a realm of complication.

Our trail opens onto a fifty-by-fifty-foot square surrounded by a dozen small buildings in odd, asymmetric places. In the center is a small tower—an obelisk of limestone with a bell perched atop and a lonely altar at its base, exposed to the sky.

The smell of charcoal smoke makes my mouth water.

The ringing sound is getting louder.

The most striking detail of all lies on the far side of the square. I get the sense of openness. Deep green shadows lie beyond the furthermost structures.

Green?

After a moment, I realize that another canyon exists there as well. This entire village is a narrow plateau perched between *two* valleys—the one we climbed up using the switchback and a second canyon, which until now had been hidden from view.

A few budding trees, whose roots miraculously escape from cracks in the stone, line the far side, and a dense vine covers a stairway whose steps are hewn from the rock. I blink repeatedly, as if seeing a mirage. The verdant color is a stark contrast to the otherwise barren surroundings.

There must be water nearby.

Of course! This remote village couldn't exist without it.

A solitary leper, one arm and one leg wrapped entirely in fresh white bandages, emerges from between two buildings, a bell tied around his wrist. He doesn't see us. A small goat follows him.

Seeing them, the palehound runs up ahead.

But it stops in place when it gets ten feet away, sniffing the air hesitantly with a raised head.

It smells the rot.

I raise a hand in a friendly greeting, but the Xian leper looks surprised and fearful. He surveys us with wide eyes. He begins shaking his bell forcefully, causing a shrill, unbroken sound to permeate the square.

"Well that's great," Colu mutters.

Blythe dismounts and rummages through his saddlebag. After pulling out a bundle of dried meat tied off with twine, he leaves his horse and approaches the leper directly. His white sheet falls to his shoulders.

"Be nothing!" Blythe calls out above the din.

A dark face emerges in a small window on the left side of the square.

Then another on the right.

"Your Effulgency!" the leper says, taking a few steps back near the obelisk. He drops to the limestone ground and kneels. "It is not safe for you," he yells, his face to the ground. "I am not worthy of your entering under my roof!"

"Under my roof?" I ask no one in particular.

"It's a Xian saying," Colu says distractedly, as he shakes his head. "A greeting to someone you respect."

People begin filling the spaces between buildings. More faces emerge, all Xian. Beyond corners or low walls of stone, the villagers look on with interest.

I count at least two dozen before remembering what the old man said. The population of this town is sixty-something, of which around twenty are lepers.

Blythe stoops at the leper's side and gently places the bundle of meat in front of the man. "We are all worthy in the eyes of the Unnamed. Each and every one of us."

"Move aside!" yells a woman in the distance, the harshness disrupting Blythe's soothing voice. "Move aside!"

Near the far-right corner of the square, from the vine-covered stairway, comes a middle-aged woman. She storms into the clearing muttering complaints and then stops once she sees us. She wears a flowing sheet that matches the light-gray limestone, but her face is uncovered. Deep wrinkles surround her yellow eyes. Her thick and unkempt black hair is tied back in a braid.

"Fuck me," Colu mutters, then dismounts and walks back toward the cliff edge.

Blythe looks up from the leper. Because his back is to me, I cannot see his expression, but a smile crosses the woman's face, as evident as any ray of sun entering a curtain-drawn room. She takes a step toward him.

Blythe stands. "Dearest woman," he says. "Blessed be the Unnamed, for I have been guided here to you." He walks toward her, but instead of embracing her, as I was expecting, he takes her hands in his and they bow their heads together, their foreheads touching.

For a moment, nobody makes a sound. Then the woman raises her head and looks at the rest of us, frowning in confusion.

"Is our graycloak not traveling with you on the way of unwanting?" she asks Blythe. "I do not want, for I do not own the dark. Yet I must confess, so long have I wanted this one thing. To lay my eyes upon her."

Blythe lets go of her hands and finally pulls her into a tight embrace. The look upon her face is one of absolute confusion. And perhaps a little fear.

Chimeline leans over in her saddle. "Who is that?" she whispers.

I motion with my head. "That's Blythe's . . . I'm not sure what the term is. Chosen mate?"

For a moment, Chimeline processes my words. Then, she inhales sharply and brings a palm to her mouth, finally understanding. "Good Unnamed. That's le-Daerke's mother."

LAKE

With Blythe following the closest, le-Sante silently leads us past the obelisk and in the direction of the darkened green shadows at the far edge of town. She doesn't move in the same hectic manner as she arrived. Her gray cloak dances with the warm, soft tones of the setting sun. The storm in her has passed. All that remains is a flood.

After passing a dozen buildings and several onlookers crammed into narrow alleyways, we turn a corner around a hewn wall.

Chimeline sighs in awe. Even Colu lets out a groan of surprise.

Down a stepped limestone pathway, the entire rear side of le-Mon-Sogara is covered in verdant plant life.

Dry grass carpets the sand. A half dozen white-flowering trees stand at the bottom of the stairs. Limestone benches have been placed underneath their low branches, and there's a small fire nestled in the center of them. An old man tending it turns in our direction, and I recognize him from the well house. The one with the crimsonhawk.

He gives us a hesitant nod.

Past the trees, the cliff falls away into the second canyon, which was only hinted at from the obelisk. The other side of the crevasse is close—perhaps fifty feet away—and is covered in patches of hanging vines as well as the same umber stone found everywhere else. A miraculous trickle of water comes out of a crack and flows down the mountainside. I hear the luxurious sound of it falling into water hidden from view.

I take a few cautious steps down the limestone stairs toward the trees and benches and then walk past them, toward the edge. I smell the sweet bouquet of white flowers above as I look down.

It's too dark to make out any details. The dying sun cannot make its way in, although some yellow light flickers hundreds of feet below. Weak and amorphous shadows move against the far rock wall.

"You must be tired from your journey," le-Sante says to all of us, extending a hand to an empty bench. "Please, sit. I will bring nourishment, provided by the Unnamed." Even though her words are kind, her tone rings hollow.

"Do you need help?" Blythe asks, almost clinging to her instead of sitting.

She extends a palm. "No, Your Effulgency," she says coolly, before walking away. When she reaches Colu, she pauses briefly but says nothing. She keeps walking.

Still squatting by the fire, the old man cups his hands and blows. Flames spring to life. "Not sure you would find this place."

I glance back to the top of the limestone stairs. le-Sante disappears around the corner.

Sitting down on a bench where I can easily face the old man, I lean forward, my elbows on my knees. Chimeline sits next to me while Colu takes the bench next to Blythe's, on the opposite side of the fire.

"Where is he?" I ask the old man directly. "The effulgent Chireseal."

The elder stares at the fire while he replies. "It is not my place to answer that question."

I exhale in annoyance. "Why not? You clearly meant for us to find him."

He points at Blythe. "I meant for the effulgent to find him. Not you."

"It is alright, my son," Blythe says. "We are all on the way together."

The old man briefly clenches his jaw then nods once, like some reprimanded child. "I don't know him by a name. But he matches your earlier description."

"So he *is* here, then."

The old man ignores me. "I only revealed this because of you, Your Effulgency," he says. "I thought that, despite the company you keep, you had a right to know. Even though I took a vow to keep it locked within my heart."

"You did well, my son," Blythe says. "Secrets are funny little things. Most people harbor them like they clutch their purses of gold. But if the secret you own is the truth, then the truth must be freely given—"

"What about his wagon?" I ask the old man, silencing Blythe with an extended hand. "Is it here too? There was a large black rock inside of it."

The old man looks shocked that I interrupted Blythe, but he says nothing. Instead, he cranes his neck, peering over the edge of the grass-covered cliff and then back to the top of the stairs. "That is for the stemma to answer."

"Stemma?" I ask. "What is that?"

He scowls at me through the flames. "Not *what*. *Who*."

"He means le-Sante," Blythe says.

I frown in confusion.

Blythe tilts his head from side to side, as if embarrassed to speak about it. "It's a word used to describe her special role. She blessed me with a graycloak and is forever esteemed within the effulgency. Typically, stemma— whether men or women—go on to lead smaller, remote towns, when an effulgent or graycloak cannot be sent."

"How do you not know this?" the old man asks me sharply, motioning to Blythe. "You are fortunate enough to travel with an effulgent, especially after what happened to them . . . " He shakes his head slowly. "Yet you seem unaware of this blessing."

Colu laughs. "Blessing my ass."

The old man stares at Colu with eyes redder than the fire they reflect.

I don't say anything. After a moment the man stands, looking down at his smoldering creation, seemingly lost in thought. Meanwhile, the silhouette of le-Sante reappears at the top of the limestone stairs, the sky behind it ablaze in the same color as the fire.

The old man glances up at her. "The stemma will tell you more. My part in this is done. I only pray to the Unnamed that I did the right thing." He nods to Blythe. "Your Effulgency."

"Be nothing," Blythe replies, as the man departs and passes a descending le-Sante on the stairs, her hands full of small stacked wicker baskets.

Blythe and Chimeline rise to assist and quickly hand out the baskets. The smell of roasted vegetables gathers in the still air under the cover of dense leaves, and my mouth waters. Uncovering my wicker basket, I see that it contains a small helping of mixed rice. It's too dark to see details, but I taste sweet potatoes. And dates, perhaps.

All is quiet as we eat, gathering up the rice with our fingers. But I feel le-Sante's eyes on me as she stands in the distance like an armored sentry.

Despite my hunger, I set down my basket before finishing the rice in it.

"We know that you're sheltering an effulgent here," I tell her. "It's imperative that we speak to him."

She narrows her eyes but doesn't reply. She takes a seat on Blythe's stone bench, keeping a few feet of space between the two of them. Her back is perfectly straight.

Chimeline passes around the waterskin.

"His name is Ch—"

"I know of this person you seek," she says. "He will be here shortly. They both will."

"Both?" I ask.

She looks away.

I glance at Chimeline, Colu, and Blythe. All three of them have the same confused expression.

"While we wait," she says to Blythe, with perfect posture and palms on her thighs, "I would like to understand how the graycloak died."

She runs her palms up and down her thighs. Her expression is hard to read in the firelight, but I feel that even clear daylight wouldn't help matters.

I notice then, just underneath the slender sleeve of her gray robe, a white bandage wrapped around her left wrist.

Blythe looks up into the low branches. Behind him, past the drop-off, the same golden light has risen in the gap, throwing the canyon walls into sharp relief. The chasm is slowly getting brighter. Someone is approaching. Climbing, somehow.

"She was a healthy and wonderful child," Blythe eventually responds. "And she turned into a fine woman. Truly. A fine graycloak. She made me very proud."

le-Sante frowns slightly. "Proud?"

He nods. "She was very strong in the way of unwanting. You would've been proud of her too."

She opens her mouth and pauses, as if unsure of her words. "I didn't know, Your Effulgency, that the way of unwanting had room for pride."

He smiles sadly. "I didn't know either, until it was too late."

Chimeline leans into me. "Perhaps we should give them some privacy."

I nod and begin rising, but Blythe extends his hand. "No," he says. "We are all on the way together. What happened to her . . . we were all witnesses." Blythe looks back up toward the dense canopy of leaves and white star-shaped flowers. One of them slowly falls, twirling silently, until it rests on the dry grass between Blythe and le-Sante.

"Witnesses to what?" le-Sante asks, as she picks up the flower. She hides it in her clutched hand. When she sits back up, her haphazard braid falls across the front of her shoulder. I realize then that no white flowers exist on the ground.

Blythe's answer never comes.

"She was murdered in al-Kimer-vis," I say softly. "Just a few days ago. I'm sorry."

le-Sante turns her head toward me like an owl, her body staying still. "Along with the other effulgents? We heard of the horror that transpired."

Blythe shakes his head. "No. No, that all happened before we arrived."

I sigh. My answer and her false assumption would have sufficed, but Blythe has to ruin it with his cursed honesty.

"I thank the Unnamed that you were spared," she says, after a moment. "Who owned the dark, then?"

Across the fire, Blythe lowers his head, putting prayerful hands together against his forehead while resting his elbows on his knees. Colu finishes eating and wipes his hands on his already-soiled pants.

"A black arcanist," I answer.

Behind his hands, Blythe nods.

le-Sante takes a deep breath, continuing to stare at me with her back straight. "The crimsonhawk master says that you are a black arcanist."

"I *was* a voider. But I am no longer."

She scoffs. "And the Xian mountain lion no longer feasts upon human flesh."

"Dem is on the way of unwanting," Blythe says flatly, looking toward the grass.

le-Sante flashes him a strange look. For the first time, I see an emotion on her face, but it's complicated. Shock? The look quickly fades. "A black arcanist on the *way*?" she eventually asks, but it's not a question that seeks an answer. I cannot decide if she's either doubtful or impressed. "And since when, Your Effulgency, have you begun using names?"

Blythe lowers his pressed hands. "I have begun many things, le-Sante. I have found that the way of unwanting is as wide as the River Xi."

She stands, recoiling.

Blythe also rises—much more slowly—and tries to gently put his hands on hers, but le-Sante swats them away.

"le-Sante," Blythe says calmly. "Be calm, Stemma."

le-Sante wipes her eyes with the back of her hand and looks up at the white flowers a few feet above her head. "I am sorry, Your Effulgency," she says, sniffling. She shakes her head repeatedly as she avoids his gaze. "This is all too much for me. You come here after all this time, bringing with you so much darkness. I struggle to give it all away."

Blythe attempts to hold her hands again. This time she avoids them by pointing to Colu without looking at him. "And you come with *this* man? Do you know who he is?"

"I do," Blythe says.

"He forsook the Unnamed!" le-Sante replies. "And now it seems as if his blindness of spirit has affected his body as well."

"The years haven't been kind to you either," Colu grunts.

Outrage covers le-Sante's face, but before she can respond, Chimeline says, "Please, let us not bicker. We have been through many hardships on our journey. And harsh words do more hurt than this harsh climate."

Colu points to le-Sante. "I'm just stating the truth. I lost my eye in a bar fight, but at least I don't have leprosy."

Chimeline turns to Colu with a scolding expression. "You cannot talk to her like that. We are her guests!"

Colu only spits.

le-Sante nods to Chimeline. "Thank you for showing the way, but this man's behavior is only a reminder of the blessings that came my way."

Colu grunts. "Really. I offered you everything I had, including my heart, and you still chose Blythe. What has that exactly gotten you? Life in a leper colony. I suppose I should say congratulations."

"I am exactly where I want to be," she says. "And yes, leaving you was the best decision of my . . . Who is Blythe?"

The canyon brightens. Giant shadows move against the far rock wall.

Chimeline bites her lip, but Colu chuckles while pointing at Blythe.

"You took a name?" le-Sante asks Blythe incredulously.

"I did."

le-Sante turns away. I get the sense that she is caught between the old world and the new one. Pulled by both obedience and objection.

Blythe doesn't seem to be concerned by her reaction. A meager smile crosses his face as he raises his arms slightly. "le-Sante, do not be troubled, for the Unnamed is clearly behind this. Bringing us all together in such a way."

"Please stop calling me by my name," she replies in almost a whisper.

Light rises past the cliff edge. The tree trunks cast moving shadows in our direction.

All of us stand. I hold a hand out before my eyes.

Two people emerge from the canyon. One of them holds a rectangular glass-walled oil lantern. They must be climbing a stairway built into the very cliff face.

Once the pair reach the top, they enter our tree-sheltered space.

"Your Effulgency," le-Sante says, bowing deeply. "I leave you with the visitors." Without waiting for a response, she retreats up the stone stairs, back to the village. The sky and the buildings are no longer red but violet.

Instantly, I recognize Chireseal. The gems on his face reflect the lantern's light, creating small, muted rainbows. He's dressed in white-and-tan riding gear. For a moment, my heart rises in triumph. After all this time, we've found him. The Axiondrive must surely be near. And nearer still are some much-needed answers.

But my gaze immediately moves onto his companion, who is completely unexpected. Someone a hilma addict might see while hallucinating.

She is familiar.

She wears a skintight black outfit that seems wet given the way it reflects the light. Not much of her skin is visible, but from what I can see of her face and neck, it's entirely red—as if she's been exposed to this desert sun for days. Her eyes are pink.

"Dem," Chimeline whispers while tightly grabbing my hand. "The visions."

I squeeze her hand back in understanding. As I recall Temberlain's words, it's as if he's standing here, saying them right in front of me.

An Agh-Severian. Scrawny, red tinted. Like the kind of ugly bird that could stand on one leg.

Chireseal runs his hand over his bald head as he surveys us. He then speaks a few words to the woman in Effulgian.

I look desperately to Blythe, who's scrutinizing them with an open mouth.

The woman replies to Chireseal in Effulgian. As she speaks, she sets down the lantern at her feet.

Chireseal nods, rubbing his hand over his face.

More back and forth occurs between the two.

"Blythe, do you know what they're saying?" I ask out of the corner of my mouth, without taking my eyes off the pair.

"Blythe?"

But it's Chimeline who replies. "The red one is asking if we're the ones who performed eleutheria on the Axiondrive," she says quietly. "She's curious about how we were able to do it without . . . a tool. Something called a drill."

I look at her in shock. Of course she can understand them. They're speaking the same language as the enervated.

"She also wants to know which one of us is . . . the empowered."

"Alright, enough," Chireseal says loudly, silencing both conversations. He puts his hands on his hips. "How did you find me?"

For a moment, everyone is silent.

"Dear brother," Blythe eventually says, arms outstretched. "The Unnamed guided us every step of the way, for we came to ensure your safety. And to ensure the destruction of the Axiondrive."

Chireseal looks annoyed.

Blythe turns to me, inviting me to speak. But my mind continues to wrestle with Temberlain's visions and the reality of the red-skinned woman standing in front of me. The past and the present have mixed like the River Xi when it hits the sea. White and black waters swirling, both cloudy and clear.

"The Axiondrive must be destroyed," Chimeline eventually says. "Even though it's been emptied, the azuremen have the capability of reusing it."

Chireseal looks at her with a stunned expression.

"It cannot be destroyed," the Agh-Severian says.

"How did you know that?" Chireseal asks Chimeline.

Blythe raises a finger. "We have always known—and taught—that there is inherent evil in voidance—"

"That's not what I meant," Chireseal says. He shakes his head and says something to the Agh-Severian in Effulgian. The two quickly begin arguing, their windlike voices becoming a storm.

"What's going on?" I ask Chimeline worriedly.

"Chireseal is telling the red one about my diary." She wrinkles her nose.

I step closer to them, standing almost between Chireseal and the Agh-Severian and breaking up their conversation. The latter is short. The top of her braided black hair reaches my chin.

"Both of you, listen to me," I say. "I've chased you all the way from Winter's Baiou. I've lost friends of mine in this pursuit. We all want the same thing—the destruction of the Axiondrive. But before we do that, we need answers. *I* need answers."

Chireseal takes a deep breath then stretches his neck left and right.

"Who are you people?" I continue. "What is going on? The azuremen. The giving houses. All of it."

Chireseal glances at his companion before shaking his head. "What you ask . . . It's beyond your understanding."

"Please," Chimeline urges, stepping forward. "You must have faith in us. Our lands have been overrun and our homes destroyed. We need to know what you know if we're ever to stop them."

Chireseal studies her with an almost-eerie sensibility.

"I admire your courage," says the Agh-Severian, "but they cannot be stopped. Not by you. Not even by us. Your world is now part of their domain. It is best to lie low, and when you die, make sure you die naturally."

"Sounds like a great plan," Colu mutters.

Chireseal subtlety extends a hand at his side, quieting the Agh-Severian before she can say anything further. "I'm sorry," he says to all of us. "I really am. But you shouldn't have come here."

"Shouldn't have come?" I shout, my patience reaching its end. I point to Blythe. "Tell that to your brother! His daughter is dead because we followed you!"

Chireseal wipes a hand across his head then looks upon Blythe with rare compassion. Stepping around me, he approaches him and places his hands upon Blythe's shoulders. "I appreciate the sacrifices you have made. What you did with the drive . . . " He gently pats Blythe's shoulder. "You got it weightless for me."

Blythe nods, straightening proudly.

"I was able to move it," Chireseal continues. "Instead of bringing in Lake. She was late getting here, and the azuremen were faster than I expected."

"What lake?" I ask.

Chireseal, his back to me, ignores my question. But the Agh-Severian raises her hand meekly. "I am Lake."

I shake my head. "I don't understand."

Chireseal pats Blythe's shoulder a final time before turning to me. "I know. That's what I'm trying to tell you— this is all beyond your understanding. But know this: you've done well. Thank you. All of you. But we have it under control now. Your job is done. You can go home, and like Lake says, lie low."

"Go home?" I ask, incredulously.

"There is no such thing as home," Colu says.

"Fine," Chireseal says, shrugging. "Then stay here. It's safer than most places. You might die from leprosy, but at least your souls will be free."

"Did you murder all those guards?" Blythe asks. The way he changes the subject makes me think that the question has been on his mind for quite some time.

Chireseal looks at him, blinking rapidly. "What guards?"

"The ones on the pier with the Axiondrive."

He taps his boot on the grassy ground as if trying to remember, then nods. "Oh, them . . . Yeah, that was unfortunate. Sorry about that."

"You own the dark, Brother."

Chireseal shrugs again and turns his back on us, retreating toward the cliff edge. But before he descends, he stops and glances at Blythe. "I own a dark mission. And it cannot fail." Then, quieter, to Lake, he says, "Let's go."

The woman picks up the lantern and the pair begin to walk away.

Leaving us with no answers.

"You're from Efful, aren't you?" I blurt.

He stops in place.

I point to the red-skinned woman. "Lake. You are from Agh-Severian."

Her mouth hangs open for a moment before she replies. "Agh-Severia, yes."

Temberlain shook his head subtly as he looked through the immense back window at the passing stars. At this speed, they were straight concentric lines. The ones near the middle were strings of vibrating color against the inky blackness of space.

"You've traveled far—across the stars—in order to come here," I say.

Chireseal turns around fully and crosses his arms over his chest. For a moment, the only sound is the trickle of water falling into the abyss.

"Alright, you have my attention," he says.

RELIC

The Agh-Severian, Lake, leads us down the narrow stairway in the cliff, her lantern raised high.

"So, Dem's wife fell completely inside of the pool, but you only *touched* it?" Chireseal asks Chimeline loudly, over his shoulder and over the soft sound of falling water.

"Yes."

"For how long?"

She shrugs. "I don't know."

I know that Chimeline is uncomfortable reliving that memory, but Chireseal has been pushing it ever since we started walking. For an effulgent, he's strangely selfish.

"It was only her finger, and only for a moment," I call out from behind her.

"And that's when she first flashed white," Chireseal confirms.

I nod.

"Be careful," Lake says from the front. "The steps turn slick down here."

We near the bottom of the hundred-foot-high crevasse. The cliff faces are only twenty feet apart. The meager waterfall, originating far above, hits the body of water just below us. When I lean over to the left, looking down past the hewn stairs, I can see our distorted reflections. A mist covers everything.

"Then what?" Chireseal asks.

Chimeline braces herself with her right hand against the damp cliff wall. Despite the narrow passage, I stay to the left of her, perilously close to the edge, and put my arm around her waist.

"I began speaking with Marine," she says.

"Who was in soteria by then," Chireseal finishes, finally understanding. "You were speaking to her in soteria."

"Yes," Chimeline answers.

"About what?"

We reach the bottom of the stairs. A flat, wet, and wide ledge of tan rock surrounds the pool of water and allows us to walk around it toward the other side of the chasm. Lake continues to carefully lead us, her lantern a single yellow star in the night. Reflections from Chireseal's gems surround us.

"Mander was getting away," Chimeline answers.

Chireseal stops and turns around. The six of us are centered between the cliff walls, standing upon the raised ledge and exposed to the night sky. To my left is the waterfall and black pool. To my right, the ledge slowly disintegrates into boulders then smaller rocks and finally sand before the darkness overcomes the meager sphere of light. But I don't need to see any further. In either direction, I know that only a maze awaits.

"Mander," Chireseal says, almost chewing the word as if it were tough meat. "He was the empowered who raised the Axiondrive?"

She nods.

"Why would he run?" Chireseal asks. "He had the upper hand."

Chimeline looks up at me, unsure.

"The Celestium," I say, "where all of this took place—it collapsed from the power of the voidance he was using. His attempt to put Chimeline in soteria unleashed enough force to shake the entire building. The cliff fell away. We were stuck on the plateau, hundreds of feet above the bay. I didn't have a voidstone. Chimeline was unconscious. Mander was on the beach, getting away."

"Alright. Then what happened?"

Chimeline wrinkles her nose. "Marine said that Dem had to jump. That I had to soften his landing so he wouldn't die."

Chireseal's eyes dart between the two of us before locking on Chimeline. "But you're *not* an empowered," he says to her. A look of annoyance briefly flashes across his illuminated face. "Voider. Whatever you call it here."

"No."

"Then how could you soften his landing?"

"Marine explained how to do it."

Chireseal laughs once then blinks incessantly. "Quick learner."

"I was able to use Marine's voidstone," Chimeline says. "There was one on her body, which was floating in the water."

Chireseal frowns as if trying to paint the mental image. "You used axion—which was on her body, floating out in the water—while you were atop a cliff?"

"Yes. To be honest, I wasn't exactly sure what I was doing at the time. It was mostly instinct—and following Marine's direction."

"But that's impossible," Chireseal says in disbelief.

I understand his disbelief. I felt the same thing at the time. I still do.

Chimeline doesn't respond.

Lake says something to Chireseal in Effulgian while studying Chimeline. Chireseal wipes a hand across his bald head, looking at the black pool in utter confusion.

"That is correct," Chimeline answers Lake, but then she addresses both of them. "I never asked for it. But it is who I am now."

"You are . . . an axionlighter," Lake says, before kneeling. Her black hair is so long that it graces the wet rock.

Chireseal turns back to Chimeline and nods once, giving her a polite smile with tight lips. I cannot tell if it's sincere.

"So that explains how you understand us," Lake says to her, standing again. "You've been speaking with the enervated."

"I, ah, yes," she answers. "Marine helped me in the beginning, but I've been able to communicate with them for some time now."

Chireseal snaps his fingers. "That's the point of your diary, then," he says enthusiastically. "You're writing down what they said to you. About the azuremen." He waves his hand between Lake and him. "And our worlds."

"Yes. You could say that," Chimeline says hesitantly, looking at me in desperation.

"I would love to read this book," Chireseal says. "May I see it?"

"Unfortunately," I say, clearing my throat before Chimeline can answer, "it's lost."

"Lost?" Chireseal blurts out.

Everyone turns to me. Chimeline wrinkles her nose again. Blythe looks as if he's holding his breath.

"We left Winter's Baiou in haste," I add quickly, and shrug to feign indifference. "We left many things behind."

Lying to them isn't something I want to do, but we've already shared so much of our story and have heard none of theirs. I'd like to know more about our new friends before divulging what's in Chimeline's diary.

Chireseal stretches his neck in both directions. "That is very unfortunate."

"We should head inside," Lake says quietly, gripping the ends of her hair and squeezing out the water before looking up mistrustingly at the stars between the cliffs.

Chireseal nods distractedly, frowning at me and looking confused. Then he extends his hand toward the other side of the crevasse. "By all means, Lake, lead the way."

I peer into the distance.

It was lost in the shadows before, but now I can see that an entire section of wall near the ground on the other side of the cavern is missing, eroded away into an immense kidney-shaped area of blackness.

Our trail leads directly into it.

Moments later, we pass underneath the curved cliff wall.

Chireseal laughs mockingly to himself. The sound blends in with the gentle dripping of water coming from somewhere inside the dark. "This is going to be interesting."

Lake continues ahead of us, illuminating more of the cave.

Once through the kidney-shaped opening, the room opens into a hollow space that's so gargantuan I'm suddenly at a loss for words. Looking up into the dim stalactites and glittering quartz, I'm reminded of the largest effulgency temple in the citadel, but even that would be a shack compared to this.

Lowering my gaze, I realize that much of the floor ahead reflects Lake's light.

A slender stream near my feet connects the black pool outside with a much larger body of water. Directly ahead it opens up wide, covering the entire left half of the cave.

An entire underground lake lies before us.

Lake keeps walking.

Soon more details emerge on the right. My heart rises when I see the wagon. The Axiondrive is still nestled inside, reflecting no light whatsoever and looking like a hole revealing a distant place where no men dare go.

Lake keeps walking.

What's revealed next makes the wagon look as if it were made of tinder and birch bark, by a child, and then lost, only to be found again many years later.

I'm not sure what they are. Two large, blue-tinged silver, seamless, and curvaceous objects gleam in the lantern light. Their surfaces shimmer as if underwater. My gaze darts to the left, but the underground lake is too far away. It wouldn't cause these reflections.

I've seen these before. But where?

They're obviously human-made. One is about the same size as the wagon, and the other is quite large—perhaps four or five times the size of the other but similar in shape. Maroon letters in a language that I cannot understand are painted on the side. And a few symbols as well.

Blythe rushes toward me. "Dem," he says. "They're just like the relic."

In Fiscarlo. The glass cage.

"They're ships, Dem." Blythe beams, grabs my arm, and shakes it as a young boy would do to his father. "Good Unnamed, they're effulgency ships."

As Lake approaches the bluish-silver objects, both awaken in glowing shades of green. Soft chimes echo in the cavern.

Chireseal and Lake immediately stop and bow their heads. Lake sets her lantern down on the rock floor.

"By your permission," says Lake quietly. "By the Unnamed's will. By the bond that unites us all."

"By your permission. By the Unnamed's will. By the bond that unites us all," Chireseal replies.

I glance at my friends. We all share a confused look.

Lake notices. "These ships—one innership and one cargo vessel—they contain axion," she says, extinguishing her lantern with a twist of a key. She looks back at the glowing pair that cast the cavern in a strange and almost sickly light.

"Sometimes our duties require us to use axion," she says. "We hate it, and we avoid it at all costs, but when we must, we offer the kahtrah. We pay tribute to enervated who are willing to give us the power of axion, and in return we pledge our unending servitude. It is our way to honor them."

"It's a strange war that we fight, isn't it?" Chireseal adds quietly, as if speaking to himself. "In order to free them, we must abuse them."

Blythe breaks the ensuing silence by bowing his head. "We thank you for your gift," he says.

A heartbeat later, Chimeline, Colu, and I follow.

"We thank you for your gift."

VOIDREAMING

Within his newfound world of axion, Temberlain tumbled.

Colorless, miscellaneous structures of particles blurred past him: a large section of the broken cage, a coiled length of ribbon connecting the control unit to the Axiondrive, the control unit itself, the lower half of a corpse—probably the half he wasn't clutching.

Were they moving or was he?

Temberlain grasped the dead empowered's neck tighter and brought whatever remained of the body into his chest, embracing it as he would a long-lost brother. He felt the curve of the skull, the wideness of the shoulders. But his intuition told him that below this there was nothing—most likely that part of the body had been caught within Sixteen's serrater's bolt. Now that the drive was offline, even the modest 0.3 g artificial gravity in the chamber was eliminated. He was weightless, and so was everything else. Yet the feeling of . . . absence . . . was present.

His body shook as his back slammed against the chamber wall.

Temberlain panicked when he briefly felt his grip on the neck loosening, but as his body rotated, he used the opportunity to push the corpse more fully into himself. Temberlain only had one arm. If he lost touch with the axiongraph, he would die.

Sixteen would be firing again. Any microrotation now.

He built a spherical membrane. And only then did he begin orientating himself.

Temberlain still moved, but slower now—the collision against the far wall had absorbed most of his momentum. His back slid against the gentle curve as he looked out toward the center.

Directly in front of him and still motionless was the Axiondrive, as black in the world of axion as it was in the world outside. Oval shaped and mostly symmetrical. Ten feet wide and fifteen feet long, it took up a significant portion of the chamber. He was still on its underside. FTL-side. The southern pole, if this room were a planet.

Just above the drive near the mirror-side, he could see the Agh-Severian's visored face behind glistening particles, like a sun rising over a mountain range. She pointed at him then looked across the room at something Temberlain couldn't see. Someone.

Sixteen.

The room broke apart again.

He couldn't hear the buzzing of the serrater. Everything was muted behind the screams of the enervated. But he saw the fabric of reality crease as multiple bolts of axion particles cut through more of the cage, moving in an arc that started from the south pole and curved north, finally stopping just to the right of him. Perhaps a dozen shots altogether. What followed was a storm of mutilated malineum.

If he couldn't see Sixteen, then she couldn't see him. The drive eclipsed the view.

But Temberlain kept sliding up against the back wall, headed north. Mirror-side.

Keeping his membrane intact, he began constructing a pressure differential.

More of the chamber slowly became visible over the top of the drive. The Agh-Severian clutched a section of cage that floated free and more of the drill. Hundreds of wires undulated against the surface of the drive, and in the center of these wires spouted a fountainhead of . . . what? Spheres of some sort—

Sixteen appeared over the surface of the drive.

One of her hands was stretched in front of her face, as if she was shielding herself from harsh light. The other held the serrater, trained on him.

Temberlain didn't hesitate. Simultaneously, he dropped his spherical membrane and released the parabolic one. A narrow cone of energy left his chest and crossed the chamber, just over the north edge of the Axiondrive and directly into Sixteen.

For a microrotation, he saw her dissolve into nothing. Her former glistening shape became countless speckles of fading light against the gray wall that curved behind her.

But this view was mostly caught within the corner of his eye.

The combination of zero gravity and his pressure differential had caused an opposite reaction. Temberlain's body launched backward, his back following the contours of the outer spherical wall, past the southern pole and up north again on the opposite side of the room. Particles blurred everywhere and nowhere.

He hit a piece of malineum, and the world of axion was ripped from him.

The bleedersnake!

Suddenly, light was inescapable. He shut his eyes, but the brightness could not be tamed. His head pounded. Someone was screaming. Was it him? The Agh-Severian? The enervated?

Frantically and blindly, he reached out with his remaining hand, trying to find the corpse again, as he ricocheted back toward the center, spinning into the unknown.

Into the fountainhead of the eleutharian drill.

REFLECTIONS

Chimeline swims over to where I sit at the darkened pool's edge. Her lashes are thick and heavy with water and her eyes reflect two colors at once: the nearby warm, flickering gold of the lantern and the sickly green axionlight of the ships at the opposite end of the massive cavern.

She sets her crossed arms down on the red rock's ledge and rests her chin on them. The remainder of her body hides underwater.

Her smile fades as she studies me. "What's wrong?" she asks.

I close her diary and clutch it tightly.

"Why do we say 'Temberlain's Ashes'?" I ask her.

"What do you mean?"

"We've learned a lot about Temberlain from your visions, but one thing that's troubling me is how it all ties in to what we know now."

She wrinkles her nose in surprise and contemplation. "I remember reading about him in that white book Blythe gave me. There was a great fire, and out of that fire was born the effulgency. It was generations ago. He was . . . the first effulgent."

I nod. "But what caused that fire?"

She shrugs. "I don't know. Why do you ask?"

Instead of answering, I carefully place her diary back into my leather sack. I purposely keep it in the shadows, orientating my body between it and the lantern, even though Chireseal and Lake are far away, near Blythe and Colu. They're giving Chimeline and me privacy while she bathes.

"Dem?"

"Do you know what happens to him?" I ask, avoiding her question.

"To Temberlain?" she says, shaking her head while still resting it on her arms. "No. What you've read is what I've seen," she mutters. "Nothing more."

I sigh. "Yeah, but you said that when you have these visions, they're lifelike. More than just the enervated telling you a story. You can see it. Feel it."

She nods.

"It reminds me of eleutheria," I say broodingly, looking at the disheveled wagon in the murky distance. "When the enervated pass through." Meeting her gaze again, I say, "Anyway, I was hoping that you'd have some sense of what's about to happen. What *did* happen to him. When he touched the white."

She tilts her head in thought.

I lean in and almost whisper, even though I don't have to. "I think that he's going to become an axionlighter, Chimeline. Just like you."

She doesn't say anything.

"I'm speculating, mind you," I tell her, leaning back, "but I think that what the eleutharian drill did to the Axiondrive is very similar to what Mander did to the voidstone in the Celestium. They both turned white. Somehow, those voidstones became doors."

"But then Temberlain would be taken in soteria. Like Marine."

I shake my head. "Not if he touches the drill just right. Glances it, maybe. Like when you touched the white substance in the Celestium. Just enough to send part of his body inside."

"Soul," she says, a faraway look in her eyes.

"What?"

"Not part of his body. Part of his *soul*."

I purse my lips in thought. "How can you divide a soul?"

She shakes her head. "It's not dividing it. Not in the way you imagine. It feels like . . . " She looks down at the black water. "A reflection."

For a moment, neither of us says anything. Lake laughs brightly near the cavern entrance and the sound finds its way around us, dancing like lapping water.

"Can you get the towel?" Chimeline asks.

I stand and walk to a nearby stalagmite, where I hung it so it wouldn't get dirty on the sandy floor.

"So that's what this is all about?" she asks as I return. I spread the towel wide as she steps out of the black pool naked, drips of water hitting the ground with an unforgiving sound. "You think that if something bad happens to Temberlain, it will happen to me?"

She wraps the towel around herself, shivering.

"Yes," I finally admit. "That's what I fear."

She laughs once, and it comes out forced—I'm not sure if it's because she's still caught within a shiver. "Well, first of all, we don't know what happens to him," she says. "We don't even know if he becomes an axionlighter at all."

"But—"

"Second, maybe that's the point. Perhaps the enervated are sharing his story with me—with us—as a warning. If that's true, then we can use this warning to our advantage. The past is the only thing that's set, Dem. Not the future."

I utter a groan of uncertainty.

She leans in and kisses me on the cheek. A cold droplet of water runs down my neck. "I'm not used to a man worrying about me. It's nice, but you don't need to."

Before I can respond, she walks back to the stalagmite and retrieves a new set of putty-colored clothes: drawstring pants and a tunic.

As she returns, I look down at the leather sack that holds the diary.

"Part of my worry is your lack of it," I say, running my hand through my hair. "I find it strange that you're not more concerned about all of this."

"Can you dim the lantern, please?"

Stooping, I twist the key. The warm glow around us disappears, and for the first time since arriving at this pool I can see the damp edges of stalactites far above, all lined with soft green.

She unclasps the towel, letting it fall by her side. Then she hands it to me and retrieves her folded pants in return.

"Don't worry—I am concerned," she says, as she steps into the baggy pants. "There's just not much we can do about it right now."

I sigh heavily.

"You have to realize something," she says, as she tightens the drawstring around her waist. "From an early age, I was groomed to do one thing and one thing only. By the time I was fourteen, I'd dispatched three men. Two years after that I left home, and I haven't been to Scorpiontail since. I started making more gold than I could ever imagine. I shipped all of it back home, so that my two younger sisters could live normal lives."

She retrieves her tunic from me and begins putting it on over her head.

"So I'm used to people not worrying about me. I'm used to being told what to do." Her voice is muffled by the tunic. Her face reappears, and she fishes out her damp hair from the neckline. "All my life people have used me as a weapon. Being an axionlighter isn't much different—it's just one more thing that's out of my control."

"Well, it may be out of your control, but that doesn't mean that we can't be careful."

She reaches for the towel again and wraps her hair up in it, a snakelike coil atop her head. "Is this why you lied to the others about the diary?"

I turn and glance at the four near the opposite edge of the cavern before staring at the leather sack. "I don't trust them," I answer flatly. "Chireseal and Lake."

She raises one eyebrow. "Why not?"

"Chireseal looks at you as if you're one of Mander's lab rats."

"Have you seen the way *you* look at me?" Her playful tone is softer than her words.

"I have your best interests at heart." I motion to the cavern entrance. "Him, I'm not so sure."

"He seems devoted to the cause."

"Hey," Colu calls out. "Lovebirds. You two done over there?"

"Yes," I reply.

"There's a line of people waiting."

"We're done."

Leaning over, I grab the lantern and twist the key to illuminate us once again within a sphere of gold. I pick up the leather sack and turn to Chimeline, but she's looking up into the dark heights, biting her lip.

"What's wrong?"

She lowers her gaze. "Nothing. I'm fine." She forces a smile and then kisses me again on the cheek.

"You sure?" I ask.

"Yes."

I set the lantern and leather sack back down on the stone and then turn to her, bringing her lips onto mine. And for a moment the world is simple again.

Like it used to be.

CONFEDERACY

The interior of the Effulgian cargo vessel is smaller than I expected. The light resembles daylight and is nothing like the external green hue. It seems to emanate from the very walls. The ceiling is low—all of us except Lake need to duck, and the six of us barely fit within the short and cramped aisle. The floor is made of a polished dark-gray metal that's warm on my bare feet.

"You can sleep here," Lake says, reaching out and tapping one of the four bunks that hang from the curved side walls—two on the left and two on the right. They contain thin white mattresses, but there are no blankets. "Chireseal and I will sleep in the cavern tonight."

"That is unnecessary," Blythe says, his clear and pressing voice filling the space and echoing back with a strange tinny sound. "I need no such luxury built upon the backs of innocent souls."

"None of this consumes axion," Lake says empathetically. "It's reserve power. Coming here—*that* is what tortured them. Now they rest, to travel with us another day."

"The dark seas you've crossed must have taxed them beyond belief," Blythe says.

"Ours is a dark mission."

Colu presses his hand into one of the mattresses. When he takes it away, his palm print glows lavender.

"The head is in the rear," Chireseal says, standing leisurely within the side exit of the ship, looking inward, his arms above his head. He seemingly hangs within the doorway.

"Head to what?" Blythe asks.

"He's talking about the shitter," Colu says.

"You have . . . a washroom in this place?" Chimeline asks incredulously.

Chireseal nods while tapping his hands on the outside surface of the ship. "Yeah, but . . . " He clears his throat. "Now that I think about it, you might find it confusing. You should probably just go outside."

"Chireseal!" Lake says.

He shrugs.

"You know what we need an explanation about?" I say. "You."

Blythe nods.

"Please understand," I add, "we appreciate your accommodations, but we don't need to relieve ourselves right now. We don't need beds right now. We need the truth."

Chireseal and Lake look at each other, and Chireseal slaps the exterior surface again a few times, as if drumming a tune. Then he turns around and descends the metal ramp down to the sandy rock floor. "Come on, then," he calls out. "Truth time."

"I'll fetch some ghultea," Lake says.

We sit around a small campfire twenty feet away from the glowing cargo ship. Its inside light has been exhausted, and the open side door and ramp now resemble a dark, toothless mouth. To my right and only a few feet away is the jagged cavern opening. The smoke from the small fire disappears into the dark heights, but I see some of it curl through the opening, obscuring part of the moonlit crevasse outside. The six of us sit on an odd mix of stones—some recently moved from other parts of the cavern, some so large and heavy they have to have been here for years.

"You already seem to know where we're from," Chireseal begins. "But do you even know what that means?"

"Of course I do."

"No, you don't," he says. "You're a parrot repeating the words of its owner."

Lake lets out a disapproving sigh.

"I mean no disrespect," Chireseal continues. "But you have to understand, asking for the truth is no small thing. In order to comprehend it, you need a frame of reference."

Blythe looks at me in consternation. So does Chimeline. Colu takes another exploratory sip of the thick, bitter tea that Lake prepared and grimaces.

"Mander spoke about many otherworldly things," I begin. "He raised the Axiondrive and used it to find the three lighthouses to call his people. The . . . empowered." I point upwards. "He said that there are kingdoms just like ours, but in the sky. *Across* the sky. That every star is a sun, and some of those suns shine their light on kingdoms just like ours." I take a breath as Chireseal looks on, studying me. "So, assuming that he was telling the truth, I think that you're from one of those kingdoms."

Chireseal takes a sip of tea. "Yes. The bastard was telling you the truth."

I nod, not surprised. "He seemed to take too much pride in it for it to be a lie."

"Yeah. Well, good. So, right. We're from kingdoms of other suns." He slaps his palm on his thigh after an awkward pause. "Well, good," he repeats. "It's great to get that out of the way. That's probably the hardest concept to get into your thick skulls. If you can handle the idea of not being alone or special in this universe, you can probably handle the rest."

"Universe?" Chimeline asks.

Chireseal's mouth hangs open.

"The name for, well, everything," Lake replies, arms open.

"How many kingdoms are there?" Colu asks.

"About a thousand," Chireseal says. "That we know of." With his free hand, he draws a circle in the air in front of him. "They're called worlds. Planets. We all live on the surface of a sphere. Like an ant crawling upon a child's ball. The sky, the clouds, the land, the sea—it's all on the ball. And everything else is blackness. Infinite blackness."

I inhale sharply as Temberlain's words come back to me. He mentioned a planet.

As he raised himself up on his palms, he turned to the massive translucent wall. Gone was the heavy tinting. Gone were the starlines that had streaked past like cloudrops on the window of an innership passing through atmospheres. Replacing this view was a planet more beautiful than words could describe. The whites, blues, and greens were so vivid they seemed to create the words, the very idea of color.

"What is it?" Chimeline asks me.

I shake my head slowly. "It was all there. In your diary."

Chireseal looks at all of us then takes another sip of tea. "I am from a planet called Efful. Lake is from a planet called Agh-Severia." He holds up his cup. "This ghultea that we drink is from a planet called Sidarche."

"Efful," Blythe says loudly, sitting straight up. "Our forefathers have written about that place. It is where the effulgency comes from."

Chireseal nods. "I was born on Efful. As were your ancestors."

"So . . . it is a real place," Blythe says. "As real as here?"

Chireseal nods, a genuine smile reaching his mouth. "Yes, it's real."

"Is it paradise?" Blythe asks, leaning in further. "Our home?"

Chireseal's smile vanishes as he looks down at his ghultea. When he looks up again a moment later, a rare look of seriousness covers his face. His eyes are moist in the sickly green light. "Not any longer, my brother. Not any longer."

Blythe stares back, unblinking. "The azuremen. They're there too."

Neither Chireseal nor Lake immediately replies. The only sound is the crackling of burning wood and the trickle of water from somewhere in the cavern.

Eventually, Lake says, "Yes, they are there, but it is not the azuremen that are the problem. It's those who oversee them. Their leadership, if you will. The confederacy."

I frown. "The confederacy?"

Chireseal tosses an arm-sized log onto the fire, causing sparks to fly. "The Halcyon Confederacy," he says. "They are the ones in control."

My mouth drops open as I look to Chimeline.

The Halcyon Roadmap. *Mander knew.*

"Every planet known to the confederacy has been turned," Lake says.

"Turned?" Colu asks.

She looks toward the moonlit crevasse. "The same things that you've seen here, recently. Introduction of axion. Establishment of giving houses. Enforcement of the confederacy's rules of giving via the azuremen. A gradual but complete social, economic, cultural, and technological paradigm shift that will engulf the entire planet."

"Welcome to the Age of Axion," Chireseal says, as he sets down his cup on the stone ground with a *clink* and then stands. Stretching his arms over his head, he takes a few steps toward the cavern's opening, his body a silhouette against the moonlight.

"So then how do you two fit into all of this?" I ask, alternating my gaze between Lake's eyes and Chireseal's back. Her face seems even redder in the firelight.

"We're the good guys," Chireseal says, his back still to me.

"What do you mean, exactly?"

Lake answers. "We oppose the confederacy and all that they stand for—including axionism: the empowered's use of axion and the abuse and entrapment of souls."

"You're empowered traitors, then," I say.

"Not exactly," Chireseal says, spinning to face us, but he's still a silhouette. "We may be traitors in the eyes of the confederacy, but we are not empowered. Nor is the confederacy solely made up of empowered."

I give him a confused look.

"While it's true that the crux of the problem is the empowered within the confederacy, there are those without the gift serving there as well. Just as there are those with the gift working with us."

"The *gift*?"

Being empowered is simply a birthright," he explains. "The ability to harness axion directly. How or if one chooses to use it is where things get complicated."

"Empowered are born on every planet," Lake adds. "One out of every hundred thousand or so are born with the gift. You even have them here. You call them voiders."

Chireseal takes a few steps toward us. His face becomes awash in red. "Dem, you are an empowered."

I recoil. "I have renounced voidance."

"And I admire that. You cannot renounce who you are, but you can renounce what you're capable of."

"What you choose to do *is* who you are," Blythe says.

Chireseal looks at Blythe, his lips pursed in contemplation. "Indeed." He turns back to me. "And you are not the first empowered, Dem, to realize the error of their ways. There have been others like you who have risked everything to join us. But their numbers are few."

Blythe lifts his finger. "Maybe they don't know the truth about voidance—"

"They know, my brother," Chireseal says. "They know."

Chireseal furrows his forehead then addresses Chimeline. "You, being an axionlighter, are also an empowered. You weren't one before, but you now have the gift, as if you were born with it." He shakes his head. "I've never seen such a thing. Heard of it? Yes. Seen? Never."

After a pause, Lake adds, "The rest of us—those born without the gift—are considered ashen."

"Ashen." Blythe spits out the word. "What a hideous term."

Lake nods. "The universe is full of ashen, and the vast majority of them simply abide by the rules handed down by the confederacy."

"They even relish it," Chireseal adds, his face still dancing with red-tinged shadows.

Lake keeps nodding slowly. "Most embrace the Age of Axion simply because it's all they've ever known. And, for the most part, it's an easy life. Easy, that is, until it's time to give."

"But by then it's too late," Chireseal adds. "For the souls of the next world have no voice in this one."

"So . . . " says Chimeline slowly, wrinkling her nose. "You are the few who are fighting the Halcyon Confederacy."

"Yes," Lake says, and again silence hangs.

Chimeline softly clears her throat. "What confuses me is how the two of you knew about Mander." She turns and faces the Effulgian ships. "You came here *using* axion. Just like the azuremen did. But Mander was communicating only with the empowered. Or the . . . confederacy."

Chireseal's knees pop as he sits back down on a stone. "We have their communication codes."

I glance between Lake and him. "What does that mean?"

He sighs as he leans forward, placing his elbows on his knees. His hands form a fist. "When Mander broadcast his signals from here, the nearest axionship picked it up. Those signals were unencrypted, but none of us were in that part of the Virel Arm to hear them. And even if we had been, we wouldn't have known to look for such signals." He waves his hand, as if pushing the thought aside. "It doesn't matter. What matters is that that single axionship retransmitted their conversations with Mander across *their* network, and we picked up on *those* communications. Because we have their codes."

"It's like a command key ring," Colu says.

We turn to him.

Colu shrugs. "We did the same thing when passing navigational instructions during the war. Every galleon had a brass ring with engravings, and the other galleons had the same ring. They were swapped out every moon phase. You know, in case you Northerners got hold of our parchments."

Chireseal nods. "Yeah, same thing. So, we had one of these brass rings, and because of that, we could decrypt the confederacy's comms. We found out about this planet on the far edge of the Virel Arm. We discovered that they were sending an exploratory axionship with haste to investigate the beacon." He looks to Lake and then to Chimeline. "So that's how we came to know."

Colu laughs deeply, drawing everyone's stares.

"What's so funny?" Blythe asks.

"That's *it*?" Colu asks incredulously. "Just you two? That's all they sent?"

Chireseal blinks.

"I mean, I just don't get it," Colu continues, leaning back against the large rock he's sitting on. "You're, like, supposed to be a fucking rebellion. A force to be reckoned with. And you get golden information. Solid gold. A new kingdom has been found, and those blue fuckers are on their way to rape the shit out of it. And your rebellion sends in *two people*?" He laughs harder, losing control. "I mean, no offense, but you guys have no chance."

"No chance at what?" Chireseal asks.

"Killing them!"

"Who said that our goal was to kill them?" Chireseal says.

I look worriedly at Chimeline, then Blythe and Colu. Colu's laughter slowly dies.

As the silence returns, a thought comes with it. I glance back at the wagon in the cavern's depths, and everything becomes clear. I cannot even see the Axiondrive—it's lost among the blackness. But I can see their strategy.

"You're not here to help us," I say. "You're only here for the Axiondrive."

Lake opens her mouth, looking forlorn and uncertain. But Chireseal nods without a hint of guilt. "That's correct," he says.

Lake looks toward the jagged cavern entrance. "We are too few. We cannot possibly take on the confederacy."

"Fucking cowards," Colu says.

Chireseal looks at him sternly. "We have done more for the cause than you can possibly know."

Colu stands and walks over to him. The two stare at each other until Colu finally turns his head to the side and spits. He looks back at Chireseal once more and then turns away and walks to the edge of the pool.

"We would help if we could," Lake says. "But it's impossible."

"The confederacy cannot be stopped with force," Chireseal adds. "Azuremen cannot be neutralized. Even tens of thousands of ashen here would be no match for their power." He leans forward and extends his hands, seemingly desperate to get his point across. "The only thing we can do is take away their axion. They rely upon it. If we can just get the stuff before they can, we have a chance at whittling away at their power."

"A fire only burns when there is air," Lake says, motioning to the pit. "We're stealing their air."

"Where are you taking it?" Blythe asks.

Lake points to the cavern ceiling.

"Somewhere safe," Chireseal says. "Off this planet." He looks at Chimeline with the same clinical interest I've seen a dozen times before. "As we told you, axion can't be destroyed."

My gaze instinctively moves to my pants pocket, which contains Marine's ever-shrinking voidstone.

"But it *can* be hidden," he continues. "And we have some very good hiding places."

"So why are you still here then?" Colu calls out from the edge of darkness. "You have everything you need from us. Just fucking go."

"We're waiting for a window to open." Chireseal looks up, as if he could see the stars. "There's an axionship orbiting this planet. They're watching us from above."

Chimeline and I share a confused glance. I mouth the word *orbiting*.

"It doesn't matter," Chireseal says, raising his voice in impatience. "What's important to understand is that they're watching us. Always. Except for certain windows of time, when the axionship is near the apogee." He makes hasty motions with his hands again, drawing circles. "Every few days, we have about a six . . . ah, a fullbell window of time to do something without the axionship seeing."

I nod. "You're waiting for this window to open up, and then you'll leave in the same manner that you arrived." I stare at the larger Effulgian ship. "Only this time, with your precious cargo."

"Precisely."

Chimeline inhales sharply. "That's why you were in a hurry."

Chireseal raises an eyebrow.

"At the Lemon Tree Inn," she says. "You said that eleutheria had to be done that day." She glances at me before looking back at him. "You had to get the wagon. You had to steal and load the Axiondrive . . . leave the city. All while they couldn't see you. Otherwise they'd know where this place is."

"Yeah," he says, leaning back. "But that's not even half of it. I knew that the azuremen were coming. They were close, and I couldn't let them get to the drive first."

"You know," Colu says, while looking up at a stalactite, the white of his one eye striking against the darkness, "if these confederates can really see everything as if they're the fucking Unnamed, they probably saw *us* travel here. We might have led them straight to you."

Blythe utters a groan, either of concern or disapproval.

"Relax," Chireseal says. "They're looking for the Axiondrive, or something large enough to contain it." He waves his hand in our direction. "Not four strangers on horseback. There are nomads constantly traveling back and forth in these lands."

Chimeline sets down her tea and grips my hand. When I look into her eyes, I see a reflection of sickly green light.

"What is it?" I ask her quietly.

Instead of replying, she turns to the two ashen. "What if they're looking for something else as well?" she asks contemplatively. "Some*one*."

Chireseal narrows his eyes. "Are you worried because you're an axionlighter?" he asks, but he doesn't wait for an answer. "Don't be. The confederacy doesn't know. And even if they did, they'd probably treat you like any other emp—"

"It's not that," she says, interrupting him. Letting go of my hand, she looks at all of us and swallows. "What if we're being hunted?"

Lake and Chireseal share a disturbed look. "Hunted?" Chireseal echoes. "They have no reason to hunt you."

Chimeline looks at me worriedly. Knowingly.

I squeeze my lips shut as her meaning becomes clear. Turning to Chireseal, I say, "That's not entirely accurate."

"What's not accurate?"

"That they have no reason. They do."

"What do you mean?"

"Remember what you said about the azuremen, that you can't neutralize them, even with ten thousand people?"

He nods. "Yeah. It's impossible."

"Not true," Colu says from the darkness. He throws a pebble into the black lake.

"What do you mean?" Chireseal asks him, before looking back at the three of us by the fire.

Chimeline turns to me, biting her bottom lip. She looks as if she's deciding whether she should tell them the truth.

I give her a hesitant nod.

Chimeline turns back to the pair of ashen. "We killed one."

THROUGH A CRIMSONHAWK'S EYES

Our faces are lit by a mixture of strange, dancing colors: red from the campfire, green from the ship, and white from the moonlight coming through the cavern's opening.

"So let me get this straight," Chireseal says. He points at Chimeline. "First, you weave a membrane," he says, before pointing at Colu, who stands alone in the darkness at the edge of the underground pool. "Then, you're dumb enough to charge an azureman and stab him in his heartplate. Just brilliant," he says dryly. Finally, he turns to me. "And you're savvy enough to sever the heartstone's connections before the azureman can react." Chireseal shakes his head and taps his foot. "Luckiest sons of bitches in the Virel Arm."

Blythe clears his throat. "If I may, Brother. We had the blessing of the Unnamed."

Chireseal glances at Blythe across the fire. "Of course. The Unnamed helps us all. But you also had the help of someone else." He studies Chimeline as Colu throws another pebble into the black water. "You had an axionlighter."

Chimeline looks at the rocky ground, massaging her temples with her fingers. "I only weaved a membrane."

"Against an azureman," Lake says. "You weaved a membrane that held back an azureman."

None of us says anything.

Chimeline's sharp inhale is barely audible above the distant waterfall outside the cavern, but it breaks the silence nonetheless. She continues to massage her temples.

"What's wrong?" I ask her, leaning in.

Chimeline raises her head, but her eyes are closed in concentration. "I think I feel something."

"Feel what, Child?" Blythe asks.

Her eyes frantically move behind closed eyelids. "It's an azureman, I think. Maybe more than one. Maybe."

"How far away?" I ask.

She shakes her head. "I don't know. Far. It's just an itch."

Chireseal and Lake both stand. "What's happening?" Chireseal says. "Talk to me."

Chimeline opens her eyes but stares at the fire. "I can feel axion when it's near," she says. "And I think I feel it now."

Chireseal turns to Lake. "Get the counter."

Lake runs to the cargo ship and ascends the ramp.

"What is she getting?" I ask Chireseal.

"Proof," he says, and begins pacing.

I hear hectic, metallic shuffling from inside the cargo ship.

Colu approaches, strapping his leather sword belt around his waist. "More azuremen coming?"

"We'll see," Chireseal mutters.

"It's just an itch," Chimeline says, slapping her palms on her thighs while exhaling. "An itch I cannot scratch. I'm sorry. It might be nothing. Maybe it's your cargo ship."

Lake emerges carrying something small. "Found it," she says, descending the ramp.

The square object she clutches lights up, illuminating her downturned face in brilliant cerulean blue. Her forehead is creased as she nears. The device she stares at looks like a thin book with its cover still closed.

Chireseal stops pacing as she approaches. Lake raises her head, fearfully searching the darkness before addressing me. "Are you carrying axion? I'm picking up . . . seven fragments nearby."

"Yes," I answer, doing the math in my head. "We do have seven. Why?"

Lake's forehead creases further. "One is quite large."

"But empty," Chireseal adds, peering over her shoulder. He touches the surface of the device. "See?"

"It's probably the heartstone that you're feeling," Chimeline says.

Lake and Chireseal look at her. "You have the azureman's heartstone?" Lake asks.

"Of course," Chimeline says. "Dem and Blythe performed eleutheria on it."

Lake slowly nods, then exhales. She seems to relax slightly. "That's it, then," she says to the hovering Chireseal. She touches the device with her fingers as if drawing on it. "Just the seven, all right here."

"That thing your hands. It indicates axion?" I ask Lake. "Like . . . on a map?"

She nods. "Azuremen. Avorsi. Empowered. Anyone carrying axion."

"Avor . . ." I ignore the strange word and focus instead on what I can understand. "How far does the map go?" I ask.

She glances up in momentary concentration. "About a mile in all directions, but it depends."

"What do you mean?" I ask.

"Well, I think the rock might be blocking the signal."

"Here," Colu says. A moment later the bloodfruit-sized sphere of axion flies through the air, directly at Chireseal.

He turns dexterously and softly catches it in both hands.

"Be careful!" Blythe yells at Colu.

"Why?" he asks. "They already said that this shit can't be destroyed."

Chireseal beholds the heartstone in his palms, his mouth slightly open.

"Good Unnamed," Lake whispers. The blue light looks strange on her red petrified face.

The two of them share a brief glance before looking down at Chimeline, who keeps rubbing her fingers against her temples, watching the fire.

Lake turns off the device. Her face is once again similar in color to the fire. "Well, if they know about this place, they sure aren't showing it."

"I don't like it. Doesn't feel right," Chireseal says, as he walks to Colu. "You have the rest of them?"

"Just the empty ones," Colu replies. "Five of 'em."

He hands the heartstone back. "Give them all to Lake. She'll take them with us, along with the Axiondrive. Assuming we get the chance to leave this cursed place."

Colu mutters in understanding.

Chireseal heads toward the cavern entrance and stops just before the line of moonlight, looking up at the meager waterfall in the distance.

Lake soon follows and stands by his side. She leans into his ear, and they share a few whispered words.

Eventually, they both nod and return.

Chireseal stoops by the fire and uses a burning stick to light the lantern. "We might not be getting a good-enough reading down here," he says as he works. "We're heading back up to the village."

"Then we're coming with you," I say.

He nods as he shuts the lantern's door. When he stands, he's staring at Chimeline. "Let's go."

I kneel on the ground next to Chimeline's now unconscious and glowing body. le-Sante is kneeling as well, but she isn't concerned with Chimeline. She picks up the white flowers that have dropped since sundown. Many paces away stands the crimsonhawk master, perilously close to the cliff edge, searching the dark skies.

The fire has gone out. The soft axionlight of Chimeline's body eclipses the useless lantern that rests on the ground nearby.

"When is this 'window' you referred to?" I ask Chireseal. "We might be able to escape before they get here."

"There is no more window," Chireseal answers flatly. He stands a few feet away, staring intently at Chimeline with his hand on his chin.

le-Sante picks up the last of the white petals and stuffs them into her fist. "What is it that you require?" she asks him as she stands.

"We don't know that yet, Chireseal," Lake says softly. "We won't know until she wakes."

"There is no more *window*," he says, louder this time. "I feel it in my bones. They know about us." He points at me. "No. I should say that they know about *you*. But it doesn't really matter, does it? We can't leave with the Axiondrive now because they've probably repositioned the axionship and are watching this cavern. It's over."

"What is it that you require?" le-Sante repeats.

"A time machine!" Chireseal shouts, almost pouncing on her. She recoils. "Can you take me back to a few days ago?"

She looks at him in hurt and confusion.

"Chireseal," Lake says admonishingly.

He extends a shaking palm and lowers his voice, taking a deep, controlled breath. "No. I'm sorry. We don't require anything now. Thank you."

But I interject. "Wait," I say.

le-Sante looks at me with apprehension.

"Can you get a blanket for her?" I ask, gesturing to Chimeline. "She gets cold when this happens." I place my palm on her forehead again and nod. "Yes. She's a little cold."

Chireseal extends his hand toward le-Sante. "Something warm and clean. Not from the lepers."

le-Sante bows. "As you wish."

"We don't know what the confederacy knows," Lake says to Chireseal as le-Sante quickly departs. "Maybe we can slip by unnoticed."

Chireseal mutters something.

"You're being paranoid, Gemface," Colu says. "The moment we killed that azureman, his knowledge died with him. Same with the two marked."

Chireseal and Lake both turn to him. "'Marked'?" he asks.

Colu looks at me.

"There were two voiders," I explain. "One was from the North. Another was Xian." I make a slicing motion up my forehead and into my short, tousled hair. "They had the black mark of axion cut into their heads. Burned in."

Chireseal looks up at the trees, exhaling deeply while tapping his foot. "They are called avorsi."

"Avorsi?" Blythe asks.

Chireseal keeps looking upwards at nothing. "Turned empowered."

"When the confederacy came here," Lake says, "they rounded up the empowered, no?"

"Yes," Blythe says. "In the Union, the king mentioned that all voiders were to report—"

"Yeah, yeah—they reeducate them," Chireseal says, as he lowers his head. He speaks too quickly, obviously impatient about having to explain. "The Halcyon Confederacy considers the empowered the utmost supreme beings in the universe, and as such they take careful strides to ensure that all of them are aligned with their cause. If any empowered *don't* fall in line, they turn them into avorsi." He repeatedly taps his finger on his forehead, hard enough to probably cause pain. "Empowered are too important to just to throw into axion like the rest of us useless ashen. Instead, they cut into their minds and take over their free will."

"They become puppets of the confederacy," Lake says.

"Animals that revel in pain and can work unending voidance," Chireseal adds. "Until they die like dried-up husks."

I look down at Chimeline's glowing body. "She said the Northern marked was like a trained palehound," I say softly.

The crimsonhawk cries out across the canyons.

"More importantly, she was still able to destroy it. Both of them," Chireseal says, motioning toward Chimeline. "Alone."

I nod.

He puts his hand on his chin again. "She obviously doesn't need the enervated's help then. She's mastered axion fully. In only a matter of days."

"I wouldn't say that."

"Then how do you explain that all of you aren't dead?"

Colu lets out a deep laugh.

Chireseal turns to him. "And I'm not paranoid," he says. "The azureman that you killed is not human. It's a machine. Like our cargo ship."

"I assumed as much," I say. "When we broke apart its blue face armor, there was a bird's nest of colored string."

"There's something else. These machines talk to one another," he says.

I turn toward Chimeline, remembering what she said in the tax collector's house.

Chireseal waves a hand around. "They're all linked by an invisible tether. You cannot begin to understand how it works. Suffice it to say, they share their thoughts."

le-Sante quietly returns with a thick gray woolen blanket. She hands it to me, bows, and departs again.

When she's gone, Chireseal continues, more softly, as I spread the blanket over Chimeline. "Everything that azuremen saw, felt, heard . . . Everything until the very end, when you ripped its heartstone out, was seen and felt and heard by all other azuremen on this cursed planet." He points to the heavy sky. "And therefore them too."

A piercing cry makes us all jump in place.

The crimsonhawk dives.

It spreads its wings, becoming wider than its master is tall. The feathers of its body are a glorious white underneath, but not as white as its eyes, which shine bright in the axionlight.

Chimeline stops glowing the moment the bird lands on its master's arm.

For a moment, her body shakes.

"What's happening?" Chireseal asks. He stands over me.

I ignore him as I put my hand around her neck and shoulders and help her sit up.

She blinks rapidly then looks around in brief confusion. She splays out her fingers wide in front of her face, studying them for a moment before shivering.

I gather the blanket tighter around her upper body.

"Did it work?" Chireseal asks. "Talk to me."

"There are five of them," Chimeline says quietly. "They'll be here by sunrise."

FATE OF THE *APSIDES*

Chimeline was right. The sky *is* different.

Moonlit clouds obscure some stars, but I know that something else hides up there in that sea of seas.

I understand now what she meant when she said that she didn't like the stars. At the time, I thought that she was acting like a child. But she's wiser than all of us.

As I lie on my back and behold this limitless canopy, I don't feel a sense of endless possibilities. I don't dream. I feel only an oncoming weight, as if the Unnamed's entire creation has been turned upside down and is pushing me into this sandy ground.

After everything we've been through, after all the sacrifices we've made, we should be winning this war.

Instead, we're losing it.

"If *I* can feel *them*, then *they* must be able to feel *me*," Chimeline says, taking me out of my bitter thoughts. I turn from the night sky and refocus on the group sitting on the ground around Chireseal's flickering lantern. Nothing new has been said in a quarterbell. Everyone is repeating the same things in a different way.

"If that's true, we won't be able to hide our way out of this," Lake says, her face awash in blue. She's clutching her device again, watching for signs of the approaching azuremen, even though Chimeline has said repeatedly that they're a long way off.

"We never could," Chireseal says, as he glances at the sky. "Whether they're tracking us from above or somehow with axion, it doesn't matter. We're trapped."

"That's why we should leave now!" Lake says, briefly raising her head from her device. "While we have the chance!"

Chireseal shakes his head fervently. "I told you, that's suicide. The axionship would see us leaving orbit. They'd send a trireme and we'd be caught before we even left the system."

Lake exhales sharply. "You don't know—"

"It's not an option, Lake!" he snaps. "I don't want to talk about this again."

"But—"

"That's an order!"

She looks back down into her radiance of blue.

"The confederacy probably assumes that the Axiondrive is here," I say softly, trying to calm the group. "Before we killed the azureman, he . . . it asked us where the drive was. It was the only thing that seemed to matter." I run my hand through my hair, shaking some loose sand out. "So the question is, what does the confederacy want? Revenge? Or the drive?"

"The drive," Lake says immediately.

Chireseal nods. "The confederacy doesn't care about revenge. The azuremen mean nothing to them, apart from their heartstones. They're just machines."

I point to Lake. "When they come close enough, will they be able to detect the drive? Just like you can now?"

Lake purses her lips and nods.

"Like I said," Chireseal utters. "We're trapped."

"Then we fight," Colu says.

I fish out the hideous gold necklace hanging around my neck. "I have a full voidstone," I say, before turning to Chimeline. "Chimeline and I can hit them with voidance. I'm sure the enervated would give us their blessing. There's never been a more just cause."

Chireseal lets out a caustic laugh. "There are *five* of them, Dem."

I study Chimeline, her expression a mystery in the flickering golden light. "Maybe we can divide and conquer," I say. "We know their weakness now. We just need them to open their heartplates—"

"What are you going to do, Dem?" Chireseal says, standing. "Ask them to open up for you like some whore's legs after you throw her some gold?"

I don't answer him.

He walks to the cliff edge and points to the east. "There are five of them coming," he says loudly. "Five."

Colu sniffs. "We killed one. We can kill five."

"You think so?" Chireseal turns back to us and makes a sloppy circle in the air. "This shit hole? le-Mon-Sogara? Do you realize that one of them alone could raise its hand and set it ablaze in a ball of fire if it wanted to? One of them *alone*."

"We could trap them in the cavern," Colu says, shrugging. He motions to Chimeline. "She could be the lure. Her and the drive. Then somehow, after we get all five of them in there, we get her out and bury them. Seal off the mountain or something. They'll suffocate."

Chireseal wipes his gem-studded face with his dry hands. "You don't understand. None of you understand. They don't need air to breathe."

Remembering Temberlain's visions—the mutiny—I point to Chireseal and Lake. "Don't the two of you have advanced weapons?" I ask them. "Something stronger than a blade?"

Chireseal retrieves something small and shiny from behind his back. "Serraters. They'd make a fight against an empowered. But five azuremen?" He frowns while shaking his head and putting the weapon away. "It's not enough."

I snap my fingers as a thought comes to me. "Then we split up."

Everyone looks at me as if the suggestion is ludicrous.

"Hear me out," I say. "We get a few covered wagons that all look similar. Five, if there are that many here." I point to the crevasse. "With the one in the cavern that holds the drive, that would make six. Each of us would take a wagon in a different direction—"

Chireseal shakes his head. "The azuremen would know which one was real."

"But not if we ride fast. We get Xian horses and outrun them. Get out of range of their . . . " I wave my hand in the air. "Whatever voidance they're using to sense the drive. And then once we're far enough away, we head to different places. Go further south. Maybe to the Jewelled."

"They'll be tracking us the entire way from above," Lake says.

"Sure, but they won't know which one is *real*."

"There are azuremen south of here as well, in the Jewelled," Chireseal says. "You think that you're running away, but you're just running toward them."

I pause.

He pounces upon the silence. "I appreciate the idea, but it's a stupid one. You're just delaying the inevitable."

"So that's it, then?" Blythe says, as he raises his head. He's been silent, his hands in a prayerful position, all this time. His voice is full of unusual agitation. "We just give up? We lose our faith in each other and in the Unnamed?"

Chireseal stares at Blythe. "I think that your prayers are all we have left, Brother."

The bleakness in the air becomes overwhelming. We're all parched, starving, and exhausted. We've been up most of the night arguing and strategizing without success. We're fighting each other instead of the enemy. All our plans are like the labyrinthine caverns that surround this forgotten place—leading nowhere, circling back to the same conclusion: we cannot beat them.

Chireseal is right. Only prayers remain.

"There might be something else," Chimeline says, pulling me out of my despair. She looks up at Chireseal. "The power of Temberlain."

Chireseal and Lake share a glance. Chireseal mouths *Temberlain.*

Chimeline looks to me in consternation. "I think that we should tell them, Dem," she says. "It may be all we have left."

"Tell us what?" Chireseal asks, narrowing his eyes.

Both guilt and hope swell as I turn away from Chimeline and peer into the shadows underneath the trees, where my leather pack is. Maybe Chimeline is right. Perhaps this is the only thing we have left. The cryptic warnings of an enslaved people.

I get up and walk away from the light.

"Where are you going?" Chireseal asks.

I ignore him as I retrieve the small white-leather book. When I rejoin the group, I hand it to Chireseal, who runs his fingers over the cover.

"What is this?" he asks, wearing a frown of confusion.

"Chimeline's diary."

I glance at Chimeline to gauge her reaction—her face is relaxed, but almost too much so. I cannot help but fear that she's resigned herself to whatever words fill those pages, or whatever interpretation comes from them.

"You said it was lost," Lake says.

"I lied."

She looks at me with a hurt expression.

"I'm sorry," I add. "I didn't trust you at the time."

"Well, we don't have time to read it now," Chireseal says, thumbing through it. "But you said that these visions didn't reveal anything more than what you already told us." He tosses the book to Lake as she sets her blue-lit device on her lap. "I don't see the point."

I take a deep breath. "Yeah, well, I lied about that too."

Chireseal stares at me for a moment then sits back down. He brings his fingers to his temples and begins rubbing them in tight circles. "Alright. So let me guess. Chimeline's dreams are about Temberlain?"

I glance at Chimeline in shock then look back to him.

"That's fascinating," Lake says, looking up from the diary. "How can the enervated be doing this?"

"Who cares about *how*," Chireseal says. "I want to know *why*."

"I think that it's some type of warning," Chimeline says.

Chireseal looks at her curiously. "Why would an empowered like Temberlain issue you a warning?"

"Maybe the answer to that question lies in your knowledge of him," I say. "What do you know about the man?"

Chireseal looks at Lake briefly, but the woman doesn't notice. She's analyzing the pages of the diary.

"A famed axionship disappeared from the far reaches of the Virel Arm," Chireseal explains. "The *Apsides*."

I nod.

"Temberlain was part of the *Apsides*' officer crew."

"Wait," I say, as my mind catches up. "You said that it disappeared?"

Lake shuts the book with a *snap*. "Gone. No FTL communications. Nothing. Like it never existed in the first place."

"That's what all of us grew up believing," Chireseal says, glancing at Lake. "Until Mander's beacon."

"What do you mean?" Blythe asks.

He motions to the crevasse just past the cliff edge, a few feet away. "That Axiondrive?" he says. "It came from the *Apsides*, when it crashed here on this planet over a thousand years ago."

My eyes fixate on the dark chasm before I look to my friends in awe. "We already knew that there was an axionship crash," I say, trying to piece the logic and memories together. "The crash caused Blackscar and Xi Bay. Caused the voidstones. But . . . " In some respects, I had already postulated this. I remember telling Chimeline about it on the way to the Union. Still, though, my mouth hangs open as the vision in Chimeline's diary come into focus: the globe of blue and green surrounded by infinite blackness.

That's our world. That's us.

"When Mander's signal reached the confederacy, they charted that signal's location," Chireseal says. "Since your world was within the momentum cone, they knew that it was likely the location of the *Apsides*' remains."

"Momentum cone?" I ask.

He taps his foot. "A region of space where the *Apsides* could have wound up after its last known location, based on mathematics."

"We were sure once we got here," Lake says. "Partly because of the presence of axion fragments. Voidstones, as you say. Then, after we ran our translation implants, we started to converse with the natives." She motions toward us. "With your people. When we noticed that you have a certain curse phrase—"

"Temberlain's Ashes," Colu says.

Lake nods while Blythe shakes his head.

"Temberlain is our revered forefather, and we should show him some respect," Blythe says. "All of us."

Chireseal clears his throat. "You might have gotten that part wrong, Brother."

Blythe stands. "You blaspheme."

Chireseal extends a conciliatory hand. "No, I conclude, using logic. Listen, I've glanced through most of your effulgency writings. They're very impressive. Despite the passing of centuries and generations, despite having no technology whatsoever, you've done an exceptional job of preserving most of the truth. The evil of voidance, as you say. But we don't know what Temberlain's part was in all of this. The only thing we know for sure is that he was an empowered officer of the *Apsides*."

Blythe exhales with a faraway look in his eyes. "Faith guides me on the way of unwanting. Not the dusty annals of your history."

Chireseal clears his throat again. "Well, I *do* go by those dusty annals. And all I'm saying is that I doubt he was a hero."

"It's true," Chimeline says. "He was a hero."

We all turn toward her. Blythe once again brings prayerlike hands to his lips as he looks down upon her with both admiration and reassurance, but then this look transforms into worry. "Child, what's wrong?"

She inhales sharply and closes her eyes. A moment later, she lets out a moan of pain.

"Is it the azuremen?" I ask, leaning in.

Chireseal and Lake both stand. "They're here?" Chireseal asks. "You said sunrise!"

Lake lets the diary drop to the sand and scrutinizes her device.

Chimeline's body tenses. "He was more than anyone—"

Suddenly, she opens her eyes and reaches into the air with both hands, as if trying to brace herself for a fall. "No—"

Her body goes slack as she collapses to the ground and begins to glow a soft white.

"I'm not picking up any readings," Lake shouts, her voice full of fear.

"It's a dream," I call out, as I rush to the nearby cluster of trees and retrieve the blanket that le-Sante provided earlier. Coming back, I drape it across Chimeline's body. The radiance pours through it like sunlight through gauze.

"Why don't I see them?" Lake says.

"The azuremen aren't here," I say absently, while I clear the sand underneath her head of rocks and twigs. "She's having another vision. A Temberlain vision."

"You're sure?" Chireseal asks.

"Yes." I turn to them. "The last vision she had—the last thing I read—was that Temberlain was falling into the Axiondrive as it was in the process of eleutheria. There was a drill. He . . . I think Temberlain became an axionlighter."

"An eleutherian drill?" Lake asks incredulously, taking a step closer and momentarily looking up from the blue light. "You're saying that there was an Agh-Severian present in the drive chamber with Temberlain?"

I nod.

"Is that equipped with a tracer node?" Chireseal asks Lake.

She looks at him distractedly, as if he has just pulled her out of her thoughts. "Ah—"

With a sigh, he rips the blue-lit device out of her hands and begins to analyze its thin edge.

"It's on the bottom," Lake says with annoyance, pointing. "What's gotten into you?"

"If Temberlain was an axionlighter, we need . . . " He exhales. "I can't see shit in this light."

"What do you want a run a trace on?" she asks.

"Her," he says, motioning to Chimeline with a meager nod while continuing to search.

"On what stream of axion?" Lake asks.

Chireseal ignores her. With a groan, he stoops down opposite me next to Chimeline, using her body as a light source to help him see the bottom edge of Lake's device. Running his finger against it, he eventually presses something.

I hear a *beep*.

"What stream, Chireseal?" Lake asks again.

"The dream!" Chireseal answers, as something extends out of the device—a thin wire with a glowing white tip. "The dream *is* a stream. At least I think it is."

"But there's no graph," mumbles Lake.

"Her *body* is the graph!" Chireseal shouts.

He sets Lake's device flat on Chimeline's stomach. On it I can see a matrix of gray lines and blue circles indicating where the voidstones are located.

"What are you doing?" I ask him.

"Don't worry," he says, as he works. "This won't hurt her."

Before I can react, he pulls the wire out further and touches her forehead with the glowing tip.

A mélange of colors appears on the device and a cacophony of sounds erupts, breaking the silence of the night.

Immediately, I recognize what I'm witnessing.

The white drive chamber.

The black Axiondrive, coming closer, filling the field of vision.

A fountainhead of light.

The cage breaking apart. Glistening marbles of red.

Someone screaming.

Translucent spheres.

"Is this what I think it is?" Lake asks. She alternates her gaze between the device and me. Meanwhile, Chireseal's outstretched hand shakes as the device's output becomes momentarily cloudy. He presses the needle up against Chimeline's skin more forcefully.

I nod, transfixed. "We're watching through the eyes of Temberlain."

Blythe and Colu come near and stand around Chimeline as if we're lowering her into a grave.

Lake covers her mouth with her hand.

"This is it then," Chireseal says, without taking his eyes off the dream. "We're watching the past. But in a way, we're watching our future."

VOIDREAMING

The child sharply inhaled and touched his mother's skin hesitantly, as if the blue light could burn. "Mother . . . you're a sponsor."

With a loving groan, she shifted the five-year-old in her lap and extended her forearm further so that he could see it without straining himself. For the first time in years, there was no fabric to move out of the way. She wore a sleeveless sari tonight for two reasons. The first was that it would help her combat the oppressive jungle heat. The second was that it was time Temberlain knew the truth.

The number *02* glowed faintly in the night, mimicking the whispersalts' phosphorescence, which hovered over the gargantuan verdant leaves all around them.

Her thigh ached. Temmy was getting too heavy for her to cradle like this. Already becoming a young man. A glorious empowered.

But she held him tighter nonetheless, like how the nearby jungle vines embraced the thick trunks, coiling, climbing to three distant suns. She knew that their days together were limited. He would get his axiongraph tomorrow. A few days after that, he would be gone forever. The confederacy would take him away so that he could change the world.

So that he could change the universe.

Temberlain's mother smiled sadly as she looked him in the eyes. "Yes, I am a sponsor," she finally answered.

"But I thought that's only for ashen."

"Sponsorship is not required of me anymore, Temmy, but I received these numbers years ago."

"Why?"

Always why.

"When you were born, they discovered that you were an empowered."

He nodded. "You told me that."

"But I haven't told you everything. The moment that happened, we all received dispensation. From the confederacy."

He furrowed his brow and repeated the unfamiliar word, mispronouncing it.

"Dispensation," she corrected slowly. "Me. Your father. Sashoi and Britenian. Our immediate family will always be cared for by the confederacy. There will never again be a reason for any of us to give—or to be a sponsor."

"Because of me?"

She smiled even wider. "Yes. Because you are the greatest gift of all."

She could tell by his blank expression that he didn't understand. Which was fine. Humility would be needed in the tests to come.

"But then . . . why do you have a number?" he finally asked, staring intently at the blue mark.

She raised her eyebrows in approval at his relentless curiosity. Always seeking the truth. She had long planned on having this conversation tonight, and this is exactly how she had assumed Temmy would react. It made her wish that she'd had the conversation a year ago. His boyish innocence masked a sharp mind.

A specific example will be best.

"Do you remember Grandma Xerja and Grandpa Jelerlin?"

Temberlain's face crumpled in thought before he looked at her and nodded. "I remember the visages. They lived on . . . Sidarche?"

She nodded. "That's right, Temmy. Sidarche." She tousled his hair. "Good memory."

"They died a long time ago."

She frowned a bit. "Not too long ago. About a year. We'd already received dispensation by then."

She could see the gears moving behind his eyes.

"They were getting very old, Temmy. Their DNAR treatments weren't working anymore. They were slowing down. Getting sick."

He nodded.

"So, about a year ago, your grandparents decided to make a very important choice, of their own free will." She let out a deep breath. "They were . . . are . . . heroes."

"Heroes?"

She tousled his hair again. "Of course. They gave themselves to the confederacy before the end. They *chose*, Temmy."

She took a deep breath as a loon cried out far away, somewhere past the palms, out on the saltlake. "Since I was their only child, I received both of their gifts. I didn't have to split them with a brother or sister, like you would have had to do."

"Did they get sick because they lived on Sidarche with those treepeople?"

She shook her head.

"But you always say that things are better here."

"Well, that's true. This is Efful. We're at the center of the universe. But age is age, Temmy. Death comes for us all."

Her eyes moved past him to a nearby hovering whispersalt coming out of the dark jungle and into the starlit clearing. The plantation's formal garden was like a living statue, always needing to be honed. She reminded herself that even on Efful, the wildness always needed to be cut back. There was a constant struggle for order.

She sighed into the night, and it sounded like the whispersalt's translucent wings.

"Does it hurt?" he asked. "Going in soteria?"

She pursed her lips and for a moment said nothing.

"Mother?"

"I don't know, Temmy," she said, pulling her arm away and readjusting her son so he was on her other hip. She turned her head so that he wouldn't see the tears starting to fall down her cheeks. And when she did speak again, she whispered so her voice wouldn't break.

"The important thing to remember is that giving is *love*," she explained. "It is love for the Halcyon Confederacy, which gives us all so much more in return."

Temberlain didn't say anything.

"It's much like love for another person," she continued. "Sometimes you need to give away the thing that means the most to you in order to help that person achieve greatness."

The whispersalt sensed her salty tears. It floated close and then landed upon the crown of her head, illuminating her face. She gently swatted it away, and it receded softly into the denseness beyond, wings like eyelashes.

She remembered what she'd told Temberlain years ago, as the whispersalts silently descended upon their plantation's saltlake. She'd said that they were the stars coming home, going to bed to dream for another day.

"And now it is my turn to give, Temmy. Something even greater than myself. And no one will get a number for this." She hugged him tightly as the loon cried out again. "To the universe, I have to give *you*."

It hurt. Beyond belief.

As the hundreds of spheres struck Temberlain, he tried desperately to find the origin of the pain. Was it in him? Or in *them*?

He'd lost his hold on axion. The corpse was gone. The two-headed bleedersnake. Yet what he was seeing was . . . not of this world.

The hate.

He forced open his eyes as he stared into the burning white.

It was too much. He closed his eyes again.

His body was pinned against the black surface of the drive. A section of cage lay over him. Everything inside the chamber had fallen apart. The drive was no longer in the center. He was being pushed down. Somehow there was *weight*, but how—

Thoughts of his reality dissipated as the passing lives of the enervated took back control.

Countless lives.

All taken.

All abused.

And so much anger!

Temberlain forced open his eyes again to stop the torrent. The white pain of reality was better. He would gladly go blind.

Just beyond his fingers' reach was a small funnel of white that penetrated the drive. Undulating wires writhed above the drive's surface like an upside-down Garthenic jellyfish burrowing into rippling water. Translucent spheres streamed out of the opening, many of them passing through and over him as they escaped. With his eyes forced open, he saw the enervated both in the physical world and in his mind, their souls overlapping with his, blurred and borderless.

His fingers were white.

No. His arm was white. His entire body was glowing white.

They were taking control.

The enervated.

Temberlain closed his eyes and tried to fight back.

His mind was a muscle. He clenched it tightly, remembering the confederacy's teachings. His mother's teachings.

This is love, he reminded himself. *Giving is love: a sacrifice for something greater.*

He repeated it as if it were armor.

But the blows didn't cease.

Slowly, he began to see a pattern. Some of the enervated had given freely. Some of them hadn't. Some were old.

Some had never been born. Rich, poor, dark, light—the souls passing through Temberlain were as diverse as the planets making up the Halcyon Confederacy.

Only one thing was shared.

Anger.

The endless pain they'd been exposed to all this time—it changed the world outside the Axiondrive, but it also changed the world *inside* it. These enervated powered the *Apsides*: The artificial gravity, the FTL array. Countless other functions. And in return, the axionship powered their suffering.

Why?

He felt like a child again. He remembered the whispersalts, imagined them feeding on his own tears this time. His armor crumbled to rust.

Nothing mattered when there was this much suffering involved. An endless cycle. There was no effect that could rationalize this cause.

The Halcyon Confederacy is built upon hate.

The world shifted, both within and outside Temberlain. His body slid away from the drive as the chamber groaned and rotated. The cage tumbled off him and fell to the floor. The spheres tapered off, leaving him alone.

He was free.

A serrater bolt to the face woke him.

"What the—?" someone said.

"Shoot him again!"

Another bolt. Thunder dispersed by lightning. Oil in water.

The fluttering rainbow of colors against the curved backdrop of the chamber forced him to momentarily close his eyes to fight the oncoming nausea.

A membrane. How?

Who?

"He's using axion!"

"No he's not. Look at him. He's lost the graph!"

Temberlain blinked himself back to reality. It was darker in the chamber. Far darker. He was pinned against the outer wall by a section of cage.

He felt different. Something familiar, yet different.

Axion.

Somehow, he was inside. Here, but also there.

The last ribbons of the membrane dissipated in front of his eyes.

Did I weave it?

No. I wasn't even conscious. Besides, I don't have—

Temberlain glanced down at himself, half-expecting that his arm and axiongraph were back—that everything had just been a bad dream.

The blackened stump remained.

Yet he knew instinctively that he could work axion. Even without a graph. An enormous supply of enervated were nearby. He could feel them. He could command them remotely, as if the millions of souls were clutched in his hand.

Guiltily, he pushed the evil thought away. Unlearning such hate would be harder than cutting his remaining arm from his body. To think that he used to consider the enervated the consenting building blocks of the new utopia. To refer to those poor souls as supply. They were no such thing. They were prisoners.

The drive!

He spun toward it.

It rested a few feet away and below him, also against the outer curve of the chamber and buried within the destruction of the malineum cage, like a black egg in a nest of straw.

The shining whiteness was gone. Its surface was a matte abyss, yet a narrow funnel remained from which wires bloomed.

Kneeling atop it and only a few feet below where Temberlain lay pinned, the Agh-Severian frantically worked on the drill. Bright light emitted in a narrow beam from the collar of her glossy suit offered her ample visibility. She glanced up, but the work light pointed in Temberlain's direction hid her expression from him.

Lowering her head once again, she pulled and straightened the wires coming out of the funnel.

On his other side, three ashen mutineers clung to the same remnant of cage. They still wore their emergency FTL-differentiation vests, now useless. Two of them had serraters trained on him. Also useless, it seemed.

Why did their serrater fire not kill me?

In a heartbeat, it came to him.

The enervated. It was the only possibility. After a lifetime of him using them, they saved him.

But for what purpose?

The moment he'd touched the white light, he'd become one with them. And in that moment, they had shared their pain—an eternity of pain. Suffering and anger beyond belief. His eyes were now opened.

They must be freed.

He spun back toward the Agh-Severian.

"It's not empty," he told her. "There are still enervated trapped inside."

Perhaps his eyes had adjusted to the dark, or perhaps this time she wasn't directly facing him with the work light. But he saw her expression. It was a mix of distrust and shock.

"Listen, I can feel them inside," he said, pointing through a gap in the cage. He tried pushing the malineum cage off him, but it was too heavy. There was blood on it as well, and his hand slipped in it. "You have to finish!" He grabbed hold again and pushed with all his might.

This time, the cage remnant moved.

It shifted and then crumbled toward the ground. The pressure left his chest. His body slid down the curvature of the wall until it collided with more debris, bringing him within arm's reach of the drive and the Agh-Severian.

The mutineers also fell, into a pile of debris across the room. One of them jumped out of the way as the cage nearly fell on top of her.

One sprang to his feet and pointed his serrater at Temberlain's face.

"Stop!" the Agh-Severian shouted. "Stop it!"

The mutineer didn't fire but looked as if he wanted to. "You have axion hidden on you?" he asked Temberlain.

"No."

"Then how . . . "

The three mutineers shared a glance as Temberlain shook his head.

"I don't know," said Temberlain. "I don't know what's happening."

The Agh-Severian took a deep breath while staring down at the funnel between her knees.

"We have to—"

"What do you think I'm doing?" she interrupted, meeting his eyes. "Drill's damaged. Either by your use of axion or the serrater fire. There are still millions of enervated in there."

"Can you fix it?" he asked her.

She looked at him for many microrotations and then wiped her sweat-stained face with the back of her hand. "I'm not sure. I need more time."

"Let me help," he said. "Somehow, when I touched the drill when it was white, I became one with them."

Her mouth dropped open slightly.

One of the mutineers said to her, "We can't trust him."

"Listen, they're saving me," Temberlain nodded toward the Axiondrive. "They were the ones who created my membrane when you fired at me."

The Agh-Severian turned her attention back to the drill. The mutineers looked skeptical.

"If any confederacy come here, I'll command them to stand down," Temberlain said. "They'll listen to me."

"That's not what I'm worried about," the Agh-Severian said. She wiped her face again. "We've fallen into orbit."

Temberlain braced himself on the rubble and looked around.

It was true. There was gravity. He was shocked that he hadn't noticed it before. But then again, the feeling of being continuously partially in axion was a more-foreign feeling.

A deep groan reverberated throughout the room as the meager lights flickered.

Gone was the omniscient brightness that this room typically employed. Only a few saffron-colored halos sputtered around the seven hardline exits that formed the equator at a strange angle. Half of them were buried under rubble.

"Is the ship past the T line?" Temberlain asked her.

She nodded gravely.

"We saw it from the hardline while coming here," added a mutineer. "We're nearly on top of it."

Temberlain sighed in frustration as the Agh-Severian went back to work.

"They're doing this for a reason," he mumbled to himself. "They're doing this for a reason."

Slowly, he got to his feet, bracing himself on a malineum rung as the debris shifted slightly under him.

The mutineers still pointed their weapons, but at least this time they didn't fire.

"Can you use their power to fix this?" the Agh-Severian asked.

Temberlain cursed while he thought.

She seemed to understand what needed to be done to repair the drill, but he had no clue. Freeing souls was the realm of the ashen, not the confederacy.

"It doesn't work that way," he said. "The enervated gave me the power, but I still need to understand what needs to be done. And I don't. Not unless you can explain it to me."

She grunted. "We'll be dead by then."

He wasn't sure how many microrotations he stood there holding on to the wreckage of the *Apsides*. Temberlain watched the Agh-Severian reconstruct the eleutherian drill while wondering what part he had yet to play in all of this.

After some time, the feeling of gravity became worse. It was almost a push instead of a pull. The sense of some oncoming force.

Maybe this is the end.

Temberlain jumped in place as a few wires suddenly began violently undulating, tapping against the surface of the Axiondrive and breaking the tomblike silence of the room. The Agh-Severian crawled out of the way, rotating herself around the other side of the funnel as a light began to stream out of the drive.

The mutineers cheered.

But the white was not blinding, and the translucent spheres were nowhere to be seen.

The Agh-Severian touched her collar, and her face became covered by a silver mask that reflected the destruction of the room.

Something felt wrong.

Temberlain sank to his knees in the rubble as the pulling feeling became worse. More distinct.

It wasn't gravity. It wasn't the ship falling into the planet's atmosphere.

It was something *on* the ship.

Five vessels of axion. Much larger than graphs.

Azuremen.

Temberlain could feel their hideousness. Five invisible strings connected his soul to theirs.

And they were moving in his direction.

He looked past the exterior walls as if they didn't exist, following the invisible strings to deeper parts of the axionship.

One thing became certain as he briefly shut his eyes: the approaching azuremen were together, approaching a singular hardline. Descending a lift.

"There are azuremen coming," he said. But no one could hear him over the staccato sound of the drive, so he quickly repeated it at a shout.

The Agh-Severian looked up at him.

"How close are you?" he shouted.

She brought her hand to her collar, and the mask collapsed. She angled her face away from the funnel and blocked it with a hand. "I need more time! One of them is snapped!"

Temberlain closed his eyes for a microrotation and thought.

This is why they're protecting me.

"Go," he shouted to the three, spinning toward them. "Get on an escape pod, if there are any left. You'll die here."

They looked at him with disbelief, as the Agh-Severian once had. But they lowered their serraters.

"Go!" Temberlain repeated. "I'll hold off the azuremen."

They looked to the Agh-Severian for guidance.

"Do it!" she instructed, as she reactivated her mask. She dug her hands deep into the drill's mechanism.

The three mutineers huddled and spoke to one another while pointing to Temberlain.

"You don't have much time!" Temberlain said. "You need to go now!"

The three nodded and begin crawling over the wreckage, headed toward the equator of hardlines.

Temberlain moved with them as the three neared the exit to the hardline where the invisible strings led.

"No! Not that one!" he yelled. "They're coming from that way!"

"But that's the direction of the pods!"

"Take another hardline and double back! It's the only way!"

After a pause, they nodded and crawled higher against the curved wall to a more-distant exit. Sixteen's remains were splattered across its door.

The circular door opened.

Temberlain looked back into the chamber, his only hand raised above his head, grasping the frame as the *Apsides* shook.

The Agh-Severian glanced up from the drill, her face still shrouded in a mirror. She nodded once then went back to work.

Temberlain wished that he could say a proper goodbye to her. He wished that he could embrace her. She was most likely going to her death, just as he was, but she was the greater person. She had believed from the start.

He turned away from her and faced the door.

Once he stepped through, exiting the flickering, saffron-lit room and walking a few paces into the hardline, the door closed behind him with a *hiss* that sounded much like an exhale. Temberlain exhaled too.

The sounds of the drill were snuffed out behind the closed iris. Except for the intermittent groans and shakes of the ship, there was complete silence.

It was also beyond bright.

No artificial light existed in the hardline. Instead, through the tinted, translucent walls and past the hub's blue-glowing FTL array, the gleaming planet of green and blue swallowed everything. For a moment, he gazed upon it with awe. He could see rivers, archipelagos, snow-capped peaks. Closer in, streams with heads of sun-glistening light emanated from the *Apsides*. Hundreds of escape pods fleeing a past of pain.

Falling into the future.

Half a mile away, the torus door on the opposite end of the hardline opened.

Temberlain heard heavy footsteps echo forth, but he didn't immediately turn to face them. He couldn't help but admire this future. A future he could never have.

He was proud of the ashen—of what they had accomplished. He only wished that he could have partaken in this from the beginning. His life could have been so different.

At least I'm here now. My clarity is a gift.

He wasn't scared for himself, but he was still scared. Of all the trials and tests in his life, this one would be the greatest. There was only one thing left for him to do, and he needed to do it properly: Delay the azuremen—or destroy them. So that the enervated could share in this freedom. Freedom for the living and freedom for the dead.

"Officer Temberlain."

He turned to face the azuremen.

The translucent cylinder suddenly seemed smaller than it once was, but Temberlain knew that it was only because the five azuremen marched down its length, single file.

"We need to bring the Axiondrive online immediately," said the one in front.

"FTL comms is still down," added a second, its voice sounding almost the same, just a slightly different pitch. "First priority is reestablishment of comms."

Temberlain began walking toward them, feigning confidence. He spoke slowly and pointed toward the planet. "We're past the T line," he called out. "Assuming there was something we could do, the first priority should be non-FTL thrusters, wouldn't you agree?"

They continued to speak while marching. "Second priority is reestablishment of non-FTL thrusters, to escape the celestial body's T line. Restoration of the *Apsides* is a low probability at this point. First priority is establishment of comms in order to send a location. This is per Halcyon emergency procedures."

Temberlain sighed while nearing the midpoint of the hardline, now feigning concern. "Fine. But there's damage to the drive." He swallowed. "There was an act of sabotage. The drive has been compromised."

All the azuremen—one in front of each other—stopped in place in perfect syncopation.

Temberlain stopped as well, about fifty feet away.

The five looked at him, almost *through* him—as if he were made of the same translucent material as the hardline.

"Eleutheria was performed," Temberlain said.

"We know" said all of them in unison.

"The drive is useless," Temberlain lied, his voice almost a shout. "Unless you have millions of ashen to put in soteria, I think we need to explore other options."

"There are plenty of resources remaining," said the leader.

"Maybe in the five of you." He pointed at them. "Have you thought about that? Can you do this by yourselves?"

The leader shook its head. "We need the Axiondrive, and the Axiondrive is still at 71 percent capacity."

"I don't understand," Temberlain said, his goal simply to delay them. "I killed the Agh-Severian who had the drill, but it was too late. The souls were freed by then." He waved his arms out. "I saw them leave! They're all gone!"

"Your understanding is not required" said the five together.

Temberlain was almost shaken to his knees as a massive shudder cascaded through the ship.

The azureman in front stepped forward. "We don't have time for further interaction. Emergency protocols are in effect. Move, Officer."

"Why? What do you hope to achieve?

"Move."

But Temberlain didn't move.

In the few microrotations of silence, Temberlain heard only two things: another cascading groan and his heartbeat.

When the azureman in front raised its hand, Temberlain knew that his charade was over.

The remaining four followed.

In the centers of their palms, small circles of light quickly turned from black to blue to red.

But Temberlain was ready.

As the red stars fired down the length of the hardline, he summoned the enervated from the Axiondrive just past the hub door.

An instantaneous army arose. He turned white.

His plan had been to create a parabolic reflective membrane that would divert all five stars back to the azureman. But the power Temberlain wielded was far greater than anything he'd ever encountered. It was as if he'd opened a gate to the Garthenic Ocean, but instead of water, there was rage.

The five red stars amplified at his breast. And a sun shot back.

When it hit the azuremen less than a microrotation later, they were already in the process of creating their own membranes, but these were only partially woven. His sun tore through the membranes as if they were made of gauze before swerving out of control.

It hit the hardline, carving into its cylindrical surface.

The hardline split apart.

The five azuremen were pulled out into the vacuum of space.

And so was Temberlain.

Instinctively, he created a second membrane—a tidy sphere around his body to trap the vital oxygen while it remained. In the spinning sphere, he repeatedly lost and regained sight of the azuremen as the *Apsides* receded in the distance.

All six of them were falling toward the planet.

He glimpsed the FTL array. It glowed blue with an exhaustion much like the hidden crime of how it had come to be. The heat there must be unfathomable.

Then, a crack.

The *Apsides'* hub split apart.

One by one, the seven hardlines followed. They snapped in a series of explosions, freeing the torus from the hub.

Minuscule fragments of malineum broke away and captured the radiant light of the perfect yellow dwarf. The hub opened like a gigantic clamshell. In the middle was the Axiondrive, a black pearl. The rubble of the cage dispersed around it, gray and yellow dust. Within it, the Agh-Severian's lifeless body floated, her mirrored face reflecting the world she would never inhabit.

Temberlain knew that some oxygen remained within his membrane, yet he still found it hard to breathe.

Frantically, he hoped that she'd completed eleutheria. But a heartbeat later, he pushed this childlike thought away. He could still feel them. An army in the millions.

She had failed.

Pieces of the *Apsides* started to enter the upper atmosphere around him, glowing bright red. The escape pods had departed already, but he could see some below in the planet's atmosphere—white specks, still falling.

The azuremen were falling with them.

They'll survive planetfall.

He knew, then, what needed to be done.

Temberlain opened himself back up to the enervated.

They answered.

The FTL array's blue heat was nothing more than a miniature human-made nebula—a cloud of hydrogen, helium, and other ionized gases. The byproduct of the FTL engine.

A miniature nebula that can give birth to a miniature star.

He began to compress the molecules into a single point.

It wouldn't be possible using an axiongraph. Even with an azureman's heart—with all five of them—he could never build a membrane this immense.

But he had millions of enervated on his side.

Gradually, the blue gases became denser, turning into a sphere. Flashes of lightning blossomed within its roiling thunderhead.

Temberlain soon felt that the reaction was out of his control. He let go of axion there. The membrane surrounding the FTL array dissolved, yet the sphere of gases continued to collapse, now under the force of its own gravity instead of outside provocation.

The process of fusion was underway.

Closer in, another process was at work.

Hypoxia. Oxygen deprivation.

His training came back to him. Within the illusion of safety in his tidy membrane, he knew that deoxygenated blood was now being delivered to his brain. He felt numb. Unconsciousness would follow. This is how he would die.

And like all dying men, he remembered.

Temberlain saw the stars descending upon the saltlake. He was a child. He saw his mother, who believed in lies. It was not her fault. He loved her. She'd learned the lies from someone she'd loved, and he'd learned the same lies from her.

Somehow, this cycle of hate and anger and pain must be broken. But how?

Maybe this new world was a chance. A purified place.

His mother was talking to him now. Holding him in her arms.

The universe turned white. It swallowed him whole, with the azuremen too. He shut his eyes, but the ghosts of their hearts followed him. White specks against black. An opposite unfolding. It was all that was left.

No. The Axiondrive was there too. He felt the enervated in the sea of plasma. The outer shell of their prison had broken apart, but a cage was still a cage. Thousands of fragments, falling, falling.

A meteor storm of axion.

His membrane spasmed with tension. But it held.

He didn't want it anymore.

He wanted to be nothing.

As the whispersalts silently arrived upon his plantation's saltlake, his mother embraced him one last time. She told him that he was a star going home. He would dream for another day.

Temberlain dropped his membrane.

THE PLAN

Lake's device is eerily silent and black. Chireseal takes the glowing tip away from Chimeline's forehead. Only then does the screen utter a crackling sound. Its dim-blue matrix returns.

Nobody says a word as Chimeline stirs, her soft glow flickering to nothing.

Chireseal leans back and retrieves his lantern, setting it close by. It bathes us all in a lapping orange glow—a stark contrast to the axionlight. Beyond this ring and at the top of the stone pathway, dozens of townsfolk silently watch us in the predawn shadows. They've been there since the voidream started. The light and noise must have drawn them. le-Sante is there among the crowd, holding her lantern and resembling a statue. Gray sheets cover the people's bodies, making them almost disappear against the low limestone walls.

Chimeline inhales sharply, coming back to consciousness.

With a hand behind her shoulder, I help her sit up. She looks around, blinking rapidly. "I saw . . . " She swallows. "Temberlain died."

I nod, squeezing her shoulder. "We all saw."

She looks at us in confusion. "How?" Sitting up fully, she wraps her arms around her bent knees.

I lean back and point to the device, which is in Lake's hands again. "They were able to do something with that thing that allowed us to see what you saw in your voidream."

"Woman," Blythe says, briefly resting a hand on hers. "You are truly something special in the eyes of the Unnamed, and therefore in the eyes of all of us. I am humbled to be in your presence and learn the way of unwanting from you."

Chimeline nods respectfully, but there's a distant look in her eyes as she stares at the lantern.

"You will not suffer that same fate," I say. "I will not let that happen."

Colu grunts. "Well, now we know where the phrase Temberlain's Ashes came from."

Chimeline looks at me. "But what if that is my fate, Dem?"

"No—"

"What if that's always been my fate?"

"These visions come from the enervated," I say. "They're giving you a warning—a warning of what *not* to do. The dangers of overextending yourself."

"Temberlain killed five azuremen," she says slowly, her gaze unmoving. "And there are five azuremen coming for us right now. That is not a coincidence. The vision is telling us how to defeat them."

I shake my head vehemently. "We don't know that," I insist. "These visions began a long time ago. The enervated had no way of knowing that our path would eventually lead here, to these five."

Chimeline doesn't respond.

"Besides, Temberlain's battle was not here, on land. It was up there." I nod toward the sky. "And he didn't even use pure voidance. He used axion to cause a chain reaction in that . . . FTL drive. Which we don't have."

Lake and Chireseal exchange a glance. "That's not entirely accurate," he says.

"What do you mean?"

He motions toward the cliff. "Our two ships hidden in the cavern—they both have FTL arrays. Much smaller than the *Apsides'*, but the same reactor."

I feel Chimeline grab my forearm. When I look at her, I see an intensity that I hadn't expected.

"It's *not* a coincidence, Dem. The enervated are showing us what we must do. Five azuremen, an FTL array, and an axionlighter."

"No," I say, pulling away from her. "You are not going to recreate some enormous firebomb. It's too dangerous."

Chireseal sighs heavily and says, "I think she's right."

Blythe leans in. "It may be the enervated showing us, or it may be the Unnamed. Regardless, we *have* to be open to whatever they say." He slaps his palm on his thigh to accentuate the word.

I look at both of them. "Temberlain killed himself—and any survivors on that ship—with that explosion. That blast was so powerful that it shredded the Axiondrive!"

"We can take precautions against that," Chimeline said. "I'll weave a membrane."

"Better be a fucking good one," Colu mumbles.

"Where are the azuremen—how close are they?" Blythe asks.

"They should be here by sunrise," Lake says, glancing at Chimeline.

Chimeline nods.

Colu looks up to the horizon and I follow his gaze. A fringe of light is there.

"I wager we have a fullbell until we see the sun," Colu says.

"Are you picking anything up?" Chireseal asks Lake, motioning to her device.

"No," Lake says, shaking her head in frustration as she touches the screen repeatedly. "But if they're a fullbell off, as she says, they'd still be out of range."

Bells ring out in the distance, and I raise my head. A group of lepers stands apart from the rest in the shadowed summit.

Chireseal straightens and takes a step toward me. I stand as well. His expression is soft, but his eyes are focused. "I know you have reservations, but I think this is our best plan. If we don't take out the azuremen now, they'll not only kill us, but they'll continue their reign of terror on this planet. They'll find the drive and refill it. It's our best option. And it's our only option."

Despite my reservations, despite my instinct to protect her, I cannot come up with a better strategy. The enervated have been providing these voidreams for days now, and it's all led up to this. Even though it defies logic, the parallels cannot be a coincidence. I'd been hoping for—no, I'd been *expecting* something else. Some gleaming gem of wisdom that I could personally leverage to save this world and everything I hold dear.

The reality couldn't be further from this expectation.

The days of Dem are over.

There is so much master voider still in me, impossible to erase, even though I've cast off that cloak of shame. Why do I need to be the one with all the answers? The one in danger? The one in whom salvation rests? It's because I've grown accustomed to a certain power—a power that was stolen.

Now the greatest power I have may be my ability to step aside.

I run my hands through my hair, saying nothing.

"Well, if that's what we're going to do, we don't have much time," Lake says, still looking at the blue matrix. "We need to warm up the array."

Chireseal mutters a curse. Then he turns toward the cliff edge and stares out at the eastern horizon, arms crossed.

"What about the Axiondrive?" Blythe asks. "It must not fall into their hands."

"It won't," Chireseal says, without turning.

"So how exactly are we going to pull this off?" I ask, looking down at Lake and then at Chireseal's back. "Chimeline uses one of your ships—"

Chireseal raises a hand by his side. "Hold on. I'm thinking."

I sigh and crouch beside Chimeline. Pulling out the still-full voidstone from under my shirt, I hold the gold setting gently. "Listen," I say, struggling with the words. "I . . . I have faith in you. I know that you can do this all on your own. But I can help if you need me to."

She meets my gaze. "By doing what, exactly?"

I stare at her for a moment. Her words were sharp, but her expression is soft. "I don't know. Whatever you want me to do."

She gives me a timid smile and places a hand over mine. Chireseal hastily returns.

"Alright, here's the plan," he says quickly, crouching beside us and placing his elbows on his knees. "We can't use the cargo ship for the fusion reaction because we need it. Eventually. To take the drive off-world."

Lake nods.

He points to Chimeline. "The axionlighter and I will take the smaller innership into the canyons."

"Where, exactly?" asks Lake.

He waves an arm out across the horizon. "It's a maze—we'll go far enough inside to draw them away from you, but not so far that they can't find it."

I purse my lips. "Why—"

He silences me with an outstretched hand. "Just listen."

I nod begrudgingly and summon my patience.

"The problem is, I'm not sure if they're going to home in on *you*," Chireseal says, pointing to Chimeline, "or the drive." He turns to me. "That's where you come in."

My heart rises with the promise of a purpose.

"Alright," I say.

"The drive is in the underground cavern, and because of that, its signal is muffled." He gestures to Lake. "That's why she can't see it with the counter—just the seven fragments you're carrying."

I purse my lips. "So . . . you're saying that the azuremen won't be able to detect the drive either?"

He tilts his head. "That's the problem. I don't know." He motions toward the obelisk in the distance. "When I move Chimeline deeper into the canyon, the five azuremen are going to pass this village. Remember the front path you climbed? The one that zigzagged up here?"

We nod.

"Well, they're going to walk right by it." He shakes his head in thought. "They could climb that path too, if they wanted. Reach the summit, descend the backside, and find the hidden cavern and waterfall. And the Axiondrive."

"But that's only if they feel the drive's presence?" I ask.

He nods. "Yeah. If that happens, we're all dead. We need them to take the bait."

I purse my lips. "So . . . you want me to seal the cavern?"

He nods slowly. "Yes. Whatever you can do to put more rock in that opening—between it and them. And put up a membrane too."

"Alright," I say. "I can do that." I turn to Chimeline. "But what about the enervated?" I ask her. "Temberlain had a nearly full Axiondrive to pull from. You don't have any voidstones. And I need mine."

"I'll have their five heartstones, which will be enough."

She'll be using the azuremen's own voidstones to kill them.

The thought fills me with a strange mix of delight and malice.

"Have you ever activated the array outside of a vacuum?" Lake asks Chireseal.

He shakes his head. "I may need to override a few things."

"What about the blast itself?" she adds. "And the fallout?"

Chireseal groans and stands. "Yeah. No, I thought about that. It's a huge problem."

"What's a huge problem?" I ask.

He doesn't answer, but Lake does. "When Chimeline streams the axion like Temberlain did, it's going to create a fusion reaction with the drive's exhaust. It's not going to be as large as what happened with the *Apsides*, but . . . " She looks up at the waning night sky. "This entire place. I'm pretty sure it will be destroyed."

"Good Unnamed!" Blythe erupts. "What about the people?" He points to the watching shadows on the summit.

Lake doesn't reply.

"What about the people here?" he repeats, louder.

Again, no answer.

"Well, this is no plan!" Blythe says, slapping the sandy ground. "We cannot murder an entire town full of innocents!"

"We can take them into the cavern with us," I say. "It's big enough. They'll be safe behind the membrane."

Chireseal shakes his head. "We'll run out of air."

"But we only need to be in there until after the blast subsides," I say to them. "Right?"

Lake shakes her head.

"Why not?" I ask.

"Fallout," Chireseal says. "When this bomb goes off, this entire place will be engulfed in fire. But after that fire dies out, an invisible poison will be left behind that's just as lethal."

"How lethal?" I ask.

"Anyone who enters this place will die. The air and the land will be poisoned with radioactive energy."

"How long will be it unsafe?" Colu asks.

"About a thousand years," he answers.

"Fuck me," Colu utters.

"Well, we can't just give up on them," Blythe says, looking to the group.

"Listen," Chireseal says, lowering his voice while peering past the ring of lantern light at the looming crowd. "Half of them are dying anyway. Maybe it's a blessing."

Blythe gasps. "Brother! Death is something only the Unnamed may bestow."

Chireseal holds out his hands in deference, and for a moment, the only sound is the nearby waterfall past the cliff edge.

"I'll lead them away," Colu eventually says.

We all look to him.

"Lead them away?" I ask.

He nods.

"Where?" Blythe asks.

Colu spits. "I'll take them further west, around the lo-Kimer range. To Xiland." He turns to Lake. "Will that work?"

Lake looks at him and nods. "If you start now."

Colu stands and fetches his sword belt.

"Wait," I say. "Are you sure this is good idea?"

"No," he says, while clasping the belt around his waist. "But I'm not going to die while being useless, and from what I can tell, I'm useless here." He raises his sword halfway out of its sheath then sets it back, looking up at le-Sante holding the lantern. "If taking them away is where I can help, so be it."

There is stillness.

Then Lake opens a pocket in her skintight black suit and pulls something out of it.

"Here," she says. "You'll need this for when you return."

She tosses Colu something that looks like a gray pebble.

He looks down at it and his face twists in confusion. "What's this shit?"

"A personal membrane. Crack it open like an egg and then just carry it on you."

He shrugs and pockets it absently. Almost as if he never intends to use it.

I stand and walk over to him. "You *are* planning on returning," I say quietly. "Correct?"

He sighs and raises his arms slightly before letting them crash back down at his sides. "I don't know. Seems like this place is going to be an even bigger shithole fairly soon."

"After we deal with these five, there's more to accomplish," I say. "We could use your help."

Colu looks at the sandy ground and shakes his head. "I don't know, Dem." When he raises his head again, his one eye is unwavering, but his voice is not. "I don't know. We'll see."

"We should head down," Chireseal says. He extends a hand to Chimeline, who grasps it. He helps her stand. "Chimeline and I need to move the innership." He motions to Lake. "You work with Dem and Blythe to get cavern sealed up. Bring the horses. Some food as well. Anything out here will be gone."

Lake nods.

"One moment," Chimeline says to Chireseal. Then she steps toward Colu and me. Blythe joins her, and the four of us form a tight circle.

Blythe places a hand upon Colu's shoulder. "Though you frequently leave the way of unwanting," he says, "you always manage to find your way back again. I hope that it will be this way with us as well, dear friend. I hope to see you again. I will pray for it."

Colu nods and clasps Blythe's shoulders, tapping his back a few times. Then he leans in for an unexpected embrace. He whispers something into Blythe's ear, and Blythe nods, his eyes glassy in the lamplight.

Colu then turns to Chimeline and takes her hands. "As for you, all I can say is good luck, Woman. Seems like the fate of every kingdom is in your hands now."

"So it seems," Chimeline says.

"It's probably for the best. Dem or Blythe would find some way to fuck it up."

Chimeline flashes him a dry smile, but it quickly fades. She puts her fingers to her temples.

"I'm starting to pick something up!" Lake says, looking down at her device, her red face awash in blue. She taps the screen a few times and then looks to the east. "Five new fragments. Azuremen sized."

"One mile?" Chireseal asks.

"Yes," Lake replies.

"I feel them too," Chimeline adds, wincing.

"Alright, let's go," Chireseal adds. "No more goodbyes."

Still wincing with her hands to her temples, Chimeline hesitantly turns to me.

"I'll let the stemma know of our plan," Blythe says urgently, heading toward the limestone steps. He keeps talking as he goes. "il-Colu will guide them. May the Good Unnamed guide il-Colu."

"Come on," Chireseal urges Chimeline, tapping her forearm. "We need to move the—"

Without turning to him, Chimeline raises her palm, silencing him, and then places this palm gently on my chest. The tension in her face drains away. Then she leans in and kisses me on the lips, quickly, three times. Whispering into my ear, she says, "I will come back to you."

I take her into my arms.

My heart beats fast, as if I had run from the Royal House to the Third Ring. Right beside it is the weight of voidance. Lost in her black hair, I never want to leave. But the strongest thing I can do right now is let go.

So I let go.

"She'll be fine," Chireseal says, as he pulls her away. "I'll be with her the entire time."

I watch the two of them approach the cliff and begin descending the stairs. She's looking down, her face hidden from me.

Colu turns my way. "Dem, can I ask you something?"

I keep watching Chimeline until she disappears from view. "What is it?" I eventually ask him.

He peers at le-Sante, who's standing upon the summit. "Is it possible to use voidance to . . . you know. Cure her?"

I follow his gaze then shake my head. "Technically? Yes. I think the leprosy isn't far enough along in her and it should be reversible."

I place the full voidstone necklace back under my tunic, so it's out of sight. "But that's not really what you're asking, is it?"

Colu briefly looks at the ground, nodding repeatedly. "No, it isn't. I just thought I'd ask." He lets out a single laugh. "You know, even if you said yes, she probably wouldn't accept it. Probably thinks the disease is some fucking gift from the Unnamed."

"It's fine," I say empathetically. "If I were in your position, I would have asked for the same thing."

He adjusts his eye patch and lets it snap back into place. "I never thought about it before, but voidance is a lot like hilma."

"How's that?"

"There's a constant urge to use it to solve all your problems. But it *is* the problem."

I nod slowly, thinking back to the plantation where the two of us met. He was still a skullman, and I was still a voider. Now the paint and the cloak have been discarded, and the only thing left is the naked truth.

I'm nearly knocked off-balance by his sudden embrace.

"This is farewell, for now," he says, his gruff voice muffled by the soft creasing of leather. "I owe you my life. And maybe more."

"Goodbye, il-Colu," I reply, hugging him back. "Goodbye, my friend."

And with that, he turns and leaves.

SOMEHOW, THROUGH THESE IMPENETRABLE WALLS

"I used to preach that it was easier to move a mountain than to give away all that one owns," Blythe tells me, as he places a soft hand on my shoulder. The action summons me back from one world of darkness to another. "It seems that you have done both, my friend."

I know that it's his attempt at making me feel better, but it doesn't help.

Hiding my voidstone underneath my tunic, I feel sick about what I've just done. Even the tips of my fingers are numb, so extreme was the voidance I just worked to seal the entrance of our cavern from the sunlit waterfall and crevasse beyond. And create a membrane on top of it. The pain all of that must have caused . . .

I sit on a rock and face my friend. The pale glow of the cargo ship is our only light now. It casts his bald head in a sickly green.

With a groan, he sits on a nearby rock. "It is alright, Dem. The enervated understand."

"I hope so."

Blythe looks around, raising a hairless brow in awe. "This place is like a voidstone, and we're the enervated entombed within."

The palehound sitting next to him yawns, letting out a nervous whine.

I nod.

"Our only visitors will come randomly," he continues. "Somehow, through these impenetrable walls, they will bring us pain, for benefits we will never see."

Lake steps out of the cargo ship while looking down at her device. She descends the ramp distractedly but glances up once her feet touch the rocky ground. Noticing that I'm done, she bows her head and quietly says, "By your permission. By the Unnamed's will. By the bond that unites us all."

Blythe and I repeat the phrase.

Lake approaches. "Well done, Dem. There is no axionware that can do what you have just done. It takes custom precision to do something like that."

"Axionware?" I ask.

"A device powered by axion. A serrater, for example. Or this." She raises the flat blue-lit device in her hands.

"Can you still see the azuremen on that?" I ask her.

She shakes her head and points at the sealed entrance. "Not anymore. There's no way for their signal to get through."

"So you won't know when Chimeline creates the . . . " I sigh as I struggle with the word.

"Reaction?"

I nod.

"No. At least not on this." She looks toward the dark heights, where the edges of damp stalactites bear the same greenish glow as everything else down below. "There may be other indications, however."

Blythe and I exchange a glance.

The few horses we brought in neigh in the distant darkness. They mingle by the black pool of water, drinking. I already smell the lingering earthy scent of their shit and wonder how long we can stay here.

"So now we wait," I utter in exasperation.

"Yes," Lake says, taking something silver out of her belt loop as she sits down on a flat boulder. She sets the small device next to her, along with the screen.

"Is that a serrater?" I ask her.

She glances at it and nods.

"How does it work?"

"What do you mean?"

"Well, I assume you're using voidstones to power them, somehow," I say. "But how is that possible without a person invoking and directing the voidance?"

"It's rather hard to explain," she says, picking up the serrater. "The technology in here won't make much sense to you." She taps the back of it. "Axion is the main power source, but it's only a fragment—programmed to perform one function."

"Programmed?"

"Through circuitry," she says, running a finger up along the barrel. "And a small battery, of course."

"What's a battery?"

"It's another power source."

"Why do you need two sources of power?"

She rubs her face, looking tired. "Because invoking axion requires energy."

"But you said axion *is* the energy."

"It is," she says. "But it's not free. Like any tool, its use requires power."

I frown at her, not quite following.

"Think of it this way, Dem. When you use axion, you exert energy. You feel tired afterward. Exhausted, even. The battery becomes drained, just as you do. The difference is, where you need rest in order to recharge, a battery recharges itself with the very axion it's invoking."

I shake my head in confusion but don't ask her any more questions about it. Because something else is bothering me: the mystery of the enervated's protection.

Would they protect me against this serrater? Against any axionware?

She sets it down on a nearby rock.

As I look upon the small silver weapon resting there, its edges reflecting the green glow of the ship, I try to determine the answer but come up empty.

The rules of protection seem as cryptic as voidance itself. The enervated saved my life countless times yet abandoned me when I needed them the most.

There must be some pattern. Something I don't yet understand.

Despite the cool dampness of the cavern, Lake unzips her black suit at the neck, to the top of her chest, revealing more red-tinted skin.

"Good Unnamed, I wish we could feel the breeze," she mumbles. "It's so stagnant in here."

Suddenly, I realize that the person in front of me may hold the answer to this question.

"Let me ask you something about the enervated," I say, then pause to choose my words carefully. "Do they . . . protect you?"

She looks at me strangely. "Protect me how?"

"From an axion attack against you."

She scoffs playfully with raised eyebrows. "No. I wish they did. Would make my life immensely easier." But her eyes eventually narrow and fixate on me. "Why are you asking me such a strange question?"

"They protect us," Blythe blurts.

She scoffs again, but this time her smile is gone. "What?"

Blythe extends a hand to me, palm up. "I will let the master voider explain. This is out of my realm of expertise."

Lake leans forward but looks dubious.

Taking a deep breath, I provide the highlights of my story, starting with Mander at the bell tower and the fountain. I tell her that I would have been dead if it weren't for the enervated thwarting his voidance. Then again, in the Celestium. And finally, on the beach. Time and time again, voidance against Blythe and me should have worked, but it didn't. And we're sitting here today because of this fact.

"Perhaps Mander was inept," she responds.

"No." I shake my head. "He was many things, but not inept."

"Dem and I believe it's because we performed eleutheria," Blythe adds.

"Yes," I say, with renewed enthusiasm. "Which is why I thought you might be protected as well. You've performed eleutheria, just as we have. So they know your soul."

She blinks a few times then shakes her head. "No. I'm afraid not. I have never, in all my years and travels, heard of such a thing. And I don't know what you mean by *know your soul*."

"They have seen the sphere of your being," Blythe says.

She furrows her brow. "When I do eleutheria, it's different. I have a drill, which is axionware, while you . . . well, you two somehow do it manually."

"What's the difference?"

"Oh, it's very different. Before coming here, I never could have imagined such a thing." She motions to me. "An empowered." Then to Blythe. "An ashen descendant of Efful." She waves her hand between the two of us. "Two non-Agh-Severians working together without a drill. It still confounds me. The primeval quality of it. Chireseal told me that you enter the fragment while wielding axion."

"And then we find the white room containing the enervated and lead them out," Blythe adds.

She wraps her arms around herself. Perhaps it's the dampness getting to her. "That sounds treacherous."

Blythe nods as he puts a hand to his heart. "We believe that after we performed eleutheria the first time, the enervated knew our names. Saw our souls, as if we were enervated ourselves. The spheres of our beings. And from that time forward, they were able to protect us."

"But not always," I add.

Lake narrows her eyes again. "What do you mean?"

"The marked," I quickly respond. "Avorsi. It was able to do things to me in the nightmarket . . . " I shake my head. "I would be dead if it weren't for Caracant and Daunt."

"Who are they?"

"Xian voiders who ran from the confederacy. Refused to give up their voidstones."

"Ah."

"Don't forget about the azureman," Blythe adds. "The enervated couldn't protect us against that hideous thing."

I nod. "True."

"But normal empowered you're immune to?"

"That's what it seems."

"How do you know that it's just you two who are immune?"

I look at Blythe sadly.

"What is it?" Lake asks.

Blythe turns toward the dark pool. "I believe that Dem is referring to my daughter."

"What about your daughter?" Lake asks.

"I'm sorry, Blythe," I say quietly.

"Be nothing," he tells me, before taking a deep breath. Then he turns back to Lake. "She was slaughtered by a voider nights ago. I believe that she would have been protected if she'd participated in eleutheria—something that she'd been wanting us to teach her. But in my pride, or sloth, I kept it from her."

The horses bray.

Lake nods then stares at the ground for some time before looking back up at us. "As I said, in all of my years, I've never heard of such a thing. You should have told us this earlier."

"We didn't know that it was unique."

"It is," she says. "It's very unique."

"You never enter axion," I say. "Perhaps that's the difference. You use a tool, whereas Blythe and I touch the very souls of the enervated."

She purses her lips. "Yes. I think you're right."

"But why would the enervated be able to stop Mander and not an azureman? Or an avorsi? Voidance is voidance, right?"

"No," she says. Her mouth hangs open, and then she closes it. "Wielding axion varies greatly, depending on the source."

Blythe and I look at each other.

Lake says something I cannot understand, presumably in Agh-Severian, before she continues. "I wish Chireseal were here," she says. "He'd have a strong opinion on this. He always has opinions, and most of the time I have no desire to hear them. But this time . . ." She eventually slaps her red hands on her shiny black pants. "Well, he's not here, so you'll have to make do with mine."

I nod, waiting.

"Mander was an empowered," she starts. "Same as you, Dem, or any other voider in this world." Then she points at the cavern ceiling. "And of course, same as any confederate empowered bearing an axiongraph. What's the commonality?"

Neither Blythe nor I reply.

"People," she says. "You're all living people with the gift."

"Alright," I say, following along.

"Now, I'm no empowered," she continues, "but I know that there's a limit to what they can do before they begin to damage themselves—"

"Voideath," I interrupt.

She nods. "Exactly. So, I think that what happened with Mander is that the enervated in his stone simply rebelled against what they were being asked to do. Because they personally knew the effects. Personally knew that you were trying to help them." She shrugs. "This is pure conjecture, of course."

"Rebelled?" Blythe asks.

"They are slaves. Any slave can revolt against its master. It's just a contest of wills."

"A contest of wills between the enervated and the empowered," I mutter, lost in thought. I nod as the notion becomes more logical in my mind. "To a voider, this would make it seem as if the desired action were a thousand times—no, a million times—more difficult to perform. Boiling a sea instead of bath water."

Lake nods.

"The choice," I continue, "would be to either give up and let the enervated have their way, this one time, or to stay determined. Which would probably lead the voider into voideath."

Lake stands and paces.

"But the avorsi," she says, glancing at me. "They were not stoppable."

"Correct."

She gathers her black tendrils over one shoulder as she walks back and forth. "Fascinating."

I wait for her to continue.

"When the axion is cut into their brain, the person is lost," she says. "That much we know. They become like an animal. There is no will left."

"You're saying that you can't have a contest of wills against an animal," I surmise.

"Yes," she says. She stops next to the serrater resting upon the boulder and looks down at it intently. "And no." She pauses in thought. "Maybe avorsi are less like animals and more like axionware," she mumbles.

Blythe and I exchange a confused glance. "We're not following," I say.

She continues to stare at the serrater. "What if the body *is* the battery?" She nods to herself then turns to us. "You've seen them up close?"

"Avorsi?" I ask. "Yes. Too close for comfort."

"Then you know how they look, physically. Dead. Gray. Sickly."

Remembering the Northern and Southern marked, I nod. Despite their power, they looked as if they were one step away from death. Walking corpses.

"They say that the avorsi do not live long," Lake continues. "And now that I think about it, that may be why. Because the avorsi's bodies are being used to power their axion. They don't suffer from voideath, as you call it. Instead, their flesh and blood are taxed, just like the battery in this serrater, until they're depleted."

Blythe turns toward the darkness of the cavern. "Like riding a horse through the desert until it dies of exhaustion and dehydration."

"Exactly."

They're trying to protect you. But I will drive this vessel into the ground before I allow them to have their say.

Who is I?

Who is them?

I run my hand through my hair as I remember the strange words which were spoken to me as I was losing consciousness in the nightmarket. "So you're saying that the enervated still rebel against the avorsi," I say, "but there is no instinctive defense mechanism—no contemplation of voideath."

"Yes. You're killing them, I wager, but just not as fast as they're killing you."

"Are azuremen the same thing?" Blythe asks.

Lake sits again. "No. Azuremen are more traditional axionware," she says. "Machines with immense fragments, batteries, and very sophisticated programming."

"Programming?" I ask.

She points to me. "The confederacy has been able to replicate the logic you perform naturally into systematic routines. And, like an avorsi, there is no will. So when the enervated rebel, the axionware can simply repeat that command within a loop, until the battery is drained."

I shake my head as I think back to the Port of Yamerind. "Then why didn't that azureman's battery fail when it attacked us? It didn't weaken in the slightest."

Lake looks up at the glowing stalactites. "Thanks to a few brave separatists, we gained access to the internal designs of azuremen years ago. The heartstones power themselves. The left ventricle of the heartstone powers the batteries, which in turn power the azureman. The right ventricle—itself larger than most fragments—is dedicated to executing the traditional axion commands." She looks back down. "It's an endless cycle."

I try not to dwell on the fact that five of them are coming for us at this moment, somewhere outside the sealed cavern. And Chimeline is the only one able to stop them.

"What about that thing?" I eventually say, motioning to Lake's serrater.

She scoffs. "Well, I'm certainly not going to test out my theory on you, if that's what you're asking."

I grin for the first time in a long time. "You think if you fired it at me, it would work?"

She raises her red brow. "I don't know. If the enervated are truly able to rebel, I'm guessing that the bolts wouldn't find purchase. At first. Maybe they'd swerve away. Or simply knock you back instead of going through you." She shrugs. "It's impossible to say. But I think after a while, if there were enough bolts fired at you—either through multiple sources or one wielder using one device repeatedly—you'd eventually be hit."

"Let's pray that we never have to find out," Blythe says.

Lake smiles sadly while gathering her black tendrils. "Well said."

Blythe puts his palms together and brings them to his face, leaning over in silence. Maybe he's praying for that right now.

Lake and I listen to the dripping of water deep in the cavern and the occasional whinny of a horse.

"So Agh-Severians are the only ones who can perform eleutheria?" I eventually ask her, trying to keep my voice low.

She raises an eyebrow. "That's very perceptive of you," she says. "How did you know?"

"In Temberlain's visions, the woman with the drill was an Agh-Severian. And you came here planning to do the same. It strikes me as either an amazing coincidence or something more."

She smiles sadly. "No, it's not a coincidence. It is an ancient and secret rite of our race."

"Why only your people?" Blythe asks.

She raises her hands and turns them in place. "Because of this. Our skin is immune to axionlight."

I think back to when Marine fell into the white pool.

"You can touch it? When the surface . . . liquefies?"

She shakes her head vehemently. "Nobody can touch the substrate during inversion. Anyone who does is immediately placed in soteria. Even we Agh-Severians must be incredibly careful."

"So . . . what exactly are you immune to?"

"The axionlight that is emitted during eleutheria. It's so strong that it elicits dementia in most people if they get too close. Some have tried wearing protective gear. Even membranes. But . . . " She shrugs again. "I don't pretend to understand it. All I can say is that the light doesn't impact us. We're able to stay conscious during the entire procedure, which takes considerable time and finesse, by the way. In order to reach all the souls."

"You must be proud," Blythe says, lowering his hands. "That your people are known for such a holy practice."

She laughs once, sardonically. "Proud? Yes. Hated?" She nods with pursed lips. "That too."

"Hated?" he asks. "By the confederacy?"

"Correct. The confederacy," she repeats, almost spitting the word. "They keep a close eye on my people. Closer than most. They try their best to infiltrate our chapterhouses. To identify the eleutherites. But they always fail."

I don't understand half of what she said, but one word rings in my ears.

Confederacy.

"When will all of this be over?" I ask her.

"Within a fullbell, as you call it—"

"No," I say, shaking my head. "I mean after the azuremen are destroyed."

She points a thumb toward the wagon with the Axiondrive. "We take it off-world and hide it."

I sigh in exasperation as the problem solidifies in my mind. Suddenly, a burning irritation consumes me. Not just because of the thought itself, but because I haven't had the thought until now. I've been climbing a rock not knowing that there was a mountain.

"After *that*," I say, my voice louder than it should be. "How do we destroy the confederacy? Hiding axion isn't a long-term strategy."

Lake leans in. "It *is* a strategy, Dem. We know that the confederacy's power is dependent upon axion. And since it's impossible to destroy axion, we hide it, wherever we can."

I look away.

"We've been doing this for a long time," Lake continues. "My great-grandfather was part of a similar operation. He performed eleutheria on a drive before it was hidden. And it's stayed hidden for all these years."

"That is wonderful," Blythe says.

"You do realize, though, that it's not good enough," I finally say, meeting her gaze again. "Freeing souls is a noble effort, but it's no endgame. In order for these atrocities to end, the confederacy needs to be taken down. For good."

"I don't disagree," Lake says. "But you don't know what you're asking. The confederacy is much larger than the resistance. And those in the confederacy are much more powerful than we are. Their willingness to use axion makes them a force so dominant that we cannot simply overthrow them."

It's impossible to destroy axion.

A childlike hope enters my mind, and at first I almost discard it as it appears, due to its absurdity. Yet the possibility remains as stubborn as me.

Could something so small—so insignificant—be the key to taking down the most powerful force known to humankind?

Feeling foolish and hopeful in equal measure, I carefully search my pants pocket for the nearly weightless stone wrapped in fabric. It's there, waiting for me.

Is it impossible?

Slowly, I take it out and hold the wrapped stone in my palm. In the dim ambient light, the emerald cloth looks black.

"This is Marine's," I say reverently to both, as if I'm speaking over a dead body. Blythe nods—he's seen this before—but Lake frowns in confusion.

"The one whom Chimeline was speaking to," Lake says. "Your wife."

"Yes," I say.

"And she's still in soteria?" Lake asks, the high pitch in her voice making it clear that she finds the situation incredulous.

I nod. "She refuses to leave."

"What?" she asks. "Why?"

Instead of answering, I stare at the cloth in my palm as the memory of my last conversation with Marine consumes me. I hear Lake and Blythe speaking, but it's as if I'm in the void again—their words are muffled by pain.

Blythe gently shakes my shoulder. "Dem, perhaps you should speak to her again."

I close my eyes. "She hates me, Blythe."

"*Hate* is a strong word."

"You have no idea," I say, opening them again and alternating my gaze between the two. "She has forgotten everything else in this world. Colors. Feelings. Memories. People. She has even forgotten Mander. That sick bastard who brought all of this down upon us. All she remembers now is me."

"That is good!" Blythe says encouragingly. "It's probably because of the love she—"

"No. There is no love in her voice. It's complete hatred. She blames me for everything. It's as if all her hate and anger has been directed on a single point, and that single point is me."

"So you think that's why she won't leave?" Lake asks me.

"I don't know," I say. "For a long time, I thought it was because she was teaching Chimeline. But Chimeline says that she's ready." I motion to the sealed entrance. "Which is obviously true. Anyway, that was the last time I spoke to Marine. I told her that it's time for eleutheria, but she responded by insulting me."

"And when was this?" Lake asks.

Guilt returns as I realize how long it's been. "Just before we arrived at this village."

"You should try speaking to her again," Blythe says. "Maybe this time it will be different."

I shake my head. "I don't know what other words I can offer her."

"Maybe offer her silence," he says. "Let her provide the words."

"Maybe," I say, raising my palm slightly as I look at Lake, eager to change the subject for multiple reasons. "Anyway, all of this is beside the point. Have you ever heard of an axion fragment turning to ash?"

Her frown returns. "Ash?"

I nod.

"You mean the outer shell fragmenting?"

"No. Not like what happened with the drive and the creation of the voidstones here. Nothing like that. I'm talking about *ash*. Black dust."

She shakes her head.

"Well . . . ever since Marine's been in soteria, her voidstone has been slowly shrinking. Turning to ash."

She stares at me, not blinking.

"I'm not sure what's happening," I continue. "But I wonder if it means it's being destroyed?" I shake my head slowly. "I don't think so because she's still trapped inside. How can you destroy axion if the enervated are still—"

Lake does something with her device and it turns a bright white, harshly illuminating us. I squint. The cloth in my hands suddenly looks as it should during the sun's zenith. It's a brilliant emerald color.

There are specks of black on it.

Lake rests her device against a boulder and kneels in front of me, extending her hands. "May I?"

I give her the stone.

Slowly, she pulls back the fabric, one layer at a time. Each time, more specks of ash appear. Even though there isn't a trace of a breeze in the cavern, they float away, as if caught in one.

"These are from the fragment?" she asks, without looking at me.

"Yes."

"You're sure?"

"Positive." After a pause, I add, "I've studied the ash in the void. There is no lattice structure to it. It's not like other indivisibles."

She glances at me in confusion before looking back down. Inhaling sharply, she slowly unveils it completely.

The stone appears to be the same size as before—grape sized. But then the outer layer crumbles, losing shape, becoming a cloud of ash that half-obscures the stone as it dissipates in the air between us, thinning, becoming nothing.

What's left behind is smaller than a grape.

Lake looks up with a haunted gaze. Her hands are shaking.

"I know," I say. "It's strange—"

It's not just her hands. My hands are shaking too.
The entire world is shaking.

FIVE

You've brought visitors, Marine says coolly.

At first I say nothing. Within the void, I turn to the glistening form of Lake. She sits next to me, still clutching my forearm. *Good*, I think. I feared that this would be too much for her, but then again, she's adept at eleutheria. Being in the void might not be that much different. Ironically, I'm the one who's anxious. I'm the ship lost at sea. She's the lighthouse guiding me home.

Blythe grasps my other wrist.

I brought two friends, Marine, I say carefully. *Blythe is an effulgent. You might remember him.*

He was one of the flies caught in the web. Where was it? Only a moment passes before she answers her own question. *In the Celestium. Yes. I think there was a Celestium.*

There are many reasons I brought these two into the fold, the least of which was to see if Marine remembers Blythe. So much of her world seems to have fallen away, like the eroded, sun-bleached cliffs that washed into Xi Bay. But some roots remain, half buried in the sand.

When Lake speaks, she does so carefully and formally—as if meeting King Andrej X for the first time, in the throne room.

I am Lake, an eleutherite from Agh-Severia. I wish to convey my deepest sympathies regarding your enslavement, but with your permission and by the Unnamed's will, I have some questions for you before we free you. The answers to these questions have the potential to turn the tide in the war.

For a moment, there is nothing—just our three glistening bodies against the murky indivisibles of the entombed cavern beyond.

Agh-Severia, Marine eventually says. *I know millions from there.*

Of course, Marine has never set foot off this world, but there must be a bridge between her white room and all the others. Like cellmates in a limitless prison. She's been everywhere and nowhere.

We need to know why your voidstone is shrinking, Lake says.

Marine ignores her. *Did you leave your loved ones behind too?*

What do you mean? Lake asks her.

When you came here in your ship. With the other ashen from Efful. You must have crossed the black sea. So far away from Agh-Severia.

Yes.

So you left your loved ones behind in order to free people you don't even know, Marine says.

That is true, Lake admits. *But it is nothing compared to the sacrifices the enervated have made. The sacrifices you have made. I serve proudly.*

Who is there, waiting for you? Marine asks. *Whom did you leave behind?*

Marine is doing the same thing she did with me earlier—she's trying to avoid the tough conversation.

I keep my voice level to help offset the harsh words. *Marine, we don't have time for reminiscing. We need to ask you about your voidstone. Anything you can tell us would be helpful.*

Time, she replies, letting the word stretch out, letting it seep into the darkness. *You must forgive me. I don't remember what that is.*

In the void, I look up and stare at the indivisibles of my membrane and the sealed entrance. Is she being facetious? How much time has passed since the cavern shook, sending stalactites to the ground? Chimeline and Chireseal will hopefully be returning soon, if things went according to plan. Chimeline will have the ability to open the cavern from the outside. Until then, there is nothing for us to do. Chireseal ordered us to wait and preserve the membrane. This conversation in soteria is the only way we can help. While Chimeline and Chireseal fight a battle, perhaps we can find a way to win the war.

Marine, I say, *do you know what is happening to your stone?*

There's a pause before she replies. *You said it was getting smaller.*

Yes! Lake interrupts, clearly emotional. *It is. But do you feel it getting smaller?*

Oh no. Quite the contrary. This white room has gotten so large. I don't remember the Royal House, but I'm sure that this room must be larger than that place. I don't even see walls anymore. If you came here . . . if you truly came here to visit me and you opened the door for good, I don't know if I would even see it.

Lake's glistening form turns to me.

Do you want us to go there, Marine? she asks softly. *Open up the door for good?*

Silence.

Blythe speaks up. *It is my undoubted belief, dear child, that you will be content in the arms of the Unnamed. All you need to do is accept.*

More silence.

I'm tempted to pile words onto Lake's and Blythe's, but I fear that Marine may still be angry with me.

First, you need to accept Chimeline, Marine replies. *And the man from Efful.*

What do you mean? I ask her harshly. Within the void, I stare at the voidstone in my glistening hand.

They are near. Accept them.

Are they in trouble? With the azuremen?

Trouble? No. The only trouble is the weight of hate.

Lake and Blythe turn toward me, perhaps equally confused by the cryptic words.

For now, the mountain is your *door*, she says. *Not mine.*

Marine, you're making no sense.

The effulgent says that all I have to do is accept the Unnamed. But he's wrong.

I wait for her to continue. Blythe moves, but he stays silent as well. Maybe Marine is preparing another personal attack. Maybe it's something else.

I need to first accept myself, Dem. I need to accept you. And all the pain. The anger and the pain. You cannot go to the Unnamed carrying those things—at least not if you want to go on your own. You need to carry nothing.

Child, Blythe says. *Have you tried praying?*

The indivisibles on the rock face in front of me suddenly move. Something is happening near the sealed opening.

Marine? I call out.

But she's already gone, haunting some distant corner of her ever-expanding world.

As I let go, a muted sandstorm of light hits me. It's coming from a horizontal slit in the rock face. The opening is much smaller and higher off the ground than the original—about five feet wide and two feet tall. A twisted smile in the skull in which we hide.

Lake and Blythe stand by my side. All of us raise our hands in front of our faces, shielding our eyes from the sudden brightness.

Quickly, details emerge as our eyes adjust.

Behind my shimmering membrane, beyond the jagged opening, Chimeline hovers within a glittering sphere, many feet above the ground. Past her is nothing. No waterfall. No ivy carpeting the walls. Only the stark wind—screaming and dry.

Chireseal floats beside her within his own membrane, his body slightly curled like a babe within the womb, chin resting upon his chest, unconscious.

There's movement near Chimeline.

At first I think that it's simply her hair. Her long, black tendrils flutter in all directions, as if caught by a turbulent breeze.

But multiple black orbs also slowly swirl around her head, disappearing on one side only to reappear as they orbit their sun.

I quickly count the heartstones.

Five.

PART FOUR

SHIP OF FOOLS

A DARK PAYLOAD

Once through the membrane, the spheres surrounding Chimeline and Chireseal collapse. They splatter against the rock face and ground yet leave no residue behind.

Chireseal falls, still unconscious. The five orbs hit the ground as well, sounding even denser than his body—five *thuds* that speak volumes as to what they contain.

Lake scrambles over as Chimeline floats toward the floor. Her bare feet gracefully find purchase.

"Is he alive?" Lake asks her, cradling Chireseal in her lap.

"Yes," Chimeline says, her voice almost an exhale. She's clearly exhausted. "They tried to overwhelm him with their . . . energy. Whatever comes out of their hands."

"What?" Lake asks, her expression one of anguish. "They hit him?"

"Partially, as I was building the membrane. He was forced back against the rock."

Lake examines the back of Chireseal's head.

I move to embrace Chimeline, but she takes the subtlest of steps backward. I'm not sure if she's simply tired and still gaining her balance, or if it's something else.

"Any complications?" I ask her hesitantly.

She shakes her head but doesn't meet my gaze. "It went exactly according to plan."

I see it now. Her cold power still rages, here in this semidarkened cave. An impenetrable radiance. She doesn't shine with axionlight. She's tarnished with the weight of experience. Whether consciously or not, she's pushing everyone away, including me.

"We should perform eleutheria," Blythe says, oblivious to the tension. "Good Unnamed, these five heartstones!" He kneels, collecting them. The palehound approaches and sniffs them warily.

"We don't have time," Lake says, looking up from Chireseal and pointing to the rippling membrane that protects us from the killing wind and sand outside. "That's not going to hold for much longer."

"I could build another one," I say, then quickly add, "If the enervated are alright with it."

"Another one will also only last for so long," Lake replies. "The radiation is simply too much. We need to leave. Now."

"Leave?" Blythe says, stuffing the heavy heartstones into a leather sack one by one. "Where?"

Lake gently sets Chireseal's head on the floor and then stands. She continues to stare down at him, hands on her hips. "I don't know. I need to talk to him when he wakes. But for now, we need to load the payload and get on board."

Chimeline, Blythe, and I share a glance. It's obvious that Lake's hiding something, and I think I know what it is.

"You're not just worried about the radiation, are you," I say to her. "You're worried about them. The confederacy."

She nods once.

"How are they a threat to us anymore?" I ask her, pointing to the sagging leather sack in Blythe's hands. "We just took care of five of their azuremen."

Instead of answering, Lake storms toward the wagon, parked in the dim recesses of the cave. As she walks, she beckons us with a wave. "Come on. I need your help. I'll explain as we work."

The three of us follow.

About a hundred feet past the curve where the pool hits the rock edge, we reach the dilapidated wagon. The white tarp soiled with reddish dust is ripped in multiple places. Underneath it sits the emptied Axiondrive.

"They may have been watching us," Lake says, as she pulls upon the tarp. "Because of what you did to that azuremen in Winter's Baiou."

"Watching from their axionship," I say, looking up toward the cavern ceiling.

She nods as she begins hastily untying the tarp cover from a grommet. I assist on the other side once I understand what she's trying to do.

"But being watched is one thing," I say. "Being in imminent danger is another."

She pulls on a leather cord then pauses and looks up at me. "You don't understand their capabilities. They could send down innerships—reinforcements—in . . ." She waves her hand in annoyance. "A fullbell. If they wanted to."

"And you think they'd do that? They know exactly what we're doing here and who we are?"

"We just destroyed five azuremen. As far as I know, that has never happened—ever. If we didn't have their attention before, we certainly do now."

Once the ties are free, the four of us pull off the soiled tarp, revealing the pure blackness of the Axiondrive. It weighs so little that it begins moving on the wooden platform, jostled by the friction.

Lake squats, pulls out a knife from her shiny suit, and cuts away two crude pieces from the tarp, about one foot square each.

"What's that for?" Blythe asks.

She motions toward me. "For the empowered. The drive may be empty, but axion is still axion." She looks at Chimeline. "Do you need protection as well?"

She shakes her head.

Lake stands and hands me the two pieces. "Just help me guide it toward the ship," she says, as she moves toward the back, disappearing from view. "Slowly."

I cannot see Lake, but I assume that she begins pushing. The drive easily moves off the wagon. For a moment, it floats in midair, at the same level as the raised wooden platform. But then it slowly falls until it grazes the stone ground, causing a soft scraping sound to echo throughout the cavern. Chimeline and Blythe stay on either side of me, palms to the black surface. I push with my palms as well, using the two squares to prevent myself from entering the void.

"I think Chireseal would agree that our best strategy is to evade them," Lake says, over the din. "The explosion will have caused tremendous heat. Also a cloud. We might be able to escape without detection before they send others."

"More azuremen?" Blythe yells.

Lake shakes her head. "Empowered. Other confederate soldiers. An axionship—even an exploratory charter ship—can carry a few thousand. Okay. Stop here."

I feel the drive push into me but I hold fast, keeping my palms against the surface. It comes to a rest, and relative silence returns.

"Someone help me with Chireseal," Lake says, walking to him.

Blythe runs over and grabs his arms. Lake grabs his feet. They carry him up the ramp and into the cargo ship, disappearing into the green light.

Suddenly, Chimeline and I are alone.

I notice that she's resting her forehead against the Axiondrive, looking at the ground.

"Are you alright?" I ask her, putting my hand on her shoulder.

She flinches, but I don't take my hand away.

Peering around her black hair, I see that her eyes are closed tightly, as if she's holding back tears.

"Come here," I say, and pull her away from the drive. Her head falls into my shoulder. Eventually, she grabs hold of me, and her sobs come.

A humming sound comes from the ship. I cannot see what's happening, as it's on the other side of the Axiondrive, but the ambient green light in the room gets brighter, reflecting off everything except the drive itself. I don't care about that, though. I care only about the woman in my arms.

Chimeline speaks into my ear. "The hate is so overwhelming. That's what's getting to me. I'm not sure how much more I can take."

"Hate?" I ask her. "What hate?"

The humming sound ceases.

I push her gently away from me and stare into her wet eyes.

"The enervated," she says. "Their hate for the confederacy is . . . it's certainly understandable," she says, with a wrinkled nose. "But you don't realize how perverted it feels. To constantly be inside it, and to be the only one who can make it grow wild." She takes a deep breath as Blythe and Lake round the Axiondrive.

"Ready?" Lake asks. Seeing us in our embrace, she clears her throat. "I've, um, activated the bay."

Chimeline nods as she lets go of me.

Together, we take a few steps around the Axiondrive, and I open my mouth in awe.

The cargo ship now has two decks.

It's been raised at least another ten feet off the cavern floor. The ramp is now a ladder that hangs vertically. The lower deck must be the bay—the space that will house the Axiondrive. It looks organic. A gigantic transparent-blue embryonic sac.

A membrane.

Following Lake's lead, we push the drive a few more feet until it's absorbed within the membrane. It snaps into place as we finish—some form of voidance must be guiding it.

The ship offers a gentle chime.

"Alright. All of you, on board," Lake says, wiping her hands on her shiny suit as if there were blood on them. "Chimeline, you'll need to open this cavern a bit more, but only when we're inside the ship and I give you the command. Alright?"

Chimeline nods.

Lake climbs up first and disappears into the ship. The palehound circles the foot of the ladder, barking once, then twice.

Blythe approaches the ladder but then stops, looking back into the darkness by the pool. "What about the horses?" he calls out, craning his head.

Lake's red face reappears from the opening. "No. They have to stay."

"But they'll starve here!" Blythe shouts.

"No, they won't," Lake says. "They'll die within a fullbell."

Blythe brings his hands to his head. "And the palehound?"

She shakes her head again. "Leave him."

Blythe's face twists in disgust as Lake disappears again. Chimeline and I near.

"I am not leaving this creature," Blythe says, as he stoops and picks up the palehound with a deep groan—it must weigh close to fifty pounds. "I am not leaving it," he repeats.

Chimeline and I look at him with concern, but the palehound doesn't object. It remains passive in Blythe's arms, although its pink eyes are wide with anxiety. Rung by rung, Blythe climbs.

"Leave him?" Blythe exclaims, in a mocking tone, once he nears the top. "Well, he would not leave you!"

I motion to the ladder. "Go ahead," I tell Chimeline, and she starts to climb. I follow.

Once I reach the top, I see that the interior door—or wall, whatever was previously there—is gone, revealing an immense curved front window and two rows of seats to the right in a space about ten feet square. Lake is already seated at the front surrounded by many different-colored glowing screens that resemble the one she had in her hand. She presses one of them, and the ladder retracts. The door behind me closes.

A rush of air fills the cabin. My ears pop.

The palehound whines.

Blythe takes a seat next to Lake, and a red strap automatically wraps around him. Chimeline and I step around Chireseal's body, which is in the aisle. His hands and feet are anchored to small red-tinted rungs built into the floor.

We move to stand behind Lake and Blythe.

Lake looks over her shoulder as she places a palm on a glowing circle on a screen in front of her. "You're going to want to sit down for this."

As soon as we do, we begin to move.

SUMMONED ONCE AGAIN

I'd considered this place a wasteland before, but I was wrong. In comparison, it used to be a garden. A lush paradise, now burned to a husk.

As we pass through what remains of the membrane, the cargo ship brushes against the rock below. Lake puts both hands on her illuminated screens, exacting precise control as we stabilize within the narrow crevasse. Through the curved windowpane I can see only a hundred feet in front of us—everything else is lost in the slowly billowing cloud of white, red, and gold.

To the left, harsh shadows caused by our ship's exterior lights indicate where the hewn stairs used to be. The path up to le-Mon-Sogara. Many are gone: blasted or burned away. I look to the right, where the waterfall used to be, but even that cliff face looks different. The proud mountain—a permanent fixture if ever there was one—seems twisted into a humble slave, shoulders bent under the commands of a hideous new master.

We begin to climb.

The sand below us glistens through the chaos. As the ship rotates, I see the cavern opening, stretched wide from Chimeline's voidance.

"Look!" Blythe says brightly, leaning forward while pointing.

Two of our horses rush out into the storm-filled crevasse.

"They're free," he adds with a smile.

Lake glances at him but doesn't say anything.

The beasts turn sharply to the right and begin galloping down the length of the crevasse over smashed boulders.

Blythe brings his hands, palms pressed together, to his lips as he continues to watch the horses. "You see, Dem? The Unnamed provides, even for the humblest of his creations. Perhaps the others will follow . . ."

His voice tapers off as the horses slow to a halt.

"Why are they stopping?" he asks.

They make a few tidy circles, as if lost, and then fall onto their sides.

A few heartbeats later, their writhing bodies are lost to the white and crimson haze.

"Same thing would happen to us," Lake says indifferently.

In a moment, we breach the plateau.

Almost nothing remains of the town of le-Mon-Sogara. No structures, from what I can see through the haze—only the subtle forms and patterns of low squares, where they used to be.

Outside the windowpane, red sparks fall like snow.

Then I recognize something. The obelisk still stands, resembling a lonely dagger buried hilt-deep, as if it were the weapon that pierced the heart of this place.

My roaming gaze falls upon Chimeline, and I realize with unease that she caused all of this. She is the dagger.

Her eyes are closed, but her expression is not one of peace nor rest. It's twisted somewhat, and she breathes heavily. Her hands grip the chair's armrests.

I'm about to put my arm around her, thinking that she has motion sickness. The sensation of flying in this strange ship is disconcerting. But then she opens her eyes and I immediately know better. Her haunting gaze is fixed on Blythe's leather sack, which contains the five heartstones. Even as she stares, her face—her entire body—diverts to the left, away from it.

She must feel the enervated. Perhaps she even feels what *they* feel. She mentioned their hatred.

That's it. As I study her more closely, this is the emotion I see. It's not fear, nor pain. It's anger.

"Alright. Clear," Lake mutters, seemingly to herself. She slides her hand forward on the screen and the ship accelerates, knocking me back into my chair and making me look straight ahead. Immediately, the corpse of a town is behind us, the red haze and sparks becoming a blur.

A groan comes from behind.

"Hey! Get me out of these!" Chireseal yells. "And who brought this palehound on board?"

Lake glances behind her, and I feel us slow down. I'm not sure if we come to a complete halt. The town was our only constant. We're in a haze that continues to slowly swirl, but it could be from our continued movement or its own chaos.

She gets out of her red harness and walks the short length of the ship. I turn around briefly—the palehound licks Chireseal's face while Lake removes his restraints.

A few moments later, they return together, his arm slung around her shoulder.

She kicks the white wall hard, and a chair opposite and facing me unfolds smoothly.

"How long was I out?" Chireseal asks, as he falls into it. A red strap silently embraces him. He winces as it pulls his body into a more upright posture.

"Not long," Lake says, as she returns to the controls. I feel us accelerate again.

"Tell me you got the drive," he says, through clenched teeth.

"Of course," Lake says. "I figured that we should evacuate the area. In case they send reinforcements to ground zero."

"Right. You did right," he says, gingerly touching the back of his head. He then stares at Chimeline, who has closed her eyes once again. "How are you doing?" he asks her.

She doesn't answer.

"Chimeline," he says, louder this time. "How are you feeling?"

Still no answer.

I motion toward Blythe's leather sack, resting on the floor. "I think the azuremen's heartstones are affecting her."

He shakes his head and looks toward the windowpane. "What she did . . . I've never seen anything like it. We could win this war with her."

"She's not a weapon."

Chireseal scoffs.

"I mean it," I add, my voice harsher.

"We're *all* weapons, Dem," he says. "Make no mistake about that. And you'd better get used to it, because whether you realize it or not, you're part of the resistance now." He nods toward Chimeline. "So is she."

"Prayer is the Unnamed's weapon," Blythe says, staring straight into the storm. "It is the one and only way to fight. And I have found that an open palm is always better than a closed fist."

Chireseal shakes his head again, as if clearing his thoughts or pushing Blythe's response away.

I feel us slow down.

"Why are you stopping?" Chireseal asks Lake.

She turns back to him. "I can't read shit from the navs. Radiation must be scrambling the sensors. I'm flying blind."

Chireseal taps his foot. "So if *you* can't get a reading . . ."

"Then they can't either," Lake says, nodding. "Yeah. As long as we're in this cloud, I think that we're safe."

"But once we reach the edge?" Blythe asks.

"We're not going to," Lake responds, leaning back in her chair. "We're going to sit right here," she says, letting her gaze pass over all of us, "until we figure out a plan."

For a moment, nobody says a word. The palehound lies down next to Blythe and yawns, its red fangs a stark contrast to the ship's white interior.

Chimeline opens her eyes. "You still want to take the drive off-world," she says. "Correct?"

I glance at her, surprised that she's been following the conversation. I'd assumed that she was locked away within her cage of hatred.

Lake and Chireseal also both seem surprised but nod. Chireseal stares at the impenetrable mist outside. "Want to? Yes. Can we? That's the question."

"We have to assume they're in a geosynchronous orbit," Lake says. "I have no way to measure the altitude of this anomaly. Probably meso-layer. But even if that's the case . . ." She shakes her head. "It's risky."

"But what's the alternative?" Chimeline asks.

The ensuing silence in the answer.

Lake finally taps her fingernails on a screen. "The explosion will have drawn their attention. They're probably sending down innerships to the caverns now." She motions to Chimeline. "To the exact location where the axionlighter created the detonation."

"The last place they received signals from their azuremen," I say.

She nods.

"So you're thinking that now is the right time?" Chireseal asks. "While they're distracted?"

Lake takes an enormous breath while bringing her hands to her temples. "I don't know. It's a gamble."

"What if we just hide it?" Chireseal asks. "Again." He points to the white floor. "On this planet."

"Where?" Lake asks. "They're watching every move we make."

Chireseal leans in. "If I recall from the maps, there's a jagged edge nearby. A plateau northwest of here."

"The lo-Kimer foothills," I say.

He nods. "They must run for hundreds of miles."

"Keep talking," Lake says.

"Well . . ." He uses his hands to illustrate, creating a vertical plane with one palm while pointing at it with the index finger of his other hand. "It might be a blind spot. We ride the edge. Unless the axionship is in the northern hemisphere, they probably won't notice."

Lake groans.

"I know," Chireseal adds. "It's not perfect. But what if we can send a signal and await orders?"

She glances at him with concern but says nothing.

Chireseal points to the sack on the floor near Blythe. "We have the azuremen fragments," he says. "I might be able to chain them together with the ship's drive."

"Wait just a moment," Blythe says, alternating his gaze between the two of them. "Are you talking about using black arcana?"

Chireseal cracks his knuckles. "Listen, I don't like it either, but we're stuck here on the edge of the Virel Arm and there's no way we can send and receive an encrypted signal that far without significant axion."

Blythe drops his head back in exasperation. "This is a ship of fools," he says to the ceiling. "I thought that you had a plan."

"We *did* have a plan," Chireseal answers, his voice raised. "SER-234! But that went out the window the moment you decided to follow me. Why couldn't you have just taken my advice and gotten as far away from here as possible?"

An image of the Lemon Tree Inn brushes across my memory, yellow upon white, but I push it away.

"SER . . ." I say. "What exactly is that?"

"A gas giant."

Lake extends her hands, palms out, as if pushing the sky away. "Jettison the cargo. Set the drive's trajectory for the planet, and the Axiondrive would be swallowed up in the dense gravity."

"Destroyed?" Blythe asks.

Chireseal shakes his head. "Not destroyed. Just hidden enough to effectively mean the same thing."

I can't help but look out at the mist and think of our similar situation. We're hidden, for now, but we seem to be destroyed as well. Everything does.

"If we're caught down here, we're done for," Lake eventually says. She points. "Up there . . . at least we have a fighting chance."

Chireseal nods. "Make a run for it—"

Suddenly, his words are muted, overtaken by screams surrounding me. Needles enter my skull, and I writhe in my harness, seeing nothing but white.

I've felt this pain before. But as I stare at Chimeline, it's evident that it's not coming from her. She's studying me, her black eyes wide and filled with concern. They all are, leaning in and addressing me. But I don't hear their words. I hear someone else—someone I'd never imagined being summoned by again, and certainly not in this way.

LORD DEMOCRYOS, says the silky voice. MY ONCE-LOYAL SUBJECT. I AM IN NEED OF YOUR SERVICES ONCE AGAIN.

FORK

Blood drips from my ear. The droplets' sporadic collisions with the shiny white floor between my legs echo in the otherwise silent cabin.

The palehound slinks over and eagerly licks them.

Leaning forward with my elbows on my knees, I watch him work beneath me. Though there is silence, the king's words still reverberate around my skull. A droplet of blood lands on the palehound's hairless neck and slides down. The beast gazes up at me with pink eyes that look like developing pearls and then licks my ear. I let it.

Lake taps the surface of her screen with her nails.

"I think he's coming back," Chimeline says softly.

"Shake him," Chireseal says. "We need to know who he was speaking with."

Chimeline shushes him then places a gentle hand on my forearm. "Dem?" She squeezes it.

I look up at her.

"Can you hear me?" she asks.

I nod and push the palehound away before checking my ear. My hand comes away clean, but I still wipe it on my already-soiled pants.

Everyone is still in their seats, but looking at me.

"Who was that?" Chimeline asks.

As I look at her serene yet tortured face, I know why I've been sitting here saying nothing, biding my time. It's not because of the pain still radiating in my head. It's not because I'm trying to understand the king's words.

It's because I don't know if I believe him. And if I *do* believe him, what does this mean for Chimeline and me? For the war at large? What he's asking of me . . .

Without voidance, it would be suicide.

"It was Andrej X," I tell her.

Her dark eyes widen.

"Your king?" Chireseal asks, leaning in. "From the North?"

"Yes."

"I thought he was in Winter's Baiou."

I shake my head. "Not anymore. He's here." I motion to the gray outside the window. "Just west, past this cloud. He's with Colu in the deepsands."

I tilt my head because I don't know if that's true. When I could look upon Andrej's sweaty face glistening in the candlelight, when his words were spoken inches from my face, it was clear that he was manipulating me.

Here, in this mist, it's impossible to tell if the king is being sincere.

"Maybe not," I say. "The king wants my help."

"Your *help*?" Blythe almost spits the word out. "Why would a man who has murdered countless—"

I hold out my hand. "Just let me relay his full message before you make any judgments."

"Is he still enlisting black arcanists?"

"How else could he voidspeak with me?"

"I thought that they were all taken," Chimeline says. "Daunt and Caracant said—"

"Maybe it was an azureman," Blythe says.

I shake my head. "The king said the five azuremen guarding them left in the night. Right before the explosion. He has a few voiders loyal to the throne. Some who still secretly have their voidstones."

Lake purses her lips. "The five did come from the west. That part checks out."

Chimeline doesn't look convinced. "Is it possible that there were more than five and some remained with the king?"

"No," Lake says, without hesitation. "The confederacy would have sent all nearby azuremen to reclaim the drive. It's that important. But they would also never allow your uninitiated empowered to be armed with axion. And to my knowledge there are no confederate empowered here." She purses her lips.

I look at her curiously. "What are you suggesting?"

"That he used an avorsi."

I snap my fingers. "Yes. He said that there were a few marked. They're guarding the cache."

She looks at me in confusion.

"The hundreds of confiscated voidstones—the ones taken away from the voiders by the azuremen." I point to the window. "The marked are guarding them."

For a moment, nobody says a word.

Chimeline softly grabs my forearm again, looking apprehensive. "Did you voidspeak with Colu?"

"No."

"So you don't know if he's still alive," she says. "Or the lepers, for that matter."

I raise my eyebrows. "No. I don't. But Andrej X knows that I'm here . . . that *we're* here, near le-Mon-Sogara, and have the drive." I clear my throat. "Anyway, all of this is beside the point. What's important is that he wants to reinstate me as the master voider so I can fight back."

"Against the confederacy?" Lake asks.

"Correct."

More silence. Blythe's mouth is open.

"Ever since the confederacy arrived," I say slowly, trying to repeat what the king said word-for-word, "Andrej X has been playing along, biding his time. Because he knows that he cannot beat them." I meet each gaze, one by one. "But now he figures that there's a chance. Colu told him what we did to the five."

"Playing along?" Blythe snaps, looking at me with a hurtful expression.

"What?"

"You said that he's been playing along. Is that what you call knowingly sending hundreds of my brothers and sisters to their slaughter?"

I close my eyes momentarily. "Those are his words, not mine. I'm sorry."

He looks away from me, his face placid again. "Being nothing and standing for nothing are two different things," he adds. "Your king stands for nothing and thereby falls for anything. He fell for the confederacy. But now, despite all its dark allure, it's just a leash around his neck. A leash that he must be longing to remove." Blythe takes a deep breath, shaking his head. "He doesn't want your help to destroy the confederacy. He wants your help to reclaim his power."

"I agree," I say.

Chimeline leans in, wrinkling her nose. "Does the king even know the truth about voidance?"

"He has to, right?" I say. "It was in the message that we sent back with Reddles. But we all know how that ended."

Chimeline nods gravely.

"He knows and doesn't care," Blythe utters.

"You're ignoring the most important detail," Chireseal adds flatly, with crossed arms.

We all look at him.

"The king knows that you have the drive. You mentioned as much. That's what he wants. Everything else is bullshit. He wants the drive."

Our gazes connect, and I nod. "I don't disagree. With either of you," I add, glancing at Blythe.

I look down at my feet. "Ever since he voidspoke to me, I've been telling myself that this is just a ploy. He now understands, more than ever, the power that the Axiondrive would give him—*if* he had voiders under his control who could wield it. I think that he's also deeply afraid that the blood rule will be overturned amidst this chaos."

"Blood rule?" Chireseal asks.

I raise my head. "Voiders and effulgents can't rule. It has always been this way. To limit the power of the throne. Xiland is the same way."

He nods.

"The king knows you, Dem," Chimeline says softly. "He knows that you would never use voidance to claim the throne. Despite your shared history, despite all your disagreements, there's no one he can trust except you."

"Brother," Blythe says, before I can reply, his face twisted into a frown. "You cannot be seriously considering this. Becoming the master voider again."

I don't reply.

"Dem?" Blythe repeats. "Please tell me that you are not considering his offer."

I address Lake and Chireseal instead. "There's no question about what we'll do with the drive. You're taking it far away from here, hiding it in a place where the king or the confederacy will never find again."

They both nod.

"*We're* taking it, Dem," Chimeline says. "All of us."

I put my hand on hers.

"But some confederates will stay here, right?" I ask Lake and Chireseal, pointing at the white floor. "We may have taken out five of their azuremen, but that's just the tip of the spear. We know at least a few avorsi remain."

Lake and Chireseal exchange a worried glance. Chireseal taps his foot. "The extent of their forces on this planet is now limited," he says guardedly. "At the moment."

"Don't you think that there could be azuremen on other continents?" Lake asks him.

Chireseal brings a hand to his chin, his index finger circling one of his facial gems. "That's included in what I would consider limited."

"You're referring to Scorpiontail?" Chimeline asks.

Lake nods. "That and other lands."

"How do you know that there's not more of them?" I ask.

He glances up as if he could see past the low, curved ceiling. "The axionship orbiting above us is small. By comparison."

"It's what they call an exploratory charter," Lake adds. "Speed over capacity. To prove that the beacon was authentic and prime the planet. There are no confederate forces on board."

"But mark my words," Chireseal says, still brushing his gem, "they're sending reinforcements as we speak. The empowered are on their way."

"So are our people, I imagine," Lake adds. She looks deferentially at Chireseal, and he nods.

"Thanks to this axionlighter," he says, dropping his hand and motioning to Chimeline, "this lonely corner of the Virel Arm is now the center of the universe. It might as well be Efful."

"How soon?" I ask Chireseal.

He purses his lips. "Before reinforcements come? It's impossible to know. Depends on how close their nearest carrier is."

"Give me an educated guess."

He looks to Lake and she responds. "It could be anywhere from a day to a year."

"Good Unnamed," I say.

Blythe puts his hands to head. "I don't understand why you're asking all these irrelevant questions instead of answering mine, which is quite simple. You know that we cannot win this war with voidance. This war is *about* voidance." He turns to me. "I know you. I know that you would never agree to becoming master voider again. War or no war."

The desire to stare at the floor returns, but I keep my gaze locked on my friend, saying nothing but fearing everything. There is a fork in the road ahead. Do I take it, despite all my inclinations? Despite Blythe's disapproval?

I feel Chimeline's gaze on me, so I turn to her.

She's studying me with cryptic eyes. As if she already knows what I'm thinking.

She has a purpose here. She's a weapon, as Chireseal said. The greatest of weapons. But her job is to hide the Axiondrive. To temporarily leave this world for the black sea. Given the increased scrutiny, I doubt Lake and Chireseal could do it without her.

What can Blythe and I do with the Axiondrive? We've already done our job. We've already emptied it. How can we be of any help? We're only in the way.

But we *can* fight back here. We *can* begin to save this land from the confederacy. With words *and* voidance.

I dig into my pocket and retrieve my remaining full voidstone, heavy with pain. I feel horribly reliant on it. The more I try to let it go, the more I feel that I'll be dead without it.

The fork in the road, I realize, is more than just physical—yes, some of us will stay here, and some will journey to the black sea. But it's more than that. Is it acceptable to use voidance to fight the confederacy? When is enough enough?

I return the stone to my pocket as the answer comes to me.

I proclaim the words like a prayer in the silent white cabin. "By your permission. By the Unnamed's will. By the bond that unites us all."

Chimeline squeezes my arm. I interpret it as understanding. Blythe frowns. The other two nod.

"You've said it before," I add, looking at Lake and Chireseal. "Sometimes our duties require us to use axion. But how do we know *when* it's acceptable?"

"It's never acceptable," Blythe says.

"Our rule is simple," Chireseal answers. He looks at Blythe and utters something in Effulgian—a short phrase that reminds me of being in the void.

Blythe utters something back, looking disgusted.

Chireseal turns to me. "It's hard to translate into your tongue. The closest I can come up with is 'axion for no axion.'"

"Blythe," Lake adds softly, "think of it this way. Soon, we'll be taking this Axiondrive off-world. To hide it forever. That takes axion. Traveling among the stars is impossible without it. Like trying to sail your oceans without the wind."

"Hiding an Axiondrive is one thing," Blythe says. "Using black arcana to fight a war is another."

"That's not the goal," I remind him.

"So you actually intend to accept the king's offer?" Blythe says, looking at me accusingly.

"Yes," I say, placing a hand on his shoulder. "But I need your help."

"I will not help you help this king. I will not help you use voidance."

Chireseal opens his mouth, but I silence him with an extended palm.

"This all started out on a road not so long ago," I tell Blythe. "Although it seems ages. When two men from different worlds grasped hands and decided to cross a bridge into the unknown. They opened their minds, and from there they opened prisons of untold torture. Faith and reason, working together."

He nods. "The evil source of voidance could never have been discovered without it."

"And still, it is the answer."

He bites his lip.

"We will both go down there—you and I," I tell him. "We help them fight back against the oppressors, but we also educate."

"Educate how?"

"We keep to the code: Chireseal's code. Axion for no axion. We take back the cache of voidstones and help the king arm his remaining voiders in order to fight the confederacy."

"But—"

"Under the condition that they swear to the code and agree to surrender the voidstones when we're done. At which point we'll perform eleutheria. Axion for no axion."

Chireseal puts a hand to his chin again, looking down at his tapping foot. "You think you can take out the avorsi?"

"Yes," I say, glancing at Blythe again. "With voidance, of course. You cannot talk down a rabid beast."

"So that's it?" Blythe says, slapping his thighs and then throwing his hands in the air. "We just distribute the voidstones again to all the voiders and *hope* that they deliver on their promise?"

"Blythe, if the king is left to his own devices, one of two things will happen. Either the remains of the confederacy will rape this land with their giving houses, or voidance will flourish in their absence. This is an opportunity. And it must be seized."

Blythe brings prayerlike hands to his mouth. Eventually, he nods.

I look at Chireseal. "And you must finish what you came here to do. Get rid of this Axiondrive and come find us when you're done."

Chireseal turns to Lake. "Alright," he says softly, almost at a whisper. "Take them to the edge and let them down. But make it quick. I don't want to be anywhere near avorsi." The gems on his face pick up a rare ray of light coming through the mist. Multicolored spots cross the curved white walls of the ship.

Lake swivels forward in her chair and taps the screens.

Chimeline looks down briefly and then back up at me, nodding once, as if she has accepted the situation. Her black eyes are wet, reflecting the swirling mist outside.

"This is not goodbye," I remind her.

The two of us move within our seats as the ships slowly accelerates, and Chimeline falls into my embrace against the wall. I know that it's by accident, but I relish it anyway— the last few moments where our hearts beat as one. I try to push away a memory of moonlight. It was the king who brought Chimeline and me together. Will he also be the one responsible for our permanent separation?

"I'll come back to you," she says.

"I know you will," I tell her without hesitation, smiling proudly. "I've never doubted you."

And it's the truth. I don't know if I can pull off what I need to do. What Blythe and I both need to accomplish. But I know that she can.

She was always an axionlighter, even before she fell into that pool.

FORGIVENESS IS DISORDER

The cargo ship's side door opens wide, and the silence of the cabin is assaulted.

Chireseal turns from the windowpane and shouts, but I cannot hear him. He points to the opening behind me—a field of violent, swirling sand. Next to him, Lake studies her glowing screens under a wrinkled crimson brow.

I embrace Chimeline, wrapping myself in the chaotic darkness of her hair, my back facing the open door.

"I love you," I say into her ear.

"I love you too."

Beyond these soft words, Chireseal is shouting.

"Dem," Chimeline adds, moving her hand to the back of my neck and pulling away just slightly. Her nose grazes my cheek. "I feel voidance nearby. Please, be careful."

"I will." I can feel the sand making its way in, stinging my face and neck.

The ship lowers slightly, and the reverberating sound in the cabin reaches new levels.

In my peripheral vision, beyond the flying wisps of black hair, I see Chireseal hastily get out of his harness and approach Blythe. He shouts something to him.

Blythe closes his eyes and jumps out of the ship. I cannot see anything—no ground, no sky. After Blythe falls away, he's lost to the swirling sand as well.

Without hesitation, the palehound leaps after him.

Chireseal approaches me next and leans in.

"I know you can't see the ground, but it's only a few feet below!" he shouts. "Don't lock your knees!"

I nod.

"Now go!" Chireseal says, slapping my back. "I'll take good care of her!"

But I'm already lost once more in her embrace, holding on too tightly. I know it's too tight. I know that I took her for granted. From the time we floated in the black airship above the Northern Kingdom, those bitter winds taking us where they willed, to now. Suddenly, I want nothing else. My life of luxury that led me here. The war against it that followed. Why did I invest my life in these bookends, which proved to be empty? Full of only naivety and sacrifice.

I want to live forever inside the space between. But it's too late now. I was too focused on teaching her to appreciate her. Too focused on the destination to appreciate the journey.

Like working voidance, it was short-lived.

She can't see my tears. So I push her away and spin into the abyss.

The sting that meets me doesn't compare to that of my regret.

The bulbous cargo ship retreats into the mist like some strange fish lurking within the depths of Xi Bay. The point where it disappears becomes a dark pincushion toward which the billowing gray petals endlessly return, folding in among themselves, poison eating poison.

I sit up in the sand, in the same place where I landed, and crane my neck upwards. To the southeast, the cloud extends as high as I can see, obscuring the destroyed remains of le-Mon-Sogara and much of the surrounding desert and mountainside.

Soon, the sand around Blythe and me becomes still. Everything to the northwest is startingly clear. We're exposed underneath a perfectly blue sky, but I cannot see the horizon. I'm in the low point of a deepsand, surrounded by shallow dunes.

There's something else—even more vivid than the sky—lying in the sand next to me.

Marine's wrapped-up voidstone.

It takes me less than a heartbeat to realize my mistake. "Good Unnamed," I utter, running a hand through my hair. "What have I done?"

I've brought her to the most dangerous place in the world.

Blythe is oblivious. He crawls up a nearby hill of sand. The palehound easily beats him to the top.

"There!" he says, stumbling and then pointing over the crest into the desert. He lets out a deep groan of annoyance. "Couldn't Lake have gotten us closer? They're over a mile away!"

The roar of the cargo ship has disappeared, leaving a soft rustle from the gentle wind. Individual particles of sand blow into me, creating a tapping sound that resembles rain.

I hear the army, far away. Echoes of a hammer on an anvil. A trumpeted tune that seems as if it's meant to stir the soul. But it doesn't. I'm already looking at one.

"Dem, we should go."

"Not yet," I say weakly, kneeling.

A few black specks lurk between folds of fabric. Some of them dissipate in the faintest of breezes.

I expect that when I touch the cloth, more will escape, so I remain frozen in place, only staring at it, wondering what I'm going to do.

Blythe stumbles back down the hill. "Dem, what's wrong?"

I look up at him, squinting in the harsh sun.

He must see the emerald cloth because his eyes open wide. "You wish to attempt eleutheria, Brother?" he asks, short of breath.

I open my mouth before shaking my head. "I don't know if she'll agree. But we need to try. If something happens to us when we meet the king . . . if the confederacy gets a hold of this voidstone, she'll be in torment for all eter—"

"Let's try to convince her," he interrupts, panting. "Right here. Right now."

I keep staring at the fabric. He grasps my shoulder and kneels beside me. "Do not be burdened with fear. Be nothing. I am here with you. And I will be with you in the void as well."

"Thank you," I tell him, glancing at him. His face is so smooth it reflects the sun. "You have always been such a good friend."

He smiles.

I slowly peel back the folds of greenish blue.

A cloud of ash immediately escapes into the dry air, black particles so small they make the grains of sand seem like boulders.

I look up, trying to follow them. For a moment, the blue sky seems darker, but then a drop of sweat falls into my eye. By the time I blink it away, there's no trace of the ash.

I bring my attention back to my upturned palm.

The pea-sized fragment remains on the bed of emerald.

Immediately, I remember the training stone that Marine used to wear on her ring. It looks exactly like it, just without the setting. The first time she tried to light candles in my room was with my large voidstone, which I'd carelessly left on the desk while I was out in the hallway lying to my footman.

Somehow, we've returned to the beginning.

Blythe grasps my hand. "Ready?"

I exhale. "Ready."

As I touch the fragment with my index finger, I'm instantly reminded of the sheer power of this evil substance. It doesn't matter if it's as large as an Axiondrive or as small as a pea.

The sunlit world still disappears.

Dem. You've been busy. So busy that you haven't even visited me.

As is typical, I don't know what to say. Am I supposed to feel guilty?

Chimeline told me what she did, she adds, before I can respond. *What she did to the five azuremen. Already I can feel the souls resting.*

Yes, I say. Seeing an opportunity, I add, *Soon, Blythe and I will perform eleutheria on them. Then they'll be free as well.*

She doesn't respond, so I continue.

Chimeline has them in her possession. The five heartstones. So they're safe. But you, Marine, are not safe. We're close to the king's army. There are probably confederates with them.

Again, no answer.

I turn toward Blythe's glistening form—the constant sign of life. It's very weak. Almost murky. I know that this is because Marine is the only enervated inside. At the edges of my vision are the colorless grains of sand, each more unique than if I saw it with my naked eye. If I flew close enough, I could enter each one and find the packed indivisibles within. But the void is the place for conversations and temporary manipulations only. Not the place for true change.

It's time. After all this talking, it's time.

Marine, we're coming in, I say. It's as much of a warning for Blythe as it is for her.

Turning my attention back to the pea-sized stone—the only thing black in the otherwise colorless void—I approach.

Soon, the fragment takes up everything, including my periphery. It might as well be as large as an Axiondrive. It swallows creation.

We break the surface, entering her prison.

Marine, can you tell us where you are? Blythe asks. I turn his way, seeking his glistening indivisibles in the murk, but then panic as I remember that we're past that point now. We're delving.

We need the point of light.

We need the white room.

Just keep going, she says. *I'm here.*

It will help, Child, if you keep speaking to us, Blythe says.

As always, I feel us move together as one, through this sea of nothing. But it's different this time. Every other time we performed eleutheria, Blythe spoke Effulgian. Words I didn't understand to enervated I didn't know.

I've been busy too, Dem, Marine says.

Busy? What do you mean?

I've been throwing things out.

Throwing things out?

Just making this place more like home. Decluttering. It was too large before. Now it's as cozy as the dormitory. Just large enough for a bed and a closet.

Her words make no sense. This place is not like the world outside. It's as sterile as the deepest of dungeons.

Do you know what? she says. *I can remember these things now.*

What things?

Just some of those small things that brought me happiness. The dormitory. Sleeping in when it snowed. There was a park in Giriya where the swans of Northinglight would come to escape the winters. There was a stone bridge there. Does this help, or am I speaking too much?

Yes, it helps, Blythe says, without hesitation. *Thank you, Child.*

I've tried to tell the other enervated about this. About how to make their homes smaller. But they don't know how to do it and they tell me to stop calling it my home. They're just so angry all the time. Even when they rest. They collide among themselves. They poison each other.

Poison? I ask, both curious and desperate. I keep looking for the point of light.

This globe. This sphere of delicate glass. If I ever collide with another enervated, I think that I'll break. But the others don't break. Their memories just mix together like spilled paint. Pain likes to mix with other pain, I think.

I don't know what to make of her rambling, but I am glad of two things. The first is that her anger seems to have dissipated—if only for a moment. The second is that she continues to speak to us, acting as a lighthouse in this storm. Without her voice, Blythe and I would be lost forever.

What I figured out, Dem, is that this soul is only so big. It can only hold so much, and so when I chose to forgive you, and when I chose to forgive Mander, and even myself, suddenly, these smaller moments started to come back. And I was able to make this my home.

Up ahead, I see a pinpoint of light.

We see you! I shout out.

It sounds to me that you are on the way of unwanting, Child, Blythe says. *I am proud of you.*

She doesn't answer.

The pinpoint of light grows, becoming a small square. The exterior wall of the white room. As we progress, it becomes larger and larger—along with my morbid curiosity.

Why hasn't she refused eleutheria already, like all the other times? Why hasn't she brought up not being ready? Training Chimeline? Or any of her other excuses? Is it because she's forgotten these things, choosing instead to cherish rose-colored memories?

I decide to keep the past in the past. None of our former conversations about her reluctance will help. This is going too well. All we need is for her to leave the room of her own volition. For her sphere to penetrate and lead us back out of the black. We're so close.

We're here, Blythe says. *Are you ready?*

Is he speaking to her or me?

As he prepares to open the wall, I prepare for the torrent of color and pain. In some respects, I've gotten used to this—if any soul could become used to this revolting feeling. It's a certain mental tension, as if I know that I'm about to reach out and touch a water kettle that has been sitting on the fire all night long. This is my burden, and I tell myself that it's nothing compared to theirs. I'm willing to partake in the sharing of their pain, if this is what's necessary to restore their freedom.

But Marine? What memories are coming my way? Am I about to see myself?

My entire soul hesitates, as if I stumble in the nothingness.

Dem! Blythe says. I feel him rush close again, near my side. *Dem,* he says, softer. I *am with you, Brother.*

As the white wall falls away, perspective and scale both fail me. I would faint if I had a body. This entire world is unbelievable, but what I'm witnessing is the unbelievable with the unbelievable.

Usually, when Blythe opens the inner room up, a mammoth cage of white presents itself—full of thousands of spheres that ricochet around and pass through us like a river breaking through its dam.

Not this time.

Marine's sphere—the only one—is nestled within a tiny cube. There's absolutely no space to spare. At first, I think that her sphere is gargantuan. Then I realize that it's the prison that's small.

Is this because of the fragment size? Or something that she has done?

Dem, do you know what I chose to remember about you?

I say nothing as I stare, dumbfounded, at the translucent sphere in front of me.

I chose your first teaching. I wrote it down when I gave you my letter. Do you remember the letter?

When you left? I ask. *Of course I remember it.*

I remember it falling to the marble floor, folded in thirds, my body shaking in disbelief.

You said that the indivisibles move about randomly. That there is a great disorder to the natural world, and the power of a voidstone holds no permanent sway.

It's true.

At the time, I thought that the same was true with love, she continues. *With any love. 'Things fall apart.' That's what I said. Just as you had said.*

I remember, Marine.

I feel Blythe next to me, his soul reaching out, ready for her embrace. But she is motionless, choosing to stay in her prison.

You were right, Dem. Blythe, you were right as well. Even in this prison, voidance has no permanent sway. There is a limit to what they can do to us, if we only allow ourselves to be nothing. Because hate is order. Forgiveness is disorder.

Suddenly, I sense a change within this hidden world.

An edge of light begins curving around us like a sunrise breaking over a black sea. I chase it with my mind's vision, and it keeps moving.

No. Not light. Colorlessness. It's creeping in, slowly, everywhere I look.

At the edge, the black is crumbling. Falling away into the sunrise.

Marine! I call out. *What's happening?*

I am leaving, she says, all too calmly.

Leaving? What do you mean?

Blythe was right all along. Be nothing.

Marine, I don't understand.

Be not afraid.

At the edge, color has arrived. Actual sunlight. I see three universes in one: the world outside—blue and yellow—as well as the colorless void and the delved depths of this black prison. But the last of these is breaking away, piece by piece, around us.

Dem, I think I know what is happening, Blythe says frantically.

He doesn't need to explain because I have the same thought.

It's the ash, but this time we're on the inside, watching it fly away. The continual destruction of the voidstone's outer layer. Slowly, this stone has become smaller and smaller, and it will continue to happen.

Until there is nothing left.

Marine! I say, feeling the utter panic in my soul's voice. *I think this stone is . . .* I struggle with the very concept. *We need to leave. Now!*

As the edge continues to burn away, I fear for my own life. And Blythe's as well. We're delving. There's no way out except if the enervated guide us, and in this case there is only Marine. Such is the risk with eleutheria.

If this stone dissolves to nothing, then what happens to Blythe and me?

What happens to Marine?

We can't afford to find out.

Marine! I call out.

Child! You must guide us! Blythe adds.

The walls around her shatter into countless lines of white as a crystalline sound explodes everywhere in this normally soundless place. Nestled within this sound is her voice. I feel the warmth of the sun, and nestled within this warmth is her soul. She's passing beyond me, but not through me.

I choose to forgive, she says.

AN ENTIRELY DIFFERENT KIND OF NOTHING

"It's gone," I say, squinting as my eyesight adjusts to the living world. The emerald cloth is all that remains. A few specks of dust fly off as I cast it away.

"It's all gone," I repeat, wide-eyed.

"Dem," Blythe says, grabbing me by the shoulders and giving me a good shake. "It's alright. If it's destroyed, then she is free. Marine is free."

I close my eyes and take a few deep breaths, letting the heat penetrate my soul. As sure as the sun, I know it to be true.

But it's all too much to comprehend.

When I open my eyes again, I collapse and lie down in the sand, facing the blue sky. The palehound licks my face once before returning to Blythe, who sits next to me.

"Marine never even left the room," I mumble, trying to remember exactly what happened as that hidden world so quickly broke apart. "We didn't . . ."

"I know," Blythe adds, after a moment of silence. "I don't understand it. Somehow she performed eleutheria on her own."

I look at him. "But that's impossible."

Blythe nods and looks away. "It *should* be impossible. But who are we to question such a miracle? There is so much we don't yet know."

I shake my head, as if to clear away the fog. Blythe is right, of course, miracles aside. If meeting Chireseal and

Lake taught us anything, it's that there's so much we don't know. But Marine leaving the voidstone on her own flies in the face of what should be possible.

"Perhaps she had the Unnamed's help," Blythe adds with a speculative shrug. "If I noticed one thing in her words, it was that she was as close to the way of unwanting as one can be." He raises prayerlike hands toward his lips and frowns deeply. "Except for one phrase. She said that forgiveness is a disorder." Hands still to his lips, he shakes his head slightly. "That is *not* on the way of unwanting. It is the exact opposite."

"She said that forgiveness *is* disorder," I reply, clearly remembering her words. "Not *a* disorder. I think that they might mean two different things."

"I do not understand the difference. Forgiveness is the perfect state of union with the Unnamed. It is peace. It is order."

"It doesn't make sense to me either. Much of what Marine said to us in the void sounded like the ravings of a madman. But what if she was actually trying to tell us something important?"

He drops his hands with a slight nod. "Perhaps the clues lie in what happened afterward."

"What do you mean?"

His eyes meet mine. "Think about what happened when she left. How did it make you feel?"

"It was . . . beautiful. I don't know how else to describe it. She passed beyond without our taking her there. It was as if she knew exactly what she was doing."

"Yes, Brother." He smiles at me.

"What's your point?"

"That she didn't need us. The way she was speaking—she was guiding *us*, not the other way around. Timing things according to *her* schedule. Which leaves only one explanation."

He extends a hand. I take it, and he pulls me up.

"She was waiting to leave until we came," I surmise, taking a white sheet from Blythe, who offers it to me. I wrap it around my head. "So that she could say goodbye."

He nods.

A breeze curls around us, swirling within the depression of the deepsand.

"But it's more than that," I tell him. "She also destroyed a voidstone in the process."

He utters a sound of agreement.

"That voidstone was normal-sized a fortnight ago," I continue. "Now it's . . ." I raise my hands to the sky. "Ash. You cannot destroy a voidstone. It's impossible."

"I would say, Brother, that it *is* possible. We just witnessed it."

"We didn't just witness one impossible thing, Blythe. We witnessed *two*: voidstone destruction and self-imposed eleutheria."

Blythe smiles and nods. "Truly the work of the Unnamed."

"How can you so easily accept the impossible?" I snap. "This flies in the face of everything we know."

"Patience, Brother." He lays a hand on my shoulder. "You are a man of science. Accepting that which you do not understand is not easy for you. Look to the way of unwanting. Let go. All will be made clear in the Unnamed's time."

"We don't have the Unnamed's time."

I wish Chimeline were here. She would know what all of this means.

"Maybe there was something different about her stone that caused it to turn to ash on its own."

Blythe doesn't look convinced. "Different how?"

I purse my lips. "She was the only enervated trapped inside."

"So?"

"To my knowledge, that's never happened before." Stooping, I run a hand through the sand, letting the infinitesimal grains flow through my fingers. "Perhaps if only one soul is trapped, the voidstone shrinks."

"Why is it so important to understand the hows and whys of the miracle we just witnessed?" Blythe asks. "Why can't you just be thankful?"

"Because if we figure out what happened to Marine, it will make freeing the rest of them that much easier. It could change everything."

Blythe gazes at me underneath his white sheet, unblinking. Then he nods slowly. "Perhaps we could test this theory of yours on one of the heartstones. Or the stone you carry. I could speak to the enervated about it. See if one of them will volunteer to stay—"

Blythe goes quiet as a deep, oscillating, humming sound swells around us.

"What is that?" I ask.

He shakes his head in confusion, looking around.

I try to locate the source as well, but it comes from everywhere at once. It's more mechanical than natural.

"Dem," Blythe says, over the humming. He's pointing west.

I adjust the white sheet shielding my head and peer into the shimmering distance. Halfway between us and the king's army, which remains at least a halfbell away, a slender trail of dust rises like a lonely smokestack.

Blythe peers underneath his hood. "Is that the king?"

"No," I say, my brow creased. "Andrej's too lazy to get on a horse if it's not part of a parade. It's one of his messengers, no doubt."

Both the frequency and pitch of the humming increases.

"Could that strange sound be coming from him? Or his forces?"

I shake my head. "I don't think so." But the last word is curved slightly upward, hinting at it being a question. A part of me worries that something isn't right. That this is a trap and these rumblings are the first indication.

A stronger breeze swirls within the pocket of the deepsand. It picks up Mander's ripped emerald fabric at our feet and drags it up a dune toward the gray poison cloud to the southeast. For a few heartbeats, I stare at it. It flutters like a ragged battle flag until another gust of hot wind takes it even higher.

Movement far above catches my attention.

Near the very ceiling of the dark cloud that extends upwards as far as the eye can see, something has emerged: a pinprick of light screaming into the deep blue.

Grabbing Blythe's shoulder, I crane my neck further. The white hood falls around my neck.

"There!" I say.

A slender trail of poison cloud extends behind the cargo ship, as if pulled from a ball of soiled cotton.

"Thank the Unnamed," Blythe says on an exhale, bringing prayerlike hands to his lips.

"They're leaving this world," I say, with a mix of emotions. Joy, fear, and sadness. It's hard to appreciate what I'm witnessing—how dangerous it must be. The closest thing I can compare it to is the void. Where Chimeline, Lake, and Chireseal are headed is an entirely different kind of nothing. So impossibly far away.

I want so desperately for Chimeline to be here next to me, but I also want her gone. She must safely fly away to safely land again. And so, despite all my reluctance, I try to convince myself that this is what's best. She is an axionlighter. Within this entire so-called universe, she is in the exact place she should be.

Saving it.

But as quickly as my heart rises, it falls.

Removing my hand from Blythe's shoulder, I use it to shelter my eyes from the sun.

Squinting, blinking away the stinging sweat, I peer into that impossibly deep blue, following the trajectory of the single glistening point of light, which bears all that I love in this world.

Something dark awaits it.

Did it just appear? Or has it always been there and I simply didn't notice? Faint, like a transparent moon, but gray instead of light, and half its size. More oblong than spherical.

"Oh, no," Blythe says, his voice heavy with worry.

"The axionship," I say. "It's the axionship. Good Unnamed—it's massive."

Blythe falls to his knees.

Wiping my face with my pooled hood, I stare helplessly.

There is nothing to do except watch. And wait.

Over the course of many heartbeats, the oscillating gradually morphs into a sustained high-pitched *whirr*. The sparkle of the cargo ship dims. It gets harder and harder to see. Ironically, this fills me with trace amounts of courage, surrounded by an ocean of humility.

I've never felt smaller.

"I think that they're still moving," I tell Blythe. "They must be moving away from us, because it's harder to see." Receiving no reply, I add, "They will escape, Blythe. Lake and Chireseal know what to do. They have to." But as soon as I hear my words, I know that they ring hollow. I'm only trying to convince myself, like some lost child grasping on to a stranger in a crowd.

Blythe remains silent.

Glancing down, I see that he's not even paying attention to me. He's kneeling, his face pressed against the sand.

Soft thunderclaps roll across the landscape.

Looking up again, I see that multiple white lines have exploded from the axionship. They slowly trace pathways across the deep-blue sky, like fingernail scratches upon a windowpane. A dozen at least. As I watch, another dozen escape, born from tiny blossoms of yellow.

Holding my breath, I'm paralyzed. I don't know what these are—acts of voidance, axionware, or something else.

But I'm certain that they're designed for destruction.

"Please," I eventually whisper, without taking my gaze off the point of light and the approaching lines, feeling poisoning dread coarse through every vein in my body, headed straight to my heart. "Please."

As the distance between the lines and the point shortens to almost nothing, my body tenses completely. I fear another blossom of yellow—a larger explosion, but this time from the cargo ship.

Instead, a ring erupts around it.

It silently emanates outward, like a ripple after a pebble is tossed into the sea.

As the perfect circle passes over the approaching white lines, more yellow blossoms erupt, one after another, until all the lines are crossed.

The lines stop moving. Their tails fade.

Heartbeats later, multiple soft thunderclaps roll from horizon to horizon.

I blink repeatedly as I struggle to comprehend what I just saw. Lake had said that the cargo ship had no weapons. No defensive capabilities.

I glance down again. Blythe's head is still pressed to the sand.

Collapsing next to him and on my knees, I pull him up into an embrace. Tears are already falling down my face.

"Is it over?" He blinks as he stares at me with an expression that borders on peaceful.

"I think so," I say, wiping my face with my hood again. Both tears and sweat come away. My hands won't stop shaking. "The cargo ship is still there."

He peers into the sky with an expression of both confusion and elation. "Our prayers were answered. But it seems that more prayers are required, Brother."

He falls prostrate to the sand again as I look up, wondering what he means.

"No," I breathe. I'm already on my knees, but if I had been standing, my legs would have given out.

There are hundreds now.

The white lines emanating from the axionship are so plentiful that they resemble a wide, growing brushstroke.

The axionship moves simultaneously. Its core glows blue—even bluer than the sky. Cutting to the left, the dark shape briefly eclipses the shining cargo ship before moving toward its opposite side. A second brushstroke of white emerges.

Just as the first attack is about to hit, the ring returns.

Rings.

Again and again, ripples upon more ripples.

So much light strobes and blooms in the sky amid roiling smoke that I cannot make out any details except for the axionship, which floats in front of it all like some dark eye socket in a skull.

I stand as the thunderclaps return. This time they don't stop.

Caught within the shock waves, granules of sand slide down the sides of the dune I'm standing on. My feet sink an inch deep into the desert. The palehound begins barking incessantly.

But I stay standing. It's the only thing I can do.

Eventually, the thunderclaps cease, echoing to nothing.

The white lines dissolve into wispy gray patterns. The axionship is still. It doesn't attack again. There's no movement at all up there except for the swirling and weakening vapors.

Desperately, I search for the single point of light within the dying chaos.

I find it.

Piercing the mist, it shines forth like O'Eridani, the End of the River. As true as the north star.

"Blythe!" I say, without taking my eyes off it. "They're still there! I see the ship!"

"Of course they are still there, Brother," he says, standing again and brushing the sand away from his forehead. He looks at me and then smiles, giving me a rough pat on my back. "You must learn to have faith!"

A streak crosses the entire sky.

Both Blythe and I inhale sharply.

It's the cargo ship. O'Eridani has become a shooting star.

"Good Unnamed," Blythe says. "That's it. They made it."

I run my hand through my hair in awe. And then I begin to laugh.

It's a joyous laugh with nothing held back. Not even tears.

Blythe joins in, and we embrace once again, smiling with uncontrollable joy while looking at the abandoned sky. Only the palehound's growling makes us stop.

It springs to life next to us, snarling, facing west.

I turn toward the approaching figure.

The man on horseback is about a hundred feet away. He's close enough now that I can see that he's unarmored and rides a white horse—a Xian one, undoubtedly. He carries a flag that bears the king's sigil along with the man's noble station.

He's the chamberlain.

The Xian steed is spotless, its oiled white hair glistening in the sun. The man in the saddle straightens his back and raises the sigil proudly. As he does this, I see his blue number glowing on his forearm, as clear in the daylight as in the dusk.

I already hate him, but I do not fear him. I do not fear the king. I do not fear the confederacy. What I just witnessed is the greatest armor of all.

We are going to win this war.

A THREEFOLD RUIN

With dramatic flourishes, the chamberlain stops his horse frequently to allow us to keep up. His head covering is similar to ours, except his is embellished with a wide fringe of gold. Every time he stops, he peels back his hood to play with his fawn-colored hair, chin-length at the sides, and finger his mustache. He says few words, but his downward gaze full of annoyance tells me enough. He'd probably rather be eating dates under the tent he just came from.

We eventually enter the sprawling encampment at a trailhead. Dozens of bronzed men and women work around small dirty tents and cooking fires. The palehound wanders toward the smell, but Blythe calls him back with a whistle, and I'm shocked that the beast listens.

The ground is flatter here. No dunes. It's also easier to walk—perhaps underneath this sand hides bedrock. We're close enough to the plateau that I presume it's possible.

Servants polish armor, cook meat over firepits, and hang uniforms on cords tied between tent poles. More uniforms are laid out in the sun—Xian girls on their knees cover them with a powder that is slightly whiter than the sand. Their noses and mouths are covered by rags, but their eyes are striking in their sadness. They look up at us as they mindlessly rub the dirt away.

The company of soldiers is next.

Some practice swordsmanship in clearings, shirtless and drenched in sweat. Some rest within a maze of larger tents, sleeping with their helmets over their faces. Strong breezes ripple through, but they're not enough to take away the stench of body odor. A group we pass plays antitwin. They stop moving their small wooden game pieces and eye us with suspicion.

From what I can see, many soldiers have blue numbers.

It takes us a tenthbell to navigate the maze, but eventually we break free of the chaos and enter a calm clearing.

A trumpeted tune rings out. Covering my head once again with my white hood, I peer into the near distance.

Three structures stand about a hundred feet away from us as well as each other, all unique except for one unifying feature—their repulsiveness.

The first is a small yet vibrant-blue tent with an elegantly peaked and gilded top. Underneath is a perfect black cube of about ten feet. A person in a robe whose color matches the tent stands next to it, hands clasped in front of themselves and watching us from within the shadows of their hood.

The second structure is a transparent dome under which are the dozens of lepers from le-Mon-Sogara. They all sit cross-legged or lie on the sand within the perfect half-sphere. But as we approach, one of them stands.

It's Colu.

"They're trapped?" Blythe asks, turning to me.

"Yes. They're in a membrane," I say with a clenched jaw, my anger growing.

"We must demand their release."

The chamberlain keeps heading toward the third structure: a massive white tent with ripples of turquoise light glowing within its shade. It's surrounded by green palms. Dozens of identical flags on poles driven into the sand ripple in the breeze.

I form fists as I realize the horrible irony.

Given our harsh environment, all three of these structures are perfect to the senses—model architectural representations that almost defy one's imagination. They could be mirages in this unforgiving desert. If only they were.

One represents slavery of the soul. Another, slavery of the body. And the third, the abuse of power that enables both.

These are not architectural marvels. These are ruins.

I storm toward the membrane.

"Ah, excuse me," the chamberlain calls out from horseback. "His Majesty awaits us! We must not dally under any circumstances!"

I ignore him.

As I get closer to the dome, I notice small black disks resting in the sand every few feet. They form a circle at its base.

From within his prison, Colu approaches. His eye patch is gone—only a black husk remains.

Stepping between two of the black disks, I stand an arm's-length away.

Even though I'm not in the void, I can see the individual threads making up this membrane. Hundreds of buzzing lines fan outward from each of the disks, weaving with their neighboring threads, forming Xs in the sunlight as they curve away from me over my head.

"Who did this?" Blythe asks, coming to stand next to me.

I point at a nearby disk. "This is voidance, but it's not coming from a voider. It's coming from these markers."

"I don't understand."

"Confederate axionware," I answer. "Do you remember how Lake explained it?"

"It's all black arcana to me."

Colu shouts from behind the membrane, pointing at the immaculate white tent, but his voice is muted.

Blythe reaches out.

"Don't—" I begin to say, but I'm too late.

The moment Blythe's fingers touch the membrane, a crackle of white lashes out like a webbed whip. Crying out, Blythe falls backward to the sand, writhing.

The chamberlain returns on his horse. Someone walks next to him.

Blythe stops moving. Completely.

Cursing under my breath, I kneel by his side. "Blythe!" I call out. I quickly inspect his body for injury, finding nothing. He's still breathing.

Suddenly he opens his eyes and sharply inhales. "Black arcana," he rasps, blinking. His hands shake, but beyond that he seems unharmed.

I help him up.

"Black arcana," he repeats.

"You okay?" I ask him. I don't know what sort of membrane this is or what it just did to Blythe. I'd have to enter the void to learn more.

Thinking back to our conversation in the cavern, I postulate why the enervated let this happen. It was axionware. Not an empowered.

"I am alright, Brother," he says.

I glance behind us. The approaching pair are about fifty feet away. The woman walking next to the chamberlain is Xian. She staggers in the sand.

Quickly, I stoop and put my hands on either side of the black disk in front of me, careful not to touch the emanating lines. It's hot—almost burning.

"Dem, be careful! What are you doing?"

"If we move these disks, we might be able to create a rift in the membrane."

As I speak, I pull on the disk, sliding it back about a foot. The lines distort and crackle, bulging away from the half-sphere.

Still stooping, I move back and do it again, pulling the axionware further from its neighbors. Then I do it a third time.

To the left and right of me, the wall buzzes madly, darkening.

"I think it's working!" Blythe calls out. "Here, let me get ano—"

Suddenly, I'm pulled away at least ten feet. My body hovers equally as much above the ground. My limbs are forced into an X position, and my body tilts forward at a forty-five-degree angle.

I cry out in shock.

Frantically, I try to move, but the sensation of weight that keeps me in place is overwhelming.

I can't move my neck. I peer to the right, trying to find Blythe. I can barely see him—blue sky fills most of my peripheral vision—but he appears to be in the same predicament.

Below are two indentations in the sand formed by our dragging bodies.

The palehound circles, snapping his teeth.

"I am shocked that the effulgent is alive," the chamberlain calls out. He brings his horse in front of us. Looking up, he squints despite the shade of his hood.

He then lowers his voice and dispenses with all the flowery edges. "Check these markers once we've taken these two back to His Majesty."

I hear a grunt of understanding behind me.

The chamberlain clears his throat repeatedly, as if he's ready to sing a tune. "Democryos, His Majesty would very much appreciate your cooperation. After the recent display in his glorious skies, his patience is short. He wants answers."

The Xian woman steps between the mounted chamberlain and Blythe and me. She keeps her head down and doesn't say a word. She's barefoot and her tan pants are ragged at the ankles. The palehound backs up, raising his haunches and showing his teeth.

She stops directly under me. Beads of sweat fall from my brow onto her head and body.

For a moment, she just stands there, head bent as my sweat continues to land on her hair and skin, creating a *tap tap tap* sound.

The palehound suddenly whimpers and goes quiet, putting its tail between its legs. It walks in a circle and lies down on the sand.

Finally, she looks up.

It's Caracant. Or what remains of her.

She's been turned into a marked.

A wide black scar cuts into her scalp, leaving a slight depression at the top of her skull. There's no hair growing there. The axiongraph is only slightly darker than her skin.

Caracant stares at me with a blank expression as my sweat falls on her upturned face.

"You need to follow my instructions," says the chamberlain. "Not release our prisoners."

"They are not your prisoners!" Blythe says, his voice strained.

"His Majesty proclaims that they are."

"Well, I beg to differ."

The chamberlain makes a high-pitched groan, sounding almost like a wild animal. "Yes, you do seem to be begging."

The avorsi Caracant doesn't move. She simply stares at me with apathy.

Directly behind her is Colu, watching from the membrane, his hands on his head.

"Dem, tell them!" Blythe calls out.

But I'm speechless as mixed emotions course through me.

I remember the nightmarket. What happened there. The enervated could not protect me from the Northern and Southern marked, just as they apparently cannot protect me from this one either. If Caracant were given the order to kill me right now, I'd be dead in an instant.

Which means that the king needs me alive. Perhaps he was telling the truth after all.

I try to look past the blank gaze, to remember the kind and soft-spoken voider I met in the hidden hearth. Her silk wrap of crescent moons framing her gentle face. Daunt's wife.

They found her. Somehow, they found her.

"il-Caracant?" I ask, my voice soft. "Caracant, do you remember me?"

Nothing. No reaction.

"Where is Daunt?" I add.

But she's gone. The woman Caracant doesn't exist. This is just a husk of a person, her mind cut into with voidance. Even if I had limitless time, no act of voidance or natural healing could probably bring her back.

"As I said," the chamberlain says, "His Majesty usually lacks nothing, but today he lacks patience. You can walk on your own two feet, or you can be dragged. What say you?"

"We'll cooperate," I say. "Let us down. We'll go to the king."

Caracant turns and walks away.

Blythe and I roughly fall to the sandy ground. My limbs are free again.

"I appreciate that," the chamberlain says, as Blythe and I dust the sand from our bodies. "I really do. You will make my job so much easier if you simply take into consideration that you are still His Majesty's loyal subjects. As we all are."

I glance at Blythe. He looks outraged. I give him a subtle nod, trying to encourage his patience. The king may not have any, but we need to embrace it because we're in the winning position. The king doesn't know what has just occurred above his decaying kingdom. We need to enlighten him. And in the interim, there is still danger. Avorsi, axionware. We must be careful not to trip on these last steps in the race.

"Shall we proceed?" the chamberlain asks, turning his horse around and heading toward the white tent and palms.

Caracant follows just as obediently as we do.

THE WAR HORSE AND THE DONKEY

"Is that my trusty war horse?" King Andrej X calls out from behind palms and over the soft cries of a violin.

As the chamberlain dismounts and leads the way into the gleaming white tent, I struggle to reply.

Weeks ago, I would have reflexively responded "Yes, Your Majesty." But I am no longer the man he thinks I am, nor do I view him as anything close to majestic. After seeing what they've done with Colu and the lepers, I am confounded. I want to berate him—to treat him like the lowest footman's apprentice in the Royal House. Yet I know that doing so would be pointless. This boy of a man needs his ego stroked if I'm ever to convince him of the truth.

I summon whatever patience I have left.

"It is I, Democryos, Your Majesty," I answer loudly, as I round the bank of low palms.

What lies before me stops me in my tracks.

A large pool of turquoise water sits in the center of the peaked white tent. It must be at least twenty feet square and a few feet deep.

Blythe inhales sharply. "Such waste!" he says, under his breath.

"And who is that?" the king asks in mock surprise, peering through the foliage. "Did you bring a donkey with you? I didn't realize that any were left."

I ignore his goading insults and take in more of the surroundings.

The king sits on a white stone seat within the shallow end of the pool. The foot-high water reaches his shins. He's looks to be naked underneath a thin white robe, which is wet at the bottom. On the opposite end of the pool—the one closest to me—the water is darker. Deeper.

"His Majesty asked you a question, Master Voider," the chamberlain says.

"Blythe is an effulgent, Your Majesty," I coldly answer.

"Come close, come close," he says, beckoning us toward the pool with a meager wave of his arm. "I need not shout nor strain to hear. Time is of the essence."

Blythe and I share a disgusted glance before slowly approaching.

The palehound stays close to Blythe.

As we walk past perfectly aligned palms, I can't help but recall the last time I was alone with Andrej. It was at dinner, the night I left the city. That was when he first called the effulgents his donkeys, and me his war horse. Now, instead of impending darkness, there is oppressive light. Instead of fifty candelabras and fifty empty chairs, there are fifty surrounding palms. Instead of on a blue-and-gold webbed rug from the archipelago, his feet rest comfortably in a pool of pure water. I recognize the violinist. Near the edge of the tent, the man strums an idyllic tune. This time, he wears a white shirt and pants instead of a black formal suit. And from far away comes the sound of a hammer on anvil.

King Andrej X has brazenly moved his world of luxury from the citadel of the Northern Kingdom into the furthest reaches of the Xian deepsands. Everything is ignorantly and blissfully the same.

And it took voidance to achieve.

I'm sure that the confederacy is behind this. I cannot make out the numbers on the king's forearm, but I can see that it's three digits. That tells me enough. He's already taken advantage of Mander's *Halcyon Roadmap*. There are probably dozens of ignorant Northerners lining up to give their poor souls to the king.

Yet he wants to fight the confederacy? Bite the proverbial hand that feeds?

"Dem, sit," he says, looking up. "We need to talk."

But there are no chairs.

"Take off your sandals," he says, pointing. "Both of you. Let your feet recuperate in my splendor."

Blythe groans, and I subtly extend my hand at my side. "Just do as he says," I say, under my breath.

Acquiescing, I let my bare feet hang over the pool's edge, which looks to be sand that has been compacted so much that it resembles stone. Blythe remains standing.

The water is frigid. The stark sensation resembles the onset of voideath. My eyes snap to the king, who's watching me with a sickly grin.

"Refreshing, isn't it?" He chuckles with eerie amusement.

The palehound lowers its head, its pink nose almost touching the surface of the water. Then it backs away, sniffing the desert air and looking at Caracant with bared teeth.

"Your Majesty," I begin, looking him in the eye. "I have obeyed your summons because I remain your loyal servant. However, my friends do not deserve to be treated so." I motion to the glistening dome in the distance, barely viewable between the surrounding palms and from underneath the fringed top of the tent. "May I ask why they are being detained?"

He raises an eyebrow, but the chamberlain speaks up. "You are in no position to be asking His Majesty anything."

Blythe clears his throat. "None of us has true authority except the Unnamed. And when we partake in selfless acts, ones that are on the way of unwanting, we—"

"They're lepers!" the king exclaims, as if we're daft. "I can't have lepers wandering around my camp, spreading their disease among my men!"

"But Colu—he is not sick," I say, after a pause.

Andrej looks somewhat unfocused, as if he's addressing the space between us. "Who is Colu?"

"He is not a leper, Your Majesty. He is—"

"If he wasn't before, he most certainly is now." Andrej says. "Breathing that same contaminated air." He weakly waves his ring-adorned hand. "Those wretches must remain in that membrane for the good of my people. I will let them go when our company departs this wasteland."

Blythe voice deepens. "No man is a wretch in the eye of the—"

"Silence!" the king shouts, slapping the arm of his throne. He stares me down. "Dem," he says, more quietly, "control your donkey, or else I will be forced to put him down."

The violinist misses a note. An off-tune screech fills the tent. For a heartbeat, the only sounds are the flapping of the tent and the distant clanging of metal on metal. Then the musician continues his silken song.

"Be nothing, my friend," I tell Blythe.

After a pause, Blythe kneels at the edge of the pool. Leaning forward slightly, he peers at his reflection. "Thank you for the reminder, Brother," he whispers.

The king sits back, putting his hands to his temples.

"I know, I know." He then shivers despite the oppressive heat. "I don't have time."

Is he speaking to himself?

As I stare at him more closely, I notice that his face glistens. The desert air is scorching, but we're within the shade of the tent, and the water his feet are submerged in is cold. I'm no longer sweating. He shouldn't be either.

He plays with his perfectly parted hair but then seems to notice that his hand shakes, so he takes it away. His teeth keep clenching and unclenching.

Something isn't right.

He turns to me. "Ah, Dem, let's get down to business, shall we?"

On that we can agree. Remembering why we came here in the first place, I look around for the other voiders. If he truly wants to make a move against the confederacy, I need to know our numbers.

Frowning, I realize I didn't see a single voider while walking through the camp—aside from Caracant, who doesn't even count anymore.

"Where are the voiders?" I ask.

He looks at me in annoyance. "What?"

"You said that you have a few voiders loyal to you. Some who still secretly have their voidstones. You also said that you have a cache of voidstones, but I haven't seen—"

"I know!" he shouts, but he's not looking at me. He's rubbing his temple and looking into the water.

The violinist stops again, and the king turns to him, his face flushed. "Fucking oaf! If you cannot hold a tune, you are of no use to me. Leave at once!"

Still cradling his instrument between his chin and shoulder, the musician bows and exits the tent, favoring the unforgiving sun instead of walking past us within the shade.

With his almost-frantic focus back on me, Andrej says, "It's time that we share what little we know with each other, Dem. No, no, no." He waves his hand back and forth. "Don't worry about your sins. They are forgiven."

I pause momentarily, and the chamberlain immediately steps forward.

"Thank His Majesty for his generous forgiveness!"

"His forgiveness?"

The chamberlain's eyes narrow, and he raises a finger. "You committed treason by disobeying His Majesty's orders and fleeing the citadel." He raises a second finger. "You stole His Majesty's property—a secret airship, not to mention His Majesty's favorite harem girl." Another finger. "You murdered the dozens of soldiers guarding the Axiondrive." Another finger. "You stole the Axiondrive and took it south. Into enemy territory!"

I'm about to explain that I didn't murder those guards, but the king interrupts. "And now it's gone, Dem!" He raises a hand to the lofty roof of the tent. "Somehow, it escaped, into the blue!"

I brave a quick glance at Blythe, struggling with what I've just heard. The king shouldn't know that the drive was on the cargo ship. He shouldn't know what happened in the skies. It's barely understandable to me.

Unless the confederacy is here.

"Who took the drive, Dem?" he asks me. "We need it if we are to win this war."

"Your Majesty—"

"Where did they take it?" he snaps.

I look around in sudden dread.

He rubs his palms together. The metallic *clink* of his rings sound like a water clock's chimes.

I glance at Caracant, wondering if somehow an avorsi could be a messenger. Lake said that they were like axionware. I'm convinced that there are no deep thoughts running through Caracant's skull, but perhaps the confederacy can see and hear through her. Similar to how the azuremen communicate. If that's true, information and instructions could be directed through her back to the king as well.

"Your Majesty," I say guardedly. "Perhaps we can talk more freely if you send away your avorsi."

His eyes flash to Caracant.

He's heard the term, then. That confirms the confederacy are speaking to him.

"Absolutely not. It stays here."

My heart sinks in realization. I've been lured. This is all a trap, as I'd feared.

Andrej probably wanted the drive so that he could give it to the confederacy, in return for his continued kingship. Or perhaps even his life. Who knows the arrangement this slippery man had made.

But now the drive is gone, and his arrangement must be coming apart.

"You have no intention of fighting back, do you?" I ask him, feeling anger swell inside me. I've been fooled, yet again. "You're a coward."

The chamberlain gasps as I stand. Blythe looks up at me in fearful confusion then follows.

The king grips his chair's armrests, wincing.

"How dare you!" the chamberlain cries out. "You shall immediately beg for His—"

Andrej silences him with an outstretched hand. "Get me a towel," he says. "Go!"

"At once," the chamberlain says, quickly disappearing around the palms.

I study the king in silent apprehension. His wincing is one of discomfort, not humiliation. His demeanor has slid from smugness to impatience to . . . something else. He's in physical pain. His breathing is heavy. He concentrates on every single inhale and exhale.

"This fucking savage wasteland," he pants. "This heat . . ."

The chamberlain returns with a large white cloth. He submerges it in the pool, wrings it out, and hands it to the king. Andrej immediately wipes his face with it fervently, starting with his forehead and then digging into his eyes and ears, as if there is sand there. When he's finished, he grips the balled-up washcloth in his hand.

He's still wincing. His mouth is slightly open and his lips move, but nothing comes out.

"What's wrong with him?" Blythe asks me, under his breath.

"I don't know," I whisper.

"They say . . ." the king begins loudly, but then he groans. He wipes his ears again.

The cloth comes away bloody.

The chamberlain hovers over the king, but then Andrej swats him away. "Leave me be!" he snaps.

The chamberlain backs away sheepishly to the left side of the pool, standing midway between Blythe and me and the king.

"We're all going to die," the king says weakly. "He's returning. And he's run out of patience."

A trickle of blood falls down the side of the king's face.

"Dem." Blythe leans in at my side. "What is happening?"

The palehound begins whining. It starts backing away.

"Someone is voidspeaking to him," I say. It was a hunch before, but now I'm certain.

"The avorsi?" Blythe asks.

I shake my head as I put my hand into my pants pocket. The full voidstone is still there.

On our left, the chamberlain glares as us while putting his hands on his hips. "You shall not have a private conversation in the presence of His—"

The air distorts behind the chamberlain, and in the next instant, he's ripped apart by an invisible but earsplitting wave.

His body is severed into uncountable pieces that fly across the pool. The right edge of the pool shatters. The water turns red and spills over onto a shallow depression in the nearby sand. Rendered slime hits the peaked white canopy and drips off, splattering into the pool below.

Blythe and I instinctively jump backward. Everything around us is covered in water and blood, emanating in a fanlike shape from where the chamberlain once stood. Even the king is half covered on his mock throne. He frantically wipes his face with the washcloth. Caracant stands nearby, oblivious. Her face and body are covered in dripping pink slime.

To the left of the pool, where the field of gore begins, the air is still distorted.

At first, I see only moving palms, moving sunlight, moving blood and water. Like a curved mirror in front of me, the mirage reveals only what's nearby.

Then, as I stare in awe, the mirage is washed away.

A pale effulgent in a gray uniform with red shoulder straps appears. His body is motionless and perfectly straight, but his head swivels left and right as he coolly takes in his surroundings.

His skin is darker near his temple, as though he has a large birthmark.

But then I recognize it. A design that I don't know from my memory but someone else's.

Temberlain's.

The effulgent has an axiongraph.

NEEDLE THROUGH CLOTH

For a few heartbeats, the empowered studies Blythe and me and even the palehound. Then he turns his attention to the king. He seems unaware of the guts splattered across the white canvas above, which sporadically fall into the pool.

"I've been extremely lenient with you." His words are directed at the king. They're soft and whispery, like the Effulgian language, but formed clearly. "Lenient to a fault. And my tolerance has reached its end."

Andrej fidgets in his half-destroyed throne. He looks like an overweight child covered in raspberry sweet fruits.

In contrast, the empowered is a slight man, and shorter than I am, but he stands as straight as a board. His lean physique underneath his tailored gray uniform speaks to both his physical strength and his rigor. He reminds me of Reddles, but a foot shorter and without a blade of hair on his body.

Andrej wipes his face with his bloody rag. His skin is more soiled afterwards.

"Officer Turenne . . . I . . . I am close to gaining the information. I just need more time," he says, pointing at me. "My master voider has come. He will serve his king by providing answers."

Turenne glances at me as I might glance at an ant crawling up the Royal House's kitchen wall.

Meanwhile, our palehound leaves Blythe's side and heads straight toward the empowered, walking through the chamberlain's guts.

"You are close to gaining nothing," Turenne says with a scowl, as the palehound tightly circles his legs. Surprisingly, it then nestles itself next to him, sitting on its haunches in the blood, looking up at Turenne with tender, wide eyes. "This man may be empowered," he continues, "but he's also a native. He knows little more than this palehound."

"He *does* know!" Andrej continues to point. "He's the one who killed Mander. He knows all about your people!"

Turenne glances at the palehound and then gently rubs its skull, seemingly lost in thought. "A palehound descendant from Efful," he says to himself. "Now this is a pleasant surprise in an otherwise unpleasant day."

His head quickly swivels toward me.

The ground begins to vibrate.

Around us, sand, blood, and water reverberate. The dozens of alabaster pots lining the tent shatter, one after another. Soil, roots, and ferns spill out. The tent above billows like a sail, thrashing wildly.

And then as quickly as it started, it ceases.

Turenne stops petting the creature, but his hand still hovers above its skull. His eyes widen and his mouth opens slightly.

I've seen this look before. Mander had it on the beach.

Turenne mumbles something in Effulgian.

"Blythe?" I say, out of the corner of my mouth.

"He said 'That's impossible,'" Blythe whispers.

I'm not sure what this man just attempted with voidance. Perhaps he wanted to render us into slime in the same manner as the chamberlain, perhaps something else. But whatever it was, it didn't work. The enervated must have thwarted him—something that he has apparently never experienced before.

The revelation gives me guarded courage. I remind myself that I'm not invincible. But I'm also not dead. In the face of such an imbalance of power, I consider this a huge advantage.

He turns fully to face us.

"What axionware did they give you?" he asks. His eyes scan my body, as if searching. "Something new. A shielding device?"

Straightening my back and squaring my shoulders, I meet his gaze defiantly.

"I have nothing but the enervated."

He lets out a short exhale through his nose. "Listen carefully," he says to both of us, speaking calmly and quietly. "I know that you were not responsible for the theft of the drive. However, I do know that there are rebels here whom you've been aiding. It is they I want." He forms a fist in front of himself while staring off toward the dark cloud in the southeast. "If you give me any information on their whereabouts, or on what happened in the canyons, I will let you live." He turns back to us. "And not just any life. A very comfortable life. The quality of the information you share with me right now will directly impact the quality of your future."

"The quality of our future?" Blythe asks admonishingly. "Can you bestow on me the blessings of the Unnamed? For that is all I need. And if not, you are as worthless as the hideous voidstones your power is dependent upon."

Turenne gives the briefest roll of his eyes and then focuses on me. "We *will* find them, sooner or later, *Master Voider*," he says, emphasizing my former title mockingly. "Your refusal to cooperate is simply a delay in our Halcyon Roadmap. You should ask yourself if your life is worth that delay."

The officer goes quiet, patiently waiting for my answer. He places his hand on the nestling palehound's head again, gently rubbing it.

Everything is calm. The chamberlain's remains have stopped falling from the soiled tent. The musician is long gone. The king and Caracant are both silent. Blythe is praying. The only sounds are the gentle billowing of the tent in the hot desert breeze and the continued clanging of a blacksmith working in the distant encampment.

My mind is equally calm. I knew my answer before there was even a question.

"This is the last time I will ask you," Turenne says. "Where did they take the drive?"

"I don't know. But even if I did, I would never tell you. Your Halcyon Roadmap is at an end."

The officer smiles at me, and even nods. But his hands are fists at his sides.

"Officer Turenne," the king says. "My master voider is headstrong, but weak in the heart. If he won't listen to you, then just kill the ones he loves. That will turn him around."

The officer's gaze flashes to Blythe. Out of the corner of my eye, I see that my friend is still praying.

"I only see one other here," the officer says.

"Not the donkey!" the king exclaims. "The lepers. His friend C—"

"What about his beloved king?" Turenne interrupts, without taking his eyes off me.

Andrej makes a sound—something halfway between a cough and whine. "What?"

"You heard me," Turenne says.

"I . . . I don't understand," Andrej says. "His Majesty does not understand."

"Does your master voider not love his king?" Turenne asks, his voice raised high like a banner.

Andrej clears his throat, but when he replies, he leans forward and addresses me instead. "Dem," the king says loudly, his voice full of empty assertion. "You should listen to the officer! He has the power—"

Turenne glances back at him. In the same instant, the king's head becomes severed from his body. Blood geysers from his neck.

"—to end your life or make it."

Andrej's head falls forward into his lap and then rolls onto the ground at the foot of his throne.

Blythe screams.

With a splash, the head drops into the pool. Blythe backs out of my field of vision.

My heart beats wildly, but I stay as motionless as Turenne. I remind myself of my strength. I remind myself of the enervated. I postulate why Turenne just did what he did—the murder was probably as much about intimidation as it was about the end of the king's usefulness to the confederacy.

At Turenne's feet, the palehound whines and begins to back away, but the man commands it with a single Effulgian word, holding out a finger while coolly looking past me and to my right.

I turn briefly. Blythe has left the tent. It looks as if he's headed toward the glistening dome.

Turenne's display of power may, ironically, make this the perfect time. Before he sets his sights on Colu and the lepers.

I could destroy Turenne. Right now.

As soon as I wonder whether this would be acceptable to the enervated, I know the answer. This man is a confederate. And not just any confederate. He's an empowered officer. Even Blythe might agree.

The officer blinks then turns slightly to his left to glance at the glistening dome in the sunlit distance.

Now.

Swiftly, I shove my right hand into my pants pocket and reach for my voidstone.

The empowered must know what I'm attempting. By the time my fingers connect with my voidstone, he's staring straight at me once again.

Colorlessness. The wind swirling.

Without hesitation, I fly into his glistening indivisibles, right between his eyes.

Roughly, without much precision, I penetrate the indivisibles there. Pushing them apart, I create a narrow channel I can follow, like a needle through cloth. No finesse. All forward motion.

But before I'm barely past the surface of his skin, I hit something solid. It's not his skull. Here, a rock—even metal—is usually clay in my phantom hands.

He built a membrane.

I push harder.

His indivisibles give, but barely. I progress a single step, but the equivalent of the entire Northern Kingdom must be crossed.

Letting the wind rip into me, I embrace the possibility of voideath. The enervated answer, a column tearing me at the edges, built of screams of pain and promise.

Somewhere, I'm screaming as well.

Another step forward as the needle continues on its path. In front of me, the officer's indivisibles—as large as suns—erupt.

It's working. I'm penetrating his membrane! I have so far to go, but it's working.

But then everything falls apart.

The world of axion is stripped from me. Sunlight returns. One type of scream replaces another.

I feel myself fall.

Intense pain radiates from my right hand—the one that gripped my voidstone. It's gripping it no longer. It's a pulsing hot ball of pain.

Blood and water surround me. I'm on my knees. Feeling suddenly weak, I place my left hand in the blood to stop myself from falling over. Pieces of flesh—the remains of the chamberlain—wash up against me.

Sweat beads over my body. I'm suddenly cold, except for my right hand, which continues to burn, refusing to let me think about anything else. I look down at it, blinking a few times to try to clear away the confusion.

There's a large rip in my pants. The entire pocket area is torn away, but my right hand is somehow still inside, caught within a few slender threads of fabric.

I'm missing three of my fingers.

"Get the effulgent," I hear Turenne say. "Bring him here and drown him in the pool. Make it slow and painful."

I look up.

Turenne stands a few feet in front of me. His hands cover his face.

And just beside him stands Caracant. She's gripping my voidstone necklace. And three of my fingers.

She blinks a few times before turning toward the glistening dome. I see Blythe there, far away, kneeling in the sand. His pangs of exertion are clear in the dry, still day. He's trying to move the disks.

"Wait," Turenne says, lowering his hands. Blood flows down the bridge of his nose from a small bloody circle in his forehead. The bright red runs past his grimacing lips.

"Don't kill him," he says. "Incapacitate him. Incapacitate all of them. Bring them here, and then summon the giving house."

Caracant lets out a grunt of understanding.

Carefully, I move my right hand, trying to free it from the half-destroyed pocket, but it catches on one of the strands and sends a fresh wave of pain riding over the ocean of dull excruciation. Letting out a weak cry, I cradle my right wrist with my left hand and lean back on my heels.

Turenne takes a step nearer, staring down at me. "You had the audacity to attack me?"

I don't respond.

"We will see if your idiot king was right about one thing in his pathetic life. I'm going to place all your friends in soteria. Every single one of them. And then we'll see if you talk."

EIGHTEEN EFFIGIES

Using my teeth, I hastily rip off a piece of my shirt and create a tourniquet for my throbbing right hand. I get off my knees. My bare feet are ankle deep in a mire of blood, water, sand, and guts. Three gray fingers float in the pool in front of me. Past it, the king's headless body rests upon the broken throne. I keep alternating my gaze between it and the eighteen frozen bodies that surround him.

Sixteen lepers, Blythe, and Colu have all become effigies, trapped in various poses in the sand.

They're alive but petrified by Caracant's powers. Some were seized within the motion of stumbling, while others were caught midstride. Blythe kneels and prays, his hands to his face. A few lepers lie in the sand, frozen in the act of crawling. One is in the fetal position. Colu's hand is near the hilt of his sword, his stance wide as he looks at Caracant with his one frozen eye.

None of them make a sound. Even the colors of their forms are muted—membranes tightly drape them all, casting them in a sand-colored sheen that makes them look as if they were fashioned from the desert. Besides Turenne, the palehound, and me, the only one who is free is Caracant, but she's as lifeless as the others. She looks only at Turenne, with dead eyes, much like the palehound, eager for another command.

As for Turenne, he evidently no longer feels threatened by me. He's left me within the shade of the tent and stands just outside, basking in the full strength of the sun. The palehound sits obediently by his side. His back is to me as he silently awaits at least two dozen approaching soldiers, a hundred feet away. Past the destruction of the palms, and even from this distance, I can make out certain details. On their shoulders they carry a large black cube on a raised platform of woven timber. Their slow progress and hunched forms indicate how incredibly heavy it must be.

A blue-robed, hooded stranger leads the procession.

I've failed.

This was supposed to be easy. Despite the sheer power of the confederacy, the enervated were on our side. We had the upper hand. The cargo ship's escape from the axionship was proof at a celestial level—a greater sign I could not have conceived. I simply had to convince the king of the truth and ensure that things didn't get out of hand here before our friends returned.

Staring at my three gray fingers, I realize my mistake. I attacked Turenne first, when I should have gone for my only known weakness—the avorsi. I should have killed Caracant and set my sights on Turenne later. But hate got in the way. I wanted to kill Turenne more than anything. I wanted him to suffer.

Why couldn't I be nothing?

The only thing I can do now is hope. Hope that Chimeline, Lake, and Chireseal are more successful than I. The last thing I saw was a star streaking across the sky, and I hold on to that vision like a voidstone because it's the only thing that I have left. They are safe now. They *must* be safe. Because the fate of everything is now in their hands.

If only she would voidspeak to me again. I could warn her about Turenne. About all of this.

"Set it down right there," Turenne says calmly.

I turn my attention back to the approaching soldiers. They stand a few feet from him, dripping sweat, and begin lowering the cube, their exertion apparent. Meanwhile, the blue-robed person approaches Turenne and bows once in deference.

They exchange words in Effulgian.

Even though the blue-robed stranger's face is half obscured by shadow, I can tell that the person is a woman. Underneath her sleeves, a blue metallic-looking shackle covers her right wrist, identical to the blue-robed man in al-Kimer-vis. At first, I'm not sure if it's jewelry or some sort of restraint. Then I realize that it's exactly where her blue number would normally be. A thought comes to me. I theorize that it signifies (and perhaps even prevents) this blue-robed person from ever becoming a sponsor. Her role, if left unchecked, could be a conflict of interest.

The two seem to be arguing. The stranger shakes her head, and then Turenne's voice picks up sharply. Finally, the woman visibly acquiesces by nodding once, slowly, and turning in place.

"We leave now!" she cries, in a commanding tone.

Clapping once, she begins walking back toward the encampment, far in the distance, keeping her head straight. Once she passes the winded soldiers with their hands on their knees, they begrudgingly straighten and fall back into rank.

I stare at Caracant. She hasn't moved an inch.

She stands only a few feet from the pool.

I briefly consider walking over and pushing her in.

Physically, I'm stronger than she is—even with my throbbing hand. I could drown her, just like I drowned Mander. But the problem is that she—or Turenne, acting through her—would resort to voidance in a heartbeat, and then everything would be over.

Turenne also has a serrater. The small silver weapon glistens in the sun on his tan belt holster. This axionware is also a potential threat to me, though he probably doesn't realize it yet.

I'm out of options. Except for lying and delaying. My words are all that remain.

"I will tell you everything," I say to Turenne's back, trying to hide the panic in my voice. "If you let my friends go."

"Right," he says quietly, but I get the sense that he's ignoring me. He cranes his neck to look past the side of the cube, studying the retreating soldiers and blue-hooded woman in the shimmering sunlight. Apparently satisfied that they're far enough away, he nods to himself and takes a few steps toward the black object.

The cube is massive. His head only reaches the midpoint. The surface reminds me of a voidstone—it's perfectly matte, reflecting little sunlight. From my vantage point, I can see only two sides of the cube. Turenne stands in front of the left one.

"Turenne," I add. "There's no need to place anyone—"

Turenne raises his hand to silence me. Then he glances back. It's the first time since taking my voidstone that he's looked at me.

"Then start talking."

I open my mouth but hesitate. It's enough for Turenne to lose his patience.

"That's what I thought." He exhales.

"Wait!"

Turning back toward the cube, he sets his palm on it. A brief reverberation crosses over me, and then the center of the side he's touching opens like a blooming flower, shining an incredible white.

I'm reminded of the azureman on the wharf. An inverted voidstone is revealed in front of me, radiating a brilliance that eclipses the light of day. I raise my good hand to shield my eyes. Behind him, Turenne's shadow crosses the pool. Everything and everyone casts shadows under this hideous power.

Through squinted eyes, I can see a translucent vertical membrane rippling in the tight space between Turenne and the white petal—it's his creation, I'm assuming. To protect himself from being placed in soteria.

"Who's first?" Turenne asks himself, spinning around.

The closest statue—a young female leper on the ground in a half kneeling, half crawling position—instantly comes to life. Her sand-colored membrane dissolves in a splash, and she collapses in the sand. She's balding due to her sickness, but despite that and the sores covering her face, I can tell that she's young. Perhaps Marine's age.

As if pulled by an invisible string, she's dragged across the sand toward Turenne and the cube.

The young woman lets out a panicked scream, but her voice is sharply cut off as Turenne shakes his head.

"No need to scream now," he says. "There is plenty of time for that later."

Her body rises in front of him and the shining flower. The membrane stands in front of her like a gauze flag trembling in a storm. The light is so strong that both Turenne and her are silhouettes.

Her mouth is open, as if screaming, but no sound comes out.

Turenne slowly steps to the right, to the perpendicular side of the cube. I hadn't noticed it before, but a blue circle pulses there, in the center. He places his hand on it.

"Turenne!" I shout. "There are two rebels! I will tell you their names—"

"And sponsors," Turenne says loudly over me, "shall be forever honored."

"Turenne!" I cry. "Don't!"

The curtain in front of the girl drops.

Another reverberation passes through me as the white light becomes even stronger. My hand still out in front of me, my eyes still squinted to the point of being nearly closed, I watch on in horror.

A heartbeat later, the girl's silhouette changes. It stretches toward the petal. At first, she looks as if she's pregnant, but then her entire body fragments. White lines invade her silhouette from all directions, breaking it apart. Curving like the lines of a seashell, they keep spiraling, tearing, until nothing remains.

It takes only a moment, and then the light dies.

I blink rapidly, but her white afterimage is burned into my eyes. Orange and black float everywhere. It's so dark, suddenly. I turn toward Turenne. His inner forearm glows a bright blue as he withdraws his hand from the cube, smiling. Then I turn toward the remaining seventeen statues. Wherever I look, I'm haunted by the woman's memory.

Her body is gone. Completely gone.

Inside the cube. Why else would it be so heavy? How many corpses does it contain?

"I'm sorry," Turenne says slowly. "You were saying?"

I'm filled with such hot rage, it's hard to even think.

"Master Voider, you'd better speak, or I will continue until this tent is empty."

"If I tell you about the rebels," I say with a clenched jaw, motioning toward the statues, "will you let them go?"

Turenne shakes his head. "No."

I let out a weak gasp. "I thought that in exchange—"

"I will kill them," Turenne says matter-of-factly, as he takes a few steps away from the cube and toward me. "But I will spare them from being placed in soteria."

I swallow.

He gazes at the seventeen. "Let's see . . ."

"There were two rebels," I quickly say.

He looks back at me, waiting.

"Chireseal and Lake," I say. "Lake is an Agh-Severian."

He raises his hairless brow. "Go on."

"They had two ships with them. They sacrificed one in a trap . . ." I point into the distance, where the remains of the dark cloud still billow. "In order to kill your five azuremen."

He purses his lips. "Yes, I was wondering about that. What exactly did they do?"

"Something with the FTL array," I say, recalling the phrase.

"Interesting," he says, tapping his lips with a finger then nodding. "You see? This is good intelligence. This is progress. It is worth some mercy in return."

He looks back at the seventeen.

The membranes surrounding three of the lepers dissolve, and the lepers' bodies collapse to the sand. A moment later, all three cease to exist. They explode outward in a tight cone of sand, blood, and rendered flesh. Some of the gore splatters on the frozen Colu and Blythe, who are positioned slightly to the side.

I cry out in shock, taking a step back.

Turenne draws a tight circle in the air with his finger. "No, no, no. Keep going," he says. "I am trying to encourage you. Do you know what they did with the FTL array?"

My heart is beating out of my chest. I distractedly shake my head.

"Which one of them is the empowered?" he asks. "Or are they both?"

I don't answer. He points to his axiongraph. "Which one of them had one of these markings? And what did the marking look like?"

"No," I say, before thinking, reflexively shaking my head. "They didn't have that."

He frowns. "You're lying."

Turenne turns back toward the remaining statues.

"No, wait!" I shout, extending my left hand—the one that doesn't throb with pain. "I'm telling the truth! There was another."

He looks back at me. "Another?"

Suddenly, I'm pressed against the proverbial wall. Torn between revealing Chimeline and watching my friends become enslaved for eternity. And I have only a moment to decide.

I choose my friends, knowing that Chimeline can handle herself.

I need to warn her.

"She's not only an empowered," I say. "She's an axionlighter."

Turenne lets out a laugh but cuts it short.

For a moment, he studies me in silence. It's the most time that has passed between his threats. Even though his expression is serene and indecipherable, the silence tells me he wasn't expecting my reply, and he's taking it seriously.

"Go on," he eventually says, his voice low.

"I will tell you everything about her. But please. Please let these people go. Let them walk away from here unharmed."

He glances toward the collection of statues. Another leper collapses then disintegrates a moment later into a fountain of red.

I flinch and take another step backward. My bare foot slips on something that feels like bone, and I almost stumble.

"The next one will go in the box," he says. "Now tell me about this axionlighter. Where is she from? Efful?"

"No. She's from here."

His mouth hangs open briefly. "A native?"

I close my eyes, hoping that what I'm doing is the right thing.

"Talk!" he screams.

"She . . . Mander tried to place her in soteria. There was a scuffle, during which she touched the pool of white." I run my good hand through my hair. "I don't understand what happened, but it changed her from that moment on. Ever since that happened, she could work voidance. She wasn't an empowered before."

His gaze darts back and forth, looking at nothing.

"She can work voidance without touching a voidstone," I add.

His mouth moves in a way that suggests he's chewing on the words I just gave him. But then he blinks and glances at the dark cloud.

"It was this axionlighter who manipulated the FTL array to create the detonation?"

I nod.

"And she lived through it?"

This time I shrug, feigning ignorance.

Taking a few steps into the sunlight, he looks up into the blue sky with a hand sheltering his eyes. He speaks to himself in Effulgian and then walks back underneath the tent, alternating his gaze between the remaining thirteen effigies and me.

"This deserves some mercy," he says quietly, his gaze continuing to roam. "Who are you closest to?" he asks me, though it seems he's talking to himself. "The effulgent? Or the soldier?"

"Please," I plead, getting down on my knees and sinking in the bloody mire. "Please let them live. I'll tell you more, but only if you let them live."

He purses his lips. "I think the one-eyed soldier."

"No!" I scream, my hands out in front of me.

Turenne smiles as he stares directly at Colu.

The tan-colored curtain surrounding him disintegrates.

But as Colu falls to the sand, he deftly rolls head over heels.

A heartbeat later, the desert erupts in a cone blown backward from where he just stood.

Colu's hand was already near the hilt of his sword, and it continues to move there as he shifts out of his roll and comes to a standstill, on one knee.

Thoughts of doom fill my head. He stands no chance against Turenne a second time. Blythe and I should have forced Colu to join us in eleutheria earlier—he would at least be immune to Turenne's attacks now. Without the help of the enervated, his sword is useless. He's a dead man, and it's my doing.

But a single heartbeat later, he pulls something out of his pants pocket. He's not going for his sword. He's going for something else.

It's small and gray. Like a bird's egg. Or a pebble.

In one quick, smooth motion, he smashes it into his other palm, breaking it. A shining sphere bursts to life around him.

And not a moment too soon. As the sphere is forming, a second wave erupts directly in front of him.

But this time, the wave breaks. Sand flies to the left and right of him. The membrane holds, rippling violently.

Then I remember. In the cavern. Lake was worried about something called radiation.

"What's this shit?" Colu had asked her.

"A personal membrane," she'd said. "Use it for when you return. Crack it open like an egg, and then just carry it on you."

In the curved, reflective surface of the wet-looking sphere surrounding Colu, I can see Turenne's face, distorted with rage.

Colu stands, feet wide apart, and brandishes his sword.

CRATER

"Behind you!" I warn Colu, pointing at Caracant, who stands a few paces away.

He nods but keeps his eye on Turenne while holding out his sword parallel with the ground. In his other hand is the pebble.

"You have a toy," Turenne says, his voice even but as chiseled as his cheekbones. "You ashen with your silly little toys."

Turenne leans forward, as if pushing a wall with his forehead.

Colu's membrane begins to crack.

I cross over the corner of the pool and charge Turenne.

As I connect with his side, we both fall into the soft, bloody mess.

On the far side of the tent and behind Colu, Caracant places her splayed-out hands together. Something bright begins to shine between them. It's as brilliant as the black cube's inverted voidstone, but saffron colored instead of white—and the nearby air is distorted. Already I can feel the heat, even over twenty feet away.

Like at the nightmarket.

I lose sight of them as Turenne and I roll in the remains of the king and his chamberlain. The sand erupts around me, once, twice. All the hairs on my body go straight. He's not even trying to grapple with me using his physical body. He's using voidance instead. I'd be dead many times over if it weren't for the enervated.

Using this to my advantage, I try pinning him to the ground with my right forearm while frantically reaching for his serrater with my left hand. I have no idea how to use it, but reclaiming my voidstone is impossible.

Above me, the tent rips in an attack of voidance, letting in a scar of sunlight.

Briefly, my uninjured hand connects with the cold smoothness of the serrater, and I reach for it with all my strength.

It slips away in my bloody grasp.

We roll again, and Colu and Caracant reenter my line of sight.

She raises her sun above her head and steps forward, directly behind Colu's sphere.

Behind the cracked membrane, Colu twirls his sword in front of himself in a quick semicircle, never letting go of the hilt. Once the tip faces backward, he grabs the hilt with both hands and stabs backward to the side of himself.

The blade enters the center of Caracant's chest.

She looks down at it nonchalantly as the sun over her head flickers out. But she's still standing.

A wave of adrenaline courses through me. I knee Turenne in the crotch and shove him to the side. The hairs on my skin dance again. Dozens of vases shatter behind me.

Turenne lets out a bellow of rage and frustration.

I reach for the serrater a second time.

My fingers find purchase, and this time I don't let go. I pull the serrater free from the holster.

But simultaneously, my other hand erupts in newfound pain.

I cry out, letting go of the weapon. Turenne is biting down on the stumps of my fingers, through the torniquet. Blood pours down his chin.

Blackness crawls at the edges of my vision.

I try calling out to Colu for help, but the words can't escape my mouth. I try to kneel, but Turenne kicks me hard in the face, and I go down in the wetness. I swallow blood and have no idea if it's mine or not.

He kicks me again—this time in the stomach.

I wretch in the filth.

"Enough!" Turenne shouts. "Enough of these games!"

By the time I get to my knees and wipe the gore from my eyes, Turenne is picking up his serrater and placing it back in the holster. He stands, feet and arms apart, looking straight up at the scar in the tent.

Everywhere, sand is flowing toward him. I could almost mistake it for a gust of wind, except the wind doesn't move like this.

He's drawing in the air.

This was in Chimeline's visions—when Temberlain tried to escape. He called it "axionilation."

He's going to destroy everything.

"Run!" I shout to Colu, but it's too late.

The world turns white.

An earsplitting *boom* is followed by a sharp ringing that fills my ears and stays there. And then, weightlessness.

I'm falling.

I spread out my hands and feet to catch myself.

I keep falling.

A harsh stinging batters my skin. It feels like sand whipping around me in a frenzy, as if I'm falling through an hourglass. I'm part of it now.

Buried and out of time.

The white room? Am I in soteria?

No. I can hear Caracant's primal pangs of exertion. I sense the heat of the sun. My right hand throbs in excruciating pain. And I smell . . . cooked meat.

Blinking my eyes open, I hold out my left hand to shelter them from the light.

Slowly, my eyesight adjusts. Color eventually replaces the white, but there is only one shade in this new place—that of sun-bleached sand.

The tent is gone. The pool is gone. Everything is gone.

I continue to hold my hand out over my eyes as I sit up in the sand. Sun devours this place.

We're in a giant deepsand.

No. It's a crater, perhaps a hundred feet in diameter. The ridge rises twenty feet above us. We're in the center.

The black cube rests nearby, but it's half buried in the sand. One of its corners points straight upwards, like the tip of a sable obelisk.

Then I notice a few small rocks on the crater floor. They're darker, and faint smoke rises from them, as if they're the morning's remains of charcoal cooking fires from the night before.

One rests at my feet.

It's the elongated skull and curved spine of an animal. A palehound.

It's covered in smoldering flesh.

I crawl away in disgust.

Blythe is twenty feet in front of me, sitting up in the sand and looking around with the same confounded expression that I must have.

The lepers that surrounded him are all gone. But observing the odd-shaped, smoldering chunks of flesh, I realize with dread that in some way, they're still among us.

Good Unnamed.

Caracant and Colu are alive—they stir a few feet apart from each other. They're about the same distance away from me as Blythe, but to my left instead of straight ahead. Colu's sword remains stuck in her chest. Both of her hands grip the blade.

I peer around questioningly. The membrane surrounding Colu is barely intact. It's no longer spherical but an amorphous shape that sways in the wind. There are places that reflect the sun, and places that do not.

Turenne is on his knees, about twenty feet to my right. His hands are at his sides, palms forward, and his posture, while straight, is relaxed. He blinks repeatedly, saying nothing.

Not quite axionilation, but he's obviously taxed.

The release of energy he created must have formed this crater, destroying everything except for Blythe and me, whom the enervated protected. And luckily Colu too, who had the membrane, although now it's in tatters. I'm not sure how Caracant survived. Perhaps Turenne protected her.

I stare longingly at the serrater, wondering if I have an opportunity to grab it while Turenne's disoriented. But before I can react, his head smoothly turns toward me, as if he knows exactly what I was planning.

He studies me with red eyes.

"How are you alive?" he spits.

I'm in too much pain to answer.

Gradually he stands and then takes a single stumbling step back. He begins to ramble in Effulgian.

Caracant's high-pitched, animalistic cry pierces the quietude as she grasps the sword's blade tighter and moves it side to side. This must be causing her incalculable pain, but the sounds coming out of her mouth seem built more out of frustration than agony. She clearly doesn't have the strength or leverage to remove it nor stand. She spreads her legs, spasming like some beast caught in a hunter's trap. Blood pours down her forearms and onto the bleached sand between her thighs.

"I told you once, and I'll tell you again," I struggle to answer amidst shallow breaths, turning back to Turenne. "The enervated are protecting us. Your power is useless. Your time here is over."

He shakes his head and watches Caracant suffer. There isn't a hint of empathy in his expression. Far away, behind him, dozens of soldiers line up at the top edge of the crater, looking down upon us.

"Yet my avorsi can get through," he says, pointing at her and then putting his finger on his lips. "How insulting that my crude instrument has more influence than I do. She took away three of your fingers, while I cannot even pluck one hair from your uncouth skin."

Suddenly, like a puppet with its strings cut, Caracant lets go of the sword in her chest and drops her palms to her sides. She's sliced almost completely through her hands—their skin looks like strewn books with maroon spines.

Caracant turns her lifeless gaze toward me.

Simultaneously, my body is consumed in agony. An intense burning radiates across my left side. I convulse immediately, crying out while writhing in the sand, then curl up into a fetal position.

Blisters quickly appear on my forearm. My skin bubbles like the suckers on a squid's tentacles. My shirtsleeve erupts in flames as the blisters crawl up past my elbow then across my chest.

Turenne stands over me. Flailing, I clutch his boot, a plea for mercy. There are no words that I can give.

But then as quickly as it started, the burning ceases. The pain is still there. Like any burn, its memory is almost as torturous as the event itself, but this dullness is a shadow.

Looking up, my face pouring with fresh sweat, I see Colu standing above Caracant with the sword back in his hand.

"No!" Turenne shouts, turning toward him while holding out his hand.

Caracant looks up at Colu as he brings the sword down upon her neck.

A brilliant stream of crimson stains the perfectly blue sky and petrified sand. Her head rolls a few feet away then stops. It's so silent that even the sound of the metal blade snapping through bone reverberates back to us in the hot wind.

"Thank you," I mutter into the sand, sure that Colu cannot hear.

Meager flames still devour half my shirt. I roll a bit in the sand, stamping them out. The sleeve falls away in ashes.

My burns still ache miserably. I grimace and summon the strength to sit up.

Still half-enshrouded by the membrane, Colu approaches Turenne with the sword.

Turenne faces him when he's about twenty feet away.

The ground between the two erupts in a cut of sand—an exploding line connecting them. Colu dodges to the side, but it happens so quickly, I don't know how successful his maneuver is. The air distorts. An earsplitting *crack* echoes back from the curved crater walls multiple times.

By the time the scalloped curtain of sand falls back to the desert floor, I can see that Colu is injured and on one knee. The clothes on the right half of his body have been ripped away. His black skin is covered in bright blood, and part of his right arm is so mangled that bone and sinew is visible.

A piece of his shining membrane flies away, dissolving into diamond-like dust as it rises into the blue sky.

Blythe approaches at a run.

"We must stand in the way!" he yells at me, pointing to the line in the sand. "Stand and protect!"

I nod and summon more strength.

The sudden movement sends fresh ripples of agony through my body, but I get up and run toward Blythe. We meet in the middle and put ourselves directly between Turenne and Colu, who stand about thirty feet away from one another.

We're almost too late. Another line of pressure emanates directly over the first.

As the sharp crack echoes to nothing, I'm briefly blinded, caught in a rising sandstorm. I feel nothing except a tingling sensation everywhere and Blythe's searching hand on my shoulder.

I spin around desperately, to see if Blythe's strategy worked.

Behind us, a triangle of smooth sand spreads to the left and right. Colu kneels within his torn membrane, sheltered within the wide section of triangle, embraced within the wake of the enervated's protection.

"That was quick thinking," I utter to Blythe, huddled next to me.

Colu pierces the desert with his sword, which he uses to stand, crying out in pain.

"Stay behind us!" I tell him. "The enervated will save you!"

He looks up at me with one eye, grimacing. "No shit," he says, spitting blood.

A brilliant red beam vibrates in my peripheral vision, brighter than the day, accompanied by a deafening staccato buzzing.

Blythe is knocked back. He spins and then falls to one knee but remains upright.

"That should have cut you in half," Turenne says behind me.

Turning around, I see that his serrater is in his hand, trained on Blythe. The tip is glowing.

I study Blythe. It's obvious that he's hurt, but not fatally. He straightens, pressing a hand gingerly to his ribs. I don't see any blood.

Colu lets out a deep bellow, storming Turenne with his sword raised high.

I try to stop him. But it's already too late.

Turenne fires the serrater again, this time arcing the red line. The hideous buzzing resonates in my bones.

Part of the beam connects with the remains of Colu's membrane, and in those places, the beam simply dies there, as if swallowed up in a mirror. But the red that moves between the gaps decimates.

Colu is sliced mostly in two—part of the right side of his torso, and his entire left leg. Even his sword is separated.

Turenne's beam continues into the ground a foot away from me, turning the sand into a black line.

The entire feat takes less than a heartbeat yet a dozen for me to comprehend. A soft, high-pitched crystalline singing is left behind—the dying rage of Colu's broken sword.

Blythe frantically crawls over and catches Colu as he collapses to the sand. Impossibly, there's no blood. Everything is cauterized.

I fall to my knees.

I'm too shocked to do or say anything. I can only stare at Colu as he stares back at me. He's still alive, but his one eye doesn't seem to be taking anything in. Perhaps this is a blessing. Perhaps he has no pain.

Blythe seems lost in confusion, gazing at the places where Colu is missing pieces.

I crawl to them and hover over Colu. His face is cradled in Blythe's lap.

"I fucked up," he mumbles. His dry, dying voice is as deep as ever.

"No, no, no," I keep telling him, shaking my head as I grasp his hand, which is still wrapped around the hilt of his broken sword. "You killed the avorsi. You did good, my friend." I don't even know what I'm saying. I just want him to die in peace.

He lets out a blood-filled chuckle then spits. "It is . . . fine."

His single eye rolls back and then finds me again.

"Dying like this . . ." He tries to spit again, but this time he has no strength. He starts to choke, but Blythe tilts Colu's head to the side. Blood pours out of his mouth, down the side of his cheek.

"Dying like this," he says, as his body is consumed in a shudder, "is better than living as a skullman."

He exhales and then becomes still.

Turenne steps near, hovering over us. He leisurely dusts away sand from his bloody uniform and puts his serrater back in its holster.

The only sounds are Blythe's soft weeping and the cheers from the watching soldiers far above.

PALEHOUND

Colu's one glassy eye is aimed directly at the sun. I close it with a soft hand. Sitting in the sand, I study his face, remembering the first time I saw it. It was painted. He was a skullman. It seems like a lifetime ago. Our problems were small problems. Our foes brandished machetes instead of serraters. We thought voidance was a gift instead of a curse.

Blythe has stopped weeping. He still kneels in front of Colu's body, but he's praying now. Sweat drips off his nose. His voice is somehow soothing, despite it reminding me of being in the void.

A rustle of leather makes us both look up.

A half dozen winded soldiers encircle us. They're wearing sleeveless tunics and leather armor, no helmets. And they're covered in sweat, their once-fair skin reddened and burned by the sun.

"Shall we take them away, my lord?" says one, panting, putting his hand on the hilt of his sword.

Turenne shakes his head. "Just hold him down." He pulls my voidstone out of his tan pants by its gold chain.

The soldier takes a step toward Blythe.

"Not him, you idiot. The empowered."

The soldier appears confused by the word *empowered* but then motions to another in his company. They both walk over to me, approaching from opposite sides.

A tinted dome appears over Turenne's head, casting him in relative shade.

"Have him kneel, facing me," Turenne says. He's not even paying attention to us. Instead, he places my voidstone in his left palm and stares at it. The gold setting and chain dissolve into glitter, fluttering away in the wind. Soon, the matte black stone is all that remains.

Using his right hand, he pulls his serrater out of his holster.

"You heard the man." The two soldiers force me up to my knees then stretch my arms painfully behind my chest. Their body odor wafts over me. Drips of their sweat fall upon my face.

Eyeing the voidstone and serrater with instinctive fear, I question what sort of attack Turenne has planned and wonder if the enervated will protect me.

I think of Mander. Whether Turenne uses voidance via his axiongraph or this stone, he's still the source, and therefore the enervated must be aware. At least that's what I'm choosing to believe.

My only vulnerability may be his serrater. And, ironically, the soldiers' crude blades.

I reflexively squirm in their grasp.

"I said hold him *still*!" Turenne barks. "Lock his head in place!"

One of the soldiers brings his arm around my neck in a chokehold while the other pushes my palm up toward my shoulder blade. It's my injured hand. A fiery pain shoots through my arm and maimed hand.

"What are you doing?" I ask Turenne. My voice cracks.

He doesn't answer. Instead, he grabs a fistful of my hair and presses the serrater against my head, hard. He rubs it back and forth across my scalp.

I cry out as I feel the cut of its precision tip.

"Stop it!" Blythe shouts.

Turenne ignores him, continuing to tear at my scalp until I feel a trickle of warm blood drip down my cheek and onto my shoulder.

Dizzy from the pain, I watch as he pulls back the serrater and adjusts something on the back end of it.

"I," he slowly explains, "am simply solving a problem."

Satisfied, he takes the voidstone and holds it between his thumb and index finger, brandishing it.

"I'm going to burn this fragment of axion through your skull and into your brain. Then I'm going to take control of your mind. Train you like a palehound. You'll eat when I tell you to eat. Shit when I tell you to shit. Kill when I tell you to kill."

"No!" Blythe cries out. "Please don't do this. We'll tell you anything you want to know."

Turenne blinks twice, as if astonished by Blythe's declaration. A faint smile touches his face, revealing perfect teeth. "Why, yes, that's true. He *will* tell me anything I want to know. His mind belongs to me now."

My rage and fear reach a tipping point as I convulse, trying to free myself from the soldiers' grasp, but my strength is no match for theirs.

"Use me instead," Blythe says, reaching out to Turenne. "Leave my brother in peace. Everything he's done has been in the name of the Unnamed—"

Turenne motions to another soldier. "Silence him."

The soldier takes two wide steps toward Blythe. He raises his hand toward the sun and then brings it down solidly across Blythe's face.

He collapses to the sand, unconscious.

"You fucking coward," I snarl.

Turenne steps forward, holding the voidstone near my forehead. Using his other hand, he raises the serrater and positions it directly behind the voidstone such that the barrel and voidstone are aligned.

"Crude last words," Turenne says under his breath as he leans forward, further adjusting the stone and serrater. "But this is a crude world, after all."

Using the serrater, Turenne pushes the voidstone against my skin.

I enter the void.

The sun is taken away from me. The blue sky dissolves. The heat on my skin is replaced with dank coldness. There is nothing left except this colorless place, and I know deep in my heart that I will never see the world again. At least not in the way it is meant to be seen.

Beauty is only for mortals.

My last frantic thought is that I should use voidance. One last time. To tear Turenne apart.

But he's prepared. A membrane surrounds him.

Colu's indivisibles are colorless, like the granules of sand surrounding him. His body is meat now, part of the deepsands. Only Blythe, Turenne, and the soldiers shimmer with radiance. They are the only things that can be considered beautiful here. And it staggers me that they look identical from this perspective. Blythe, the epitome of holiness, decency, selflessness. And Turenne, the opposite in every way. In the void they are twins, sparkling like stars in the night behind a veil of thin clouds. Such is the distortion of truth here. In some respects, I see everything as the Unnamed must see it—the way the world was created. But I also see nothing. What good is this strange vision if I cannot even tell right from wrong? Good from evil?

And if I can't see it, can the Unnamed?

When the pain comes, it hits me like nothing I've ever felt before. The pain is layered, physical and mental, coming from the outside but also from the innermost chambers of my heart.

The latter hurts more.

"I keep failing." Marine sighs, letting go of the voidstone and sitting down next to me on the fountain's circular stone ledge. Her three small membranes dissolve, and the pigeons they once encircled fly away in panic.

"Good," I reply. "That means you keep learning."

She scoffs playfully.

"Just remember," I tell her, "failure is not the opposite of success. It is part of it. Soon you'll be able to maintain four in parallel. Then five."

"Yeah, except the others can already do a dozen. Anaxarchis already passed his challenges."

I purse my lips. She does have cause for concern. All her fellow students are excelling in their classes, while Marine is lagging. Why? Is it her stubbornness? Am I a distraction? Does she simply not want it badly enough? When Submaster Herrophilus discovered Anaxarchis and her in Giriya, she seemed to be the stronger one. But the timid Anaxarchis is the one being dispatched to Fiscarlo in the winter.

The birdseed I scattered moments ago is almost devoured. The dozen or so remaining pigeons hunt and peck on the stone-paved ground of the Royal House's gardens, looking for more. Little do they know that I have one handful left. But only if Marine is up for another lesson.

The light of the summer evening has become golden. The sun is low enough that it's half obscured by the tall, ivy-covered walls that surround this private place. Besides my footman Elrich, who stands in the shadows, we're the only ones here.

Still seated, Marine spins herself around, gathers up her indigo-dyed sundress around her tanned hips, and places her bare feet in the fountain.

For a moment, I lose my concentration. Why are we even here? I am a teacher, and she is my student. But as soft golden rays cut through her shiny blonde hair and droplets of water sparkle on her smooth legs, I'm lost to her implausible beauty.

It's a power. A raw power, just like voidance. The ability to manipulate the world without saying a single word.

Hearing the clink of dishes from the nearby kitchen, I sense that someone is watching.

Turning, I glance at Elrich, who quickly looks away. His cheeks are flushed redder than usual. He's standing in the arched doorway that leads into the Royal House, next to one of the older kitchen staff. On a silver tray, she carries two small glasses of mint-infused canex. As she hands the platter to Elrich, she whispers in his ear, a smirk upon her face. She motions my way.

Everyone knows what's happening here.

"Can I ask you a question?" Marine says, bending over and cupping some clear water in her hands. She lets it run over her thighs.

"Of course," I answer.

"There have been rumors," she says, running more water over her legs. "About happenings down South."

"Xiland?" I ask.

She nods.

"What about it?"

Again, more water over skin.

"They're saying that voiders will be sent to war. If war comes."

I laugh once before realizing that she's serious. She looks sideways at me with apprehension.

I place a hand on her thigh.

"Alright." I nod. "Yes, there have been issues with the trade routes in the bay, but that's nothing to go to war over. Andrej IX is a wise old king, and he lived through enough war as a child to know that it's a fool's errand. Diplomacy will prevail."

She purses her lips. "But the prince . . ."

I lean into her ear. "Is an idiot."

Her eyes go wide as her hand covers her mouth.

"Thankfully," I add, "he has decades to become half of what his father is today."

When her surprise fades, she doesn't look convinced. "But Submaster Herrophilus said that we're to learn battlefield triage now in our curative class. That was never taught before. Why would we be doing this if it weren't serious?"

A spark of rage ignites within me. I had agreed to this one piece with the king as risk mitigation, but only under specific terms, and those included discretion. It was the prince who was pushing for it.

I remind myself to speak to Herrophilus later. The man opens his mouth wide way too often—both to let in copious amounts of decadent food and to let out profanities.

"Marine, voidance is not designed to harm. It's meant to cure. We are servants of the people." I point to the brick wall. "From here in the citadel to the furthest reaches of the Northern Kingdom."

"I know." She turns to me with slightly parted lips. They already glisten—and they haven't even touched the sugary canex yet. "But . . . Dem, whatever happens, just promise me one thing."

I lean in. "Anything. What is it?"

"You know that I've always wanted to see the world, right?"

I nod.

"But not like this," she says. "Not because of a war."

I shake my head. "There's not going to be a war."

She puts her hand on mine, which is still on her thigh. "I don't want to be abandoned in some forgotten town. And I don't want to be sent to war."

"So, what do *you want?"*

Sighing in frustration, she looks up at the garden's brick wall and then, craning her neck, at the looming tower of the Royal House.

But she doesn't answer.

I have a notion. Perhaps her recent struggles with voidance are connected to this fear, whether consciously or subconsciously. Perhaps she's lagging because she doesn't know what awaits her.

A gold sunbeam hits me from across the garden. It's perfectly positioned between low branches and reaching ivy, and it brings a thought as well.

We are the same, she and I.

She has the gift of voidance—that cannot be disputed. But her real power is beauty. She will never need to be the strongest voider. And she will never take orders from anyone. She will abuse her beauty to climb the ranks of the citadel. Not only will she graduate—she will reign in her own kingdom, whatever that might be. And I am simply a means to that end.

Her beauty will shape her future like voidance shapes the world.

Similarly, my real power is the authority placed upon me by the king, but more importantly by all the submasters and voiders who serve the Northern Kingdom, and by extension, all citizens. I am Master Voider Democryos. All voidance runs through me.

Am I abusing this power to have relations with a woman? A woman I would otherwise never have the chance of courting?

Of course I am.

But why shouldn't I?

Why shouldn't I consume this ravaging beauty with pleasure? She is willing to give herself to me, and I will take her.

We will abuse each other into oblivion.

"What are you thinking about?" Marine asks me.

"The future." I blink as the sunbeam passes, caught now behind the brick wall.

I run my hand up her smooth thigh as Elrich brings the first drink of the evening, a promise of even sweeter things to come. With my other hand, I cast the seeds away. An orgy of feeding commences at my feet.

A LITTLE YOUNG FOR YOU, WASN'T SHE?

It's Turenne's voice, filling my head with needles. But the needles are only an itch compared to the burning between my eyes.

I'M THROUGH YOUR SKULL NOW. THE AXION IS JUST INSIDE. COVERING THE OUTERMOST LAYER OF THE NEURAL TISSUE OF THE CEREBRUM, SEEPING INTO THE LONGITUDINAL FISSURE. THIS IS THE CHASM THAT SEPARATES THE LEFT FROM

THE RIGHT. I'LL NEED BOTH. TELL ME, MY PALEHOUND, WHAT DO YOU FEEL NOW?

WHAT DO YOU FEEL NOW?

"He made me sit on the bed and face him," Chimeline says, from behind her bamboo bars. "He also sat down, but in a chair, facing me. He held his voidstone. His face was behind shimmering air, but I know he was looking at me the entire time. He kept asking me, 'What do you feel now?' Over and over. If I stopped talking, he would get very angry."

"And what did you feel?" I ask her, my face pressed against my own bars, my knees cold against the dirt floor.

"All sorts of things."

"I don't know what that means," I mumble.

"It means all sorts of things!" she screams. Her voice echoes across the meager village.

I smile internally at her outburst. Yes. Anger is good. Anger is her letting go of the cage of her embarrassment. If I am ever going to find this veiled man, there is no place for embarrassment—hers or mine. Those quiet, careful times are behind me. Let everyone in the citadel know that Dem went to find his wayward wife. That she left with a veiled man. Shout it from the rooftop of the Royal House, for all I care.

Soon the veil will be lifted. This girl from Scorpiontail will be the one to take me to him if it's the last thing she does.

THAT WAS MANDER? THE VEILED MAN? AND WHO IS THIS AXIONLIGHTER?

I don't voidspeak back.

I'M INTO THE SECOND LAYER OF CEREBRUM, MY PALEHOUND. IN A SHORT AMOUNT OF TIME, YOU WILL HAVE TO ANSWER ME. THE DEEPER I GO, THE SHALLOWER YOU BECOME. BUT I AM REALIZING NOW THAT YOU'VE ALWAYS BEEN SHALLOW. HAVEN'T YOU?

The wind picks up, a storm buffeting Turenne's words. The enervated know what's happening. A destruction worse than death. But they cannot stop it.

THAT IS TRUE, PALEHOUND. THEY CANNOT STOP ME.

Voiders don't create or destroy, *I write on the blackboard, the hollow sound of chalk echoing in the wooden coffer-ceilinged classroom.* We only change.

I underline the word change. *White specks float within the stagnant air, almost like indivisibles.*

"Change," *I say out loud. It's my first word to my new class, chosen deliberately. I let the silence stretch out as I stare at my writings, keeping my back to the class. But then I realize that it's not completely silent—a* drip, drip, drip *sound invades the room. I fight the urge to spin in place, find its source, and instill discipline. But I summon my patience. This lesson is more important.*

"*We manipulate what is already there,*" *I eventually add.* "*And many times, this change is brief. If you hold on to the power of the voidstone for too long, you risk voideath. So you must always let go, and when you do, things tend to go back to the way they were. It may take a fullbell, or it may take days, but eventually, the world returns to normal. You cannot change things forever.*"

Finally, I turn and face my students.

The room is vacant except for six people in the front row.

An emaciated Cleanthes is all the way on the left. His face is covered in redskull paint, except for around his hollow eyes. The color is almost the same as his rusty hair. He wears a red cloak made of silk, and a voidstone is draped around his neck. In his hand is a hilma pipe—from it, a gray line of smoke rises to the ceiling twenty feet above.

Suddenly I can smell the heavy sweetness that borders on decay.

"You couldn't change me," he says. He looks so much like a skeleton, and the red paint has nothing to do with it. "You couldn't save me. You couldn't save any of us."

Next to him sits a blue-skinned, bloated, sopping corpse. I don't recognize him. At his feet is a pool of water, where the dripping sound originates. In the pool is the cut-up reflection of the moon, even though the sun outside coats the space through rose-colored paned windows at the far end of the classroom. There's no possibility that he's alive, yet the corpse sits upright and stares at me with blinking black eyes that resemble buttons on a pincushioned settee.

"You must always let go?" gurgles the corpse. "You never held us to begin with."

Marine stirs beside him. "Anaxarchis," she says, running a manicured hand down the length of her ponytail. "You look awful. It's like you've been living underwater." She wears the same tan and white riding clothes she wore the first day I met her, with her shirt tied into a knot at her waist.

"Ah, um, have you been underwater? To Xi Bay?" asks Mander, to her right, clearing his throat. He pushes his brass glasses up the bridge of his nose. "It's, um, a beautiful place. Um, almost. Almost, um, as beautiful as you."

She turns to him, her ponytail whipping around, before she leans in and puts her hand on her chin, tapping her front teeth with a fingernail.

"Would you like, um, to see my kingdom?" Mander asks.

Outside, past the rose-colored windows, the sun is swallowed in black.

It's as if a storm cloud has just appeared over the citadel. But no storm moves this quickly, and no cloud is this dark.

I hadn't noticed them before, but sixteen lepers sit silently in the shadow-filled last row. They're covered in bloody, yellow-stained gauze.

Above them, the glass panes begin to crack.

TELL ME YOUR NAME.

I try to stay silent. But there is this desire within me, unstoppable now.

DEMOCRYOS, I answer.

NO, comes the reply. YOUR NAME IS PALEHOUND.

The wind is everywhere.

WHAT IS YOUR NAME?

I want to float in the blackness, but I also know my name, and it is Democryos. I am the master voider.

I am . . .

Who am I?

le-Daerke's fiery eyes are suddenly the brightest thing in the room. She sits between Mander and Colu, her dark and glossy skin almost blending in with the warm wood tones of the classroom. Her effulgency cloak should be white. But it's colorless, as if she is in the void.

She turns toward the cracking windows and pulls her dagger from out of the folds of her cloak. For the first time, I can see the back of her head. It's completely missing.

The windows shatter.

le-Daerke turns to me in terror, and then her forehead creases as she bares her teeth at me. "I should have slit your throat when I had the chance. You're like all the rest. Once a voider, always a voider."

A black substance begins to ooze into the classroom from the windows, flowing down the walls like thickened syrup.

"You fucking idiot," Colu says, slouched in his desk, glaring at me with one eye as he struggles to stay upright with a hand grasping the edge of his desk. Half of his body is cut away. "You tell us that voiders don't create or destroy? You fucking destroyed all of us."

The black substance continues to flow in from the rear bank of windows. It pools on the floor then moves forward, row by row, throbbing like some copulating organism. The wave reaches my six students. It envelops their feet, and then the substance touches me, and I feel the icy coldness up to my ankles.

It's axion.

WHAT IS YOUR NAME? the voice commands again.
PALEHOUND, I answer.

LAST CLASS

"Where is the Axiondrive?"

Disoriented, I look up from the churning matte blackness that blankets the floor of the classroom, seeking the origin of my master's voice. He's actually here—not just voidspeaking, but physically present in this classroom. His words echo off the ornate ceiling.

I hear scratches of chalk on a blackboard.

Facing the front of the classroom, I finally see him. He's written down the same question and underlined it.

My master stands where I used to be, near the podium, dressed gloriously in his gray uniform. He truly is the master. The master voider.

Which must make me his student. I am his palehound, but his student as well.

Yes. I am sitting in a desk now, aren't I?

A sense of pride swells within me.

Turning left and right in my desk, I realize that I'm the only student in his class.

There used to be others in the first row, and even more lurking in the shadows along the back. But their names and faces escape me. All my memories escape me.

It doesn't matter. All that matters is that I'm here, learning from my master.

"Palehound," he says, pointing his chalk at me. "Answer the question."

"I do not know, Master." It breaks my heart to disappoint him. I'd gladly slit my throat if my blood contained the secrets that he was looking for.

"You didn't overhear anything during your time with the rebels?"

I shake my head. "They only said off-world."

He begins to slowly pace at the front of the classroom, his footsteps causing a thick splashing sound as he trudges through the inches-deep axion. "Tell me about this axionlighter," he says. "She went with the two rebels off-world to hide the drive?"

I nod. "She is from Scorpiontail. The archipelago," I quickly add.

"And you were a friend to her?"

I pause, unable to answer.

"You have my permission to remember," Master says.

Suddenly, feelings enter me.

"Chimeline?" I ask myself, as if saying the word for the first time. "Oh, yes. She was a friend. More than that, Master. I loved her." It seems strange to say the words because the only love I have now is for my master. Even the memory of her love is gone. Yet I am saying these words.

He turns to face me, hairless brow raised.

"Did you, now?" he says. He points to an empty desk next to me. "You have my permission to bring her here. To class. I want to meet her. Actually, I want to meet all three."

"I . . ." I don't want to disappoint my master, but I don't understand what he's asking.

"Concentrate. Picture them in your memories, my palehound, and I will do the rest."

"But, Master, I don't have any mem—"

"You have my permission!" he snaps. "All of your memories are there, beneath the surface. So remember!"

Closing my eyes, I frantically try to do as he says.

Random scenes come into focus before disappearing again. An argument with Chireseal. Lake polishing her lit device with her glossy black suit. Chimeline and I making love near the pool's edge in the cave. My master moves past them all, like flipping the pages of a book. Finally, we settle into the claustrophobic space within the cargo ship. The poison cloud is just outside of the front window.

A moment later, a loud splashing sound erupts to my left, and I turn in that direction.

Chireseal, Lake, and Chimeline all sit behind desks, at rapt attention. Matte black emanates from beneath all three in slow ripples, as if they were stones cast into a dark lake.

"Good," my master says, approaching them. He first stands in front of Chireseal, running his thumb harshly over the man's facial gems. Chireseal doesn't seem to notice. "We don't know about this one," my master mumbles. "This is good. We will find him and bring him to justice. You said he goes by the name Chireseal?"

"Yes, Master."

"He's Effulgian," my master says with a sneer.

Next, he steps over to Lake but doesn't touch her. "This one we do know about," he says, looking down upon her with narrowed eyes. "I executed her family a long time ago, when she was a child. She escaped my grasp at the time. Slippery little red fish." He briefly turns my way. "What do you think about that, Palehound?"

I don't understand his question, but I feel my master's emotions. He's fuming behind his composure, but this anger is centered on himself—that he let Lake get away and because of it now has a missing Axiondrive.

"You will kill her now, Master. Once you find her and the Axiondrive."

He smiles. "Yes. I will. And you will help me."

I smile back. "With delight, Master."

Finally, he grabs Chimeline's chin and forces her face up. My master swivels it left and right. "She is very attractive, for a native," he says. "And almost as young as that wife of yours. I could see why you were so taken." When he releases her chin, her head falls back into place.

"It's strange you never acclimated to us," he says, turning toward me.

"Master?"

"You like the fine things in life. The confederacy could have provided that for you, if only you'd fallen into service." He shrugs. "It's of no matter. Being a palehound suits you better."

"Yes, Master. It does."

"Does she trust you?" he asks, his demeanor turning serious.

"Chimeline? Yes."

"Then I want you to speak to her. Ask her where they took the drive."

Blinking repeatedly, I struggle to understand what exactly he's asking. Chimeline is sitting right in front of him. He could ask her himself.

Before my master loses his patience, I face Chimeline squarely, turning in my seat. "You heard the master," I tell her loudly. "Tell him where you and the rebels—"

My master chuckles, making me feel small. I have apparently made a mistake.

"No, Palehound," he says. "I meant the *real* her. I want you to speak to the *real* axionlighter."

"I . . ." The same disappointing feeling fills me, as I have no idea what he means.

"This"—my master sharply points to Chimeline, and she and her desk explode backward in a storm of splinters and flesh—"is only an illusion," he yells over the thunder. "Only a fragment that you created in your mind!"

Once the echoes die, he softens his voice. "Outside of this classroom is the real world. And I need you to speak to the Chimeline *there*."

"But I don't know how to voidspeak."

"My poor palehound," he says, stepping toward me and placing his hand on the crown of my head, tousling the hair there. "You needn't worry. I will do the hard work. All you need to do is say the words I put into your tiny little head. Do you think you can do that?"

"Oh, yes, Master," I reply. "With delight."

He drags a neighboring desk over and situates it directly opposite mine. Then he sits down facing me, leans forward, and stares into my eyes. The veins on his hairless forehead bulge.

"Then we begin," he says.

CHIMELINE, WHERE ARE YOU? I ask. It's strange to hear my voice saying my master's words. I go where he leads.

Almost immediately, I sense her presence.

DEM?

YES.

She pauses. GOOD UNNAMED. ARE YOU ALRIGHT?

YES. YES, I AM FINE.

DID YOU MEET THE KING?

I feel as if my entire being is a string being pulled in two opposing directions. On one end is Chimeline, and on the other is my master. There are different feelings at each end. The emotions around Chimeline are somewhat muted, and strange—love, apprehension, tiredness. I don't understand any of them.

My master's feelings are strong and clear. He is impatient and full of hate. Chimeline didn't answer my question. He doesn't want to talk about the stupid king. He doesn't want to talk about Dem. He wants to know where the drive is.

But my master is also being careful. Chimeline cannot know that Dem is gone and now only Palehound remains. There are layers of curtains hiding this stage. Chimeline to Dem. Dem to Palehound. Palehound to Master.

He is such a smart master.

KING ANDREJ X IS DEAD, CHIMELINE. IT WAS A TRAP, BUT . . . EVERYTHING IS ALRIGHT NOW.

She hesitates. I feel more fear on her side. WHAT ABOUT THE OTHERS? she asks.

My master penetrates my being. It doesn't feel violating. I want to delight him in every way possible. I open my mind to him.

He frantically flips through my memories again, as if they're pages in a book, until he extracts one from the deep and forces it into focus.

A splash erupts on the other side of me. Blythe and Colu appear in nearby desks, silent and facing forward. Seeing their faces, I remember them. They were my friends. But no longer. One is dead, and the other does not follow the master.

BLYTHE IS ARIGHT, I tell her. BUT COLU . . .

WHAT HAPPENED TO COLU?

In front of me, my master continues to lean forward, inches from my face. His eyes are closed in concentration now, moving behind smooth skin.

THERE WAS A CONFEDERATE HELPING THE KING. I HAD TO USE VOIDANCE. I WAS ABLE TO KILL HIM BUT NOT BEFORE COLU WAS STRUCK.

Silence.

My master's patience is waning.

WERE YOU ABLE TO HIDE THE DRIVE? I ask.

YES.

THAT'S EXCELLENT. AND CHIRESEAL AND LAKE? ARE THEY ALRIGHT?

YES. THEY'RE RIGHT HERE.

WHERE ARE YOU?

IT'S SO BEAUTIFUL HERE, DEM. THE TREES . . . EVERTHING IS SO DIFFERENT, YET THE SAME. I WISH YOU COULD SEE IT.

My master slowly leans back in his desk and smiles. He folds his hands together then brings them to his lips. He's waiting now. Waiting for the revelation.

DEM?

I'M HERE, I say. TELL ME ALL ABOUT IT. I'M LISTENING.

WELL, FOR STARTERS, THE SKY IS MORE PURPLE. AND THE MOON IS SO LARGE. AND THE WATER IS RED! CAN YOU BELIEVE THAT?

Master smiles wider.

Red.

YOU'RE ON AGH-SEVERIA?

YES!

YOU HID THE DRIVE THERE TOO?

SORT OF. LAKE CALLED IT SER-234. THERE'S ANOTHER WORLD NEAR ARG-SEVERIA MADE ENTIRELY OF GAS, DEM. IT'S NEARBY. WELL, I DON'T KNOW HOW CLOSE, BUT CHIRESEAL JUST POINTED IT OUT TO ME IN THE SKY, AND IT ONLY LOOKS LIKE A STAR WHERE I'M STANDING NOW. BUT AT THE TIME IT WAS HUGE. THEY JUST JETTISONED THE CARGO AND IT FELL INTO THE CLOUDS. THEY ADDED WEIGHT TO IT. THEY SAID THERE'S NO WAY IT CAN BE FOUND THERE. THE HEAT IN THE CENTER WILL MAKE THE AXION IMPOSSIBLE TO DETECT.

My master stands and begins to chuckle.

OH, WE WILL GET IT BACK, I say.

She pauses as my master's laughter grows louder. He reaches out and tousles my hair again. "Well done, Palehound. Well done."

DEM? WHAT ARE YOU TALKING ABOUT?

DEM IS DEAD, YOU AXIONLIGHTER BITCH. DO YOU KNOW WHAT I DID TO HIM?

Silence. I feel her muted terror being drowned by my master's elation.

I BURNED AXION INTO HIS BRAIN. HE'S MY PALEHOUND NOW.

I feel her urge to flee.

I sense her speaking hysterically to Chireseal and Lake. They're telling her to break it off. But she doesn't want to believe the words that she's hearing. She has hope that there's still something she can do.

IT'S OVER, AXIONLIGHTER.

He raises his hairless brow. "Don't you agree, Palehound?"

I smile. "Oh, yes, Master. It's over."

"We are done here, then," he says to me tersely. "I need to alert Agh-Severia immediately. Put their orbit into lockdown. Send a solaris team out to SER-234. Meanwhile, I need you back in the real world. Your first task is to fix the giving house. Then, we'll place that friend of yours in soteria. He is no longer of value."

"Yes, Master," I say, meeting his approving gaze. "But how do I leave this place?"

"Simple. Take my hand." He reaches out.

But before I can grasp it, the wooden door to the classroom bursts opens wide. A piercing light invades the room. Instinctively, I move my hand, once intended for my master's, to cover my squinting eyes.

Someone rushes into the room. Someone made of stars.

It's a storm of light. Wherever this intruder steps, the axion covering the floor is whipped away in a whirling cyclone, revealing the polished checkered floor underneath.

"How . . . ?" my master cries, while spinning and facing the intruder. He raises his arms at his sides, and a wave of black rises from the floor between the two of them.

But the intruder holds their hands of stars in front of them. A web of light spins out from their fingertips and across the front of the classroom. The web strikes the black wave. Its glistening specks explode randomly, pushing back the axion in thousands of concussions until the black covers my master up to his shoulders.

My master turns to me as he struggles in the syrupy, churning waste, and I feel his absolute panic. His dread embraces me like an icy blanket. Out of the black, he raises his hand in my direction and grimaces in exertion. "Palehound! Grab my hand!"

Leaning forward, I try to reach out for him, but the intruder of stars prevents it.

"Master, I'm trying!"

All I can do is watch helplessly as the intruder spins their web of stars between my master and me, pushing us apart.

My master screams. "Grab my h—"

His words are cut off as his head sinks beneath the surface.

The intruder wastes no time. The figure of light comes near, holding out both hands. The light climaxes.

I'm sobbing in fear and loathing. I put my head down on my desk and cover it tightly with both arms. I have failed him. I am a wretched palehound.

The entire room turns white.

I am Dem.

Raising my head off her shoulder and solace of black hair, that is the first thought that enters my mind.

I am Dem.

The second thought is that the classroom is evaporating.

All her stars have been cast into the air, into the moonlit night sky.

Her glittering form has been replaced with a real body, naked shoulders, half covered in a velvet robe even darker than the night. Her bangs cover her eyebrows, but the black hair below disappears against the fabric. Her cinnamon skin still glows, but softly now, reflecting the splendor above. The splendor that used to be her.

Exhaling, she sets her head against my chest and takes a few breaths. She seems physically exhausted, on the verge of collapse.

We stand in the middle of an empty, damp street. The full moon shines on a nearby pothole. Behind me, the evergreens and hedgerows of formal gardens emanate in perfect lines as far as the eye can see.

This is the king's palace. We're in the Northern Kingdom.

A glass-covered streetlamp stands nearby. We're just out of reach of its ring of saffron light.

We say nothing as she catches her breath in my arms. Eventually she looks up at me.

"You look like a gentleman," she says after a moment, her smooth face upturned in the moonlight. It had the look of caution then and it's cautious now, but for different reasons. Her voice is crystal clear. And I recognize it immediately.

Good Unnamed. She has brought me back.

A tear falls down my cheek.

"That's because I am one," I answer, just as I did the night I met her.

She smiles wide but still raises a disbelieving eyebrow.

"You saved me, Chimeline." I run a hand through my hair as I look around. "How did you do that?"

But I already know the answer.

Axionlighter.

"Good Unnamed, I remember everything that happened." But with this memory comes torture.

Palehound. Master.

"Turenne," I say, slowly. "He turned me into an avorsi."

She nods.

"So this isn't real," I add quietly, as I look beyond her. "None of this is real."

She doesn't reply. It's as if any word could break the spell.

"Come," she eventually says, snaking her arm into mine. We walk down the long, circular drive to the public street beyond.

Toward the Royal House.

Past the low wall of the curved street, the hillside abruptly ends, giving way to the slumbering Northern Kingdom. Next to us is a tall cypress tree, which cuts the night in its sheer ambition.

Far away, past the First Ring, the landscape fades into the matte shadows of the countryside. It's darker there than I remember.

"Even though I've temporarily pushed the axion out of your skull, you're still in a dream. But I *am* here with you, in spirit. This part is real."

"So, outside of this dream, what's happening to me?"

"You're unconscious, lying on the desert floor."

"But what if Turenne tries it again?"

"He will," she says. "But right now, he has bigger things on his mind. Like notifying the confederacy where we hid the drive. And where Chireseal, Lake, and I are hiding."

She wrinkles her nose and looks past the low wall toward the cityscape once again, leaning into me—almost hanging upon me, as if she no longer has the strength to stand.

Temporarily.

Looking at the weakened image of her in my mind, I know that she doesn't have the strength to expel the axion again. Everything in her body language is telling me that it's not a question of *if*. It's a question of *when*.

"How much time do we have?" I ask.

She closes her eyes and takes a few deep breaths. "A tenthbell. Maybe less."

When she opens her eyes again, the stars are reflected in their wetness. She has summoned the same courage as I have—to admit the same harsh truth.

"Dem, I can't—"

"It's okay," I say, pulling her into my arms.

"I'm so sorry," she cries into my neck. "I'm so sorry." She wipes her nose and then looks away. "I wish I could. I would do anything. But I'm too far away, and he's too strong."

"I'll commit voideath," I say, without hesitation.

She snaps her head upwards. "What?"

"Voideath," I repeat. "I'll put this palehound down before I can be used against you. Or Blythe. Or anyone."

"Dem . . ." She shakes her head. "You can't do that."

"I must."

"No, I mean you *can't*," she says. "You won't have enough time to draw that much power—the amount of power it would take to consume you."

She might be right, but I'm willing to take that chance.

"I can do it," I insist.

"You can't!" she snaps. "Turenne may even have the power to stop you once you start. Besides, who's to say the enervated would even *let* you do such a thing?"

I hesitate. She's right. The enervated have stopped others from killing me. They may do the same thing if I try to kill myself.

"Then you do it."

"What?" she asks, her voice breaking.

"You're the axionlighter. You can talk to them, explain what you're doing. You need to kill me. Kill me before he has the chance to overwhelm my mind again."

"No!" she shouts.

"Chimeline, you must!"

"I'm not going—" She shakes her head fervently instead of saying the words.

I take a deep breath and let it out slowly before lowering my voice. "You have to do this. You know that it's the right thing to do. Look at the damage I've already done."

Chimeline breaks down in my arms. I gently lower her into a sitting position on the low stone wall.

"Can you do this for me? Please?"

"Dem . . ."

I force her wet face up to meet mine as I stand between her legs. "Please."

After a pause, she nods once.

FALLING INTO THE SUNRISE

"Are you ready?" she asks me.

I nod solemnly.

She stands up from the low stone wall and grasps my hands.

"I love you," she whispers, looking up, deep into my eyes.

"I love you too."

Chimeline's face twists in hurt, but almost immediately it's shrouded by a veil of light.

She's become a woman of stars once again.

This time I know that it's her. I'm not clouded with Turenne's axion. She is luminescent, as she has been all the other times she's used voidance, and I know that this will be my last time seeing her.

I can still make out certain details behind the radiance. Her eyes frantically moving behind closed lids, her brow furrowing behind perfectly cut bangs, her white teeth biting her lower lip. All of this is almost invisible, but I stare longingly, letting my eyes water from the brightness, because I know I only have heartbeats left before . . .

Before *what*?

There is no white room reserved for me.

But I hope that there is a Good Unnamed.

Unexpectedly, she goes dark.

"I can't," she says with a sigh, opening her eyes and letting go of my hands. She's weeping.

I gently grab her shoulders. Were I in her position, I'd feel the same. "I know it's not easy."

"I can't do it, Dem," she cries, shaking her head.

I know that the guilt must be unbearable. Killing someone you love—even as an act of mercy—would be a tremendous burden to bear.

"I know you don't want to, but you must," I say. "Death is better than enslavement. You know this!"

"I don't care, Dem. I can't do it, alright?"

We don't have time for this. Perhaps if I get her angry?

"You're an assassin!" I snap. "The one time you're called upon to kill someone for the sake of good, you can't do it?"

She looks at me. I can see the hurt in her eyes. While it breaks my heart, I know that it's the only way she'll go through with it.

"Do you really think that's who I am?"

I shrug. "Assassin, axionlighter. What's the difference? You're a weapon. A tool."

"Stop it," she says, her lower lip trembling.

"I'm not saying anything you haven't said yourself."

She swallows hard.

"Mander tells you to poison me with moonspit, so you obey—or at least you tried. Voidance is easier than using poison. You—"

I stop midsentence, opening my mouth wide as a thought crystallizes.

Poison.

The word enters my skull, but unlike Turenne's burned-in axion, it carries the possibility of salvation. It might be the key. To everything.

They poison each other.

Chimeline doesn't notice. Her expression changes from one of hurt to one of anger. She turns her back to me. "I know what you're trying to do, Dem, and it's not going to work."

I'm not listening to her. I'm listening to Marine.

Pain likes to mix with other pain.

"Chimeline!" I shout, spinning her to meet me.

She raises her hands in protest. "No!"

"Stop! Wait. I'm thinking about what Marine said to me," I tell her. "When she freed herself."

Chimeline's expression softens, but she looks confused. "What about it?"

"What if . . ." I momentarily close my eyes to help organize my thoughts. "It's just . . . Marine's words didn't make sense at the time. To Blythe or me or anyone. But now I think I understand. She said that the enervated *poison* each other."

She folds her arms underneath her breasts, waiting for me to continue.

I take my hands off her shoulders and snap my fingers. "She said that the spheres keep colliding with each other. The enervated. Their memories just mix up like spilled paint. Pain likes to mix with other pain."

Her expression remains unchanged.

"Pain mixes with other pain! It feeds on itself!" I say, my voice almost a shout.

She wriggles her nose. "I still don't understand. How are the enervated poisoning each other?"

"Marine said that her soul was only so big," I say. "I think she meant *any* soul."

"I remember she was talking about her room only being so big."

"Yes, yes, she was talking about her room, but I think she was also talking about a soul. That it can only hold so much."

"Okay," she says with a small nod. "But what does that have to do with poison?"

"When we forgive, we throw out all of that clutter in our soul," I explain, looking her squarely in her dark eyes. "And I think *that's* why her stone shrank. It's because she was forgiving. Forgiving me. Forgiving Mander. Forgiving herself. And every time she did that, part of her prison turned to ash."

Chimeline pauses. "Dem, if that's true, then why aren't all of the millions of enervated doing the same?"

"That's the question surrounding everything," I say. "And I think the answer—the entire reason—lies in the fact that they aren't alone."

"You mean, the way Marine was alone?"

"Exactly! She was alone with her pain!" I wave my finger. "But they're not. They share their pain, like a poison that's able to—"

Suddenly Chimeline cries out, short and abrupt. She hunches over, as if punched in the gut.

I hover close. "Chimeline? What's wrong?"

She flashes white, but this time it's erratic, like lightning. Then she disappears, only to reappear again a moment later.

The shimmering ceases.

"Chimeline! What's happening?"

She seems about to fall over. I settle her back into a sitting position on the low stone wall.

Her eyes are wide open, unblinking, as if in a trance.

I gently slap her cheek a few times. "Chimeline!"

She lets out a sharp exhale.

"He's back," she says, in a panic. "He's burning the axion back into your skull."

She slowly turns her head left, toward the dark countryside.

Following her gaze, I see it.

Past the First Ring, it's not the shadows of the countryside taking over. If that were true, those fields would also be lit up with the same moonlight that paints the clay rooftops. No, it's something darker.

Axion.

My heart drops as I realize that this is no different from my classroom. Chimeline has changed the scenery, but a wave of axion is still storming the gates of my mind.

And it's just broken through.

I watch in terror as all the streetlamps and all the lights in the windows down below are snuffed out. Within heartbeats, it's an unbroken sea of black. All the common city is submerged. Only a few rooftops and the steeples remain.

Quickly peering over the edge of the wall, I try to gauge how much time we have. This street curves back on itself as it steeply descends into the city. I remember when Chimeline and I jumped, on that night I met her. There were street cleaners down below. How far was that? One hundred feet? Two hundred?

Now everything is gone. The black rises, swallowing the dry sagebrush of the cliffside, foot by foot.

"Chimeline, can the enervated hear us?" I ask her.

"What?"

"Did the enervated hear us just now when we spoke about Marine? My theory on the poisoning—"

"No," she says. "You'd have to be touching the axion. My membrane is preventing it."

"But if I were, would they understand me?"

"Yes."

"But I don't speak their—"

"You're not actually *speaking* now, Dem. We're in your mind—and my mind. It transcends speech."

I run my hand through my hair.

Then there is a chance. But is there enough time?

I glance back down the sharply descending road. Shadows lurk there, but I'm not sure if it's axion or not.

"Can you stand?" I grab her hand and gently pull her up.

She nods as she falls into my arms.

"Listen," I tell her. "We have to do this now. This is our only chance."

"I'm not killing you!" She struggles in my arms, pounding my chest with her fists.

"I know, I know," I tell her, trying to keep my voice level to install calm in her. "I'm talking about destroying this voidstone." I gesture all around us. "The one that's burning into my skull. We have one chance, but I need to speak to the enervated for it to work."

Her eyes are as wide as gold coins. "Well then do it!" she snaps.

"I need your help."

The sea has reached the cliff.

Chimeline lets out a short scream and falls into my arms as the black seeps over the stone edge to our right, feet away from us, slopping down onto the pavers.

"When the axion comes, can you protect me?" I ask her.

She stares helplessly at the black.

"Can you protect me?" I repeat. "Just for a little bit. Until I can speak to the enervated?"

Chimeline nods. "I think so. I can't drive it back this time, but I can hold it off."

As the thick axion crawls up the street to meet us, she grabs my hand tightly, interlocking our fingers.

"Dem, are you sure about this?"

I nod. "I just hope they'll listen."

"Well, they should," she answers. "They have the best teacher."

We share a brief smile and then she turns a dazzling, radiant white, shattering the darkness in all directions. I cannot see the stars, the moon, the sky, the bell towers of the effulgency temples scattered across the land.

A moment later, I feel the rising flood hit us, flowing over our feet.

Instead of paralyzing ice, instead of Turenne's voice, I hear only a glorious wind.

The enervated.

"Can you hear me?" I cry out.

The wind answers.

"I am speaking to all of you who are trapped together in the white room," I say. "All souls. I come bearing good news! You all have the power to free yourselves. Right now!"

The wind grows.

"You all know what Marine did," I begin. "You know that she performed eleutheria on herself. Without my or

Blythe's help. We also know that her voidstone turned to ash. We didn't know *how* she did this. Until now."

The flood rises to my shins.

"Marine said that pain likes to mix with other pain. But she was alone in her pain. Alone in the white room. She was separated from the poison of other enervated."

I'm trying to pace myself. I'm trying to go slowly enough for these words to seep in, yet fast enough that I can say them before my mind is ripped from me.

Looking up, I gauge Chimeline's expression. Behind that veil of light, she's looking at me through clenched features. I see pride underneath that duress.

Through the pain, she gives me an encouraging nod.

I nod back as I continue. "No other spheres were colliding with hers, filling that white room with more memories of hate, pushing it ever outwards and fueling her own anger."

I pause as another memory returns.

"Good Unnamed," I say, running a hand through my hair. "It was in front of us the entire time."

The sea rises to my knees.

"My first teaching!" I say, quicker, raising my voice. "The answer was there from the beginning! Indivisibles move about randomly! There is a great disorder to the natural world, and the power of a voidstone holds no permanent sway!"

It's up to my thighs.

"Even her prison had no permanent sway. There's a limit to the power of the confederacy. If we only allow ourselves to be nothing. It's what the effulgents have always taught. We have to be nothing."

I'd be floating by now if this were a normal sea. But the axion is thick and it grabs hold of everything. It wants me. Turenne wants me.

Stepping closer within the blackness, Chimeline embraces me, putting both shining arms around my waist. An onlooker might think it was she who needed protecting.

But I'm the one who needs it. She's the one thing keeping the palehound at bay. She is my last gate.

"I know that we've been trying to do this for ages! I know that the effulgency has always taught this, but one critical piece was missing. It needs to be *all of us*! Every enervated *together*!"

Marine's cryptic words ring clear.

Hate is order. Forgiveness is disorder.

The sea has reached my waist. The wind becomes a howl.

"Hate is like voidance! When you hate—when you fear, despair—you manipulate your thoughts and feelings, as if they are indivisibles. It's the same thing that the empowered do! You push your past around, molding the world to your liking, manipulating memories because you cannot let them go. We struggle to let go of the horrible things that have happened to us because of the confederacy. Or because of the very ones we loved who put us here!"

I scream because I can no longer hear my own voice.

The axion has reached my chest.

Chimeline's radiance floats over the surface, yet there is no reflection. This evil even swallows the light.

"By hating, you fuel voidance! You are no different from the empowered!"

Chimeline is screaming in pain.

"Forgiveness is disorder!" I call out, one final time. "If you don't want axion in this creation, you must forgive the person who placed you within it. I am speaking to every last soul in the white room. Let the universe take back control! It is not yours to own!"

An invisible cyclone surrounds us. Within it, the black is up to our shoulders.

I crane my neck, staring at the stars. There is one last thing for me to say.

"I forgive!" I cry to the stars. "I forgive Turenne. Mander. Andrej. Marine. Myself! Everyone! Each is a voidstone to me, and I let them go. Because if I keep holding on to them, I will never, ever, be free."

Chimeline's body convulses.

"Be nothing!" I shout.

Suddenly, I feel the absolute cold of what embraces me. It hits me on all sides, as if I'm suddenly buried underneath blocks of stone. I close my eyes as my breath is taken away, but not my thoughts. I hold on to them tighter than Chimeline.

Chimeline?

When I open my eyes, she's gone.

"Chimeline!" I cry out.

But somebody else answers.

PALEHOUND, says a stretched-out voice.

This is the end. I accept it. I feel Dem leaving and Palehound quickly returning. There's no hate left in me, so I don't as much push him away as ignore him for as long as I'm able.

PALEHOUND, YOU . . . RETURN . . . MY SIDE.

I try to listen to my master's broken instructions, but my attention is captured by what I see before me. Far away on the horizon, the sun rises over the Northern Kingdom.

Colorless light breaks over the black sea in all directions. Everywhere I turn, it's growing.

PALE—

This time, his word is silenced, and I feel completely cut off from him.

At the edges, the black crumbles. Falling away into the sunrise. It's spreading so quickly, almost instantaneously. It's turning everything into dust.

Into ash.

"Do you see this?" I instinctively call out. My words are meant for Chimeline, but the moment I say them I already know that she cannot hear me. She deserves to see this, after all that she's done.

"It's beautiful," I whisper. "Chimeline, it's so beautiful."

As the wave of colorless sparks nears, my arms break free of the surface. The axion isn't thick anymore. It's brittle, breaking apart into smaller and smaller pieces until I cannot see anything. The ash floats above me, obscuring the stars. The stars have become different stars. Closer to me, they're suns.

Spheres.

Translucent souls are appearing everywhere.

"You did it," I tell them, as I sense myself fading away from this place. They're leaving too, floating free. And for the first time, after all the forced eleutherias, I finally understand the complexity of what can only be called true freedom. I feel their hope and fear. They don't know what's going to happen next, and neither do I.

One of the glowing orbs passes close to me, deliberately so. I reach out and touch it. As I do, I hear a voice as clear as day.

It's true, the soul says, almost whimsically. *Forgiveness isn't the hardest part. It's the emptiness that's left behind.*

My hand shimmers with colors as it passes through.

Goodbye, Teacher.

HALCYON'S END

A desert world in twilight awaits me.

Disoriented, I lie on my back in the cool sand, staring up into inky shades of purples, reds, and blues. The pale cream moon hangs above me, and a few stars glimmer in the newly born night. So do a few circling birds. But I'm having a hard time focusing. Maybe it's the disorientation at work, but I feel as if a dark haze partially obscures my vision. Perhaps there's windblown sand or smoke trails far above.

My heart beats fast, as if I were running.

Turenne speaks somewhere close by. Even though I don't understand his language, I detect the urgency in his voice. The soft sound of pacing on sand.

Movement out of the corner of my eye draws my attention.

Sharply turning my head sideways, I watch a solitary desert locust crawling inches from my face. It emits a *click, click, click* sound as it jumps vainly in place, its damaged, translucent wings unable to fly.

I see infinitesimal black particles swirl about the lime-green insect, forming spirals that meander in the air as the creature beats its useless wings. They refuse to sit idle, refuse to lie dormant in the sand. They are everywhere and nowhere at once. And I've seen them before.

Ash.

Bringing my gaze back overhead, I instinctively raise my right hand. My blood-soaked strip of shirt wraps it tightly from the wrist to the maimed end. The sudden movement sends pain radiating across my body.

I'm missing three of my fingers.

I blink in momentary confusion. Then the memories return.

When I was Palehound—when I was stuck within my mind—I was complete in some perverted way. I had all my fingers. Reality, at least in my limited understanding, was ordered and precise. I felt no pain. Now, it almost seems as if the disfigurement of my body is the dream. But *this* is reality.

It's the reality I've been waiting for.

Slowly moving my injured hand, I try to touch the axion ash that floats in the dry air, barely discernable against the sky, but then a cool breeze comes and blows all of it away.

I smile wide, despite the throbbing pain.

Eleutheria occurred in the dream, and it occurred here as well.

"Dem?" It's Blythe's voice. "Can you hear me?"

Slowly I sit up, trying to find him.

Turenne is the one who's closest. He's still in his soiled gray uniform, pacing a few feet in front of me. He repeatedly taps a small screen that looks very similar to Lake's then lets out a shout of frustration and throws it in the sand.

Briefly, he looks up into the sky.

We're still in the center of the crater, but everything is in shadows. A soft purple-orange glow graces the top of the eastern rim's wall, where the soldiers once stood. They're gone now.

Blythe is to my left, sitting with his legs crossed. Ten feet behind him lies Colu's dismembered body, which explains the vultures overhead.

Blythe is in the center of a perfect circle of darkened black disks. Turenne must have placed him in a membrane while I was dreaming, but this membrane is now gone.

Eleutheria.

"Dem, can you hear me?" Blythe asks again.

Before I can answer, Turenne stumbles near. Adeptly, he draws his serrater from his side. The cool metal softly reflects the purple sky above.

I stare at tip of the barrel, which had a bright-red glow the last time he used it. Now it's dark.

Is it more than just me? More than just my voidstone?

It seems impossible. But what else would explain what is happening?

I swell of hopeful joy rises within me.

"It's over, Turenne," I answer flatly.

He takes a single step back. Then he grimaces and pulls the trigger.

Nothing happens.

"The entire confederacy is over," I add.

Screaming in frustration, he keeps attempting to fire. All I hear is a *click, click, click* sound, just like the locust.

Suddenly, he winces, crying out. He lets go of the weapon, and it falls to the sand near his feet.

With the same hand, he claws at the axiongraph on his temple.

It's already disappearing. The vivid black pulls away from his skin like a healed scab then breaks apart into ash that floats away in the coming night.

He sinks to his knees. His eyes are wide and even whiter than the moon, unblinking.

I feel hot blood drip down the bridge of my nose. The metallic taste enters my parched mouth as the blood passes over my blistered lips. My head spins. I must be dehydrated.

My left arm is also injured. Blisters cover my forearm, and the outer layers of my skin are burned away. The edges of my torn shirt are singed black.

Closing my eyes, I fight away spots in my vision.

"Dem," Blythe says. "Are you alright?"

I nod but keep my eyes closed due to a wave of dizziness. I'm about to lie down again but hear Blythe crawl over to me in the sand and then feel his hand on my shoulder.

"Your forehead," he says. "You have a serious head injury."

"I'm fine." I wave him away. "It's just from the stone being cut in. I just need a moment."

After the wave passes, I cautiously open my eyes. Blythe is staring straight at my forehead in awe.

"The axion is gone," he says, after a pause. "It's completely gone."

"It's not just mine, Blythe. I think it's *all* gone."

"What do you mean?"

"Just like Marine . . ." I glance at Turenne. He hasn't moved. He simply stares into the sky. Tears stream down his face.

Then I glance at his serrater. His screen. The black disks.

"We triggered a chain reaction," I tell him.

Blythe shakes his head. "I don't understand."

"In my dream. Chimeline was there. Together, we spoke to the enervated."

"What dream?"

"When I was being turned into an avorsi, I was asleep but conscious," I explain. "It was very dreamlike. Turenne tried to enslave my mind, but Chimeline was also there. She voidspoke, using her power as an axionlighter." I swallow. "She saved me."

Blythe simply gazes at me.

"She was able to hold him at bay for a short while," I say. "Enough time for me to talk to the enervated."

"You spoke directly to them?"

I nod.

"How?"

I open my mouth but don't answer his question. I barely understand it, and I was there. "They performed eleutheria on their own," I eventually say. "Just like Marine did."

Blythe grips my shoulder tight. "I was praying for you to succeed, all this time, Dem. For fullbells."

"Thank you," I tell him. "But you give me too much credit. I didn't do this. They did." I motion while I speak.

"The enervated in the serrater's stone. Turenne's axiongraph." I point to the surrounding disks. "Your membrane. It's happening to all axion."

Blythe furrows his brow. "You mean . . ." He pauses then gestures around us. "Everywhere?"

"Yes."

He looks up at the night sky. "How far does this chain reaction go?" he softly asks.

I slowly shake my head in thought. "There is no distance in the void, as Chimeline has proven. These white rooms . . . they can be anywhere. Until they are nowhere."

His mouth hangs open in disbelief. "But that would mean . . ."

"The end of axion."

He stares off into the distance. After a pause, he looks back at me. "How sure are you?"

"For once, Blythe, my faith may be stronger than yours."

Blythe looks around. "I only wish there were voidstones nearby, so that we could prove it." He bites his lip as he catches himself, then lets out a deep laugh. "Look at how we've switched places, my friend."

"Wait," I say, glancing back at Turenne. "There *is* another voidstone."

Turenne's gaze hasn't moved.

Slowly, I rotate my body and arc my neck to see what he's been fixated on this entire time.

I sharply inhale as I see it.

It's the axionship.

"Blythe, look."

Before, it looked faint. Like the moon, but much smaller and slightly oblong. Now, it looks like a solitary cloud. And the cloud is moving, leaving a smoky trail. A thin sickle of white, like the newest of moons, forms at the front.

"Is that . . . ?" Blythe brings his hands to his lips while craning his neck. "Dem, that's the axionship."

"Yes, it is," I whisper in wonder.

He stands.

"We were right all along," he says.

I'm not sure if he can see me nod. "All this time, the enervated just needed to be told."

"No," he says, blindly extending his hand to my good one, enabling me to stand. "They needed to be *taught*."

With some effort I stand next to him. We look up at the eastern sky, past the ridge of the crater.

The axionship breaks apart.

Dozens of bright white lights flash silently in a chorus of strobes buried among the cloud, but they're quickly muffled. Smoke trails multiply, spinning off, downward, in random directions. It looks as if a giant's hand is reaching out, his crooked fingers pointed toward the horizon.

Out of the corner of my eye, I see Blythe's lip quiver. He tightly closes his eyes before his entire face distorts into a swell of emotions. He breaks down into soft sobs and then turns to me, arms open wide.

I embrace him as tightly as I can, given my wounds.

"I wish the others could see this," he eventually says, past my shoulder.

"They *are* seeing it," I tell him. "Different axionships, perhaps. Different axionware. But in the end, I imagine it's all the same, wherever they may be."

"That's good," he says, pulling back and then wiping his wet face with his sleeve. "When our friends return, we will have much to celebrate."

My smile instantly fades.

When they return.

I stagger.

"What's wrong, my friend?"

Black spots return to the edges of my vision, like sagebrushes in the sand.

Blythe grabs hold of me.

"Dem, we must get you water. You are weak."

"When they return . . ." I mumble.

"Here," he says. "Let's get you down on the ground. Watch your hand."

He settles me back down. Once I'm lying fully against the soft sand, I cautiously open my eyes. He kneels next to me. We're in the center of the lifeless black disks. Above him, I can see the remains of the axionship slowly falling, like my hopes and dreams.

I cover my eyes with my good hand. I try to swallow but can't. My throat is sand on fire. Tear trails appear from my eyes and streak toward the back of my head.

"Dem, what's wrong?"

"It takes axion, Blythe," I say hoarsely, raising my hand from my tearful eyes to the sky. "It takes axion to travel across the black sea."

He blinks many times, and then keeps his eyes closed for a bit. "There is no more axion."

I shake my head.

"Where are they, exactly? Perhaps it's possible to travel via other means."

"Agh-Severia, I think," I eventually say. "It doesn't matter. It might as well be—"

Motion from behind us makes us jump in place. A metallic shimmering sings in the quiet desert air.

It's Turenne.

He stands over Colu's mutilated body with Colu's sword in his hands. The blade is shattered—only a few inches rise past the hilt, yet Turenne still grasps it in front of himself with sharp focus.

Blythe grabs my wrist and begins to stand. "You are in no condition to fight, Dem. I will defend you. It is on the way of unwant—"

In one quick motion, Turenne slices his own neck wide open. The blood looks black in the twilight. I hear it hit the sand like a bucket of water upturned.

"Good Unnamed!" Blythe cries.

Turenne collapses over Colu. One of the vultures touches down briefly before shrieking and flying off again. It's still too scared to feed.

"Good Unnamed," Blythe repeats. Then he settles on his knees, palms together, index fingers against his forehead. He rocks back and forth.

As the sound of the wind leaves his lips, I watch the cloudy remains continue to fall from the sky. The dozens of pieces have broken into dozens more. I wonder where they're landing. Hopefully over the ocean, somewhere between this place and the archipelago, where she used to live.

Chimeline.

Part of me always knew—always feared—that this would happen. That somehow this war would get the better of us. But fear and realization are two different things. Now that it *has* happened, it feels as if I've been punched in the gut. Somewhere deep inside me is a dull, pulsing agony. Unlike my blistered skin, it may never heal.

I can't even remember the last words I said to her in the dream. When everything was falling apart.

"I lost her, Blythe," I say. I'm too weak for tears, drained of everything I have. I'm drier than this wasteland. "I lost her, just like you lost le-Daerke."

He looks up sharply. "I never lost le-Daerke."

I return his gaze questioningly. "What do you mean?"

"You can't lose what you've never owned," Blythe says. "While it is sad to no longer have those we love in our lives, they were never *ours* to begin with. Chimeline . . . she was never yours to hold. Much like the enervated themselves."

I remember then what the last soul said, and I repeat it as much for me as for my friend. "Forgiveness isn't the hardest part. It's the emptiness that's left behind."

"That is beautiful, Dem. Beautiful and true."

"And hard to swallow," I add.

He points to Colu's remains. "Just thank the Unnamed that she is safe."

I'm filled with raw bittersweetness. Blythe's right. Chimeline could have easily suffered the same fate as Colu. Or worse. But Colu didn't deserve death either. He should be standing here, cursing while watching these smoke trails fall from the sky.

"She's safe with Chireseal and Lake," I admit. "All of creation is safer than before, without axion. Without the confederacy."

"Well said, Brother."

"I just wish I could tell her that she was never my weapon. But perhaps she was my prize. And I'm not sure if there's a difference between the two."

"Then pray on it," he says, as if the answer is simple.

I exhale into the growing night, knowing that's an impossibility.

"Temberlain's Ashes, I envy your faith in the Unnamed," I say softly, almost to myself, running my uninjured hand through my hair. My head is bloody and tender where the axion used to be. "Even now, despite everything I've witnessed, yours is a gift I will always envy."

Blythe's expression is one of sadness, but then he smiles and nods. "Dem, I also have faith in *you*." He sets a hand on my shoulder. "I have faith that one day you'll be able to fill this emptiness with someone. But without owning them."

For a moment, I return his gaze. Behind him, the smoke trails are smudges against the twilight. In another fullbell, all evidence of the so-called Age of Axion will be lost forever.

"Well," I say, "that's faith that I can get behind."

EPILOGUE

556

BRICKS
(ONE YEAR LATER)

Blythe turns in the seat and addresses his daughters, who ride in the wagon's covered section behind us. "Girls, make sure you're decent. We're getting close to the village. We should be there before dark."

"Yes, Father," says the timid Yisla, from behind the thin white curtain.

Yerla, always the inquisitive one, asks, "Uncle Dem, have you been here before?"

"Never," I answer.

"But you said you've been to Scorpiontail."

"I *have* been to Scorpiontail. A few times. When I was the master voider."

I hear shuffling, and then the white curtain parts. Her head peeks through, directly between Blythe and me. "I don't understand," she says.

Blythe smiles as he holds the reins.

"The archipelago has over seven thousand islands," I tell her. "This is just one of many. The first of many."

"Oh," she says. "I see." She starts to retreat but then thinks of another question.

"What's the name of this island?"

"Jwoei."

"So, how many other islands will we visit?"

"How many bricks does it take to build a temple?" Blythe asks in reply.

"Huh?" his daughter says.

Even I turn to him in confusion.

"If you can't answer the question, my dear, I fear that I must tell you a story."

All three of us groan. Yerla retreats behind the white curtain.

"But this is a story of il-Colu," he adds brightly.

That shuts me up. The memories of him return.

"Who is il-Colu," Yerla asks, her voice now muffled.

"Our friend," I answer.

"Where is he now?" Yisla asks.

"He's dead," I softly answer. "He died fighting the confederacy."

With these words, I assume that I've turned the atmosphere blue, but Blythe continues without missing a beat. His tone is full of excitement and fond reminiscence.

"il-Colu was a mason," he begins, his tone low, his words stretched out. "He worked on the grand temple in Winter's Baiou." He smiles with a faraway look in his eyes. Then he seems to snap out of his reverie and taps his knuckles on the wagon's frame over his shoulder. "Daughters, are you listening?"

"Yes, Father," they say in unison.

Blythe clears his throat. "Years ago," he continues, his voice deep and strong, "when that temple was being built, I was walking through the construction site, and I asked every stone mason I ran into the same question."

I ponder where Blythe is going with all of this as he continues.

"I asked them, 'What are you doing?'"

Blythe pauses dramatically to let the question sink in.

"Didn't you know what they were doing?" asks Yisla, in her bashful tone.

Yerla giggles.

"Of course," Blythe answers. "But I wanted to see if *they* knew what they were doing."

Again, Blythe lets the silence stretch out before continuing.

"The first man I ran into said he was laying bricks," Blythe says. "The second man said he was putting up a wall. But neither of those answers was correct. il-Colu was the third man. And il-Colu answered correctly."

Blythe turns to me. "He said that he was building a temple."

"That doesn't sound like Colu," I say softly.

"Actually . . ." Blythe leans close to me and whispers, "His words were, if I'm not mistaken, 'I'm building a *fucking* temple.'"

I laugh. "Now *that* sounds like Colu."

"Uncle!" Yerla says. "What did Father tell you?"

Before I can answer, Blythe interjects. "The point is," Blythe declares, straightening back up, "il-Colu saw the bigger picture. And so must each of us." He extends his hands, reins still clutched within them. "We are building a temple."

"What?" I ask, baffled. "On this island?"

The girls giggle, and Blythe taps the wagon's frame again.

"Not a physical temple. A temple of the mind. A new effulgency. A new way of unwanting. The Age of Axion is now finally behind us, but the age ahead is still not void of suffering. Of abuse of power. This is why we are here. To educate."

I nod.

"So," Blythe says, turning a bit in his seat. "Daughters, how many bricks does it take to build a temple?"

I hear the girls whisper frantically to each other.

Then Yerla reappears. "One hundred and forty, Father."

Blythe smiles. "And why is that?"

"You said yourself. The plan is to give a book per island, until we run out."

"Excellent, my dears," Blythe says. "Excellent. Now please get ready."

Yerla's head vanishes behind the curtain again.

I stare into the distance.

Jwoei is much larger than I'd imagined. The term *island* connotes smallness to me, but a lush green mountain range sits in the distant twilight. It will probably take us days to cross it—especially if the roads get muddy. The sun has already passed behind the mountains, throwing everything into soft shades of pink.

Our first destination is visible, a few miles ahead. The village is on a tree-barren hill past alternating coffee fields and sections of deep jungle. Although torches are being lit there, it's still light enough to make out hundreds of buildings. They almost resemble the huts in Yisla and Yerla's town of Fiscarlo. Made of straw. But where Fiscarlo's were cylindrical and drab, these are cone shaped with round doors painted the most vibrant array of colors.

At first I thought the wagon we purchased at the beachfront was special due to its yellow-and-red-painted frame, but the handful we've passed on this road all look the same. Different colors, but equally rich.

Blythe says that *Jwoei* in the old tongue means "bright bird."

I'd always thought that it meant "stinger." The first in the chain of curving islands. The scorpion's weapon.

"We're getting close," Blythe says, under his breath. "It's supposed to be in that dense section up ahead."

"Yes."

He glances at me. "Are you sure you want to go?"

I nod.

"He might not be there."

"I have to at least try."

For a long time, all is silent except for the creaking of the wagon's wheels over dried dirt.

Leaving a coffee plantation behind, we enter a denser section of jungle. Palms cover us completely, and the lush landscape extends in deep greens and shadows to the left and right. It's chillier here, and I smell the dank fertileness of the earth. Both the hilltop village and the mountain range beyond are suddenly obscured. The dirt road is our only guide.

Standing in my seat, I use a flint to light the lantern that hangs over our heads. We're soon bathed in a saffron glow.

But as I settle back into the seat, I spot another weak glow in the shrouded distance, about a hundred yards into the jungle to our right. It's greenish and unnatural in hue—reminding me of the ambient light from Chireseal and Lake's ship.

Then it's gone. Obstructed by more vegetation.

I continue to search the jungle as Blythe drives us forward, until I notice a smaller footpath leading off in the direction of the brief glow I saw. It's so overgrown here that if I hadn't been staring in that direction, I would have missed it.

"Stop," I tell Blythe. "I see it."

He pulls on the reins.

Yerla reemerges from behind the curtain. "Are we here?" A breath later, she adds, "Oh. Why are we stopping?"

"I'm going to get off here," I tell her, reaching down and grabbing my tan leather satchel. I put the wide strap over my shoulder. "I'll meet you three at the inn later tonight."

I jump off the wagon and look up at the sky, trying to find the moon, but everything is obscured by palms. "Are you sure there's a full moon tonight?"

Yerla nods enthusiastically. "It was nearly full yesterday on the ship. It should be full tonight."

"Can I have the small lantern, dear?"

She disappears and a moment later emerges with a miniature version of what hangs above. Reaching into my satchel, I grab the flint again, and then light the lantern.

"Uncle, where are you going?" she asks, a tinge of worry in her voice.

"Uncle Dem is just paying a visit," Blythe answers for me.

"To who?"

I run my hand through my hair as I search for the right term. "A fellow teacher."

Peering down at the overgrown footpath, I search for the greenish glow, but nothing's there.

"Good luck, Dem," Blythe says with a nod. "And be careful."

"Thank you."

Blythe flicks the reins, and the wagon lurches forward as the horse leads them away. A moment later, Yerla's and Yisla's heads emerge from the wagon's rear curtain. Yisla is braiding Yerla's hair, while Yerla leans her forearms over the wagon's frame, watching me as she recedes from view.

"We'll save you some dinner, Uncle," she says.

It takes me a halfbell to reach Moonlake.

I remember what Chimeline said in the sewers underneath Winter's Baiou—that she could see the light through the palm trees even before she descended onto the beach.

It's the same for me.

As I cross over onto coarse sand, I set down my lantern. I don't need it here.

It's quite possible that this isn't Chimeline's exact lake. I have no idea if there are multiple freshwater lakes with moonfrogs on this island. I doubt it, though. Regardless, it's smaller than what I'd pictured. It's roughly a hundred yards in diameter, and as circular as the moon.

The black body of water is alive with croaking and glowing moonfrogs.

For a moment, I simply stand there in awe. Surrounding the lake is a ring of sand and tall, leaning palms. The moon shines down, as if summoning the throbbing creatures to this ancient dance.

The closest copulating pair is where the sand meets the water—about ten feet away. I don't dare go nearer, knowing how toxic moonspit can be. All I do is stand in place and survey the ringed beach, determining if I'm alone.

I'm not.

Across the lake, a man sits in the sand. With the help of both the greenish glow and the moonlight, I can tell that he might be the man I'm looking for.

I begin walking toward him, carefully circumnavigating the lake while staying far up the beach—even weaving between the trunks of palm trees—to avoid stepping on any glowing moonfrogs.

When I'm twenty feet away, I see that he's drinking out of a clear bottle. I hear the sloshing over the chorus of frogs.

He's so close to the lake that his bare feet touch the water. A moonfrog sits in the sand next to his feet. It's smaller than I expected. The size of a grape.

Each is seemingly oblivious to the other.

"You're a Northerner," he says, still staring out at the black water.

The man is ten to twenty years my senior. Darker skin, like Chimeline's. He's extremely thin, bald, and shirtless. And not as drunk on sugarcanex as I presumed. He doesn't even slur his words.

"I am," I say.

"If you're looking for moonspit, I ain't selling."

I crouch in a clear section of sand a few feet away from him. There are no moonfrogs in reachable distance. "That's not why I'm here."

His eyes flash to mine briefly, eerie green light reflected in them.

Then he wrinkles his nose.

And now I'm sure that I've found him.

"You're her father."

He scowls and turns away. "Leave me alone, Northerner."

A single copy of the book is in my satchel. I consider simply setting it down on the sand and walking away.

Instead, I sit down next to him.

He continues to take periodic swigs from his bottle of sugarcanex, as if punishing himself.

"Did she send you here to kill me?" he asks, taking another swig.

"No."

He laughs. "Too bad." He takes another drink.

"You want to die?" I ask.

He shrugs. "If anyone deserves it, it's me. Although I thought she'd do it herself."

I look toward the black water. "Well, I'm not here to kill you."

"In that case." He holds up the bottle in offering, and I accept it.

The liquid burns going down. There's a trace of cinnamon and cloves. I resist the urge to cough.

"Is she dead?"

I shake my head.

"Next time you see her, then, tell her that I'm sorry."

I don't have the heart to tell him that this is impossible. Instead, I ask hoarsely, "Sorry for what?" as I give the bottle back.

"For everything," he says, shaking his head. "For teaching her to begin with."

With his free hand, he quickly grabs the glowing frog near his feet.

I flinch and almost fall back in the sand.

The man brings it within inches of his face. "You know what the funny thing is, Northerner?"

I don't say anything, as I know he's not waiting for an answer.

"Thanks to her, I've got more gold than I know what to do with." He cocks his head, as if motioning to the faraway mountain, past the palms. "Own half the town. My two other daughters, they left." He snorts. "No men in Jwoei are proper suiters now, with the wealth that they've become accustomed to. So I'm alone with these moonfrogs. My piles of gold and moonfrogs."

He leans closer to the poisonous creature in front of his face, staring at it.

"Anyway, the funny thing is, I'd give all my gold back to do things differently. I did what I thought was right, but . . ." He shrugs. "I was wrong. And now it's too late." He looks at me, squinting. "She never asked for anything. You know that?" He shakes his head. "All those years, she never once complained. Just accepted her fate."

I give him a nod. Slowly, I stand and then dig my hand into my satchel. "And quite a fate it was."

After retrieving the leather-bound book, I carefully set it down on the sand, away from the water's edge.

"What's this?" he asks me.

"*The Age of Axion*. It's the story of the end of voidance, the destruction of the confederacy, and the restoration of peace and justice in this land."

He groans. "Been hearing all sorts of rumors about that. All those fools who got numbers on their arms. Even more useless than my gold."

"Well, now you don't have to resort to rumors. Now you have the truth."

He returns his gaze to the glowing frog in his slightly closed hand. "Thank you, Northerner, but voidance doesn't concern me."

"Yes it does," I say. "She and I did it—together. This is *her* story too."

He opens his hand. The glowing creature jumps off his palm and plops into the water, causing the perfect reflection of the moon to break apart.

When he turns, his haunting green-lit eyes bore into me. Then he raises his bottle toward the moon, sloshing the sugarcanex around. "Might have drunk more than I thought."

He upturns the bottle, pouring the remaining liquor over his hand, washing his palm of the toxin. Then he throws it down next to him and picks up the book.

"How exactly do you know her?" He runs his hands over the leather cover.

I point to it. "I'm afraid you'll need to read that for the answer."

He exhales. "So if she's not dead," he says, slowly, as if he's working out the logic as he speaks, "why didn't she bring me this book herself?" Almost immediately, he thinks he finds the answer. "She hates me."

"She doesn't hate you. In fact, she forgives you."

He laughs again and flips the pages. Bringing the book up to his nose, he inhales the scent of the dried ink. "You don't know that."

"I do."

"How?" he asks.

"Because she forgives me."

Taking a few steps backward, I reach a palm tree and lean a hand against it for support. Chimeline's father stares at me for a few heartbeats then turns back to the perfect moon.

I glance across the lake.

My lantern still burns brightly.

A NOTE FROM THE AUTHOR

Reviews are gold to authors! If you've enjoyed this book, please consider rating and reviewing it on the following platforms: Amazon.com, Goodreads.com, and BookBub.com.

SIGN UP FOR
MY MAILING LIST

Sign up for my mailing list to get access to author updates, giveaways, and much more.

www.dmwozniak.com

OTHER WORKS BY D.M. WOZNIAK

The Indivisible and the Void (Age of Axion Book 1)
War. Magic. A lover's betrayal. A dark secret lies beneath them all.

Each year, Democryos sends his brightest student into the war-torn countryside to work magic. But when his wife leaves him for a mysterious stranger, he finds his own life ravaged.

Forsaking the comfort of the citadel, he searches for her, traveling through the same forgotten lands where he sent his students. Along the way, he befriends an elusive member of the king's harem, a holy man harboring guilt, and a maimed soldier. Together, they stumble upon a key—not only to the war, but to understanding the magic of voidance itself.

"Wozniak's medieval world, as described, is a beautiful one; from the sky, it "looks like thousands of curved pieces of glass" covering everything "in blues and greens." The book also wonderfully handles the notion of a preindustrial society discovering the atomic structure of nature. Yet the plot's human elements--which include romance, drug addiction, and trust across philosophical lines--often shine brightest. Revelations and combat converge in the propulsive finale, and Wozniak's strong imagination will rope fans in."
- Kirkus Reviews

The Perihelion: Complete Duology
A newly-combined edition of the critically-acclaimed duology: The Perihelion and An Obliquity. Also contains the prequel novelette, The Rue Cler Decommission.

It is Thursday, January 3, 2069: the eve of the perihelion. Night is upon Bluecore 1C (what used to be known as the city of Chicago, before the riots). Snow is falling, plans are being made, and within hours, everyone in 1C will be changed forever.

Narrated from the vantage point of six residents of 1C, The Perihelion: Complete Duology is a work set against the dystopian backdrop of near-future events. As the modern trappings of their bluecore fall apart, each must strike his or her own separate path towards salvation. Their interlaced stories become a compelling exploration of moral deviation and ultimate redemption.

The Perihelion (The Perihelion Book 1)
"Literary, character-driven science fiction at its best."
- Self-Publishing Review

"It's clear that D.M. Wozniak's future in science fiction shines bright."
- IndieReader Discovery Awards

An Obliquity (The Perihelion Book 2)
"An intelligent, superbly written, creatively unique and complex, supremely imaginative story."
- Readers' Favorite (Five Star Review)

"One of the more innovative literary dystopian sci-fi novels
you'll ever read."
- Self Publishing Review

The Gardener of Nahi
Since the mysterious closed timelike curve appeared above
the world of Cassidian, nothing has come in or out of it. So
when an innership emerges from the celestial cloud and
crashes on the beaches of the Still, a Hunion courier named
Anon Selfe is sent to investigate. When he lands, he finds
the blood and footprints of the only survivor leading away
from the wreckage. But inside there is someone else
awaiting him in the darkness: his own dead body.

What follows is Anon's desperate chase up through the tiers
of Cassidian to find the survivor of the crash – a young
woman named Myria who is unyielding in her belief that she
knows Anon from her past.

The only problem is that she claims to be from a world called
Nahi, which is not known to exist.

ABOUT THE AUTHOR

Born and raised in the west suburbs of Chicago, D.M. Wozniak discovered his passion for software at St. Lawrence High School, where he joined the computer lab as a ploy to get out of gym class. By the time he graduated in 1993, D.M. knew that he wanted to code for a living. But his senior-year honors-English teacher took him aside on graduation day and said, "Never stop writing. It's your true calling."

Four years later, D.M. graduated from the University of Illinois at Urbana-Champaign with a degree in Computer Science from the College of Engineering. After that, he started a family and a career in software. He didn't have the time then to consider that true calling.

But he never forgot.

D.M. Wozniak is the author of two two-volume speculative fiction epics: The Perihelion: Complete Duology (The Perihelion, An Obliquity) and the Age of Axion (The Indivisible and the Void, Temberlain's Ashes). His first novel was The Gardener of Nahi. He lives in Raleigh, North Carolina.

www.dmwozniak.com

9 789898 668181 8